# Story of
# Our Lives

*Hope you Enjy*
*Love Lily Rose*
*5/9/18*

# Story of
# Our Lives

**A Novel**

**Lily Rose**

Copyright 2017 Lily Rose
All rights reserved, including the right to reproduce this book or portions thereof in any form whatsoever.
Library of Congress-in-Publication:
ISBN: 099661107X
ISBN: 9780996611077
Library of Congress Control Number: 2016901591
Fay Mata, Monroe, MI

Visit us on our web site: storyofourlives.info
Email us: lilyrosestory@gmail.com or on twitter @Reallilyrose

# LILY ROSE

Holmes Cove Village, Cheshire, England.

Nine-year-old Lily Rose raised the front of her T-shirt to wipe a line of sweat from her brow. The weather was uncommonly warm for April. Her father, Charles, managed the estate of Highcliff Castle. With its thousands of acres, it was one of the largest in the country. He managed a few estates, but Highcliff Castle was one of his top priorities. The Castle had been handed down for generations and has always been owned by the Duke of Highcliff. The Duke,—Uncle Eddie, as Lily Rose referred to him and Charles have —been the best of mates since childhood. Actually, he was so close to the family that none of them referred to him as "the Duke." He was just Ed to them.

The castle, maze, and grounds were due to open for the season, and people came from all parts of the world to visit. The maze was unique and one of the most visited in England. It was comprised of thirty-two hundred evergreen trees that stood over seven feet high. Two gates, one located at each end, were for entering or exiting the maze and were securely locked when not in use.

The difficulty in solving the maze began after reaching the middle—a large fountain sat in this location, with six wide paths jutting out like the spokes of a wheel. Four of the paths led around in a circular pattern leading back to the fountain. The other two paths also led in a circular pattern but worked out to one of the exits. The goal was to enter through one of the gates and exit from the other. Loud laughter and chatter could be heard as people met each other over and over again while trying to find their way out, hoping it wasn't where they had entered.

Keaton Hall, another estate at the top of Charles's list was located just on the other side of Highcliff's private eighteen-hole golf course. The golf carts made it convenient for getting back and forth. Keaton Hall wasn't as big, but it was just as grand as Highcliff Castle. It was Lily Rose's favorite of the two. One of the wings had been converted into a beautifully furnished bed-and-breakfast, making the estate self-sufficient until the legal heir came of age. The bed-and-breakfast was open to the public year round, whereas the castle and grounds were open only six days a week during the spring and summer months.

Charles went to Keaton Hall while Lily Rose and Bill, who Charles considered his father, were finishing up the secret hatch they had installed in one of the evergreen trees on the back row of the maze. It was only two feet tall by two feet wide, but it was plenty big enough for Lily Rose to crawl through.

The duke and his ten-year-old son, Anthony, whom they all loved and adored, often visited since moving back to London. Anthony was the reason the new escape hatch was being installed. The previous week, he had taken the extra key that allowed one to reset the codes on the gates' keypad from Charles's desk drawer. He'd known Lily Rose was playing in the maze and closed both gates and changed the codes, trapping her inside. Luckily, Bill's sixteen year old son and nephew were around to rescue her. JR and Jayden had been practicing football when they heard the cries for help. After retrieving the key from Anthony and resetting the codes, the gates opened, allowing her escape. They knew something had to be done to prevent it happening again in the future.

Mary, Lily Rose's mum, was not happy when she heard about it. She loved Anthony as her own, making it difficult for her to lay down the law. She decided Lily Rose was not to be allowed anywhere on the castle grounds when Anthony was there, until she saw an improvement in his behavior. He was being such a brat lately, driving them all mental.

Lily Rose bent down in front of the tree they were working on at the back of the maze to help Bill, who was on his knees inside. She blew her bangs out of her eyes, again, as she held the latch in place. She tried to tuck her—now way-too-short—dark hair behind her ears. It didn't stay. Instead, it flopped right back down onto her face. She thought about how her mum was right, once again. After being allowed to choose the style of her first haircut, she had been advised to leave it long enough so that she could pull it back. She was told to hold off on cutting bangs or she would quickly regret it. But being stubborn and always thinking she was right, she had insisted she would love it. She had argued that she was tired of it being so long. She just knew it would to be easier to take care of shorter. Of course, she had gotten her way. She should have known it was about to become another lesson learned—Mum was good for that. Before the day was over, she knew what a major pain it was, and she now looked like a bloody boy!

Bill stood as he called out, "Okay, Snaggs," using the nickname he had given her. "That should do it. Lift the latch; let's see if it opens and if it's big enough for you to get through." He was good about coming up with nicknames. He called her Snaggs because when she was younger, one of her front teeth had fallen out, leaving the other one dangling. He had told her she reminded him of a snaggle-toothed tiger. She had put her hands up like they were paws and let out a huge roar, making Bill jump. JR and Jayden laughed so hard that they had tears streaming down their cheeks. "Snaggs" then became her permanent nickname from them.

"Doing it now, Papa," she called back as she lifted the latch and pushed the small hatch open.

"No, Snaggs, pull it toward you; it will swing both ways. Not much of a secret passage if you push it open in front of somebody, letting them see it. Plus, you can sneak a peek both ways before crawling through."

"Smart thinking, Papa," Lily Rose replied, as she pulled it toward her. She crawled through, closing it behind her. She jumped to her feet and looked up with a big smile. "It works perfectly, Papa, and you can't tell it's there; it just looks like the other trees."

"You did a fine job, baby girl. Your idea was brilliant," he said, bending to kiss the top of her head.

Her face lit up as she shrugged away the compliment. "Aww, it was nothing. Besides, I got the idea from those fake grate things over the holes inside the castle and Keaton Hall. They are just about the same size too," she added with a smile.

Bill took off his ball cap that he always wore and scratched the back of his head. "Those are heating vents."

"Oh," she said and then thought for a second before asking, "Papa, are you sure?"

"I'm, sure. Why do you ask?"

"Our secret, right?"

"Of course. You know my lips are sealed whenever you share your secrets with me."

"I know. Sorry, Papa." She lowered her voice as always when sharing one of her many secrets with him. "I use them to play hide-and-seek with JR and Jay." This was her and JR's nickname for Jayden. "Well, the ones I can get open." She hesitated for a second, then clicked her tongue, and rolled her eyes in disgust at herself. She started to quickly mumble, leaving words out—her worst habit in the world. It came out in one breathless stream. "That's why can't get all open…duh! Some are heat. How daft can I—"

"Whoa, Snaggs, slow down," Bill said with a chuckle. "You're mumbling and leaving words out again. So you're telling me you use the ones that have been closed off, not the ones in use?"

"Correct! The ones that heat doesn't come out of are great to get from one room to the other."

"How?" he asked with a grin. Knowing her, it had to be good.

"It's easy," she replied, her eyes beaming. "Well, once I got the hang of it. I keep the screws loose, not knowing which way I'm going in. I remove the screws on the one I'm going in, take the cover off, back through on my belly while I kick the one in the other room loose as I replace the one I crawled in. At first it was hard making the one stay in place on the wall until I could get back in there to replace the screws. But then I figured out I could use silly putty, so I always carry a little in my pocket. Like you say, Papa, always be prepared."

Bill burst out laughing. "Now I wish I hadn't promised. I would love to tell Charlie this one!"

"Well, I'm glad you promised because I get away from him sometimes too!"

Bill laughed even harder.

They both looked up, hearing the helicopter arriving with Ed and Anthony.

Bill complained as they quickly picked up the tools. "They're early, and you're not supposed to be here. I can't believe Charlie didn't say they were just about here."

"Papa!" She pointed to his ear and giggled. "Your earbud is out again."

Bill looked down seeing it dangling on the front of his shirt. "I hate these dang things," he grumbled and stuck it back in his ear. He said a little too loudly, being upset as he got it back in place, "*Snaggs is still here!*" There was a pause as he listened and bellowed back. *"Stop your hollering! The bloody thing fell out!"* Another pause and then, "You did what?" Another pause and again he bellowed, *"I'm not yelling, and yes I hear you! I'm not deaf!"*

Lily Rose giggled again. "What did he say, Papa?" She knew he was the only one Dad let talk to him like that.

"To get you the heck out of here or your mum is going to have all of our hides. He's taking them to the clubhouse instead of the castle. He also let some lad in over at Keaton Hall to walk around the golf course."

"He didn't!"

"Yeah, I guess the lad loves golf."

Lily Rose groaned and rolled her eyes skyward. "You blokes and your bloody golf."

"You sound just like Grammy Tessa."

Lily Rose's brow went up. "Oh no, Papa, we left the Jeep parked over by the clubhouse!"

"Well then, we better hurry and see if we can get to it before they see us."

They hurried out of the maze closing the gate and waited for the click, making sure it locked. Lily Rose added with a little groan, "Papa, we left the other gate to the maze open and the back gate leading out to the golf course. That bloke Dad let on the course might come over here."

"Nah, I'm sure he'll stay out on the golf course, but just in case he doesn't, we can double back around and close the back gate once we get the Jeep."

They stopped midstride, seeing Charles, Ed, and Anthony on the golf cart pulling up to the clubhouse.

"We're too late, Snaggs," grumbled Bill. "Use the maze and your new passage to get out back; it's closer. I'll get the Jeep and swing around to pick you up."

"Okay, Papa."

Bill talked in a hurried tone from the corner of his mouth. "Anthony just turned this way. I'll stall him to give you a little more time to make it inside the maze. Make sure you pull the gate closed behind you."

"Don't have to tell me twice," replied Lily Rose, already turning to run. Once she made it to the gate, she blew her bangs out of her eyes as she quickly entered the code on the keypad.

Anthony yelled, "Hey, Rosie, wait up!"

Lily Rose groaned. She hated it when he called her that, and he knew it. She looked back over her shoulder to see Papa stopping him. She pulled the gate open and quickly closed it behind her. After hearing the click, she took off running as fast as she could. She knew every inch of the maze; she could get through it blindfolded if she wanted. She laughed as she ran.

*Bam!* She grunted as her bum hit the ground.

# HARRY

Wthile Lily Rose worked in the maze with Bill, ten-year-old Harry walked around the grounds at Keaton Hall. He was staying there with his mum, Madison, and stepfather, Luke. He decided to give them some alone time in their room; after all, it was their anniversary. He was five when his mum and Luke had started dating. It hadn't taken him long to consider Luke his dad, even before they got married.

He walked toward the back and saw a couple of blokes playing tennis and decided to stop to watch them for a few minutes. He figured they were about sixteen, maybe seventeen. After watching for a few minutes he muttered, "Bloody hell! These blokes are brilliant!" He heard the one who had just lost the set yell out in broken English, "You too good. No quit. You join the pro tour next year." Harry figured he was Italian, maybe Spanish, from his accent.

The other bloke just laughed. "Sorry, Rafa, family business. Besides, you know bro can't get along without me!" He served the ball with a little chuckle.

Harry walked off thinking he wouldn't mind learning how to play tennis someday, especially if he got muscles like the bloke serving. His arms were so big; it was no wonder he had the sleeves cut out of his shirt.

He then walked alongside the ten-foot brick wall that separated Keaton Hall from the golf course at Highcliff Castle. He saw a golf cart flying, about fifty yards away. It looked like it was going to crash into the wall, but at the last minute it disappeared like magic. He muttered, "Either that bloke is from Hogwarts, or there's a gate." He took off running and saw an opening. He paused, briefly considering whether to go in. Curiosity, as always, won out, and he took off running through the gate.

Charles had stopped to check on JR at the guardhouse by the gate.

JR looked over, surprised to see Harry blowing through the gate. "Hey, kid, turn your little bony arse around and get out of here," he yelled.

Harry stopped dead in his tracks and looked over. "Well, that's cheerful," he said sarcastically.

"Dude, can't you read? This is private property!" JR yelled as he pointed to the sign on the gate: Private Property—Do Not Enter.

Harry eyed JR up and down. He didn't like JR's arrogant attitude. "Duh...didn't see it! The gate is open!" He added, with a sarcastic laugh, "I bet you loved He-Man when you were a kid!"

"What're you going on about?" snarled JR.

"If you're trying to look like a He-Man wannabe, you've certainly accomplished that with that long blond hair. How long does it take for your mummy to dye and curl it like that, anyway?" Not letting JR's size intimidate him, he added, with another sarcastic laugh, "You get those muscles from steroids?"

"If you don't move it, I'll show you how these muscles work by throwing your smart arse over that wall!" yelled JR, not liking Harry at all. He gestured toward the gate again. "You going back out that way or over the wall? Your choice! I prefer the wall myself!"

Harry snapped right back, "Chill, *dude*, no need to get your panties in a twist. I just wanted to walk the course—or is it 'dude-ette'?"

JR sneered as he said with disgust, "You're not too smart the way you keep running that mouth of yours!" He added with a sarcastic laugh, "What's your deal with golf? A little obsessed or what?"

"Brilliant deduction, Sherlock," Harry replied mockingly. "As a matter of fact I am! What gave me away? The fact I want to check out the course—or maybe it's because I'm dressed head to toe in golf gear?" He added under his breath, knowing JR could hear, "What a wanker! And he thinks I'm the one who's not too smart?"

Charles chuckled as he walked out, having a nagging suspicion it was Harry. "Enough already, you two."

Harry jerked his head toward him, taking an automatic step backward. He whistled and muttered under his breath, "That bloke is a He-Man wannabe." He grinned at Charles and nodded toward JR. "If you're that tosser's boss, he's a little intense, and his manners are absolutely rubbish!"

JR looked at Charles with a stunned look. "You believe the nads on this smart-mouthed punk?"

The lines at the corners of Charles's eyes crinkled as he laughed. "He reminds me of you at his age." He stared at Harry for a few seconds; he had shoved his curls up under his hat and pulled it down. Charles had to keep from chuckling as he thought, *Yep, it's Harry!* He was the stepson of Luke, his and Ed's childhood friend. Whenever he visited Luke, he had to be in disguise because Luke still wasn't ready for Madison to know about his childhood or the secrets he kept from her about his line of work. So since Charles wanted to get to know Luke's newfound family, he visited as the prim and proper, stiff-faced, stuttering Lord Standish. Little did he know that five-years later he would still have to keep up with the ruse when he visited. Harry never looked him in the eye, and most of the time, within seconds he would make an excuse and run off. Luke finally came clean on why Harry ran off when he visited. He said when he asked Harry why, he had laughed and stuttered back, "Dad...ah-ah...he drives...ah-ah...me mental...ah-ah."

Charles grinned thinking of how much they had laughed over it. As JR wouldn't know he knew who Harry was, he asked, "Is this your first time at Keaton Hall?"

Harry's mouth curled into a grin as he remarked politely. "No, sir. I'm here with my dad and mum. We're staying in room six, just like always on our—I mean, their anniversary. Dad told me to go burn off some energy 'cause I was bouncing off the walls, driving them batty." He raised his eyebrows up and down and gave Charles a little wink. "I can be a handful at times. So I figured I would give them a break and check out the course. Me and Dad play all the time at the course in Chester. Dad thinks I'm good enough to be a golf pro one day!"

"I find that to be rubbish!" JR said with a snort.

Harry shot him an angry look. "My dad says if you don't try, you'll never know." He then added, as his green eyes sparkled with unmistakable pride, "He's the smartest, most brilliant dad in the world. If he says it's so, then it is. I bet I could beat your sorry arse any day of the week; but then, it wouldn't take much. That's if you can get that hair out of your eyes to even play!"

JR responded with a low snarl. "The day you can beat me at golf is the day I'll—"

Charles looked over at JR. "Enough!" he ordered.

JR gave him a small nod.

Charles looked back at Harry and grinned. "Who knows? Maybe I'll let you play the course one day!"

"And I might just take you up on it one day," Harry replied with a grin. He added with confidence, "That's if I can fit you in. Dad says when I'm out playing on the circuit I'm going to be awfully busy."

"I bet you will be." Charles chuckled with a nod. "Go! Check out the course that you'll be coming back to play one day."

JR shook his head in disgust but never said a word. He gave Harry a dirty look.

Harry's face split into a grin as he shouted with delight, "*Thank you!*" Happiness oozed from every pore. He turned to run, but then spun back to JR looking pleased as he stuck out his tongue and then let out a triumphant laugh before he took off running.

Charles laughed.

JR looked at him as if he had sprouted another head. "You never let anyone on the course, let alone an unchaperoned, smart-mouthed punk!"

"What? He's right. You loved He-Man, and you have to admit you kind of favor him," Charles said with a laugh, not taking his eyes off Harry as he ran off. He looked at JR. "Call Jayden; he's still playing tennis with Rafa. Have him go out and shadow the lad."

JR nodded.

"I better get going. Ed's chopper will be here anytime," said Charles as he got in the golf cart.

"Charlie, Anthony is starting to worry me and Jay. You know we worship the kid and don't mind him always tagging after us, but he won't listen anymore and does the complete opposite of what we tell him to do. He's driving us completely nuts."

"I know." Charles nodded. "It's time we do something about him being such a handful. This has gone on long enough. I'll talk to Mary and Ed." He started up the golf cart and added, "Don't leave this gate until Harry comes back through."

"You got it. I'll tell Jay you want him followed until he's back with his parents," he said, not realizing Charles had just called him Harry.

Charles threw his hand up waving as he drove off, already leaving Luke a message on his phone. "I just let Harry out on the golf course if you get to looking for him. Jayden is going to shadow him until he gets back to your room. You got yourself one heck of a son there, bro. He does you proud, and for some reason, he thinks you hung the moon!" He laughed as he ended the call.

Harry made it to the third hole by the castle when he looked up, hearing the helicopter. "Wow, that's the only way to travel. I bet it's the duke," he muttered, watching it land. He saw the man who let him on the course drive up on a golf cart. He saw another man, almost the size of the one on the cart, and a kid about his age hop in the golf cart. Once they drove off heading toward the castle, he glanced over his right shoulder and saw the back gate leading up to the castle was open. He loved the castle and the maze. He and his parents visited the castle a lot in the summer. They would have a nice picnic lunch on the grounds, and then he and Dad would time each other on how long it would take to get through the maze. He knew which turns to take from each gate to get to the fountain and which path would get him back out, ending up at the opposite gate.

"Mmm…" he said, staring at the open gate. "Should I or shouldn't I? Yep, I should." He quickly decided and ran toward it. Once he made it through the castle's back gate, he looked over to his left and saw the one to the maze was also open. He didn't waste any time as he flew through it, seeing how fast he could reach the fountain in the middle. He counted off the turns as he ran. "Two lefts, one right, three lefts, two rights, now straight, passing these two openings because they are dead ends." He continued to mutter as he ran. "Now, one more left and two more rights and presto here I am in the middle. Now, to reach the gate on the opposite end I take that path over there," and off he went around the huge fountain and onto the path. He started his count again as he ran even faster. "One left, one right, two lefts, three rights…"

BAM! Something hit him like a ton of bricks, knocking him backward, almost making him fall to the ground. "*Bloody hell!*" he yelled.

Lily Rose blinked a couple of times, taking in deep breaths to recover, like JR had taught her to do when in pain or needing to calm down. It wasn't helping. Her bum was throbbing, and she was furious, instantly realizing it was the bloke Dad let in. She pushed her dark hair from her face as she looked coldly up at him with flared nostrils. She hissed between clenched teeth, "You're supposed to be on the bloody golf course, not in here!"

Holding his hand to his chest, he said with a little chuckle, "You scared the living daylights out of me, mate! I nearly wet myself!" He reached down and grabbed her hand, pulling her to her feet and was met with an icy, cold stare. His smile tightened into a hard line. "Blimey, mate! What's with the dagger eyes? It wasn't my fault! You ran into me!"

Lily Rose frowned still giving him a cold stare. "No, *you* ran into *me!*" Her chin went up a notch. She jerked her hand away and took a couple of steps back. "And don't 'mate' me," she snapped. She was just about to inform him she was a girl when she quickly looked toward the front, hearing Anthony's whiney voice.

"I can't get it open. Hey, Rosie, what's the code? When did they put in this new bloody keypad?"

"Aaargh!" she moaned, looking up at the sky shaking her head in disgust.

"Oh! You're a girl!" his eyebrows rose in surprise.

Her lips tightened as she crossed her arms defensively across her chest while giving him a look that would stop a raging bull. "Well done, you!" she spat. "I see we have a real Einstein here! Well, smart guy, you might want to turn around and beat feet back the way you came in while you can!"

"Is that right?" Harry's green eyes narrowed as his challenged hers. "What, you the maze police?" he asked with a smirk.

A pair of perfectly arched brows furrowed. "Ugh! What an idiot," she mumbled, rolling her eyes.

He stared at her blankly, never meeting a girl who didn't instantly like him, and he hated her eye roll. "I'll leave when I'm bloody good and ready, thank you very much!"

Lily Rose responded with a cocky shrug. "Knock yourself out, Einstein, but don't say I didn't warn you when you get locked in here."

He stood his ground as if he was rooted to the spot. "Oh really! You the one planning on locking me in?" he replied stiffly. "You're about as cheerful as the tosser over by Keaton Hall."

"Don't have to," replied Lily Rose with a glow of smugness, nodding to the front of the maze. "He will. Since I closed that gate to get away from him, he'll try to beat me to the other one and close me in here. He won't beat me, of course, but he might beat you if you miss a few turns getting back over there. He'll lock you in and not think twice about it! Then what are you going to do, smart guy?"

They heard Anthony yell, "Rosie! If you don't let me in, you know I'll just meet you at the other end!" He taunted with a laugh, "Hope I don't close you in before you reach it, *Rosie!*"

Lily Rose groaned as she rolled her eyes. "That bloke is getting on my last nerve. If by chance you beat him and make it out of here, you better hightail it out the back gate you came in. If he sees you, he'll hit the alarm letting a dozen dogs out just like that." She snapped her fingers. "Gotta go! Good luck...mate!" she said sarcastically over her shoulder as she took off running.

Harry quickly reconsidered staying. "Hey, wait for me!" he yelled running after her. "I lost track; how do I get back to the fountain?"

She yelled back, "Not so smart after all I see! By the way, that bloke over by Keaton Hall is my brother, you big jerk. He's not a tosser; you are!"

"Come on, wait up, or at least tell me the turns to get back to the fountain!" he yelled in a whiney voice.

"Say you're sorry for calling him a tosser!" she yelled back.

"Fine, I'm sorry." He muttered under his breath, "Not!"

"Nobody deserves those dogs on their tails, I guess," she called back, not caring she had lied about the dogs. "Three lefts, two rights, one left, and then right. Better hurry, Einstein, he can move pretty fast for a porker." He surprised her as she heard his footsteps right behind her. After quickly taking two left turns, she cut right to a dead end where the secret hatch was. She quickly backed up into the curve of a tree until she heard him pass. She almost gasped as Harry came skidding in and stopped dead, breathing hard. Her heart was thumping, thinking he saw her. She didn't move as she watched him from the corner of her eye.

"She said three lefts. She could have waited on me; how would I know she was a bloody girl!" he grumbled. "She shouldn't wear her hair so short if she doesn't want to look like a bloke! Christ, man! Get a move on before you become those dogs' lunch!" He turned and ran out.

"That's it," Lily Rose mumbled sullenly to herself. "I'm never cutting my hair again." She waited for a minute after he ran out, in case he came back. Then as quickly as she could, she took a few steps forward and dropped to her hands and knees before her secret passage. She reached in, raised the latch, and pulled it toward her. She leaned through and quickly looked both ways. Not seeing anyone, she crawled through, closing it behind her until she heard the click. She mumbled as she jumped to her feet, "See, Papa, I follow orders already! I'm going to be a brilliant agent!" (It was her secret dream to join him and her dad one day). She took off running the opposite way that Harry was heading. The only sound made was the crunching of the gravel under her feet as she quickly ran on the path alongside the brick wall.

She ran about fifty feet and stopped when she came to a small iron gate. She quickly raised the latch and pulled the gate open and ran through. She glanced over to her right and saw Papa coming in the Jeep. She looked to her left where Harry should be running out of the back gate. She didn't have to wait long before Harry came running out. "Wow," she said with a chuckle. "He's fast!"

Bill pulled up.

Lily Rose reached in and patted the two huge German Shepherds sitting on the back seat and said, "Hurry, Papa, hit the test alarm."

"Okay." He chuckled seeing Harry running for all he was worth. He reached down and hit a button on the dash. Alarms went off within seconds.

She was so giddy, she could barely contain herself as she told the dogs, "Come on, guys, play time; go find JR." The dogs jumped out of the Jeep, hearing playtime, and JR, and knew where to go. They started barking and playing as they ran off toward Keaton Hall. Lily Rose, all excited, hopped into the Jeep and said, "Pull up some so that we can watch, Papa. I caught him in the maze and told him if Anthony saw him he'd set a dozen dogs out after him."

"You didn't?" Bill said laughing as he drove slowly, hearing Charles in his earbud. "No, we're fine. Snaggs seems to be messing with the lad you let in. She found him in the maze." He paused to listen and then answered, "Jayden? Yeah, I see him; I'll swing over and pick him up."

Jayden hopped in the back seat, and said, "I couldn't find him. Then, the next thing I knew he went blasting past me and started screaming like he was getting beat when the test alarms went off. What's his problem? Does he think the dogs are after him?"

"Yep!" Lily Rose replied happily before she burst out laughing.

"Okay," Jayden said slowly, smiling watching her laugh. He asked Bill, "But why? And why are you testing the bloody alarms now?"

"Because Snaggs told me to." Bill chuckled. "She caught him in the maze, and she's messing with him. Haven't heard why yet."

"Snaggs," said Jayden, chuckling when Lily Rose stopped laughing. "What did he do to get you so fired up?"

"For one, he called JR a 'He-Man wannabe' and a tosser. I made him apologize for that one. Then he thought I was a bloke, and he also knocked me on my bum."

"What?" Bill and Jayden yelled in unison.

Lily Rose quickly explained, "He didn't mean to. We kind of just ran into each other in the maze, and he accidentally knocked me down."

"Oh, well then, I'll let him live," Jayden replied with a grin and added, "but he was right about your hair and JR. You've said it yourself that you look like a boy, and JR is a bit of a tosser!"

"Yeah, well, that's beside the point," she said making Bill and Jayden laugh.

"Poor lad," Bill said shaking his head. "You probably scarred him for life making him think those dogs are after him. You should be ashamed of yourself, baby girl."

She huffed and rolled her eyes. "Not—in—the least! That bloke has an attitude and a half!"

Bill pulled up next to JR.

Jayden saw Harry running out the gate. He laughed as he jumped out. "That little bloke is fast!" he yelled over his shoulder as he took off following him.

JR asked, "What's going on? He was yelling something about alarms going off and a pack of dogs being after him."

Lily looked over at the dogs now lying down, enjoying the chew bones JR had given them, and burst out laughing again.

# CHAPTER 1

# LILY ROSE

## EIGHT YEARS LATER

The first Monday of April just before noon, Lily Rose had finished one of her long walks while taking photos. She was now sitting on her hill enjoying the warm spring sunshine and solitude for a few more minutes before heading back to the bakery. Her mum, Grammy Tessa, and Aunt Abbey had opened the only bakery in Holmes Cove when she was five. It hadn't taken long for it to become a huge success since they *did* make the world's best baked goods, casseroles, and candies. She loved working at the bakery and living in Holmes Cove. It was small, even for a village, but it had all of life's necessities—a petrol station, pub, school, church, bank, charity shop, their bakery, a grocery store, and Jones's general store and, of course, an overpriced coffee shop serving the latest flavored latte. The gift shops and bed-and-breakfasts scattered throughout the village and on the outskirts made it even more quaint and unique, drawing tourists visiting Highcliff Castle.

Visitors who came to the village of Holmes Cove often said it was too small and too far from a large city, but she didn't agree. She felt blessed to live in such a beautiful and peaceful place and wouldn't want to live anywhere else, even after seeing amazing places around the world.

Lily Rose loved traveling and getting it on film, but she was always ready to come home. This is where she was settling down and raising her family one day, which was years away as far as she was concerned. She wasn't looking for a bloke, nor did she want one for the near future. Photography was her deep passion. She had her mind set on her plans. She wasn't answering to some nosey bloke that would most likely try to tell her what she could and couldn't do. She was traveling the world as a freelance photographer, while she worked for her father.

She tipped her head back, letting the spring sun hit her face while listening to the birds in the distance along with the swish, swish of the sprinkler watering the flowers. She let out a happy sigh, thinking life was perfect. She wondered just how many hours she had spent sitting there and looking out over the thousands of rolling acres surrounding their home. She looked down at the camera hanging around her neck and thought about the busy week ahead. She had a full schedule, which was nothing new. She loved being the village photographer and tried to be available for whoever needed her, free of charge, of course. She had been doing it for years. Some days she drove herself mental, running from one photo session to another and then working in her dark room. Occasionally, it got rough trying to keep up. It sometimes seemed like everyone wanted her at the same time, or needed their photos right away. She did her best to accommodate them, never wanting to let anyone down.

The phone alarm interrupted her thoughts, signaling it was almost noon. She switched it off and wiggled her toes one last time before slipping her trainers back on. Her stomach growled, reminding her she hadn't eaten anything all morning. Knowing Grammy would have lunch waiting on her, she picked up her phone and slipped it in her back pocket. She brushed the grass from her trousers as she stood, before running down the hill, carefully holding the camera against her body.

Lily Rose ran passed the flower garden, taking the shortcut, running across the lawn, and passed the large thatched-roof barn. She took a left, running alongside the blooming lilac trees and then ran right to the wrought-iron gate covered with English ivy vines. Opening the gate and closing it behind her, she hurried along the gravel path and then quickly descended the twenty or so stone steps with no problem, after having taken them so many times. She made her way onto another gravel path taking her to the back door of the bakery. Her long dark hair was pulled up into a ponytail. Tiny, wispy curls framed her face, which usually happened when her hair became damp or just needed a good brushing; most likely after her long walk and quick jog, it was both.

Lily Rose opened the door and stopped suddenly. Her lunch was on the table waiting for her as usual, but a bloke with curly brown hair was sitting there wolfing it down as fast as he could. He seemed to be in his own little world as he ate. He was eating so fast that she was trying to decide if he was chewing or even taking time to breathe in between bites. Smiling she thought, *Papa would say, "That boy is eating that like he's mad at it!"*

Knowing everyone in the village, she knew he had to be their new neighbor living just up the hill; plus, she had heard all about him that morning. Albert, the local bus driver, and Mrs. Jones, who had been on the bus Saturday afternoon, had been visiting the bakery that morning and had filled everyone in on the details. Albert had said the new president of the bank and his family had started moving in Saturday morning, and he had driven the teenaged son back to Chester in the afternoon. He had added with a knowing smile that apparently the lad had a hot date and needed to get back. Mrs. Jones had chimed in that she could see why and gushed on about how handsome, nice, and well mannered he was and had added he had gorgeous curly hair! Albert had gone on to say all the girls in the village were sure going to love him; the lad had a way with the ladies. He'd never had so many happy ones on his bus. He had charmed them all. She had heard enough after that and tuned them out, not interested and not in a hurry to meet him. She'd photographed, met, and known far too many arrogant, good-looking, sexy jerks like him to last a lifetime.

She shook her head disgustedly. Now there he sat, which she couldn't believe. Nobody was allowed in the back except family. She rolled her eyes knowing he had to be there for the job. *Buggar*, she thought, *I just put the help wanted sign in the bloody window before I went out for my walk.*

She had finally agreed with Mum this morning that she needed help, but had said she had the final approval of who was hired, since he or she would be working with her most of the time. Well, she already knew it was a big *No!* on this bloke. She needed help, not some bloke on the make all of the time. A little devilish voice inside her head told her to make the door hit the wall. She did, pushing it a little harder than she meant to, letting out a little frustration.

*Bam!* It slammed against the wall almost breaking the glass.

# CHAPTER 2

# HARRY

Harry opened the front door of their new home not realizing Luke had followed him up the hall. He yelled over his shoulder, "I'm taking a break. I thought I'd go down to the village to check it out. Maybe it looks better in the daylight."

"Okay," said Luke standing behind him.

Harry jumped and said with a chuckle, "Bloody hell! Dad, you scared the total crap out of me."

Luke responded with a grin, "I'm going up to tuck your baby sister in for her nap before I head back to work. I'm sure you're going to check those gates out on the—"

"You know me so well," Harry said cutting him off.

Luke nodded and said, "Keep to the left following the wall after you do. When it ends, there's a path around the bushes that will lead you down to a small gate. Then just follow the path to the walk, and it will take you right past the bakery and then down to the village. It will save you some time."

"Thanks, I will."

"Have fun. You might want to take that rag off your head. Your mum won't like you having it on out in public."

"Oh yeah, thanks I forgot I had it on. See you later," Harry said, closing the door behind him. He removed his do-rag and stuffed it in his back pocket. He ran his fingers through his curls making them fall naturally as he headed down the long driveway. The sun was shining brightly, making it a perfect spring day, but he still wallowed in self-pity despite how cheerful the weather was. He muttered as he kicked a rock, "Life sucks! It's going to be a long, boring summer living in this place!"

His parents, and three-year-old sister, Madeline, had just moved from Chester. It came about so quickly, he didn't really have time to wrap his mind around it. Dad had come home Wednesday all excited and said the bank in Holmes Cove was in need of a president again, and they called him to see if he wanted the job. The only catch being he needed to report to work on Monday morning, so they took a family vote. Harry hated to even think about moving but knew Dad had turned the job down three years earlier so that he could finish school with his mates. The job he left as the head of the audit department with the bank was great, but it took him away from home more than he wanted, having to travel to all their branches. It was usually only a few days at a time, but lately he complained even that was too long. He had to vote yes this time around, knowing the sacrifices Dad had made, missing some of Maddie's firsts. He wasn't home when they found her first tooth, when she sat up on her own, and the one he hated the most—when she took her first steps.

They worked nonstop for the next few days getting things packed up and ready for the moving truck, which was arriving early Saturday morning. He was happy Dad had gotten the job; he just wished it wasn't out in the middle of nowhere. He had walked around the village the night before to check it out. He couldn't believe it; he didn't see a movie cinema or fast-food place, not even a pizza or taco shop in the whole bloody place!

There weren't enough kids with the village being so small to offer the last year of school, which was a good thing. Dad made sure the job included transportation for him to go to Chester in the fall. Thank God! He wouldn't have to ride the one and only local bus. It had taken the bloody thing forever Saturday afternoon to get to Chester!

He had to admit, the new house provided with the job was brilliant. It was at least three times larger than their house in Chester. He loved that his bedroom was double the size, with his own loo. There was also the hot tub, huge swimming pool, and pool house. The pool house was half the size of their old house. It was more like a guesthouse, sitting twenty feet from the huge, kidney-shaped swimming pool. He could see a lot of parties going on there, that's if there were any kids his age around.

He reached the intersecting point of the long drive, which was shared with two other families. He turned right onto the drive leading him toward the gates he wanted to get a closer look at. It was the only place to look through to see the house. The whole place was surrounded by a huge, ten-foot brick wall. He was anxious to see the house knowing it had to be brilliant to match the awesome gates. They were made of black wrought iron with stone columns, each topped with a gold lion standing on its back legs holding a shield. He was sure the family had noble roots dating back to the Tudor times, his favorite time in history. He stopped walking when he got close and looked up at the top of the brick wall and gates. He was intrigued by the vast number of CCTV cameras, and his curiosity piqued. He let out a low whistle and muttered, "It's like a fortress around here. I bet they have twenty-four-hour armed guards in there, too. I wouldn't be surprised if there are landmines around the place. Dad said the bloke owned some big security outfit, but it seems this is just a bit over the top, being so far out in the boonies. What? They worried the bloody cows are going to attack?" He chuckled at his own joke as he looked through the gates. The house was mostly shielded by trees, but he could see enough to determine that it looked a lot like his—a sixteenth-century manor house made of honey-colored stone. He grumbled disgustedly, "That's just depressing. What a waste of these wicked gates; their house looks like mine! I was expecting this place to be something on the lines of Highcliff Castle or at least Keaton Hall. This whole village is a bloody let down!"

He followed alongside the wall, remembering the path Dad told him about. He walked to the patch of flowering bushes and started down a small gravel path that led to an iron gate. He lifted the latch, and as he pushed it open, it creaked, letting him know it wasn't used much. Once through, he closed it and continued down the path to the walk. "Thanks, Dad. It does save a lot of walking," he muttered seeing the bakery that sat just above the village in its own cul-de-sac. He hadn't walked by the bakery on Saturday since he went down the long drive. His stomach growled as he walked by inhaling the delicious aroma. He stopped and backed up a few steps after noticing a Help Wanted sign in the window. He got a strange feeling like he needed to go in and check it out, which was weird because he wasn't looking for a job. He and Lee, his best mate, were planning to work on their music and hopefully find a couple of new mates to get a band together again. He chuckled while opening the door, thinking it was probably the amazing smell giving him that feeling; it was doing his head in. He went in, never expecting his life would change.

CHAPTER 3

Ten minutes later, Harry found himself sitting at a small table in the back room of the bakery. His mood had shifted considerably as he happily munched away on his second meat pasty. He could see why the place was so busy and needed help. It was the best bakery ever! The best meat pasties he'd ever eaten in his life by far. He thought maybe it was because they were smaller than the ones he had eaten tons of over the years from the Cornish pasty shop in Chester. He crammed the end of a pasty in his mouth and was reaching for an apple one when he heard the back door bang open. He jumped as if he had been shot and jerked his head around toward the door.

"Oops! It must have slipped," said Lily Rose smiling sweetly.

Harry straightened up on his chair. His eyes moved directly to her perfect-sized and perfectly shaped breasts. His gaze lowered liking her slender waist and long, lean legs.

Lily Rose was trying not to stare as she thought, *Mrs. Jones had said he was handsome. Bloody hell, that was an understatement! He's drop-dead gorgeous!* Her stomach seemed to float up under her ribs taking her breath away as she felt warmth spread through her insides. When she realized she was staring and starting to blush she quickly turned to close the door before her cheeks got really bright.

Harry was just about to focus in on her face, hoping it matched the rest of her, when she turned. He was waiting for her to turn back after she closed the door, but she walked to the refrigerator away from him not looking his way. He liked the graceful way she moved and how slender and tall she was, figuring she was a couple of inches shorter than his six foot. He nodded his approval as he stared at her bum. He thought, *She has all the right curves in all the right places*. Feeling some discomfort in his man part, Clyde (the name he had given it when he was two), he knew there was no way he could stand up to meet her. His black jeans were tight enough before Clyde made an appearance. He was sure not much would be left to the imagination as he would be perfectly outlined from standing at full attention.

Lily Rose's legs felt like they were wrapped in lead as she walked. When she made it to the fridge, she couldn't stop herself from taking a quick peek over her shoulder as she opened the door and saw he was staring straight at her bum. It should have made her angry, but it did the complete opposite. It made her heart hammer even harder in her ears as heat rushed through her again. She stepped in letting the door block his view, while loving the cold air hitting her face—it seemed to calm her a little.

She took a small breath. "Hi! I'm Lily Rose," she announced, finally finding her voice while slowly reaching a trembling hand for a couple of fizzy drinks. She closed the door, looking down as she turned to give herself an extra second.

Harry was disappointed when she turned not looking at him.

Lily Rose shifted one of the cans to her other hand before she dropped it. She could feel his stare before she raised her head to meet it.

Harry let out a breath he hadn't even realized he'd been holding. He was caught totally off guard and immediately felt his pulse start to race when she smiled. It was as if the whole room lit up. He was staring at the most beautiful face he had ever seen.

Lily Rose walked toward him. She was drawn to him like she had never been drawn to anyone before.

Harry was unable to take his eyes away as if in a trance. He noticed right away she wasn't wearing any make-up but then she didn't need any. Her skin was flawless—clear and smooth. Her eyes big and almond shaped. Her incredibly long, curly lashes were dark and thick, like her hair. He couldn't quite work out the color of her eyes. They looked blue one second and green the next. He decided they were more like a light gray. They were seductive and sparkled as she smiled. He flashed her a huge smile. It wasn't the flirty one he usually flashed at the ladies; it was his genuine smile. The one that made his green eyes twinkle and dimples run deep.

She felt her pulse quicken from his perfect, little dimples. *And—oh—*she inwardly sighed—*what amazing, full lips. People paid good money to get lips like his.*

Harry knew he was staring and nervously threaded his fingers through his curls and pushed them behind his ear.

Lily Rose caught herself from letting out a groan; his curls seemed to beg her fingers to run through them. His hair was a little longer than she liked, but she liked it on him. It was the wildness of it she decided, the way his curls fell over his forehead and laid this way and that all over his head. It seemed to suit him; he wore it well. Heat was now raging through places down deep, places she never even knew she had. Her instincts quickly warned her to get her guard up at the way he was affecting her. She leaned over slightly, setting down the drinks.

"Looks like you could use one of these," she said feeling pleased with herself, thinking her voice sounded reasonably cool and collected.

Harry couldn't avoid breathing in her scent, a hint of peppermint. He had never noticed it on anyone before. It matched her perfectly, and he really liked it. He realized he needed to say something and hadn't even introduced himself after she'd told him her name. A wave of nervousness seemed to come from nowhere making him suddenly feel awkward. He could feel the muscles in his neck beginning to tense. *Blimey! What is my problem? I never lose my cool with girls!* He opened his mouth but nothing came out. He was having difficulty in making his tongue understand that one of its primary functions was to work so that he could speak.

She was doing his head in. For the first time in his life, a girl had him rattled. After what seemed like hours, instead of just seconds, he finally blurted out, "Hi! I'm Harry Thomas," and grimaced when he realized he had said Thomas. He could feel his cheeks growing hot and quickly looked away, hoping he wasn't as red as it felt. *Thomas! Really? I never use Thomas. I just managed to morph into a complete tosser before her very eyes!*

Lily Rose picked up an apple pasty from the platter as she slid into the chair across from him looking into his deep, green eyes. She couldn't help getting lost in them. *Any girl would envy those long, thick eyelashes.* She told herself sternly, *Get it together; he is just another gorgeous bloke and is quite clearly aware of it.* Well, she wasn't going to let him think she was the sort of girl who would fall so easily for his charms. Absentmindedly, she rolled her eyes seductively with pleasure as she bit into the pasty, totally ignoring him as if he had no effect on her at all.

Harry stared at her full, luscious lips as she bit into the pasty and almost groaned when apple filling squirted onto her bottom lip. He watched her run the tip of her tongue lightly across to retrieve it and thought it was the sexiest thing a girl had ever done. *Oh! I wish it was my tongue doing that! Kissing girls with full lips is the best. I'm definitely going to kiss those lips.* He had to fight to keep his expression neutral while desire flooded through his body.

He reached for his drink, taking the opportunity to chill out and gather his wits. "Thanks," he finally got out as he lifted it up at her. He flipped back the tab, leaned his head back, and started gulping it down greedily. He tried to swallow down the burp that was trying to escape as he drank. Feeling as though he couldn't breathe, he dragged air into his lungs. He began choking and sputtering the drink from his mouth and nose. It gushed out like a geyser, going everywhere!

He stared at her while he choked seeing her take his photo, making him choke more from sucking in air of disgust. A flush of color flooded his face as he stopped. *Bloody hell! I just made a complete arse out of myself, as she got it on film!*

"Looks like you're having a little trouble there," she teased and tossed him the hand towel from the table.

Harry raised his eyebrows as he picked up the towel. "Cheers!"

Her laughter exploded. She laughed so hard that she had tears streaming down her cheeks.

He tried to ignore her laughter ringing in his ears as he wiped himself off.

She wiped the tears from her cheeks as she got herself under control.

"Humph, someone has a very perverse sense of humor," he muttered making Lily Rose laugh even harder. He continued to stare while mopping up the table.

She gained control again and let out a little sigh.

He made a sound of disgust. "Are you about done taking a mick out of me? Need to work on your manners. You might put people off!"

"Come on, you have to admit that was funny."

He hmmphed once again and grunted. "Oh, just hysterical." He folded the damp towel and dropped it onto the table.

"It was certainly entertaining." She nodded as her mouth twitched. It wasn't a good sign. It meant she was forcing control. "The look on your face when it shot out your nose..." She roared with laughter again.

He folded his arms across his chest watching her. "Obviously, not done!" he replied, with an annoyed expression.

Taking a deep breath a moment later, after regaining her composure again, she said, "Okay, I'm done. But honestly, I didn't think a person was capable of shooting so much liquid out of their nose..."

He dismissed her comment with a wave of his hand to let her know he had heard enough. "Yeah, yeah, all right. I looked like a total wanker! I got the picture," he muttered.

She lifted her camera. "I certainly hope I did. I'm *sooo* glad I have it on film." She couldn't control herself and burst out laughing again.

"Well, that lasted for about a nanosecond," he muttered. Despite his embarrassment, he watched her with an amused grin. He found himself relaxing and his self-confidence grew by the minute.

Taking another deep breath, she softly exhaled. "Okay, I'm really done this time," she said, wiping away the last tear slipping down her cheek.

He leaned back in his seat. His eyes sparked in interest, deciding he liked her. "Right then, but you've said that more than once," he said with a raised brow. "Are you sure this time?"

"No, I'm not sure!" she said as she shook her head. Her teasing eyes drew him in even more.

"Nobody can accuse you of being polite, that's for sure. Did you mean to be rude on purpose?" His words were undercut by the hint of a smile on his lips, liking he was sounding like himself again.

Lily Rose shrugged, the corner of her mouth lifted as she replied, "Oh, if you want polite...you've come to the wrong place. And just so you know, I usually don't have a problem with voicing my opinion."

His confidence was back in full swing loving her banter. He teased with a wink as he leveled his chair, "I'm sure nothing about you is usual."

The wink and implications in his tone sent a heated rush through her again. To cover up the way her body reacted, she immediately asked, changing the subject, "Who let you back here by yourself?"

"It was Mrs. M., who I take is your mum, seeing as you look just like her mini-me." He added showing off his sexy, lopsided grin, "By the way, I find the mini-version much more beautiful!"

She rolled her eyes not commenting on his compliment. "So you and your family getting all settled in? I was planning on bringing a welcome basket up later. You saved me a trip."

"Now, if I were the nosey sort—which I'm not—I'd probably be asking, how do you know I'm your new neighbor?" he asked grinning.

"First let me say, I'm glad you're not, because there is no shortage of those around here. The locals discuss and share all the village gossip in here. You were their main topic this morning as a matter of fact."

"I guess they have to have some form of entertainment around here. This place is...well, boring as hell!"

Shaking her head she replied, "Actually, it's not!"

"Uh-huh, that's a matter of opinion," he grunted.

She couldn't stop from rolling her eyes again. "I heard you were well entertained by the ladies on the bus the other day on your way to Chester. Doesn't sound like you thought they were too boring."

"Bus! Is that what you call that old rickety thing I was on? It took forever to get to Chester." He started to complain as if disgusted but had a flirtatious smile on his face the whole time. "First, I spent an hour kicking my heels at the one and only bus stop because the one and only bus that comes through this place only comes every other hour. Then the driver, who has to be at least eighty and moves like a turtle, took like five minutes just to open the door to let me on, which happened every time we stopped, every other minute, for people to get on or off. We would finally get up to ten miles an hour, going good, then a mile before we even reached the next bloody bus stop, he would begin to slow back down and coast in. Plus, he would stop and ask people walking alongside the road if they needed a bloody ride!"

"That's because he's a real sweetheart," she said with a grin, "but you're right; he doesn't get in any hurry, that's for sure."

"That's an understatement. A snail moves faster," he teased. "It took so long to get to Chester, I almost just stayed on the bloody bus and rode back home to make sure I got back by Sunday night!" His cheeky smile matched the absurdity of his remark.

"Stop," she said with a chuckle, "but I have heard it takes almost an hour to get to Chester on the bus."

"What do you mean you've *heard*?" His brow shot up in surprise. "You've never been to Chester?" he asked.

"Now, why would I want to leave here?" she teased, winding him up.

His brow shot up. "And you think that's not crazy?"

"Actually, no. You seem to be under a misconception that everyone thinks it's boring as hell here," she replied as a smile curled the corners of her mouth. "We don't!"

His eyes went big as he playfully blew air out of his puffed cheeks. "Then misery loves company!"

She chuckled.

He grinned as he picked up his drink and lifted the can in mock salute. "Let's see if I can keep it down this time," he joked with a wink before he took a slow slip.

She reached for hers and held it up returning his salute. She then watched him over the top of the can as she took a sip. She thought, *Of course I've been to Chester. What kind of daft question is that? I just don't take the bus.* Then she realized what he was thinking. *This bloke thinks I'm a country bumpkin!* She almost laughed out loud at the very thought of it. Placing her can on the table, she switched the topic back to his bus ride before she ended up telling him she thought he was an arrogant arse! Congratulating herself on her restraint she said, "Albert was saying you kept everyone well entertained, and he had never seen so many happy ladies on his bus."

"What can I say? The ladies love me. I'm just full of charm."

"Humm, you're full of something all right!"

That got a chuckle from him. "I have to be honest; I did like Albert, and I really enjoyed my extremely *long* bus ride."

"I'm glad, he likes you as well. By the way," she said way too sweetly, "what do I say when the customers ask me your name? Seems you were a little confused earlier when you said Harry Thomas, as if you didn't mean to say Thomas at all."

He playfully grimaced and asked with a husky groan, "You caught that, huh?"

She nodded with a wide grin.

"How about I let you decide? Am I a Harry Thomas? Or am I just a plain ol' Harry?" he asked with a lazy smile. He ran his fingers through his hair, pushing it back from his face as he gave her one of his winks.

"Humm, let me think a second," she said, lightly tapping her chin with her index finger appearing to be thinking on it, but really trying to recover from her insides turning to mush. She grunted inwardly, *Like there is a plain thing about this bloke! And I wish he'd quit that bloody winking; he's doing my head in!*

"Well?" he teased.

"I'm thinking here; don't rush me."

Harry's eyes gleamed as he chuckled.

"Got it!" she replied a few seconds later. "How about HT? Covers both of your names, and it will keep you from getting confused again."

"Let's see. Interesting," he spoke slowly, as if deep in thought. After a few seconds, his eyes sparkled as he replied with a nod, "I like HT!"

She rolled her eyes laughing. "You don't like it!"

"No really, I do," he insisted as he nodded.

"Well, there you go then; problem solved."

He held up his hand. "Hold on, not so fast. It's only fair that I get to return the favor."

"You want to give me a nickname?"

"Yeah, at least a go at it!"

"You're up to the challenge? Are you sure?"

"For sure." He nodded grinning.

"Well then, give it a go. Let's see what you can come up with. First let me just say I really do love Lily Rose because I'm named after my grandmothers."

"No pressure there," he said with a cheeky grin. He rubbed his chin thoughtfully while muttering, "Humm, let me see, let me see." After a few seconds, he snapped his fingers. "Got it! You're going to think I'm absolutely brilliant."

"I highly doubt it," she said smugly.

He lightly shook his head as his mouth twisted with his sexiest smile, loving her banter and having a hard time trying to keep up with her quick wit. He proudly announced, "Lil?"

She fought to keep her face straight and pulse from racing. She loved it, but there was no way she was going to admit that to him. She hesitated with her answer appearing to think it over.

He lifted his brows waiting.

She slowly said, "*Lil*, you say?"

He watched her face and saw her feeble attempt to appear nonchalant. He knew she liked it. "Absolutely. It's brilliant," he assured her with a nod.

"I'm not sure I look like a"—she scrunched up her nose—"Lil!" She added a little sigh for effect and asked, "Are you sure?"

"Oh yes, I'm very sure," he answered playing along, not taking his dancing eyes off her.

"Right then," she said on a sigh. "I guess I can live with Lil since you seem to like it so much."

He flashed his arrogant smile. "You know you love it."

She didn't like that smile at all and couldn't help being a little irritated he seemed to be able to read her. "One quick question," she said, wanting to wipe the smug look off his face.

"What's that?"

She tilted her head a bit to the side and asked, "Well, do you think maybe the reason you find all the locals so boring is that you're the one who's just not that interesting to talk to?"

His green eyes started to narrow at her insult and then realized he had finally rattled her and threw his head back, howling with laughter.

Mary entered smiling at hearing him laugh and seeing Lil's flushed cheeks and shining eyes. Her warm, brown hair was pulled back in a stylish hair comb, not a strand out of place. She looked casual and elegant at the same time, as if she was off to have high tea. No one would have guessed she had been working since 5:00 a.m. or that she was closing in on forty. The faint, crinkly lines around the corners of her eyes were the only hint of her age.

Lil glanced up as she walked toward them, while removing her white-and-pink-striped apron. Lil returned her smile and thought the aqua-green sundress brought out the hazel color of her eyes.

Lil could tell by the way she looked at her, she wanted to know. *Did she hire HT?* Her mind raced, listing the pros and cons, trying to decide. Her overall impression was that he was an outrageous flirt, had a cocky attitude, and was one smooth operator when it came to the ladies...best she'd ever met. He was in a class of his own, but she couldn't deny that she really liked him and loved his humor. She enjoyed his company and their banter; they had that spark that drew people together. *So what's the problem?* she asked herself. She frowned as a mental alarm buzzed with the answer. *The bloody problem is I have never met a bloke I'm so bloody attracted to!* The sane, rational part of her brain knew she was in trouble from the way her body was reacting to him, that she was taking on more than she could handle! But the part of her brain that was silly and told her she was strong enough to resist him no matter how sinfully gorgeous he was, won out. The little voice inside her head protested, as she gave Mum a little nod.

Mary acknowledged understanding with a slight nod of her own.

Lil stood and greeted, "Hi, Mum."

HT not knowing she had come in, jumped up, and turned as she approached.

Lil snuck a glance his way. She wasn't expecting him to be so tall, and she liked it when guys were taller than her. His tight, faded black jeans, T-shirt, and well-worn, low-heeled black boots made him look like a rock star...not her type at all.

Mary said with a big smile, "You two sound like you're getting along." She glanced over at Lil. "So do we offer Harry the job?"

Lil saw him from the corner of her eye, watching for her answer. Still looking at Mary, she shrugged. When she responded she tried to sound doubtful. "Um...I honestly don't know! I do like him...Okay, mostly I do," she said as if she needed to correct herself. "He's a little cheeky though." She paused as if thinking.

HT stared, eyebrows raised, as she continued.

"Well, no...he's very cheeky. He doesn't care for our village at all, and he's just amazed that we love living here so much, and he thinks we're all boring as hell!" She paused another second for effect and glanced over to check HT's expression and had to bite back a laugh. His eyes were opened so wide that his forehead wrinkled; he was clearly surprised by her remarks.

"Oh my!" Mary said, acting disturbed by her reply.

Lil slowly dragged out her next words. "But then...he does have a few good points, I guess."

"Then maybe I should hear the good points before I decide!" Mary replied, playing along.

He realized they were winding him up. A slow smile spread across his face liking Lil more by the minute.

Lil continued with a head nod his way. "A real charmer this one. His magnetism alone will draw the ladies in. Also, he likes to abbreviate names; yours is Mrs. M. and mine is Lil. I'm sure before long he'll do the same for all the ladies in the village, and they will absolutely love him for it."

"Oh! Well, I have to admit I like Lil," replied Mary. "Do you?"

He tilted his head a bit waiting for her answer.

"I do..."

"I knew it!" He chuckled.

Lil rolled her eyes. "I didn't tell him because of that!"

He gave her yet another of his little winks when she glanced over at him.

She quickly turned away, feeling her insides warming up again. *Stop it*, she warned herself, trying to focus. She added a little sarcastically, "By the way, it seems he has a hard time remembering if he goes by Harry or Harry Thomas, so I shortened it to HT. You know, make it easier for him."

"I like HT," said Mary as she crossed her arms over her chest and pursed her lips as she looked at HT. She tried her best to appear stern as she told him, "Well, we do need to keep our lady customers happy around here, but since you don't care for our perfect little village, well, that might be a deal breaker."

His eyes shone like glass, seeing where Lil had gotten her humor. He said slowly, "Well...if you're basing your evaluation of me on that," he hastily interjected, making his eyes grow wide, "I've changed my mind. I love it here! I really, really do!"

That got a big laugh from all of them.

"The job is yours, that is, if you still want it after that little display." Mary chuckled.

"Oh, I definitely want the job, Mrs. M. I'd pay *you* to work here!"

"Great! Welcome aboard!" Mary replied as she turned and walked to the back door, stopping just long enough to hang her apron on a hook. She opened the door, looking back at HT with a smile. "I prefer you call me Moms."

Smiling from ear to ear, he replied, "You got it. Thanks for hiring me, Moms!"

"Thank Lily Rose, I mean Lil. It was all up to her," she said with a smile, closing the door behind her.

Lil groaned and closed her eyes. "Buggar," she mumbled under her breath.

"Looks like she just dropped you in the middle of it!" he teased.

Lil let out a little huff seeing his smug look again. "Yeah, well, get over yourself, Mr. Rock Star. I'm so desperate for help, I'd let her hire an arrogant, overly smug bloke with a huge ego...Oh wait a minute, I did!"

"Ouch!" he playfully winced, seeing the grin she was trying to hide and replied, "I can see I'm going to have to improve my image with you."

"Just the one when you're such an arrogant arse, not the whole I wanna be a rock star thing you have going on. It suits you."

A slow, sexy grin slid over his face. "Thanks, it's what I strive for!" causing them both to laugh.

She walked to the middle of the room and stood between two long, stainless steel work counters. "I'll show you around before I start the cleanup, if you have time."

"I can stay and help," he said, walking to stand beside her. "So where do we start, and what are my hours?"

"As to the hours, it's up to you really."

"Then what's your hours?"

"I'm usually here around seven; I have breakfast, and help out where I'm needed," she replied. "I leave when the rush is over and come back around noon. On Saturday, I work straight through; it's our busiest day. Then Sundays we're closed." She added, "Of course, you don't have to work all those hours. If you can come in around noon on weekdays and then work what you can on Saturday, it would be brilliant."

"I'll see with my busy schedule what I can pencil in," he teased.

"I'm sure it will get real busy once the girls around here get a look at you; or should I say, once you get a look at them!"

He gave her a boyish grin, running his fingers through his curls and pushing them back once again. "How about we call a truce here. Let's see if we can carry on a conversation without all the banter while we work. It's doing my head in trying to keep up with you."

"Fine, I agree to a truce if you stop all that flirting and winking. Besides, it's all wasted on me; save it for the customers," she said while she thought, *I'm willing to say whatever is necessary to get you to stop that bloody winking!*

His eyes widened in surprise. "You're into girls? Blimey, my radar isn't working!" He puffed up his cheeks and blew air out.

Lil started laughing, shaking her head as she thought *even that is sexy as hell.* "Nooo, your radar is fine. I'm not batting for the same team. I'm definitely into blokes, just not ones like you."

"Like me! I'm not so sure I like what you're insinuating. What the bloody hell does that mean?" he asked…"Hey, wait a minute. You already reneged on our truce."

"What?" she asked innocently, a faint smile evident on her lips. "We're not working yet!"

His brow rose. "I would say that's a bit dodgy!"

"It was. Sorry." She chuckled.

"Apology accepted," he said with a grin. "So let's move on to the grand tour."

She returned his grin and as she waved her hand in an arc, "This room is the largest of three," she said. She turned in a half circle and stopped facing the back wall telling herself, *Don't embarrass yourself, don't mumble, don't mumble.* It was her worst habit ever. She would tend to do it when she explained things or had a lot to say. If she was tired or nervous it was even worse; she mumbled faster and left out words. She motioned to her left. Not realizing it, she started talking with a rhythmic voice to keep from mumbling.

"The refrigerators and freezers are over there. There's another small fridge up front, blah, blah, blah. I bring all the containers and tins in here to fill; it makes it a lot easier, blah, blah, blah." Pointing to the right corner she continued with her rhythm, "The brooms, mops, and dust pans are there by the loo, which I will give you the honors to clean—"

He cut in, using the same rhythmic tone. "Oh thanks. I appreciate that, blah, blah, blah. Cleaning toilets is my most favorite thing to do. Blah, blah, blah."

"I guess that was a little annoying," she said wrinkling her nose.

"Maybe just a tad," he teased, with a grin.

She turned back to the front thinking, *Not as annoying as my mumbling.* "Mum will take care of closing the front. By the way, no customers are allowed back here or behind the counters up front."

He nodded in response. "Got the 'no-one-back-here' earlier when you were surprised to see me."

She continued talking as she walked right toward the main kitchen. "That's really about the only rule around here."

HT followed her, and they stood in the doorway.

"This is the baking room. It's where Grammy makes all the magic happen along with Aunt Abs and Uncle Joe."

"So who's the real boss?" he asked.

"Nobody is really what you call a boss. Everybody just goes with the flow and pitches in to get things done."

"I like that. It's sure impressive in here," said HT as he scanned the room.

There were six huge ovens against the back wall and two stove tops with ten burners. In the middle of the room, large mixers, bowls, a lot of containers and jars were sitting on two long counters each with wooden tops, sitting back to back. He looked to his right and saw scales and multiple bags of flour stacked on another large wooden-topped counter. There were dozens of baker racks full of empty silver trays just waiting to be filled to restart the day. Everything was neat and organized, and the silver chrome was shiny and sparkling.

"We clean in here?" he asked looking at Lil.

She shook her head. "No, they take care of this room. We stock those shelves with boxes and carry out the trays in the morning." She pointed to containers, tins, and jars on the shelves and counters as she spoke, "And we fill those. Actually, that's usually where I start."

"Right then," said HT, "let's get started." He took his favorite, blue do-rag from his back pocket and tied it around his head. "I've tried to hold back on wearing this, but I've had about all I can take of these bloody curls flopping down in my eyes. My hair is total crap when it gets this long. Hope it's okay with Moms that I wear this thing while we're open."

Lil's insides went instantly hot. "No, that's perfect! Mum will like your hair being up and off your face. She makes me keep mine tied back."

"Great. Then my mum can't give me any grief. She hates me wearing it out in public."

The next hour or so passed quickly as they talked and laughed while they worked. Neither of them had to pretend; they were truly curious and interested to hear what the other had to say.

Once they were done, Lil looked around. "Looks good. Of course, it doesn't usually take this long, but I think we did more laughing and talking than we did working. Now, all that's left is the sweeping."

"Leave the sweeping to me! I can sweep a mean floor now," he replied and walked to the radio and turned it on. "I can work faster with music." He pushed the do-rag up further on his forehead, making his curls poof on top of his head and then grabbed a broom off the back wall. "Now, time to get at that sweeping," and he began humming happily as he swept.

Trying to catch her breath and calm herself down, she grabbed a stack of cookie boxes from the shelf just in case he was looking and escaped to the baking room, not caring the boxes were kept up front. She fussed under her breath, "Blimey! I wanna run my fingers through his curls." She made a tsk sound. "Remember, you don't like blokes with long hair and do-rags? Yeah! Right! Well, apparently I do on him!"

She walked out of the kitchen and froze in her tracks hearing him sing. She was awestruck listening to his amazing voice. His tone was brilliant, lively, and rich, putting the bloke on the radio to shame. She let out a low, despairing groan as if in pain. She had never experienced anything quite like the burning that started deep down and spiraled outward through her whole body. She continued to stare and mumbled under her breath. "He is sure full of surprises! How is it possible for one person to possess so much natural charisma and magnetism?" Finally tearing her eyes away and pulling herself together, she ran for her camera. She scooped it up. She was totally captivated as her fingers moved in constant motion on the button. She could actually tell when he really got into the song, going into his *own zone*. She decided to call it "The HT Zone." His whole demeanor seemed to change. It was like every fiber in his body felt the music. His eyes even seemed to get brighter. She mumbled, "This is the hottest, sexiest photo shoot I've ever done."

HT was so immersed in the song that he didn't see her or hear the constant click of the camera. He turned when the song ended seeing her and flashed her a cheek-dimpling smile. Not taking his eyes from hers, he bent slightly forward giving her a small bow, unembarrassed at being caught. He teased, "If you liked it, you can find me here same time tomorrow."

"Seriously? I'll be here," she teased back. She raised her slightly closed hand and kissed the tips of her fingers and then quickly opened her hand as if she was imitating an Italian. Her voice rose higher with excitement as she said, "You're brilliant! Magnificent! Just superb! You have to be the best floor sweeper ever!"

A slow smile tipped the corners of his mouth as he nodded vigorously. "I know! I'm just amazed at how truly brilliant I am. Just wait; I get even better with a mop. The air guitar comes out then!"

They laughed as he pulled off his do-rag and ran his fingers through his curls, making them fall naturally.

Lil groaned inwardly as she quickly turned and headed up toward the front. She couldn't deal with the way her body was reacting to him. She had to get him out of there; she'd had enough. She said over her shoulder, "I guess that's it for today."

"Right then, I just need to put this broom back," he replied as he walked to the back wall.

She grumbled under her breath as she went to the front door, "I bet he can even pull off a bloody man-bun, which I also hate on a bloke! But I'm sure I'd find it sexy on him!" She couldn't put her finger on what it was about him that had gotten to her all day, but whatever it was, she needed a cold shower!

He walked up, taking his phone out. "How about you give me your number in case something comes up?"

She rattled it off as she unlocked the door and pulled it open. Her phone buzzed at the same time the bell above the door chimed. She asked with a raised brow, "Yours, I take it?"

Slipping his back into his back pocket, he nodded. "Just in case you want me, and it doesn't have to be about work," he said, lifting his brow up and down. "I'll be home all night if you want to bring that basket over later."

"That's wishful thinking, HT. I'm glad you've got a sense of humor though. I don't suppose it would do any good to mention that we had a truce!"

"We're done working," he teased with a wink. "Besides, I couldn't help myself. You were just too easy! You can check out just how easy I am tonight when you stop over."

She couldn't help but laugh. "Do you ever listen to yourself?"

"Nope," he said with a chuckle as he strutted out the door, "I'll see you later!"

She was grateful that he couldn't read her mind wanting to take him up on it. She stuck her head out the door as he started up the walk, "Don't hold your breath!" she said laughing at his retrieving back.

He turned walking backward and replied, "About seven is good!"

"Yes, seven is brilliant, and that's a.m.!" she called back.

He turned back around laughing, throwing his hand up in a wave. He shook his head lightly as he muttered, "I can tell already you'll always get the last word in," and chuckled. He started humming the song from the radio earlier as he started up the path.

She sighed, as she closed the door and locked it. She shook her head in disgust, knowing she was wildly attracted to him...and the worst part, she knew it was mutual. "Bloody hell!" she mumbled, "What did I just get myself into?"

Twenty minutes later, after making herself a pot of tea, Lil went to her darkroom carrying it and a large mug. She wanted to work for a few hours before dinner, and she needed to stay focused. Sipping her tea, she developed the film of HT. She laughed at how she'd let him think she had never been to Chester. She went almost every Sunday. She loved visiting Jacob, who owned her favorite camera shop. She had been buying her supplies and equipment from him since day one. He had more in his shop than any shop she'd ever been in. They could go on for hours talking about one camera or piece of equipment.

She watched the developing tray as HT's eyes slowly came into focus as he was sweeping. If there was a secret for sex appeal, he knew it well; he oozed it. He didn't have to worry about turning on the charisma; he had that naturally, along with his self-confidence. She mumbled as she hung the photos on the line, "You're gorgeous, and you sure make my body crazy. I wouldn't mind for you to be my first. Where the heck did that come from?" She shook her head as if to clear it while fiercely scolding herself. "Stop it. Get your guard up. I'm not, absolutely, most definitely not, going to let myself fall for him. That bloke will chew up my heart and spit it out without thinking twice about it. Well," she fussed, "you're not about to get mine added to your list."

She sighed as she went out of the darkroom. She headed to the loo mumbling, "Damn him and his irresistible winks, curly hair, and dimples; I need a long, cold shower!"

# CHAPTER 4

Charles was sitting behind his desk in the study waiting on Luke. He was deep in thought of how they had come full circle. Luke had finally made it back to live in his childhood home; however, he had stayed there off and on over the years using one of his many disguises as Bill's best mate Carl, a yank from America.

Charles thought of how he, Luke, and Ed had become the best of mates at an early age, meeting during their fathers' secret meetings at Highcliff Castle. They didn't have a clue of what their meetings were about or know of the Special Ops Team operated by them. Officially, that didn't exist. Like his security business, the knowledge of the team and how it operated was handed down over the years. The family and members of the team had taken pride in providing the security service for the monarchy, even though few people knew they existed.

He remembered how he, Luke, and Ed had discovered a secret room off the old duke's private library. The room was packed with leather-bound journals full of stories from, throughout generations, describing the details of each op, including accounting ledgers.

They'd been so enthralled by the secret journals that they couldn't quit reading them. They'd decided when they were nine to tell their fathers they had read the journals and knew about their special security team and that they wanted to join right away. They knew from the passages in the journals eighteen was the minimum age for entry, but didn't want to wait and hoped their fathers would make an exception, seeing as they *were* top command. At first their fathers had been unsure of what to say or do with them, but after a thorough discussion, they'd developed a plan to make them the Jr. Ops Team.

The Jr. Ops Team was sworn in to uphold the same code: honor, honesty, and complete secrecy at a small ceremony. Training was to start right away with realistic missions devised for them to solve. They were to follow clues leading them from place to place throughout the castle and grounds. Sometimes it would take weeks to solve one mission. They loved it, always wanting more. Their fathers, realizing they were naturals with each having their own specialty, immediately appreciated the potential of their Jr. Team. All three were perfect for the world of intelligence, with individual skills and the desire to pursue the tradition of their families. Luke was the exceptional one with his natural talent. He could sneak in and out of their meetings at an early age, listening in without them knowing. Immediately realizing his talent, they provided him with trunks of clothes and disguises to master his craft, "his gift," as they called it.

They seemed to have naturally grown up to fulfill their roles. Each one of them took over their father's positions, just as generations before them. Charles became top command, while Luke and Ed were trained as his co-captains.

The three of them lost their mums at an early age, and their fathers spoiled them rotten. That was where Bill came in. They felt doubly blessed because Bill had always been as much a father to them as their own fathers, more so in some ways. He was the one who kept them in check. The one who would "box their ears," or "tie a knot in their tails," as he would say, when they caused mischief. He was also the one who mothered them when they just needed a hug, letting them know they were loved.

Ed was tall, muscular, full of charm, and more handsome than a bloke should be. He was brilliant with the whole posh social scene and fit right in, wearing the coat and tails while attending all the social gatherings to hear the gossip. He was the smooth talker, clever, charming, and had a way of being able to handle and read people. He knew how to get things from them without even trying, had them telling him their life stories, and sharing things they'd never shared with anyone. So there was no doubt he grew into his role of being a duke.

Luke looked like an everyday bloke, with sandy hair, average height and build, and was mild mannered. He blended in seamlessly with the crowd and moved around like a cat. They nicknamed him, "the Chameleon (Cam)," a master of disguises. He seemed to love it the most, the danger and adventure of it all, and he was the best at it.

Charles shared some of the same characteristics as Ed but was more handsome with his piercing blue eyes. He was like his father when it came to being the thinker and the planner. He always planned every detail and move to be made. He had a photographic memory, never forgetting dates, times, or places. He didn't believe in second sight or premonitions, but like generations before him, he had an intense intuition and knew when things just weren't right. He would feel chills, as the saying goes, "Like someone had walked over his grave." He had gotten them as long as he could remember. Sometimes he had dreams, which really drove him mental until he could figure out the meaning.

He also took after his father, as well as acquired traits from Bill, since Bill had been in his life just about twenty-four-seven, since the day he was born. He could be posh and snobbish playing the role when needed like his father, but he preferred being the laid-back, down-to-earth person he admired and loved the most—Bill.

He knew he needed to come clean with the three of them about the dreams he'd been having, knowing they had something to do with the helicopter crash, that killed their fathers some twenty-five years before. He, Luke, and Ed had graduated from Oxford, and their fathers had been flying to London with Bill's father, who was the pilot, to meet them for a special night out. However, their helicopter never made it. They found out a short time later it wasn't an accident, but the motive for the murders remained unknown. It was undetermined if it was for personal reasons or because someone had found out they were the men in charge of the secret security team of the monarchy.

A little red light flashed on the inside of his desk letting him know Luke entered the secret door downstairs in the back of the wine cellar. The door led to a tunnel that connected their wine cellars.

Bill asked as he walked in, "You ready to go down? I saw Luke is here."

"All set. I left some paperwork here for JR to take care of while we're gone." He, Bill, Ed, and Jayden were going on a routine op, checking on his teams of agents located in different parts of the world. They were going to give updates on new protocols for calling in and to provide new codes. Charles had decided it was time to have his own computer system, keeping his agent's identity and location secret from the security council of the queen, "E" as they called her. He was keeping the old system up and running as far as they were concerned but only sharing information he wanted to share.

They walked over and around the fireplace, standing away from the wall. They then followed the secret passage, to the narrow stone spiral staircase. At the bottom they continued through another passageway to enter an enormous round room that looked like it came out of MI5's building in Vauxhall. It was filled with computers, printers, filing cabinets, chairs, desks piled high with files, and large TV screens covering the walls.

Charles and Bill greeted Luke with the quick guy hug, handshake, and the slapping-each-other's-back thing they always did when seeing each other.

"So how's the unpacking going?" Charles asked Luke. "Harry still busting your nads about dragging him out to the boonies?"

"He's coming around a little," replied Luke. "He was going down to the village to check it out saying he hoped it looked better in the daylight."

Charles's phone rang. "What's up, love of my life?" He laughed after hearing what Mary said. "Just a sec; I'll see what Luke says."

Luke looked up hearing his name. "What's up?"

"Seems Lily Rose decided she could use some help at the bakery after all and put a Help Wanted sign in the window this morning. So guess who just came in asking about the job."

"Harry?" asked Luke surprised.

Charles nodded. "Mary wants to know, does she send him to the back for Lily Rose's okay?"

Luke shrugged. "What do you think?"

Charles also shrugged. "I guess. We knew they would meet sooner or later."

"Tell her to go ahead then," Luke said.

"You're going to let them work together?" asked Bill with a raised brow.

"We all know our baby girl; she doesn't go for blokes like Harry," said Luke. "She won't give him the time of day, let alone the job."

"Hey, babe, it's fine with us," he told her. He listened again for a few seconds and replied, "Love you most" and then slipped the phone into his pocket.

Bill looked at Luke. "I think you underestimate that boy's charm. You forget I've helped keep an eye on him over the years. That boy has to beat them girls off, and Snaggs is female. If those two hit it off, we could have Mary and this bloke"—he gestured at Charles—"all over again. You remember Mary was just like Snaggs until she fell for him."

"Oh no!" said Luke in a long-suffering tone. "Don't even joke about that. She had him mental for what, two years?"

"*Him* mental?" Bill scowled. "Seems I remember it being the worst two years of all *our* lives."

"Yeah! Yeah! And it was only a year and a half," Charles grumbled. "I should have been truthful with her a lot sooner than I was. At least, I came clean with her. What's your excuse?" he asked Luke. "Madison is still in the dark about everything. I'm telling you, it's going to come back and bite you in the—"

"I know, I know," he interrupted, waving him off. "Don't start that rubbish again," Luke huffed. "When are you telling the kids who I really am? They still don't have a clue."

"Don't turn this around on me. We both know after that promise I made to you with Madison, I'm leaving whom you tell and what you tell your prerogative."

Luke huffed again. "You seem to forget that you only came clean with Mary because we got caught."

"Which I remember was your fault, dropping me in it like you did, coming as Erica to my birthday party."

"Hey, I had just come from a meeting with E and didn't have time to change."

"That's total bollocks! I know Ed put you up to it, winding Mary up all night, flirting with me, and letting her think we had been carrying on behind her back."

No one spoke as the three of them thought about that night. The memory made them laugh.

Charles said, between fits of laughter, "I'll never forget the look on her face when she came tearing out of that loo and straight out the front door. You had her thinking my door swung both ways!"

Luke shook with laughter as he said, "I don't know who was more surprised, her or me, when she pulled opened that stall door to demand to know what was going on between us and saw my johnson hanging there. I have never moved so fast trying to get those damn stockings pulled up and that dress pulled down."

They laughed even harder.

Once they stopped laughing, Charles said, "Man, those were the days, huh?"

"Yeah, the best," Luke responded grinning. "I didn't mind having to give up that disguise after meeting Mags. It was rubbish having to shave my eyebrows and all my body hair!"

"No, what was really rubbish was," Charles said, still chuckling, "you got to be the lovable and entertaining southern talking Carl from Georgia, around the family, while I was stuck with the worst disguise ever to get to know Harry and Madison... your close friend, the prim-and-proper stiff-faced, stuttering, Lord Standish." He started to stutter, "They couldn't...ah-ah...get away from...ah-ah...me fast enough when I...ah-ah...came around."

"It's not my fault Lord Standish is the only disguise you can believably pull off," said Luke.

"That's because I've had to play that buffoon for years at those damn security-council meetings that I hate."

"Which was your doing, I might add," Luke said. "For some reason you have E wrapped around your little finger. She sets the meetings up per your request and makes everyone haul their arses all the way out here to have them at Keaton Hall."

Charles made a tsk noise. "You know, Keaton Hall is the ideal place to be able to control the meetings. And we both agreed we needed a secret way for us to keep an eye on her top-security advisors. So I had you come up with disguises to fit in."

Luke nodded. "Yes *you* did! So stop busting my nads over it! The disguises are perfect, since most of them talk and act as if they have a broomstick stuck up their arse. You became the stuttering Lord Standish and me the pansy Lord Witmore, which has worked brilliantly. Those idiots don't have a clue!"

"He's got you there, Charlie." Bill chuckled shaking his head. "You boys have fit right in over the years."

"I'll have to admit," Charles, said chuckling, "I've had fun over the years driving them mental with my stuttering." He felt his phone buzz, took it out, and groaned as he read the text and then put it back into his pocket. He informed them, "Well, looks like Lily Rose likes Harry. Mary just hired him."

"Bloody hell!" grunted Bill shaking his head slowly. "Here we go again, I tell ya!"

"Be quiet, old man," said Charlie. "She's not going to lose her head over him. She's not going to let any bloke interfere with what she has planned. If possible she's even more stubborn than Mary. She'll stick to her guns. It will be fine."

"Yeah, I think so, too," Luke agreed nodding his head. "Harry is all about his music anyway. He plans on being in the next big boy band coming out of the UK; he won't be letting a girl interfere with that! There might be a little attraction at first but then they will settle in and just become good mates."

Bill just grunted.

"I wonder who will figure out first that they met years ago in the maze," said Charles. "I bet it will be Lily Rose. Not much gets by that girl."

"You're on," Luke said grinning. "Harry is observant. Same bet, but what's the time frame?"

"Couple of weeks is good. I'm sure one of them will figure it out by then. I feel another hundred pounds richer already," said Charles.

They laughed knowing they would enjoy the bet, regardless of the outcome.

Charles added with a scowl, "Buggar, I better keep JR away from Harry in case they recognize each other. They didn't like each other that day. I'll tell him I don't want Harry seeing him until I get back. He won't ask any questions. And I'll tell Lily Rose there's a bet, let her think it's with Bill and tell her not to mention JR till we get back. I'd better make it JR and Jayden so that she doesn't think anything of it."

"That should work," Luke agreed. "You would think a million pounds was at stake. After the bet, if they don't figure it out, are we going to tell them they've already met?"

"No way!" Charles replied without hesitation. "I would like JR and Harry to get to know each other before they know. Especially JR. You know how Lily Rose and Jayden still bust his nads every now and then over Harry calling him a He-Man wannabe."

"True," Luke said with a laugh. "He grumbles when they tease him that he would love to meet the tosser now. He'd show him who was a He-Man wannabe and how much larger his muscles have gotten!"

Bill nodded as he said, "I remember that day like it was yesterday. He had Tessa shave his head that night grumbling about Harry the whole time. It's not been much over a couple of inches long since."

"Well, he sure loved He-Man when he was a kid," said Luke. "He had me hating those bloody cartoons."

They all laughed.

After a few minutes, Luke asked Charles, "When are you guys shoving off?"

"After I tuck Raif in tonight. Did you run E's payout reports from last month yet?"

"I did; they're over on the table," Luke replied.

Charles walked over to the large table in the middle of the room. He nodded to the new computer system. "How long before you get that new monstrosity, which cost me a small fortune, up and running?"

"Watch it! Don't insult my new baby. She's going to be worth every penny," said Luke grinning. "I'll have her online before you leave. Have you gotten all the agents new codes done so that I can get them in?"

"Still in my head; I'll just give them to you when you're ready."

Luke glanced at Bill. "How daft was that question after all these years? I guess I'm still amazed how much he can store in that fat head of his."

Bill laughed as they walked over to the table.

"What are you looking for?" asked Bill.

"Not sure; give me one second here," said Charles. He wasn't looking for anything in particular as he processed the information on the printouts. He muttered, "Something has been gnawing at me for a few months after our meetings with the security council. I'm not seeing anything out of the usual here, but my instincts tell me there's more. I might just be blowing this way out of proportion."

"I doubt that," Luke said shaking his head. "Those weird feelings of yours have always paid off. I've never known you to be wrong."

Charles nodded to accept the compliment. His eyebrows were lodged in a worried line.

Bill observed him knowing something was wrong. He could see he was stressed and recognized the look on his face. "What's going on, son?"

"I think we need to go back over the old man's ledgers." He joked, trying to lighten the mood before laying the bombshell on them. "Of course, they're in his chicken scratch, not on printouts so it's going to take forever."

"Son, I know you like the back of my hand. You're having dreams, right?" Bill asked looking at him with concern.

Charles nodded.

"Bloody hell," Bill said. "I knew it. What's your old man trying to tell you now?"

"Not sure," said Charles as he reached up and began to rub the knot in the back of his neck. "I have to say, they're doing my head in. He's sitting at my desk looking over his account ledgers and then he points to the bookshelf behind him and looks at me and nods. Then I wake up. I don't know if he's telling me to look at E's ledgers because of my gut feelings at those meetings or if he's trying to tell me I missed something on his ledgers."

They were all silent for a minute thinking.

Bill said with a knowing look, "Either way, you know the dreams are related to our old men's murders. I can see it in your eyes and how upset you are."

Charles grunted. "That's what I'm thinking. Don't ask me how I know; I just know."

"So where do we start?" asked Luke.

"Start digging into all of the council members' personal accounts while we're gone," replied Charles. "Be smart about it; don't rush. We don't want to raise any flags. For now, run E's last year's statements. Let's give them a once over."

Luke nodded and went to the computer. "You have a feeling on anyone in particular you want me to start with?" he asked as his fingers quickly punched keys on the keyboard.

"No, not really. Not yet anyway."

All six printers started printing.

Charles and Bill walked over to the huge printers and started ripping off the printouts.

Still punching on the keyboard, not looking up, Luke said, "Don't forget; I need those codes out of that fat head of yours before you leave tonight!"

Charles chuckled as he walked to the table with the printouts. Still holding the printouts after he reached the table, he just stared with a far-off look on his face.

Bill nudged Luke and motioned over at him.

After a moment Charles said as he sat the printouts down. "Hey, old man, give JR a call and tell him we're on lock-down until we get back."

"Here we go." Bill grunted as he walked to the table with more printouts and took out his phone.

Luke walked over to join them at the table. "Not like we weren't expecting it."

Bill handed Charles his phone. "Here he is; you tell him. He'll ask me a million questions."

Charles grumbled, taking the phone. "I thought I was the boss around here."

"Well, I guess that's what you get for thinking." Bill chuckled.

"Tosser," Charles said grinning, putting the phone to his ear. "Yeah, you are one too, but I was talking to the old man." He chuckled. "We just went on full lock-down. I don't want Lily Rose to leave the village while I'm gone or go out back on walks. Put Ben on Raif full time. (Ben was one of his top agents, family as far as they were all concerned. He was another one who had been in Charles life since the day he was born). As a matter of fact, I want you both to bunk down inside the house, and your mum and Abs stay up at the house, too. Assign a full team over at Luke's. I want his place covered just like here, twenty-four-seven. Double the guards around the bakery and through the village. Have Toby fly to the States to help Seth keep an eye on Anthony. If Anthony complains about having two bodyguards, tell him if he doesn't like it I'll drag his arse back here." He handed the phone back to Bill. Seeing the look on his and Luke's face he stated, "I'm having these bloody dreams and feelings for some reason. I've never had feelings so intense as the ones I've been having. They come out of nowhere like the one I just had, and they're chilling me to the bone. So until I figure it out, I'm keeping ours safe."

"Now you have me nervous as hell," said Luke. "How long have you been having them?"

"A few weeks now."

"Wow, they really must have you buggared. That's why you made the job available at the bank again and had me move back here so quickly instead of taking my time over the summer."

Charles nodded. "I didn't want to alarm you. Besides wanting you and yours close, I knew you would want to be here every second you can to help figure this out. I expect Ed will be staying here as much as possible too when we get back."

"I won't be able to come up with a reason why we shouldn't go to Chester on Saturday," said Luke.

"No worries. I'll have Joe step in to help Al with Harry," replied Charles.

"Wow, you are spooked, also assigning Joe. Have you decided if we're keeping my old place in Chester?" asked Luke.

"Yeah, I think we should." Charles nodded. "I'll keep a full team there as well. If nothing else, it's worth the expense being able to land a chopper out back without being noticed. Tell Madison you think it's a good idea to keep the place in case the job doesn't pan out."

"And I'll point out that we'll always have a place to stay so that we won't have to stay with her parents!"

They laughed.

"Now, back to Harry," said Charles. "I'm putting Jayden on him full time when we get back."

Luke's eyebrow shot up. "Really?"

Charles nodded. "It keeps him close. We'll have all our chicks home so that we can keep an eye on them. All we'll have to worry about is Anthony."

Luke nodded. "Sounds good. How long is Anthony staying over there with the yanks?"

"For the summer. He's loving that film studio his granddad bought."

"I know Ed doesn't like him being over there," said Bill. "He's worried he won't come back in the fall."

"He'll be back. I'll be surprised if he stays all summer. He won't be able to stay away from us that long," said Luke chuckling. "So when are you giving Jayden the news?" he asked Charles.

"When we get back. No sense getting him upset out in the field. He might leave me there."

They shared a good laugh at that comment.

Later that night Lil was in the kitchen waiting for the teakettle to whistle. Charles walked in about the time the kettle started whistling. She poured the hot water into the teapot with her favorite herbal tea as she asked, "What, Raif let you off with just one story?"

"Mum took over; the guys are waiting on me. We both know how Bill hates waiting."

"Oh yeah," said Lil smiling. "Dad—"

"Before you ask why the lock-down…because I said so." He grinned. "No leaving the village and no long walks out back."

"No worries; I'll be busy. I have a lot of photo sessions coming up. I was asking about the lock-down because I was thinking I might invite HT to have lunch on my hill tomorrow. Is that okay?"

"For sure." He nodded and then thought about the bet. "Do me a favor though," he added with a cheeky grin.

"I know that look." Lil chuckled. "What are you up to?"

"Just a friendly little bet."

"Oh boy! What do I have to do?" she asked, playfully rolling her eyes. "You guys and your bets."

"It's what I don't want you to do. Don't mention JR or Jayden to HT and keep Raif away from him."

"Not even going to ask why not to mention JR and Jay, but why can't he meet Ra..." She laughed. "Oh, Raif heard you telling Mum the bet, which is obviously something about HT and JR, and you don't want 'little repeat' to say anything to HT when he meets him, in case JR hears."

They'd all thought Raif's repeating was unconscious at first but now knew it was deliberate because he liked making them laugh at him.

"Something like that," Charles said. "I have to start paying more attention what I say around him. He doesn't miss a thing."

"I know." Lil nodded. "The bad thing is he's gotten to where he repeats every-thing now!"

They laughed as Bill stuck his head around the door.

"Let's go, boy. Ed and Jayden are already in the chopper waiting on us. Hi, baby girl. Give me a hug and kiss; won't see you for at least a week, longer if this boy doesn't get the lead out."

Lil kissed his cheek and laughed as he gave her a big bear hug. "Love you, Papa."

"Love you most, baby girl. Move it boy," he said over his shoulder as he went back out.

Charles rolled his eyes at Lil as they hugged. "The old fart forgets who's the boss."

Lil kissed his cheek and teased, "Are you sure?"

"Good point," Charles said laughing. "Love you, baby girl; see you in about a week."

"Love you most, Dad; be safe."

"Always," he said closing the door behind him.

HT kissed Maddie's forehead as he tucked her in, after reading three bedtime stories, all about princesses of course. She *loves her princesses*, as she always says. He was smiling as he tried not to get his curls tangled in the pink plastic blinking tiara while removing it. She made him wear it while he was reading to her. He turned it off placing it on her nightstand, along with the matching wand she had him use for effects. He was still smiling as he quietly made his way across the room and out the door, silently closing it behind him. If she woke up it would cost him another story.

He flopped down in an armchair once he made it to his room, kicked off his trainers, and propped his feet on the seat in front of him. He drummed his fingers on the arm, settling deeper into the plush chair, and stared out the window, watching drops of rain collect on the pane. Again, Lil popped back into his head. No, actually she had never left. He couldn't get his mind around how she had gotten to him. He absolutely had no idea why he was so attracted to her, although she was no ordinary seventeen-year-old. If his dad hadn't told him she was seventeen, he would have never guessed it. She was more mature than any girl he had ever met. It surprised him how easily they had fallen into the sort of banter you only had with mates you'd known forever. They even shared the same sense of humor, and she constantly had him laughing. She definitely got him, like no other girl had before. He felt when she looked into his eyes she could see straight into his soul. He'd never had a girl drive Clyde so crazy and didn't know he could be so turned on without physical contact. Sure, she was fit. "No," he said out loud, "she's beautiful," and smiled as he thought he liked that she acted as if she didn't know it. That alone got him interested. She didn't even have makeup on, while most girls painted up their face, looking like Maddie did when she got into Mum's stuff.

The makings of a song popped into his head, and he quickly sat up grabbing his songbook and pen from the side table. That's how it usually started, with a thought or two. It could easily turn into hours before he put down his pen. He thought about how her smile seemed to light up the room. He couldn't believe how words and feelings flowed through him as he wrote but had to admit it was easy because of the way he connected with her. He couldn't have stopped his pen from flying across the pages if he'd wanted to as he filled one after another. After another hour he muttered, "All right, let's see what I got here." He tapped his leg with the pen as he looked it over. He saw he had written "beautiful" about six dozen times.

"I know, I know," he said laughing, as if talking to Lil. "You're beautiful already! I got it! What I'm trying to get my head around is, *What makes you so beautiful?*"

"I like that!" he muttered as he scribbled it down—"What makes you beautiful?"—and circled it, feeling an intense rush. "What the bloody hell was that?" he said with a little laugh.

He'd never written a song about a *girl* before; she had totally inspired him. Wanting to call her, he looked at his phone lying on the table. He couldn't remember ever calling a girl; they always called him. He took in a deep breath staring at his phone, trying to get up the courage to call.

"Really! I'm nervous about calling her now? Stop being such a wanker," he said snarling, as he snatched up his phone. He checked the time, almost eleven. "Maybe it's too late," he grumbled and almost put it back down. "No, you got this. Just do it already." He laughed. "Now I sound like a bloody commercial." He reasoned, "Fine, it's too late to call. I'll text just to tell her good night. I'm not going to be cool or make up an excuse for texting. I'll keep it short. I know...something simple. This will work,

"Good night, Lil ☺."

He stared wide eyed at his phone seeing what he did. He jumped up and said disgustedly, "Really! A bloody smiley face! Who does that?" With a loud groan, he stomped over to his bed and threw himself down. "I am a total tosser!" he muttered, staring up at the intricate plasterwork on his ceiling.

While HT was thinking and writing about her, Lil was turning the gold handles of her claw-foot tub, dropping in a little peppermint-scented bubble bath. She loved that Dad had it and her perfume personally blended by a top perfume company in France. While it was filling, she turned on the radio and then pulled her hair up into a knot on top of her head. She was too tired to dry it tonight, so she would wait to wash it in the morning. She lit some scented candles and finished her herbal tea and then undressed and climbed in. It felt luxurious as she sank down until the bubbles tickled her nose. Sighing deeply she closed her eyes, laying her head back against the tub. The gentle massage of the water soothed her. It was sheer heaven. Her eyes flew open and her heart raced as she raised her head, hearing the song HT had sung as he swept. She had downloaded the song for his ringtone and thought he was calling. Realizing it was the radio, she chuckled and laid her head back again, closing her eyes. She racked her brain trying to figure out what was so special about him that had her thinking about him or made her heart race from a stupid song. Then she thought about his smile, not the fake, flirty one, the real one that made his beautiful, green eyes light up and his sexy dimples appear. She groaned as she thought about him putting on his do-rag, getting that same hot feeling she had gotten then seeing his gorgeous curls piled up high. The effect he had on her body was confusing. She desperately fought it and tried to ignore how he made her feel all day. She was still trying to ignore it now, listening to the bloody song on the radio. There was no point in pretending she wasn't physically attracted to him. She was, from the first moment she'd laid eyes on him as if he had cast some crazy, magical spell. There was no explanation for the intense, well, lust she felt. *It must be because I'm just getting over my curse*, she reassured herself. That's what she and Mum called it. Her hormones could get way out of control making her overly emotional. Usually her body reacted with a negative attitude or crying over some chick flick. This was something new. She had never been so thoroughly turned on by a guy she'd just met. Actually, she'd never been like this with the ones she'd dated. She mumbled, "I'm so out of my comfort zone with this bloke that it isn't funny." She added with a chuckle, "But what harm can a little snogging do? Not like the bloke is going to take it seriously." She shook the thought away the second it popped out her mouth as the little voice of reason in her head screamed at her. *This stops now; don't allow yourself to be charmed by the biggest flirt and probably biggest player you've ever met. You've got a plan, and you're sticking to it and not screwing it up by falling for some bloke!* She lathered up with her peppermint-scented body wash and submerged herself under the water. She resurfaced, wiping the bubbles from her face, and lay back. She was getting too worked up about being so attracted to him. From past experience, she knew the interest and attraction wouldn't last long, especially with him. All of that flirting of his would get old real fast. In no time after doing one of JR's mind exercises, she was completely relaxed and had her mind back where it belonged, off HT.

The water turned cold and her fingertips were as wrinkled as prunes when she heard her phone playing HT's ringtone. She climbed out of the tub, wrapped in a fluffy pink towel and hurried out of the loo leaving wet footprints on the beige carpet. Hurrying to her bed, she scooped up her phone and pushed back a strand of hair as she read the text. Seeing the smiley face she mumbled, "You can tell this bloke doesn't worry about his masculinity." Ignoring her racing heart, she replied back with a huge smile,

"Good night, HT☺."

HT anxiously raised his arm and stared at his phone. He couldn't believe he actually cared if she was going to return his text. He jumped as it buzzed in his hand. After he read her returned text, he smiled and then yawned. His last thought before he fell asleep was, morning couldn't come fast enough.

# CHAPTER 5

The next morning at six HT's alarm buzzed. He quickly hit the button, throwing off the sheet as he jumped out of bed, looking forward to seeing Lil. He took the fastest shower ever and quickly dressed. Within a few minutes, he had brushed his teeth, combed his curls, and tied on his do-rag. Being in such a hurry to get to the bakery, he was about to do something he never did, skip breakfast. He quietly left his bedroom and hurried downstairs without turning on any lights, not wanting to wake Maddie. If she heard him he'd be all morning trying to get away from her. He quickly went down the hall and slipped out the front door.

☺☺

Lil sighed as she rolled over and picked up her phone. She sat straight up, seeing it was after six. "Aww man!" she mumbled. "I didn't set the alarm." Her heart gave a little skip seeing HT's text from the night before. She quickly fired off a text without thinking.

"Good morning, HT ☺."

HT's phone dinged on his way to the bakery. He pulled it out of his back pocket and got a jolt of excitement as he read Lil's text. A huge grin crossed his face while he quickly returned it.

Lil jumped up and headed to the loo and quickly turned back around and ran back to her bed, hearing HT's ringtone. Scooping up her phone and ignoring the butterflies in her stomach, she read,

"Good morning, Lil ☺."

HT was just about to push the door open to go in the bakery when he paused. He felt his senses prickle; something was putting him on alert. It was the same feeling he had gotten over the years. But this time it felt more intense. He felt he was being watched. His eyes darted around as always not seeing anyone; the street appeared to be deserted. Feeling jumpy, he pushed open the door and hurried inside muttering under his breath, "Bloody hell! I hate when this happens!"

Mary looked up from the coffee maker, hearing the bell on the door. "Good morning, HT," she greeted brightly.

"Good morning, Moms," he returned with a smile. "Are those cinnamon rolls I'm smelling?"

"There's plenty in the main kitchen," she answered with a little laugh. "The gang is back there waiting to meet you."

"Brilliant! I'll go get acquainted and nab a few," he said as he went to the back.

HT stopped in the doorway of the baking room announcing his entrance. "Knock, Knock." He saw two attractive ladies—looking around mid-fifties or so; both ladies had their hair pulled back in a bun. He thought, *Sisters, looking just alike.* He looked over by the ovens and saw a tall, balding bloke built like the Abominable Snowman and just as brutal looking. To say he was very intimidating with his size was definitely an understatement. He had to be at least six eight, and his muscles were boundless. His huge Popeye arms were covered in tats. HT felt the hairs on the back of his neck rise from the way his sharp eyes were glaring at him. They were alert and cautious, which rattled him a bit, no...a lot. He looked as if he was ready to pounce and rip off his head if he made a wrong move.

"Hi, I'm HT," he greeted looking back at the ladies with a broad smile. "I want to know which one of you I need to thank for making the *best* pasties in the world!"

"I'll own up to that!" Tessa said brightly, wiping her hands on her crisp pink-and-white-striped apron. Her blue eyes were warm, as she extended her hand in greeting, "Nice to meet you. And call me Grammy."

HT moved quickly forward and shook it. His eyes sparkled as he grinned in greeting. "The pleasure is all mine, Grammy."

She motioned to her left. "This is my sister, Abbey, whom we call Abs."

HT saw Joe out of the corner of his eye, move beside Grammy as he took the few steps to reach Abbey. "Hi, Abs," he greeted, still smiling as he reached out his hand. "Nice to meet you."

"Nice to meet you, HT," Abs said with a pleasant smile, shaking his hand.

"This stern-looking brute here is Joe, her husband. Don't let the size of him scare you; he's a big softie underneath it all, a real pussy cat," Tessa said lovingly, as she patted Joe on the back.

HT thought, *I doubt that*, as he gave a little nervous smile. "Nice to meet you, sir," he said extending his hand to Joe.

"The name is Joe, not sir," he said as he shook HT's hand, none too lightly.

"Sure. Sorry, si...ah-um Joe," HT stammered. He saw a small twitch in Joe's cheek. He wouldn't swear to it, but he thought the bloke was trying not to smile. It eased his nerves a little. Not much but enough, so he wasn't worried about wetting himself anymore. He said with a big smile, "Nice to be working with all of you. Just let me know if there's anything I can do to help."

"Need to get these trays out front," said Joe in a gruff tone.

HT eagerly replied, "Sure. I'm on it!" and hurried to pick up a tray. He headed to the front whistling, trying to ignore Joe, who was right on his heels carrying two trays to his one.

He grinned and said something funny to Tessa and Abs each time he went back for a tray. By the time he and Joe had gotten all the trays out front, he had charmed Tessa and Abs and could have sworn that he almost got a grin out of Joe. Well, one corner of his mouth turned up. He didn't see any sign of him being a pussycat though.

It started getting busy, so HT jumped in without being asked or taking time to eat. He laughed and talked to all of the customers as if he had known them for years. And of course he teased and flirted with all the ladies, young and old. He had everyone smiling by the time they left. His heart gave a leap hearing Lil laugh in the back. He couldn't believe from just hearing her had brought Clyde to full attention.

For a moment Lil's eyes met his as she went through the doorway but almost immediately she looked away with heat rushing through her. "How long have you been here, HT?" she asked, trying to ignore how her body was reacting to him again.

"About an hour or so," he answered smiling. "I wanted to get out of the house before Maddie woke up; otherwise, I'd still be there having breakfast with her."

"Sounds like Raif," said Lil.

They had talked about Maddie and Raif so much the day before that each felt they already knew them.

"Good morning, Mum," greeted Lil as she walked over to kiss her cheek.

"Good morning, sweetheart," said Mary returning her kiss. She looked over to HT smiling. "I'll have to get in touch with your mum once you're all settled in and arrange a play date."

HT nodded. "That'll be great. She'll love that."

The bakery stayed busy most of the morning, so Lil and HT decided instead of taking a break and coming back before lunch, they would just work straight through doing the cleanup, giving them the afternoon free. Without knowing it, they began the process of settling into a routine for the months to come.

"Want to join me for lunch at my favorite spot?" asked Lil when they were finished.

"Absolutely," HT replied with a nod, finishing off another one of the pasties Grammy had saved for him. "Aah! Delicious," he added smacking his lips and licking his fingers.

Lil playfully rolled her eyes, shaking her head.

HT followed her out the back door carrying their lunch basket. They exchanged small talk while they walked together up the gravel path leading to the stone steps, embedded in the brick wall. Once they reached the top, chatting away, they continued up the path toward the iron gate where it attached to the ten-foot-high brick wall. It usually only took Lil a few minutes to cover the distance, but it had taken them three times as long with all of their laughing and talking.

Reaching out, HT unlatched the gate and pushed it open. "Lead the way, little lady."

"What a perfect gentleman."

He whistled as he followed her through. "Well, I'm taking that as a compliment."

"Just don't get used to it," she teased.

He chuckled in response as he closed and latched the gate. He came to an abrupt halt after they had walked about twenty feet. He saw a pair of huge, matching German Shepherds baring their teeth and coming straight at them. They didn't make a sound as they ran. They were moving so fast that it looked as if they were flying, and in perfect synchronization. "Bloody hell! I hope those things are yours," he muttered.

Lil gave a command in a language HT had never heard before. The dogs stopped dead in their tracks and sat like stone statues. She gave another command, this one in a softer tone but in the same weird dialect. The dogs approached another six feet and then again sat like statues just in front of her. She gave a little nod and their tails started wagging as she laughed and dropped to her knees, wrapping her arms around their necks, hugging and patting them at the same time. Her eyes were sparkling as she greeted, "Hello, mates. What are you doing out? You knew I brought you lunch, huh?"

"Ha, ha!" said HT, not taking his eyes off the dogs. "Is it safe to move?" His voice was so low that she barely heard it.

"Yes, you're fine," she said with a little grin. "Sorry for the scare. Raif must be taking an early nap. It's the only time these guys let him out of their sight." Lil gave another soft command, and the dogs instantly stopped all movement and sat like statues again. She stood smiling at HT. "You like dogs?"

"Yeah, I do; just a tad nervous with the bigger ones. Had a scare once when I was younger."

"That's not good. Well, these guys won't hurt you, and they're ready to be introduced." She said as she nodded to the slightly taller one. Sir George stood and walked to sit in front of HT and raised his paw. "HT, allow me to introduce you to Sir George the third," said Lil proudly.

HT, hearing the dog's name was Sir, thought it would be funny to bow. He gave Sir George a little bow as he shook his paw. "Nice to meet you, Sir George."

Sir George inclined his head slightly as if he acknowledged his respectful bow, as all royalty did, of course.

HT's expression changed from nervous to amused. "How brilliant was that?" he asked in amazement.

"That's an honor. He only nods to people he approves of."

Sir George went back to sit beside the other dog.

"Now, this other one, with the little white spot on his nose, waiting so patiently to meet you, is our problem child."

HT could hear the affection in her tone and knew he was her favorite.

Lil gave the same little head nod to the dog. He also stood and walked over to sit in front of HT and raised his paw. Lil then said, "HT, this is Sir Tigger." Her eyes twinkled with mischief. She wasn't giving HT any more clues.

HT instantly liked Sir Tigger, seeing the twinkle in his eyes and hearing he was the problem child. Again trying to be funny, he bowed over, this time he was eye level with Sir Tigger and shook his paw. "Very nice to meet you, Sir Tigger," he said while holding his head down just a little too long, thinking Sir Tigger would give a little nod back. Sir Tigger couldn't help himself, loving HT on the spot for some reason, and licked him right square on the mouth, making HT laugh. That was all Sir Tigger needed. He pounced catching HT off guard, knocking him to the ground, licking him all over the face. The more HT laughed the faster and harder Sir Tigger licked and whimpered happily.

Lil laughed as she watched. After a few seconds she said, "Enough, Sir Tigger!"

Sir Tigger let out a little whine, not happy he had to quit, but instantly stopped and returned to sit by Sir George's side.

"Sorry, he has never done that when just meeting someone. I'll have to admit I thought he might get a lick in if you bent over the way you did with Sir George."

She extended her hand to help him up. She felt a current run up her arm when he took her hand. She pulled her hand away smoothly once he got to his feet.

"No worries," he teased. "I believe that's the best snogging I've ever had. Just the way I like them, lots of tongue," he added with a wink.

She laughed softly, immediately turning to the dogs, trying to ignore his wink. For some reason his wink got to her the most. She gave the dogs a command. They instantly jumped up and took off running.

They continued to walk another twenty feet or so.

Lil said, as she angled left passed the row of flowering bushes, "I just love the scent these lilac bushes give off." She didn't notice HT had stopped.

HT had glanced to his right when she turned and gasped with surprise as he came to a sudden stop. He stood staring at the huge house that rose three levels high. He gave a long, low whistle. "Now this place matches those gates," he muttered.

The house…well, it was more like a sprawling, stately mansion. It was constructed of pale yellow stone, with rows and rows of windows to let in adequate light. He saw sunrays stream through the huge, stained-glass window above the large oak entry door, and at least two dozen chimneys on the roof. He knew that meant it had as many fireplaces inside. Lowering his eyes, he took in the long, glass solarium that stretched along the left side. Realizing that he had stopped walking and Lil hadn't, he hurried across the lawn.

He caught up to her as they approached a perfectly tended flower garden full of red, white, and pink rosebushes just beginning to bloom. He let out another low whistle as they stopped walking. "Wow," he said scanning the garden. "Behind those walls is like being in a different world. This flower garden looks like I stepped into a priceless painting."

"Mum will love you said that," Lil said. "She spends hours in this garden. She loves working in here almost as much as the bakery."

He saw the huge water fountain in the middle of the garden, bubbling away as water shot up. His eyes moved from the fountain to a maze of crisscrossing gravel walking paths leading throughout the garden. The paths were bordered with low two-foot box hedges. Every so often a Victorian iron bench, lamppost, or a marble statue stood, perfectly spaced apart on the paths.

Lil had given him a few seconds to take it all in before entering the garden through the opening in the box hedges. She then turned right.

HT followed her, hearing their feet crunch on the gravel path as he stared at the water fountain. He noticed tiny, unlit lights entwined through the hedges as he followed her left on the path at the edge of the garden. He looked up from the hedges to see where she was heading and stopped dead in his tracks. "Blimey!" he gasped as he looked to his right just outside of the garden. "This place is wicked!" he said in awe. He was mesmerized looking at the waterfall inside a hill. The hill stretched out longer away from him than it was tall.

Lil turned left and walked about six feet and stopped to wait for him.

He gestured to the hill. "I bet we're heading there, right?"

"Yep!" she replied happily. "My most favorite place in the whole world."

"I can't imagine why!" he teased as he slowly moved toward her taking it all in. To the right of the waterfall, he saw another tall brick wall looking as if it had grown right out of the hill. It had the same six-inch iron railing running along the top of the wall, both wall and railing was covered in English ivy and entwined with thousands of more tiny, unlit lights. His eyes moved a little more to the right, following the wall as it turned. He looked to his right and turned slightly as his eyes ran with the wall toward the house and then beyond, heading toward his house.

"Amazing," he said turning back to Lil and walking toward her.

They walked out of the garden through another opening in the boxed hedges and stood in the middle of the six-foot gravel path that stretched outwardly to the left and right. The left branch of it went toward the barn with the thatched roof, and the right went past the waterfall to the wall.

HT walked over to get a closer look inside of the waterfall. He saw it was covered with blue mosaic tile. The reflection made the water look blue as it ran off the rocks.

He walked back and said, "I expected to see a grotto inside that sucker."

Lil just chuckled as they climbed the hill just left of the waterfall.

HT breathed in deeply when they reached the top, absorbing the beauty of the view stretching out for miles over the English countryside. After a few minutes of silence, he asked, "Do you live in that amazing house over there?"

"Yeah," she said on a sigh, enjoying the view.

"How much of that out there belongs to you?"

"Not really sure," she replied talking softly as she pointed ahead of them. "Out there and to the right behind your place belongs to Keaton Hall and then out to the left belongs to Highcliff Castle. Our land stops where theirs starts is the best I can tell you. There's not really any fence line until you get closer to the castle and Keaton Hall. I love taking long walks out across the fields. It clears my head. You'll have to go with me sometime."

"Sure, count me in, anytime. I like to run when I need to clear mine." His stomach rumbled loudly enough for them both to hear, breaking the tranquil moment and making them laugh. They spread the quilt over the ground.

Lil kicked off her trainers as they sat down. They unpacked the basket, working together like they had done it a hundred times.

"Question?" HT asked with a serious tone, hiding his grin.

She nodded. "Sure."

"Doesn't that waterfall make you wanna pee?"

"I wasn't expecting that," she said with a chuckle.

"I'm just saying. It makes me wanna go, and I didn't drink like a dozen cups of tea this morning like you did!"

"I didn't drink that much," she said rolling her eyes, "but I do like my tea."

"That's an understatement," he said with a grin.

"There's a switch on the side of the waterfall if it's bothering you. I've gotten used to it over the years."

"I'm fine. I'm just messing with you. This place is absolutely amazing. I can see why this hill is your favorite though. It would be mine too. I would eat lunch here every day, no matter the weather."

"Then, I'll share it with you! It just became *our* official lunch spot," she said. She chuckled and added, "It's all yours though if the weather is bad. I'm not that mental."

He grinned and asked, "So next question. Why Sir Tigger? And not Sir William or Sir Henry?"

Lil sat a water in front of him as she answered. "The name on his registration papers is Sir *Harry Edward* the second."

"That explains the warm welcome I received," HT said in that teasing way of his. "So how did Sir Harry Edward turn into Sir Tigger?" he asked before he bit into a meat pasty.

"Raif," she replied. "Sir Tigger was supposed to be mine. Dad gave him to me just after Raif was born. Sir Tigger was premature, and his mother passed having him, so I became his mother. I fed him with an eyedropper and kept him warm with a hot-water bottle. He slept in a shoe box beside my bed. Anyway, as soon as he was up and walking, he would end up out of my room and beside Raif's crib. I tried to keep my door closed to keep him in, but as soon as I left it open, he would be off looking for Raif. No matter what I did, wherever Raif was, Sir Tigger was. I eventually just gave up. We all came to the conclusion Raif belonged to Sir Tigger. Drove Dad mental that after all of his training he still couldn't get Sir Tigger to stop licking Raif. The more Raif would giggle the more Sir Tigger would lick. Raif was maybe six months old and would say 'tick, tick' when Sir Tigger licked him. We think he was trying to say tickle. Next thing we know, Raif was calling him Tigger. So Sir Tigger it is."

"The name suits him, I have to say. So what was all that gibberish you were saying to them?"

"I mostly just told them you were a friend and to sit and shake and then I released them to go find Raif. They were getting a little antsy being away from him since they're his bookends."

Lil held up an apple pasty.

HT nodded.

She passed it to him.

"Thanks," he said as he took it.

"Thanks?" she repeated him with a chuckle. "You sound like a yank. I've noticed you don't say 'cheers,' like most English do."

"That's Dad's doing," he replied. "'Cheers' was a code he and his best mates used when they wanted to call someone a wanker and couldn't. I thought it was a brilliant idea, so my best mate Lee and I started doing it too!"

"That's funny! I have an uncle who's a yank and was forever making fun of us when we said it. He'd say, 'Who the hell says "cheers"? Don't you English realize how ridiculous that sounds?' So we all just quit saying it!" Her brow shot up after thinking for a second. "Hold on. Wait one minute here, mister."

"What?" he asked with a cheeky grin, knowing where she was heading.

She playfully slapped his arm. "I remember you said cheers to me yesterday! It made me think of my uncle."

"Nah," he teased. "I never."

"You know you did, when I laughed at you choking!"

"I rest my case!" he said with a wink.

They laughed.

HT bit into the pasty and sighed, giving her a blissful smile. He had a million questions in his head. He had never wanted to know so much about a girl before. After swallowing he asked, "Is your papa as cool as Grammy?"

"Absolutely. You're going to love him but then everyone does."

The warmth in her eyes and her tone told him just how much love she felt for him. "Can't wait to meet him," he replied.

"I guess I should probably warn you about him though. Don't take to heart what he says. Some of it might not make sense to you."

"Oh, I'm sorry to hear that," HT said sadly. "Getting a little out to lunch, hey?"

Lil burst out laughing.

HT frowned slightly wondering what was so funny.

Lil wiped a tear away. "That was too funny. You'll see why after you meet Papa. He is definitely not out to lunch; he's as sharp as a tack. At times he says things that don't seem to make sense, sounding like one of his best mates, Carl. He's a yank from a southern state in America and uses a lot of silly anecdotes that can seem pretty off the wall. When Papa and him get going, they are hysterical. Actually, Uncle Carl, as I've always called him, is my godfather."

"The bloke who has you not saying cheers?"

She nodded. "He tells me because of him we're not the typical stiff-necked English family, that we're cool, more like the yanks. But of course Papa disagrees—says he didn't raise Dad to act like he had a stick stuck up his bum in the first place."

HT chuckled.

Lil smiled and continued. "Uncle Carl is also why everyone but me calls Mum, Moms. He use to wind Mum up calling her Moms before I was born. Drove her mental at first but then it stuck. Now she loves it."

"Can't wait to meet this Carl bloke, too. He sounds like a hoot!"

"He is. I just love him to pieces. Actually, he just moved out of the house you moved into and leased it to the bank. He took a friend of the family to the States for the summer, so you'll have to wait to meet him in the fall."

"Dad did say a yank had lived there. By the way, Dad is my stepdad, but I feel like he's my real dad."

"I can tell you are close by the way you talk about him." Lil smiled. "Do you ever see your biological father?"

"I don't see him as much as I should. He's out of the country a lot on business. We get along, just not real close. I was really young when he and Mum split. Anyway, Dad's not your typical English bloke either. He's always making fun of the snobbish, posh ones he has to deal with at the bank. He spent a couple of summers in the States when he was young and sounds like he almost married one. He doesn't talk about that part of his life much. Mum still gets a little jealous. When they first met, Dad kind of got cold feet and stopped seeing Mum for a while because of some American girl. I'm thinking it's the one he used to date." He shrugged. "Not sure."

"Uncle Carl is always aggravating Mum over one of Dad's old girlfriends named Erica. I think she was from the States," Lil said. "I'm sure you've realized we're all really close, which means the banter never stops, and they have a way of knowing everything that's going on. If you have secrets, this isn't the family to be around. They stick their noses into everything!"

"No worries," HT assured her, "my family is the same."

Lil acted as if she wiped sweat from her brow as she chuckled, "Whew, that's a relief."

He grinned and said, "I realized last night that the drive going in the opposite direction of yours is Joe and Abs. I saw them going that way last night. So I take it Grammy and your papa live in that house just through the gates?"

"Yep, and JR." She frowned, realizing she'd just screwed up mentioning him. She hesitated and thought, *Oops sorry, Dad!* "Are you eighteen yet?" she quickly asked in hope of getting his mind off JR.

"Huh! What?" he questioned, confused for a second by the rapid change in subjects. Then what she had asked registered. He nodded. "Yeah, February first." He could tell from her tone and the change of subject, she didn't want to talk about JR.

"I won't be until November seventh."

"How old is JR?" He fired right back to the person she didn't want to talk about.

"Twenty-five, also in November," she responded.

He had to hide his grin as she let out a little sigh. He took a bite of his brownie and asked after he swallowed, "Is Grammy Moms's mum?"

Lil took another bite of her brownie, to give her a moment to think. She debated how much to disclose, never sharing her personal life with anyone before; it was kind of taboo. She decided it was better to tell him some things since she knew he would be around a lot. She would just be careful of what she said this time. "No," she replied. "All my grandparents passed away before I was born, even before my parents were married."

"That sucks. Mine are still alive and kicking."

"That sucks because mine are passed or because yours are still alive and kicking?"

"Depends on how much Mum makes me visit them, I guess."

"Really?" she asked with a raised brow.

"No." He chuckled. "They're brilliant, and I visit them all the time." He raised his brownie and stopped midway to his mouth. "Hold on, back it up a minute here. It just registered what you said. Your grandparents are all passed, so…"

Lil laughed cutting him off. "Sorry, I forget Papa and Grammy aren't my biological grandparents. I guess I should mention that JR is their son. I think of him as my brother though. He's amazing. We're really close, the best of mates. He thinks I can do no wrong. Dad says he has me spoiled rotten!"

"That's why you think he's amazing! So does he?" he asked.

"Definitely, to the core! Actually, I have to admit they all spoil me."

"At least you're honest."

"I'll have you know I'm always honest. I never lie and don't care for people who do," she replied with a tilt of her head.

"Don't get testy; I totally agree," he remarked playfully, wondering if her statement was true. The girls he'd been involved with always lied but then, he never stuck around long or cared.

"Good, another thing we agree on," she said as she licked the chocolate off her fingers.

He couldn't take his eyes off her full lips as she licked them one by one, making Clyde thicken. Having to tear his eyes away, he asked, "So did Moms meet your dad through Grammy and Bill?" He pulled off his do-rag and ran his fingers through his hair, trying to ignore Clyde.

Lil let out a little groan while watching him and saw him turn to look at her. She quickly handed him a brownie and groaned again, to make him think she had groaned due to the brownies, and said with a little sigh, "Please eat this last one so that I don't."

"If I must." He grinned and took it from her. "Yum, yummy; you don't know what you're missing. It's loaded with icing!," he teased holding it up.

"Cheers!" she teased.

He chuckled and said before he bit into it, "You can talk while I enjoy."

"I guess I should start with a little family background," she replied. "Mum and Dad met first. Grammy and Papa and Aunt Abs and Uncle Joe, who is Papa's cousin, met through them. They pretty much fell in love right off. Mum and Dad had a tougher time. Seems they broke up a few times before they finally made it down the aisle. I'll leave that for some other time."

He made a little huff sound and muttered, "We can compare notes on that one! Mum and Dad had a rough patch too."

She grinned and continued, "Grammy, Mum, and Aunt Abs have always been really close. Grammy and Aunt Abs's mum, Jane, was a second cousin to my granddad. She was actually more like his little sister because his parents raised her. After Grammy and Aunt Abs's father passed away when Grammy was only three, my grandparents insisted Jane move back in with them, along with the girls. They had given up hope of ever having children since it hadn't happened after nearly twenty years, but when Grammy was ten my grandmother became pregnant. Mum gave them all a welcome shock. Mum says granddad used to tease that she was just taking her time to make a grand entrance—on his fiftieth birthday. Grammy says the day Mum was born they were all blessed with the sweetest, most beautiful little angel."

HT held the last of the brownie up. "Last bite. Speak now, or it's gone."

Lil shook her head. "You go ahead."

He shrugged and popped the last bite in his mouth as she continued.

"Now for Dad and Papa. Papa's father and my granddad were business partners and really close mates. Papa was fifteen when Dad was born, and Dad started following him around as soon as he could walk."

"Ah, that's why you said he didn't raise your dad with a stick up his bum."

Lil nodded. "Of course. Papa is always joking that Dad has been a real pain in his backside ever since. They're always fussing at each other, but don't let that fool you. They're really close and would be lost without each other."

"That's cool they're all still so close. So whose idea was the bakery?" he asked. "Moms's or Grammy's?"

"Both, and Aunt Abs's. They had dreams of opening one together since way back. All three wanted to train in Paris to be bakery chefs, and Grammy did go for a year. She'd come home for breaks and weekends, and they would spend hours in the kitchen while she taught everyone what she had learned. Mum remembers it being the best days of her childhood, laughing and baking all day. Mum was ten when my grandparents and Jane were killed in a car crash. My grandparents had named Jane as Mum's guardian in their will, but since she also passed, Mum had to move in with her aunt, my grandmother's sister."

HT whistled. "That's beastly."

"I agree," she said softly. "So after they passed, Grammy never went back to Paris to finish her training, and Aunt Abs never started. They could have, with a trust fund my grandparents left for them, but they wouldn't leave Mum. They moved in with Mum and her aunt, who wasn't much of a mother type, and she was more than happy to have a free nanny/mother. Like I said about Dad and Papa, Mum wouldn't know what to do without them. We've always been together, even when we lived in London."

"I'm confused again." He chuckled. "I thought you've always lived here."

"Yeah, we have; well, sort of."

"What kind of answer is that?"

"Again an honest one," she said laughing.

"Okay, Ms. Smarty-Pants." He chuckled. "I got it. You're honest. Now, back to London. I've always wanted to go."

"We'll go sometime then. We can even stay overnight if you want since we still have our house there."

"Sweet, count me in. Wait a minute, we stay in the same room, right?"

She rolled her eyes. "Uh, no!"

"Aww man, now I wish you weren't so honest!" he teased.

She shook her head with a slight smile. "One thing though; I need to ask you to keep that we lived in London and have a house there between us."

"For sure, absolutely," he reassured her with a nod. "Anything you tell me stops here."

"You know, even with all that rubbish you throw out I believe that. I'm not sure why, but I trust you, and I have to admit, that's a first for me."

"Same here. I trust you," he replied returning her smile. "And I'll have to admit since we're being all mushy here, that it's a first for me too. So back to the big secret of why living in London is such a big deal."

"Mum," she replied with a little shrug. "Dad's family has lived here for generations, so the locals all know him. They never thought much of not seeing him around the village very often, knowing he was so busy working with Granddad running the security company and going to uni. They didn't have a clue he wasn't living here and that he was living in London. So when he and Mum met he brought her here a few times and she fell in love with it, so they started staying here more, spending holidays and most weekends. No one suspected they had another life going on in London. Remember, I told you Mum had to move there with her aunt?"

He nodded.

"Well, Mum hated living in London, and her aunt was a piece of work, to say the least. The real snooty, posh type, one of the social climbers trying to move up the ladder. She made Mum attend social functions and associate with what she called 'her kind of people.' Mum absolutely hated living in that world. She was tired of spending her life in a social whirl and said she didn't care for the people she had to associate with. She was planning to move to Paris as soon as she controlled her own money, which was when she turned twenty-one. Then she met Dad and was thrown even more into the world she hated in London. He was big in the finance world and handled the money and business affairs for a lot of influential people. He was on everyone's A list."

HT whistled. "He gave that up to live here?"

"Why do you do that?" she asked with an impatient look.

"What?"

"You deliberately wind me up because we love living here!"

"I do? Nah," he teased, shaking his head. "I don't believe I do."

"You do exactly that," she said trying not to smile.

"Okay, you're right I do. I'll quit." He grinned.

"Good. As a matter of fact, Dad was just as ready to leave London as Mum. They wanted me growing up away from all that society rubbish and around real people. They wanted me to go to school here. So when I was three, they started working on getting the bakery ready, so by the time I turned five and ready to start school, we were also ready to open the bakery. Like I said, Mum loves it here and took to the locals right off. To them she was just one of them. Now back to your question. Mum thought if they knew about the lifestyle we had in London, they would think we were all snooty. I don't really think it matters if they know now, but Mum still has a hang up about it so why bring it up."

He nodded. "I can see that. So now your dad is just big into the security thing?"

"What makes you think that?" she teased.

One side of his mouth arched into a half smile. "Buckingham Palace doesn't have this much security going on!"

"Yeah, Dad's a little intense when it comes to that." She added with a grin, "You'll get used to it. Dad and Papa will drive you mental always babbling on about security rubbish. But then if it's not that, it's golf. They're absolutely crazy about everything to do with golf, too!"

"I love golf! It's brilliant!"

"Really! You?"

"You sound surprised." He chuckled.

"I am."

"A lot of things about me might surprise you, Lil," he replied with a wink.

"Humm, I doubt it," she teased. "So, changing the subject, I take it you're finishing school in Chester not Manchester?"

"For sure." He nodded. "And you?"

"Chester."

"Great, we can car pool. You're going to love Chester. Changing the subject again, let's talk about your love lif—"

"No," she said shaking her head. "I've been doing all the talking, so it's still my turn to ask you questions."

"If you must know, girls aren't interested in hearing what I have to say," he replied sounding a bit smug. "They're more after how I make them feel!"

She gave him a little sideways push. "Please…" She groaned, pretending revulsion. "Did you really just say that?"

"That was bad," he admitted with a grin. "We'll let that rubbish pass."

"Yeah, let's do." She nodded, and they laughed.

They lost track of time as the afternoon wore on, talking and laughing, surprised at how much they really did have in common.

HT had become so comfortable that he confessed he liked chick flicks; it just sort of slipped out.

"Jeez, I'm shocked," Lil said surprised. "No bloke ever admits to that!"

His eyes widened as he teased, "Have I finally done something right?"

"I believe you have. You definitely deserve a brownie point for that one." She lightly touched her index finger to the tip of her tongue and then halfway raising her hand she ticked off an imaginary mark.

"Don't be too quick at ticking that box just yet," he said sadly and hung his head in mock shame. "I'm afraid I have an ulterior motive."

"Oh, really! Such as?" Lil asked with a raised brow, trying not to laugh.

Wiggling his brows he admitted, "Well, it's a known fact it helps out with the ladies, you see."

"Which means?"

A glint came into his eyes as he playfully shrugged. "Absolutely no idea. I thought it sounded cool."

She chuckled, rolling her eyes.

He added with a little grin, "I really do watch them though, with Mum. It's kind of a son-and-mum thing we do to hang out."

"Aww! That's really sweet," she said, warmed by his admission. "For that you get to keep your brownie point."

"Lucky me." He chuckled as he stood up.

Lil slipped on her trainers and smiled as he offered his hand. He then pulled her up. They folded the quilt, strolled down the hill and back through the flower garden, chatting away as HT swung the basket and Lil carried the quilt.

HT asked, "You want to meet up later, after dinner? I wouldn't mind seeing this place when all those lights are on."

"Sure, it's even more beautiful."

"What time?"

"About se—oh, wait a minute," Lil frowned. "I can't make it tonight."

The smile faded slowly from his face as he shrugged faintly. "No worries," he replied, disappointment evident in his tone.

Reading his expression she said quickly, "How about tomorrow night? I have a photo session tonight."

"You want company? I can carry your equipment or something."

"You want to come with me on my photo session?"

"For sure." He nodded. "If that's okay."

"Absolutely." She nodded. "It's with Mrs. Peters and her cat, Fluffy. I'm sure she won't mind."

He gave a low laugh. "Mrs. Peters or Fluffy?" he teased. He thought about his allergy to cats. *So I will be miserable for the rest of the night. She's worth it!*

"Fluffy, of course!" she teased back. "So if you can be here at seven, it would be great. A little heads-up about Mrs. Peters. She totally adores Fluffy and thinks everyone else does too, and she has a way of getting information out of you. It wouldn't be bad, but she tends to share what she hears with everyone."

"Tragic." He grinned. "A gossip!"

"Oh yeah! The queen!"

"All right then. I'll mind my manners, be on my best behavior with Fluffy, and, most important, keep my mouth shut, not giving her any ammo."

They laughed as he handed her the empty basket.

"I'll meet you back here at seven," he said with a little wink.

"I'll be here."

"Until then, my lady," he said with a little head nod and then started down the drive.

She heard him start to sing. Her eyes followed him until he disappeared from view. She let out a long sigh and turned, heading up the walk to work in her darkroom.

JR caught up with her.

"What's up?" Lil asked.

"Nothing. I just wanted to talk to you about something."

They went inside. She placed the basket on the snack bar and asked, "You want a brew?"

"For sure." He nodded.

She went to the stove, sat the teakettle down, and turned the burner on as she said, "I have a photo session tonight."

"I heard. Also heard HT's going?" he said, taking two mugs from the cabinet.

"He is. What kind of tea would you like?"

"Whatever you want is fine."

She put peach herbal tea into the teapot. "Mrs. Peters is going to love it. A little overkill on the lock-down, huh?"

He just looked at her.

"Come on, JR," she began to protest. "Don't you think it's time we talk about this stuff instead of skirting around it?"

"Snaggs, you know Jay or I won't talk—"

"Yeah, yeah, yeah, until it's official, I know. And if Dad asks if I know, you have to come clean because you and Jay looked the other way when I went into that secret room at the castle and read those journals. Good Lord, JR. I know, he knows, I know, and I know he knows I plan to join as soon as I turn eighteen."

"That was a mouthful," he said.

They laughed.

He turned off the whistling kettle and poured water into the teapot. "Maybe he figures you've changed your mind since you can't put that camera down for five bloody minutes," he joked.

"Real funny! Like I've not worked my bum off in all those defense classes of yours and been putting up with you driving me mental with that mind-control rubbish over the years! Besides, my photography is a fantastic cover, so I need lots of practice to be brilliant at it."

"Oh! Is that it?" he replied laughing, as he poured the tea into the mugs.

"That's as good excuse as any!" she said as they walked to sit by the fireplace.

They laughed.

Lil watched as he drank his tea, thinking of how she adored him and Jay. Their physical appearances were totally different—JR with brown eyes and dark blond hair and Jay with bright blue eyes and jet-black hair—but their actions were identical. To say they were tight was an understatement. They shared secrets, spoke in their own secret language, and could understand each other without saying a word. It was a given that anything she told one of them would be shared with the other, which she didn't mind. She could never hide anything from them. They knew her better than anyone did. She always put up this strong-woman-I-can-handle-the-world attitude, unless she was with them; then she let her vulnerability show. They kept her straight on things they thought she was doing wrong and was always there when she needed a little pity. They would baby her, make her feel better, and then basically tell her to suck it up and move on and assured her that she could handle anything she put her mind to.

JR looked over and saw her staring and smiling. "What are you thinking? I'm not real sure I like that smile on your face."

"Just thinking how great you and Jay are. And…"

"Yes we are," he teased.

"Whatever," she said rolling her eyes and continued. "No kidding; I feel blessed that you love me so much and put up with my rubbish. I know I don't say it enough, but you guys are brilliant."

"Great, hold that thought because I need to talk to you as a big brother."

"Uh-oh, why do I get the feeling this conversation is about to take a turn for the worst?"

"Not at all. Well, I don't think it is."

Lil frowned and said, "Maybe you should just say what's on your mind. You're getting me a little worried here."

"Right then. I just wanted to give you a little heads-up about HT that's all," he said.

"Oh, such as?"

"Be careful with him. It wouldn't hurt to block out all that rubbish of his and keep your guard up," he said in a worried tone. "Don't go biting off more than you can chew with this bloke, playing his game."

"Don't be ridiculous, JR," she said. "I've got his number. It's just a little playful banter."

"I'm being serious here, Snaggs. The thing is I don't want him getting hurt either, causing hard feelings."

Lil gave him a confused look. "I know I caused hard feelings because Jay and Rafa are so tight, and things ended badly when I tried to date him, but why are you worried about HT?"

"Just remember this stays between us."

"Duh!"

He ignored her sarcasm. "Charlie and HT's dad, Luke, are pretty tight. Actually, Jay, Dad, and I like him too."

"Really!" Lil said surprised.

JR nodded and continued with the cover story Charles told him to say. "Charlie and Luke have known each other from their uni days, and Charlie's finance days in

London. They got reacquainted while hammering out the security contracts for the banks a few years back. Charlie was impressed with his knowledge of computers, so he hired him to maintain all of our systems. He even invited him to play golf with us at Highcliff and has been our fourth for a while now."

Lil whistled. "Wow, you do like him if he plays golf with you guys. Something tells me I'm not to discuss him playing golf with you guys at Highcliff, either."

"Right. Nothing about Highcliff or Keaton Hall until Charlie clears it."

"Yeah, yeah, I know. Again he knows I know about those meetings at Keaton—"

"Enough with that rubbish for now," he said putting up his hand. "As I was saying, I'm not real crazy about repeating what I've heard during private conversations on the golf course but then I don't want bad feelings again if things go south between you and HT."

"Okay, I got that part, and I'm sure that little speech came from Dad about causing bad feelings."

He just gave her the look, letting her know she was right.

"Fine, you're off the hook; his message received. Now what has you so buggared?"

His mouth curled into a slight smile. "I've never seen you like this with a bloke before, and quite frankly it scares me a little," he said, looking a little embarrassed.

"Like what?" she asked in an amused tone, knowing he knew the effect HT was having on her.

"Ha, ha! Let's just say...so taken with a bloke. If someone gets their heart broken, I don't want it being you." His face became more serious as he spoke. "I hate for this to sound like Luke was talking bad about HT because he wasn't. He and Charlie were just talking kids and well..." he paused trying to find the words.

"Not boyfriend material?" asked Lil with a grin. "A bit of a tosser when it comes to girls?"

"Yeah! Well no, not a tosser! I'm not explaining this very well, so bear with me here. You're used to your typical blokes who are sure of themselves, and you know their game."

"Wankers!"

"Right, and the way Luke talked, HT went through that phase a few years back, not caring how he treated girls. He's not like that now, but girls seem to still get their hearts broken. You've seen him in action; he charms them all without trying. It's just him." He let out a long sigh. "Am I making any sense here?"

"Yeah, I get it." She chuckled. "He's a nice guy and a real charmer. I shouldn't take it to heart if he makes me feel as if he's madly in love with me and that I'm the *only* one in the world."

"That's about it." JR nodded with a chuckle. "Luke did say when a girl catches his eye, he really turns on the charm and doesn't quit until he gets her, but once the chase is over he loses interest. The way he's going after you, well, it looks like the chase is on."

"Relax, I've got this. I'm not going to deny he's making my body crazy, more than any bloke I've ever met, or deny that I would love to have at least one good go at him so that I can get my hands on those curls and lips of his. I'm dying to see how he kisses. I bet he's amazing at it."

JR put his hand up to stop her. "Whoa! Too much information," he muttered.

Lil started laughing. "You're actually blushing! It's not often I get to see that."

"All right, enough; you're enjoying this too much. Let's get back to being serious here," he grumbled trying to keep from grinning.

"Don't worry," she said still chuckling. "I've got my guard up, and I was just messing with you. I'm keeping my hands and lips to myself, and I'll make sure he knows it's 'mates only' for me."

"Good. That makes me feel better, but do me a favor, make it clear to him like right now. Just in case he thinks you're interested, and he ends up obsessed!"

"He's not the type to become obsessed, JR. Like you said, he just sees me as a challenge. He'll lose interest in a few weeks when he realizes I'm not falling for his rubbish."

"One more thing—"

"He really has you worried!" Lil chuckled, seeing the worried look flash across his face.

"Laugh now, but just remember if things develop between the two of you, Jay and I have to let whatever happens, happen. You're on your own. You know Moms's law about letting things play out. We can handle the wrath of God from Charlie when we step over the line when it comes to you but not Moms!"

Lil chuckled and replied. "No worries; again, message received. I know how Mum is. You have to love her though with her 'lessons are better learned than in telling' rubbish."

"Don't forget her favorite," he said grinning. "Life is a series of lessons. The important thing is to learn from our mistakes and move on. Blimey, Jay and I have learned a few in our day."

"Me too." Lil nodded, her eyes gleaming. "Remember the time I cut my hair?" They laughed.

"You want more tea before you get started in your darkroom?"

"I always want more tea. You know that," she said jumping up. "I need to go pee first."

"Like that's something new."

HT sat on his bed and pushed himself up against the headboard—naked, of course. He always slept in the nude. He hated clothes. He had his songbook and pen, working on his new song, and thinking of Lil. He thought about how brilliant the day and night had been. He knew he was attracted to her, that much was certain, but this was nothing like he'd ever felt before. He found himself venturing into uncharted territory. She was different from any girl he had ever met. She made him feel different.

He sneezed. "Bloody cat," he muttered. "I can't believe I held that flat-faced fleabag so that she could take photos of it. I'm still sneezing my head off. No wonder with all that long white hair. It's the fattest cat I've ever seen. It's so fat that it squeaks when it tries to meow." He smiled, as he thought of how Lil laughed at him when he whispered that the thing was staring at him and giving him the evil eye. He sneezed again and grumbled, "The wanker almost made me hurl when it sneezed, blowing cat snot all over me. I know the evil thing did it on purpose." Clyde came to life as he thought of how Lil dropped her head to the side and with a soft, sexy tone, cooed, "Oh, poor kitty has a bad cold," making the fat thing purr and spray spit, along with more thick, green snot! He sneezed again and said with a grin, "She didn't care I was sneezing my head off when we left. She still tore me a new one for not telling her I was so allergic."

He felt an overwhelming need to connect with her, letting her know he was thinking about her. He picked up his phone and without hesitation texted:

"Good night, Lil. ☺"

Light from the garden filtered through a gap in the curtains as Lil yawned and slipped out of her pink, fluffy slippers and dropped her matching fuzzy robe on the ivory armchair beside her bed. She turned off the light and then pulled the duvet back and crawled into bed. She had just settled back against the pillow, covering herself and closed her eyes when she heard HT's ringtone. She quickly sat up, going warm inside. She leaned over to the edge of the bedside table and grabbed her phone. She glanced at his text. His silly smiley face made her chuckle and love it even more. She returned his text smiling:

"Good night, HT ☺."

## CHAPTER 6

The rest of the week passed swiftly. Saturday afternoon, Lil and HT strolled side by side through the garden to their hill to have lunch. The more time they spent together, the more they enjoyed each other's company, settling into a comfortable friendship.

It was another beautiful afternoon, the sun peeking out every so often through the white fluffy clouds. After eating, Lil lay down with her hands behind her head, watching the clouds float by. She thought about the past week and how she and HT had gotten so close. She looked forward to his return text every morning and the one she returned to him every night. She liked that he even tagged along on her photo sessions and seemed to enjoy himself. The ladies sure loved it. He helped a lot, carrying her equipment, loading her camera, and helping her set up for shots. She was amazed how easy it was to talk to him and knew he was quickly becoming the best friend she had ever had. She let out a loud, satisfying sigh as she closed her eyes. Maybe she would just doze for a few minutes, knowing she had a long night ahead of her.

"You sound happy over there," said HT softly as he too lay looking up at the sky. He glanced over at her. "Wake me up in an hour. I'm going to catch a few z's."

Lil replied drowsily, "Better set phone not to miss date night," as she fell quickly asleep.

"Are you playing possum over there? Nobody falls asleep that fast, and you drank like a gallon of tea!" He waited for her come back, knowing she'd never let him have the last word. She didn't make a sound. His eyebrows went up in surprise; she really was sleeping. Her breathing had fallen into a deep, even pattern.

He turned onto his side, leaning on his elbow, and propped his head up to watch her sleep. His eyes strayed to her long slender legs stretching out from her denim shorts with her cute little pink-painted toenails. He never got tired of looking at her. She was so beautiful and amazing that just being around her kept a smile on his face. He wasn't used to girls listening and really wanting to know what was going on in his head. She made it easy for him to relax and talk for hours, making him feel he was the most interesting bloke on the planet, and he liked it. He had to admit, however, she was completely baffling. She acted impervious to his flirting, almost as if it got on her nerves. He shook his head a little, screwing up his face wondering, *Does she have an agenda, and I'm just not seeing it?* Based on past experience with girls, he knew they always had one, acting as if they weren't interested, hoping it would make him more interested in them. He knew their game playing. "No," he told himself shaking his head. "I really believe she's always honest with me and always herself. She doesn't have a phony bone in her body!" He grinned seeing her camera lying beside her. *Man she loves that thing. I've never met a girl so fierce about anything.* He lay his head down thinking he was starting to like living here more and more every day, mostly because of her.

The next thing he knew he heard her sigh. He opened his eyes to see her eyelids flicker before she opened them. She shaded her eyes squinting from the glare of the sun. He quickly rolled onto his back.

Sighing heavily, Lil sat up yawning. "I feel like I slept for hours," she said, raising her arms in the air, stretching, and letting out a little satisfied groan. She glanced over not seeing him moving. "Hey, you asleep over there?"

"Who can sleep with all that snoring?" he teased as he sat up. A warm breeze whipped his hair across his face. He automatically reached in his back pocket for his do-rag, ran his fingers through his hair, pushed it back, and tied it on.

Lil couldn't take her eyes off his fingers, wishing they were hers. She took a quick breath, telling herself to stop it, and ignored the heat rushing through her body. She said with a little chuckle, "I don't snore. You better get a move on. Can't have you missing date night."

"I could just stay here, and we could have our own date night."

Lil looked half confused. "Like a date-date? You and me?"

Amusement flickered in his eyes. "Yeah, that's what I'm saying. You know a date, snogging, holding hands, me whispering sweet nothings in your ear…"

"OMG! I never thought of that; it's genius!" she teased. The image flashed through her mind, making her think she would like to do that *and* a whole lot more.

"Okay, okay, Ms. Smarty-Pants." He chuckled.

She shrugged and said, "I've given up blokes for a while anyway."

He couldn't help but laugh. "Uh-huh, and how is that working for you?"

"Very well, actually."

"Are you sure you don't want a crack at me first? Might be fun," he teased with a half smile, raising his brows up and down.

"I'm very sure." She laughed while rolling her eyes.

"I might be your keeper, as they say!"

"I highly doubt you'd stick around long enough to be anyone's keeper," she said. "I'll just wait to find my keeper once I get my career going."

"Maybe having a bloke around will make the ride more enjoyable," he replied.

She wrinkled her nose. "Or, make it more painful, having to put up with his rubbish. No, I like my plan better. No answering to anyone, being free as a bird."

"Bloody hell!" he playfully made his cheeks poof with air before he blew it out. "You're tough!"

"That's rich coming from you. What, you keep a girl for one date, maybe three at the most!"

"Three is definitely pushing it." He grinned.

"Right, my point exactly. So stop trying to make me feel guilty just because I'm independent and don't need a bloke in my life."

"It's just weird coming from a girl."

"What kind of rubbish is that?"

He tried to backtrack, making it worse. "I'm just saying, I've never met a girl who didn't jump…well, want me…" he shrugged with a little laugh. "Never mind; let's move on."

"Admit it. You're just used to having any girl you want and them confessing their undying love!"

"Of course," he replied with a cheeky grin. "After all I am me!" he teased.

She let out a playful groan along with her signature eye roll.

"You know," he said, "on anyone else I find that expression annoying as hell, but on you it's sexy."

She shook her head. "You can be a massive arsehole with all that rubbish! Do you know that?"

"Yes, mainly because you're always informing me of it," he replied, loving how she was always busting his nads.

She caught herself before rolling her eyes again. "Whatever!" She grinned. "Now that we've gotten all that no-dating-we're-only-mates thing out of the way…"

"Did we?" his twinkling eyes challenged hers.

"Absolutely," She said with a nod. "No sense in us denying the obvious—that we're attracted to each other."

He threw up his hand with a cocky grin. "Whoa, rewind. Did I hear you're attracted to me?"

"HT, will you stop and be serious for two bloody minutes. Why waste a great chance of making something great of the friendship that already exists between us over a few weeks of attraction that we both know will end? We really like each other as us just being us. Which means, I like the real you, not Harry the horny rock star!"

His brow shot up. "That's a bit harsh, isn't it?"

"No, not at all," she answered, shaking her head laughing. "You're a different person in the bakery…a.k.a Harry, the horny rock star, performing for all the ladies! 'Good morning, little lady. Step on up here and make my day! Now what can I get for you gorgeous?' And so on and on and o—"

"Okay, okay, I guess I have to give you that one," he admitted, giving her a half grin along with a little wink.

She took a deep breath trying to ignore the wink and went on to say. "So the way I see it, strictly being mates is the answer. There's no pressure. No complications. No commitments. No—"

He interrupted, "Answering to anyone, being free as a bird. I got it! I got it!"

"HT, I'm just trying to be honest here. My point is we can enjoy each other's company without having to answer to each other avoiding all the dating nonsense. That way we don't screw up the great thing we have going so that we can always remain mates."

He stood up, stretching, and rolling his shoulders to work the stiffness out. He shrugged, trying to pass the entire thing off as a joke, never being turned down before or talked to like that. "Your loss, but I'm sure you'll change your mind about that," and teased. "After all"—pointing his thumbs to himself—"who doesn't want this?"

She laughed as he pulled her up.

"Uh-huh, laugh now, but don't come crying to *me* when you realize what you missed out on."

"Puh-leez, I know *exactly* what rubbish I'm missing out on."

"Wow, that's really terrible." He placed a hand over his chest. "My heart is broken."

Lil laughed again, shaking her head. "Save it for your ladies in Chester if you're looking for sympathy. They're probably queuing up now waiting for you."

He shrugged with a cheeky grin. "I guess I should get going then. I can't be breaking all my beauties' hearts!"

Lil snorted and replied, "It would serve no purpose what-so-ever to tell you that you sound like a complete tosse—"

He threw his hand up laughing. "Enough already! You're always doing my head in trying to keep up with you, and it has me spewing out rubbish like that!"

They laughed.

"So I'll see you here tomorrow, say, around noon?" he asked.

"For sure; I'll be here, and I'll bring plenty of lunch," she joked as her smile widened, "since you seem to be a bottomless pit!"

"Harsh, but true," he said with a grin and gave her a quick hug before he turned and strolled down the hill.

He turned around when he reached the bottom. He pointed to himself with his thumbs again. "I'm just saying you're going to want this one day."

"Give it up, Casanova. That's obviously not going to happen," she said, trying to ignore the swirls of desire taking flight deep down again.

He laughed, as he turned back and strolled off whistling. Although he'd dismissed it as if he was joking, he meant every word. He had never wanted to be with a girl more.

Lil let out a little sigh as she watched him. His hips seemed to roll with each stride he took. His arrogant swagger was turning her on even more. "Blimey, that bloke is driving me mental," she mumbled as she made her way down the hill. She saw JR waiting for her. "So was that clear enough?"

"You sounded pretty clear to me. If the bloke gets his heart broken, it's all on him!"

She rolled her eyes as they went inside. "He's not going to get his heart broken! He's not really interested. He just likes winding me up."

Hours later Lil undressed, exhausted. Every muscle in her neck and shoulders ached as she slipped into the bathtub. She let out a little sigh and slid down until the water reached her chin. She was enjoying the hot, hot water with her favorite bubble bath. As her screaming muscles relaxed, her thoughts slipped to HT. She wondered what he was doing and if he *did* have a steady girlfriend. Most likely not; there was no way he could commit to just one. He sure loved the ladies. "*No, you're not going there!*" she mumbled, pushing that thought aside. "Why do I care? He can have half a dozen." She swept all thoughts of him from her mind and lathered shampoo onto the top of her head and worked it through the long strands of her thick dark hair. After she rinsed she stepped out of the tub and toweled off. She slipped into her pajamas and brushed her hair and teeth and then made her way to bed. She knew she would be out like a light as soon as her head hit the pillow, being so exhausted. Glancing at the clock on her nightstand, she saw it was after eleven. Her thoughts turned to HT once again, and she thought she must be the last thing on his mind, so he wouldn't be sending her a text. She climbed in as she mumbled, "He probably has his hands too full trying to catch up with his long line of beauties to think about me!" She laid her phone next to her pillow trying to convince herself it wasn't, in case he didn't forget about her. Just as she got comfortable under the duvet, his ringtone made her jump. She felt intense tingling as she reached over and grabbed it. She smiled as she quickly sent back.

"Good night, HT ☺."

# CHAPTER 7

Lil and HT spent most of their waking hours together the next week keeping busy. Their bond grew steadily stronger. They laughed, teased, and talked, enjoying each other's company and being intrigued by everything the other had to say.

It was a glorious Saturday afternoon, sunny and growing warmer as they strolled to their hill. A spring storm had blown through earlier in the morning, leaving everything refreshed and bright. The garden was in full bloom with endless sprays of daffodils, pansies, purple lilacs, and roses. Lil lay down after they finished lunch, while HT stretched out on his back, propping himself up on his elbows enjoying the sun.

"I was just wondering...what do you see yourself doing this time next year?" Lil asked, curiously.

"Oh, I don't know...being on this hill listening to the waterfall with you but doing more than just talking, I hope."

She sat up and turned so that they would be facing each other, with their legs stretched out in the opposite direction. She crossed her ankles and leaned back on her hands. "No really, be serious. We haven't really talked about our dreams, our plans. So..." her voice trailed off as she looked at her toes and wiggled them and then back at HT. "What is the one thing you want to do? You know, what is your real passion?"

He sat up, crossed his ankles, and leaned back on his hands, looking into her eyes. "Lee and I do have something going on for next summer. It took a lot of soul searching for me to make that choice, though."

"Such as?"

"Okay, I'm going to spill my guts here, but just so you know, this is a first for me to talk about this with anyone."

A smile appeared on her face as something warm slowly blossomed inside her at learning he was going to share a private part of himself.

He returned her smile and continued, "For a long time my dream was to be a golf pro and own a professional course. Dad played a lot of golf when he and Mum met. He took me to the driving range with him a few times, and I fell in love. I just knew golf was what I was destined to do for the rest of my life. Of course, Dad being the type of guy he is, he told me to dream big. He told me if I didn't try, I'd never know if my dreams could come true, so I should set my mind to it and work hard, but have fun and enjoy doing whatever it is I choose to do in life. I remember thinking he was the smartest, greatest man ever, and I still do. We started going to the range three or four days a week and even made a small putting green in our backyard. I couldn't get enough. Every second I was home, I lived in the backyard. Mum had to make me come in to eat."

"That's hard to believe," she mumbled.

"Hey, Ms. Cheeky!" he teased as if he was offended. "You have me pouring my heart out, being all serious here, and you want to pick on me about my eating habits?"

"Sorry, I didn't mean to interrupt you. I'll be nice. You were saying?" She smiled sweetly batting her lashes.

He chuckled running his fingers through his curls trying to calm Clyde. He gave her a little wink and continued. "Dad took me to my first real golf course in Chester when I was eight, and the owner, Bruce, was impressed. He said I was a real natural, and he would like to work with me and possibly sponsor me one day. Everybody wanted him so that was a big honor. I went every day I could and never got tired of playing." His voice trailed off and stopped. A shiver ran through him, making the hair on the back of his neck stand on end. He asked, "Did you hear that? Like a squeaky gate opening or something. I've been having the weirdest feelings that I'm being watched. It's starting to freak me out."

Lil knew it was JR. She saw him scurry up toward the house and said, "I hate when you get those weird feelings," and left it at that.

A few seconds passed in silence and then he spoke again. He glanced up toward the house, making certain no one was watching them as he talked. "Anyway, it was the best summer of my life. Especially since Mum and Dad got married that spring.

They even took me along on their honeymoon," he said with a chuckle. "That's when I fell in love with Keaton Hall. I thought it was a bit dodgy the only part we could go in was the wing they turned into the bed-and-breakfast. I told Dad when I make like a gazillion pounds playing golf, I'm going to buy this place so that we can live here and go where we want!"

Lil asked with a smile, "And what did he say?"

"I don't think he really knew what to say to that one," HT replied with a chuckle. "But he said, 'Good, son, then we can finally see what they have going on up there!'"

They laughed.

"Dad said he thought it was closing after the summer season. That they're turning it back to a private residence."

"Yeah, I heard the same thing," Lil replied. She couldn't tell him it was a fact, since she couldn't discuss Keaton Hall. "It's kind of a shame; I've spent a lot of time walking around over there and playing tennis."

"Really? I've always wanted to play tennis after I watched a couple of blokes playing there. They were really good. I mean like pro good. You any good?"

"Not bad, I guess."

"We should walk over there sometime this summer. Maybe get you back to playing, and you can give me a few lessons before they close the place up."

"Sure on the walking but not so much on the tennis," she mumbled while turning away. "I've really lost interest in playing."

He knew there was more to the story from her tone and reaction, and with a minimum amount of prodding he'd get her to spill. "No worries. I know it's rubbish when that happens, losing interest in something you thought you really liked."

"*Or somebody.*" She didn't realize she'd voiced the thought until he spoke.

He grinned and thought, *Well, that didn't take long!* "How about I quit pouring my heart out, and we talk about that somebody? The one that has you hating tennis now."

She shook her head. "No, we're not talking about him," she mumbled. "He's been the major mistake in my life!"

"No way," he protested. "You can't drop a bombshell like that and not expect me to be curious."

She edged her chin up. "Just continue, because I'm not saying another word."

"I'll move on, but I'm not letting it slide. We'll come back to talk about that somebody."

"Don't hold your breath," she said, making him laugh.

"So, to finish my story, here's the short version. I met Lee. We both had singing parts in a school play in grade school. We became instant mates and have been ever since. Fell in love with music. It's my passion, blah, blah, blah! Now, let's move on to that somebody."

Lil raised her brow laughing. "Oh no, good try!"

"What?"

"No. Blah, blah, blah!"

"It worked for you!" he teased.

"That's total bollocks, and you know it! I wasn't talking about anything worth hearing. I want to hear the long version. You always seem to keep me running my mouth, so you're not getting off that easy. Come on spill your guts a little more; give me details."

"But yours wasn't really personal, just family stuff. So you have to fess up about this somebody. Agreed?"

She opened her mouth to object but rolled her eyes in disgust.

"You know you're awfully cute, and your eyes sparkle when you're annoyed," he said grinning.

"Well, I do have my cute moments."

"Yes, you do! Wait a minute," he teased. "So are you being cute now to distract me?"

"If it works."

He shook his head slowly. "Sorry didn't. So...?"

She let out a little groan. "How do I know if the rest of your story is worth me spilling my guts on the biggest mistake of my life?"

"I'll throw in the most embarrassing event of my life."

"Fine! I agree. But it better be good, mister!" she grumbled.

"Oh, it's absolutely classic! Just remember what we talk about on this hill..."

They said in unison laughing, "Stays on this hill."

"Right then," he chuckled and said, "since I know my secrets are safe, I'll continue. Lee and I were fourteen when we got a band together. We thought we were just the coolest blokes ever! Lee even had Justin's haircut! We did a few gigs, nothing real big, but we did win a Battle of the Bands contest. Blimey, did that give us big egos. We let all that attention go to our heads, big time."

"I'm speechless," she gasped. "Somehow I just can't imagine you being so arrogant."

"Watch it," he playfully growled. "You're supposed to be nice over there, remember?"

"Oops, silly me. I forgot."

"Uh-huh, you forgot," he responded with a sexy grin and then continued. "Lee and I learned our lesson. We were so self-absorbed that we couldn't stand ourselves, let alone each other. It made us grow up fast when we realized we'd almost lost our friendship over it. What really brought me down to reality was when Mum and Dad, who think I can do no wrong, told me I was acting like total crap. Mum said it started when the whole music thing kicked in, and I should just stick with the golf. She said she hated to admit it, but she was ashamed of me for the first time in my life. That did it; nearly broke my heart hearing her say that. I promised her and Dad that no matter what I did in life, I would never act like that again. So since then, I try my hardest to be polite and treat everybody I meet with respect."

"And from what I've seen, you do," Lil said smiling.

He returned her smile.

"Are you still in a band? And more importantly, the guys will want to know just how good you are at golf!"

"No, on the band," he replied shaking his head. "We broke up from being such prats. It didn't end well. Not bragging on the golf, but I won every junior tournament I entered, also beat some senior pros, but let's keep that between us."

"Aha, that explains it," she teased. "Now I understand why you're a little strange. You're a huge golf nerd!"

He clicked his tongue with a disapproving tsk and slowly shook his head. "Lil, Lil, Lil. You're doing it again. Aren't you supposed to be nice? Has the word taken on a new meaning since last I heard?"

She just laughed and asked, "So are you getting another band together?"

"Lee and I are working on it. Dad gave me one of the garages for band practice when we get it together." He raised his eyebrows up and down, trying to play it off in case she laughed or thought it was daft. "Our plan next year is to try out for, *Brit Idol*. You know, wanting to be the next big boy band that comes out of the UK! So how cool is that? May even be on the telly! Pretty impressive, huh?" he joked, as he watched for her reaction.

"Very impressive," she said with enthusiasm. "I think you should go for it. From what I've heard, you're brilliant. You definitely have talent."

"Who are you really?" he asked with a cheeky grin, pretending he hadn't eagerly waited for her reaction or that his heart wasn't leaping from her response. "Do you like that show?"

Lil shrugged. "It's okay. Of course it will be my favorite. If you make it on, I'll be there front and center, getting it all on film!"

"No doubt you'll be chasing us around with that bloody camera! I've never had so many photos taken of me. You have to spend a small fortune on film alone, not counting the developing cost." He started laughing. "I bet they love to see you coming. Cha-ching!"

"For your information, Mr. Smarty-Pants, I develop my own film and have for years. I have my own darkroom and am proud of it, so laugh all you want and call me a dork now."

"Well, I wouldn't say you're a dork, although I would go with you're a little nerdy," he teased with a laugh.

"Now who's not being nice?" she joked.

"Sorry." He grinned. "I think having your own darkroom is brilliant. I can't wait to see it."

She moved on not ready or sure if she would ever invite him to see it. "But seriously," she asked, "what if you don't find anyone you like? Or isn't good enough?"

"Well, we try out on our own. We made a pact that no matter what, we're trying out. Simon judges a show in the States too, and last year he formed a group with four of the single girls and they won! So, maybe he'll do the same for us; that's if we even get the chance to audition for him."

"Stop it; you will. So your parents are cool with the not going to uni? Because you're definitely going to make the show and not be able to go!"

He flashed a big smile. "Thanks for the confidence. That's where the soul searching came in! I had to make a choice between music or golf and uni. Of course when I finally decided it was my music and came clean with Dad, thinking I was letting him down not joining the circuit and maybe pushing back uni, he told me not to be daft, that I should do what made me happy! The only rule Mum has laid down as law is no tattoos until I'm out of school; she hates them."

"I have to agree with her on that one. I hate those things too. They are just disgusting," she said with a shudder and grimace. "I can't believe people pay good money to get them! Like Papa would say, they look like ten miles of bad road when you get old."

"So tell me how you really feel." He laughed. "You sound just like Mum."

"Smart woman."

He let out a long sigh. "Now, for that embarrassing story I promised. I'll probably live to regret this," he admitted with a faint growl, "but here it goes. I tried to get a tat when I was fifteen. There, I said it!" The admission was more difficult than he expected.

"Oh my gosh! You don't even look eighteen now with that baby face."

He shrugged. "I just knew I looked eighteen. I had a fake ID and everything. I cut school one day and strutted into a tat shop like I was way too cool. Three rough-looking blokes, full of tats, were doing the inking. I mean, not a space on them wasn't inked or pierced. One bloke had such big earplugs; I could have stuck my head through them."

Lil laughed at the image.

He winked and gave her his biggest smile. "They were working away on other blokes, looking just as rough and inked to the hilt. Here I was this skinny kid wanting a tat. They laughed, told me to come back when my nads dropped, and asked why I wasn't in school. I should have left right then."

"You still tried?" she asked, her eyebrows raised.

"What can I say? I was a real nutter back then. I showed them the ID and demanded they give me a tat. I wouldn't give up. The more they laughed the more determined I was. It wasn't a pretty sight when they escorted me out of the shop, while everyone in the place laughed their arses off."

"You're not serious?" she asked, looking skeptical. "That didn't really happen?"

"Yeah, really—I swear it's true. Oh, it gets better. On the way home, I was thinking how lucky I was Lee had backed out of going and I was in the clear. Nobody would ever know about me making an arse of myself. Wrong! Jake, the owner, is a real good friend of Dad's. He called him as soon as I left the shop. Dad had him over that night for dinner, dropping me right in it."

Lil burst out laughing and continued to laugh until she cried.

He joined in after a second, laughing just as hard.

She wiped the tears from her cheeks as she recovered. "You're just winding me up, right?"

"I wish I was! I'm deadly serious. I almost wet myself seeing him sitting there. They laughed and busted my nads all night. He still comes to dinner. I'm never going to live it down." He chuckled and added, "He's actually a really nice guy; told me when I was ready, he would be honored to give me my first tat."

"Just promise me if you ever do get one, not on your face or neck and don't get too many. Those things really are vile!"

"I promise; say no more than what, twenty-seven?" he asked, trying to keep a straight face.

"Ah, yuck!" She made a face. "Are—you—mental?" she asked in a disgusted tone. "You'll have no space left on your body! One is enough to make me nauseated."

He gave her a lopsided grin. "I promise, none on my face and neck."

"Good, I'm glad to hear you're not that daft. They're just disgusting," she grumbled making a face and shivered to illustrate. "The mere thought of you marking up that gorgeous face of yours makes my skin crawl."

His eyes were shining like stars as he flashed her a sexy grin. "Oh! What was that? Did you say gorgeous face?" he echoed, sounding shocked.

"Yeah, yeah, get over yourself. As if you don't know," she said with a grin. "Now let's get back to talking more about your music. You write songs?"

He smiled and replied, "Yeah, I do when I'm inspired. I'm finishing up one now, as a matter of fact."

"Awesome! I'm looking forward to hearing it when you're done, along with all the others you've written. I bet they're brilliant."

"I don't know about that." He chuckled. "So what do you have going on after school?"

"If I have to go to uni, I want to go to King's University down in London."

"What do you mean if you have to?"

"I'd rather get started on my career. I want to be a freelance photographer. Of course, when I mentioned that to Dad all hell broke loose, and he told me I was going to uni and follow family tradition and go to Oxford. He also added to just get the idea of not going, along with attending Kings, out of my head!"

"Poor baby has to go to Oxford." He chuckled.

She playfully rolled her eyes.

"So why King's?" he asked.

"Well…let's just say at first, it was a great place to hide out last summer. I took a six-week course in film producing and directing there. I loved it. It got me hooked. Who knows? Maybe I'll film and direct a music video for you one day!"

"Certainly, I'm going to hold you to it." He grinned. "Sooo, why did we have to run off to London in the first place?"

"I got myself into a little mess, so it ended up being a good thing—the course, not the mess. Besides having somewhere to hide out, it pointed me in another direction with my career."

"Really? And just what kind of mess might that be?" he asked. "Wait, we're back to that somebody?"

She shook her head laughing. "Leave it to you to skip right over the fact that I changed my life plans to include videos and documentaries and head straight in the other direction."

"What? I'm just saying the 'other direction' sounds way more interesting!" teased HT. "Wait a minute." His face lit up. "I think we just got something here. That sounds like a great name for the band when we try out for the show."

"What? My Mess?"

"No, that's total crap! Other Direction! Not bad, huh?" He grinned, nodding his head.

"'Direction,' I like. 'Other'? Well!" she said, scrunching up her nose and making another one of her faces.

"Hey now, don't look at me like that. I liked 'other.' You know, shorten it to O—"

"Still no!" She chuckled, shaking her head and cutting him off. "You and your abbreviating."

"Right then." He grinned. "So let's find something we both like, to go with direction." He snapped his fingers. "Got it. *Opposite* Direction!"

"I see you're sticking with something with an *O* to use that silly *O* and *D* abbreviation."

"What? I never put an 'and' in it!"

"Same difference," she said grinning.

"Fine. Let's try it your way, Ms. Bossy Pants. We'll come up with something else. How about That Direction, Another Direction, or maybe First Direction. Hey, that's not bad; I'm feeling that one!" he said raising his eyebrows up and down. "That's a good one, huh?"

She nodded and replied, "For sure! This could be where it all starts with the making of the band name, right here on our hill." Her eyes shone brightly as she teased him, knowing he had meant *first*. "The world's next biggest boy band's name is...Good One. Or was it? Feeling that one! Or was it? Good one, huh!"

He tilted his head to give her an aggravated look. "Really?"

"Okay, I'm sorry." She chuckled. "I'll quit winding you up; I know this is serious. I'll love whatever you choose, so just pick one!"

His face lit up with a huge smile. "You just did!" he said with a wink.

She poked him in the ribs teasingly. "You deliberately picked one so that you'll be able to use that silly abbreviation!"

"Who me?" he teased back. "I did no...O such thing."

They laughed.

"Just don't forget me when you're rich and famous, since I evidently helped you pick out the name!"

"How can I forget you? You'll be chasing me all over with that camera! Besides, you're making our videos!"

"Oh yeah, I forgot." She smiled.

HT broke the silence after a few minutes of being lost in their thoughts. "What's it going to be?"

"Huh? You lost me."

"I'm giving you another chance."

"Okay...I need a little more than that!" She chuckled.

"Do we have a date night tonight, or are you chasing me off again?"

"Well, I walked right into that," she said with a little huff. "You know you can be really irritating with that rubbish!"

"But I'm charming when I am."

"Uh-huh, if you say so!"

He nodded. "I do. That's why I'm giving you a second chance. Seems to be an easy decision to me...I know you just needed another week of me, well, me being me, to change your mind on this no-dating thing."

Lil shook her head. "No, I haven't changed my mind, especially after another week of you being you and getting to know you even better."

"Uh-oh! Not sure I like the sound of that," he grumbled.

"Don't be daft. I just mean I like you too much to date you."

"And that's supposed to make sense?"

"Absolutely! Besides, we already agreed no dating!"

"You did," he said with a raised brow.

"Come on, HT. I'm really serious about this. I can see us becoming best mates for life, as long as we don't screw it up by trying to date! I'm sure you know how it is."

"No," he replied shaking his head, with a smile that girls always found irresistible. "Just how is it? Please tell me, oh wise one."

"Fine, I will. You try to date a mate, it all goes bad, and someone gets hurt. I tried it once, and it turned to total crap. All of a sudden I couldn't stand being around him." She got a blank look on her face, took in a deep breath, and started to mumble. "All that flirting and winking that used to turn me to mush, got on my last nerve. That laugh, no, just the sound of his voice made me want to throw up!"

"Bloody hell," he said under his breath. His eyebrows rose, as she continued on, not missing a beat.

Her words were running together as she mumbled faster, now with an accent. "Want you, love you, miss you. Not even going to talk about that lousy kissing, after dreaming about it forever. Oh! I just knew he had to be great. Yeah, right! There's nothing worse than a bad kisser," she added with a shiver. She drew in a deep breath and rattled on. "It was like kissing a big-mouthed fish. I wanted to hurl while he tried to swallow my face!" She made a face like a fish, opening and closing her mouth. "Ew, that's enough to put you off snogging; it sent me running straight to London to get away..."

His eyes sparkled as he threw his head back and howled with laughter.

She blushed, realizing she had been mumbling and rambling on like an idiot and probably giving him way too much information.

"I think I got that. He kisses like a fish, foreign, and almost made you hurl. That kiss sounds promising though. How about you demonstrate it again? But, this time on me." He laughed again.

Despite her embarrassment, she laughed.

"I take it, that was the no-tennis, going-to-London bloke, right?"

"Yes, on all accounts. Now you know my worst habit. It's been years since I've embarrassed myself doing that. I mean I mumble but only around people I'm comfortable with." She shrugged. "Sorry, I'm afraid you'll have to get used to it."

"You don't have to apologize. I'm glad you feel comfortable enough with me to mumble."

"You say that now, but wait until I drive you mental. I tend to mumble and talk fast when I have a lot to say or if I'm nervous or stressed out, and it's really bad when I'm tired. If the mumbling alone isn't enough to do your head in trying to figure what I'm saying, just wait until I leave out words. I can get fired up at times, and it tends to get me in trouble."

"I like it. I finally got to hear about your mystery bloke. Let's hear the rest. By the way, the feelings are mutual. I feel comfortable with you too."

"I'm glad to hear it," she replied. "And, he's not my mystery man, silly. He just screwed my whole summer up last year, and us trying to date killed a great friendship."

HT kept prying. "What did this bloke do? He turn beastly? Is he still around?" he asked in an offhand sort of way. He was eager to get more information without sounding too interested.

"No, the opposite," she said shaking her head. "He really is a nice guy. He's sweet and caring, and the family loves him. He just started doing my head in, always around, always blowing my phone up with all the texting and calling. He was forever telling me he loved me, like every five bloody minutes. I never had a second to myself. I felt really bad that I didn't return his feelings and ended up backing away from him."

He teased with a cheeky grin, "Based on past experience—"

She threw up her arms and cut in with a heavy, weary sigh. "Aaargh, I give up. Why am I even trying to explain this to you? It's not like you ever listen. You're so sure that I'm going to magically change my mind. I've never had such a hard time trying to have a serious conversation." She shook her head in disgust and rolled her eyes at him.

He rolled his right back. "And you're too stubborn to admit you could be wrong."

"Not stubborn, just right!"

She had him growling low in his throat as he stood up. "You're so smart that you have an answer for everything, don't you?"

"Of course I do," she replied trying not to grin, hearing his growl.

He huffed, "It's just amazing all those brains fit in your bloody head!"

"I know, I know," she teased as she slipped her trainers on. "I wonder about that myself at times."

He mimicked her and threw up his arms and let out a heavy, weary sigh. "Aaargh, I give up. Why am I even trying to get the last word in with you!"

They laughed.

"So, Ms. Smarty-Pants, what's your rules if, and that's a big if, I agree to this just-mates rubbish?" he asked as he held out his hand.

She took it and said as he pulled her up, "Good question. If we're making rules—"

He cut her off laughing. "I didn't mean the rule thing literally!"

"Tough," she said wiping her backside off. "I like the idea of having rules."

"And that doesn't surprise me!"

"Yeah, whatever. Now, let's think about this. Our rules need to be simple ones that we agree on so that we'll be honest about keeping them." She thought for a second. "I know our very first rule should be just that. We never lie to each other. No matter what, we tell each other the truth, even if it hurts. As you know, I'm big on being honest."

He gave her a brief nod and grunted. "Sometimes, I'm thinking a little too honest."

"HT! For God's sa—"

His laugh cut her off again. "Don't be kicking off again. I was just teasing. As you know I like the whole honesty thing too. So I'll agree to that rule."

"Good. It's great grounds to build a lifelong friendship on—trust and respect. Don't you think?"

"Yeah, I do." The corners of his mouth edged up, making his eyes twinkle. "Wanna kiss on it?"

"Kiss?" Lil raised an eyebrow. "I don't think so!"

"I promise I don't kiss like a fish!"

"No fringe benefits," she said with a little chuckle. She extended her hand. "A handshake will do. Rule one: No lies!"

"No lies!" he sighed shaking her hand. "Right then, as fun as this has been, you busting my nads about all this no dating and making rules rubbish, I'll go so that you can catch that break you seem to need from me."

"Stop! You know I don't want a break from you. I just need to get caught up in the darkroom. I'm behind again."

"I could pitch in while we hang out. What do you say? I'll stay home and help you. I would love to learn, and it'll be fun."

"I'm sure it would. You make everything fun; that's the problem. I have a lot to do, and I won't get anything done. Now, get going; I'm sure your parents are waiting on you, and I need to get started."

"There you go, being Ms. Bossy again," he teased. "So I'll see you tomorrow at noon. And don't for—"

"Lunch," she said cutting him off.

"Nice. You're the best." He gave her a hug and then leaned forward and quickly brushed his lips lightly on her forehead.

She groaned inwardly taking in his musky, clean scent. It was the first time he had kissed her. It was no more than a butterfly kiss, but her forehead and insides were burning.

He stepped back as he quickly turned to hide Clyde's reaction and trotted down the hill. Not turning around knowing there was no hiding Clyde, he threw up his arm giving her a little wave as he started singing his favorite song about her being beautiful.

She let out a long, hard sigh. "That was new," she mumbled. "I'm just getting used to him taking my hand whenever the opportunity presents itself and even his hugs. It's just him being him, being so affectionate. But now I have to ignore his winks and him kissing me and his scent! Blimey! I need a cold shower," she grumbled as she went down the hill.

☺☺

An hour later HT and Luke were standing by the car waiting patiently on Madison and Maddie. Luke leaned against the car his arms crossed over his chest as he watched the front door. HT was looking down, moving gravel around with his foot.

Luke knew by HT's actions he was struggling with something and wanted to talk. He had learned over the years he just needed to get him talking. "Seems like you're coming around more. So am I forgiven for dragging you here?" he asked, not taking his eyes off the door.

"I'll get back to you on that one."

They chuckled.

After a few minutes passed, HT asked, "Dad, how do you know if you're really falling for a girl?"

Luke didn't say anything; he knew HT would continue.

HT let out a heavy sigh and said, "Lil has me a little buggared, Dad."

"How so?" asked Luke, still watching the door.

"I've joked around a few times about us hooking up." He paused.

Luke glanced over at him. "She turned you down?"

"Yeah, both times."

"Shocking."

"Whatever." HT grinned. "Her reasoning was because we like each other too much, that we have the makings of a great friendship going, and that she doesn't want to mess it up over a few weeks of attraction we both know will fade. She started a bloody list of rules about us being best mates."

Luke almost did a fist pump; he was so glad. He kept his tone even. "So what do you think?"

"That she's mental, or I am for going along with her," he replied.

Luke shrugged. "She has a point. It makes perfectly good sense to me."

"Yeah, it makes sense, I guess." He made eye contact with Luke. "I really like her, Dad, more than any girl I've ever met."

"More than Sloan?"

"I've never been attracted to Sloan." He chuckled. "She's been one of my best mates since we were ten."

"Maybe you just see Lil as a challenge."

"You know my motto," he teased, "challenging…but not impossible!"

"And we know you always like a challenge," Luke said with a grin. Then added in a serious tone, "Why not wait it out and see? Don't push the dating thing, and take time to really get to know her. We both know you quickly lose interest once they cave."

"True," said HT with a half grin. "But, I don't think I will with her. The more I'm around her, the more I want to be! Crazy, huh?"

"So what is it about her that has you so interested?" Luke asked.

HT shrugged. "We've clicked from the second we met. She's quick witted and always has a comeback keeping me on my toes. We have lots in common, and I really like that she seems genuinely interested in what I have to say. She makes me feel things I've never felt before. She's on my bloody mind all the time, even when I'm not with her. She has me laughing one minute and frustrates the hell out of me the next, and boy is she stubborn and *always* thinks she's right!"

Luke grinned thinking, *That's our baby girl.*

"She's never, ever boring that's for sure!" added HT. "Besides you, I've never talked to anyone, or even wanted to, about my personal feelings but it just feels right with her. Like today, I was only going to tell her a little, but I got carried away and told her *way* more than I intended. And what's really scary, I was honest with the things I told her, like the tat thing!"

Luke's eyes widened with surprise, "You didn't?"

HT blew air out of his cheeks. "I know. I can't believe it either. So how do you know when it's real, Dad? Not just an attraction like she says."

Luke's heart skipped a beat at seeing the same little lad looking at him like he was the smartest man in the world. "That's the million dollar question, son," he replied. "It's like my pops told me when I was your age; it will happen when you least expect it. A girl will come around and maybe have just *one thing* that will make you forget all you thought you knew or wanted in life. When it happens, you'll fall hard and everything changes. They make you do things you don't want to, even things you never thought you'd do. And the amazing thing is you'll never be happier doing them! You'll be acting just like the rest of us sad sacks because there is no stopping it. The heart wants what it wants; it's impossible to be logical after that."

"I believe I could get a song out of that!" HT said with a chuckle. "But seriously, thanks for the advice, Dad, but no girl will have me acting like that!"

"Just keep reminding yourself of that, when you write that song, smart guy," Luke said with a laugh. After a pause he added, "Can I ask you not to push the going out and just stay mates like she wants?"

HT gave him a weird look. "Why?"

"Keep this between us?"

"Of course, Dad. You know I never repeat what you tell me."

"I do. I just don't know what Lil knows, and I don't want it getting back to Charles that I discuss our business relationship."

HT nodded.

Luke started on the cover story he and Charles had put together. "A few years back, I was assigned to do an audit on Charles's company's accounts. You know, boring bank stuff. His company has held the bank branches' security contracts for years, and while going over all his contracts we got reacquainted from our uni days. Anyways, we went to dinner a few times and began discussing business adventures and realized we both loved golf. So we started having our meetings out on the golf course. The bloke is brilliant when it comes to making money and golf. I can't beat him or his business partner, Bill."

"Really?"

"Yeah. It was killing me not being able to brag about you, but since you don't like people knowing you're such a golf nerd, I couldn't brag that you would put them to shame."

"I can beat 'em, huh?"

"Of course. Never seen anyone you can't beat."

HT just grinned.

"Hey, I just thought of something," said Luke with a sheepish grin. "I'm sure you'll be joining us when they get to know you. Keep it on the down low on just how good you are until then. I see a little revenge golf in my future. Maybe I can win back some of my money!"

"Sure!" HT nodded. "I'll give up on trying to hook up with her too, now that I know you and Lil's dad are so tight. I'll just stick with just being mates."

"Thanks, son. I just hate to see hard feelings if things turn sour between the two of you." He paused with a wave of guilt. He was trying hard to persuade himself against acting on his feelings. He heard Bill's voice in his head telling him to let it slide, boy. It'll be Charlie and Mary all over again! He didn't listen, knowing HT was half in love with her already. He took in a deep breath and said, "Son, forget that rubbish I just said. Don't let Charles and our friendship stop you if you find yourself really having feelings for her. If you do, then go for her with all you have."

"Are you sure?"

Luke nodded and thought it wouldn't hurt to give him a little heads-up so that he knew what he was getting into, since he knew how stubborn Lil was. "I feel I need to tell you something because you sound like you really do like her."

"Such as?"

"Well, Charles and I have talked about you kids over the years. You know, proud dad stuff."

HT chuckled.

"He mentioned a while back that Lil was giving him a hard time about going to college. Seems she took a course last summer, and now all she thinks about is starting her career."

HT grunted and muttered, "She took it to get away from some bloke."

"Yeah, that's what he said. Seems she's pretty stubborn when it comes to her plans, and nothing or nobody is going to keep her from them."

"She basically kicked his arse to the curb," he muttered.

Luke chuckled thinking, *That's my girl, being honest with him.* "At least she's up front about it. Doesn't mean you don't have a shot. Turn on all that Harry charm you ooze that girls can't resist."

"I think maybe I'll stick with just being mates for a while, no pushing the dating thing until I figure her out. Sometimes I think she feels the same and is just being stubborn not admitting it and then the next I don't have a bloody clue how she feels."

Luke grunted and said, "Good luck with that. I'm still trying to figure out your mum!"

They laughed as Madison and Maddie came out the front door.

# CHAPTER 8

Monday morning Lil left her bedroom, heading toward the stairs when she heard Raif rustling around in his room. She stopped in the open doorway and said, "Good morning, love of my life!"

Raif looked up with a big smile, "Morning, Lil. Breakfast?"

"Absolutely. You're up bright and early." Squatting down, she held her arms open wide.

With a big giggle, he ran as fast as his little legs could go and launched himself at her.

She stood up holding him, gave him a quick kiss on the cheek, and snuggled him into her chest. As she carried him to the front staircase, she said, "Wait a minute. You just called me Lil. What happened to calling me Sis?"

Raif giggled. He saw Charles starting down the stairs. "Hi, Daddy?"

"Morning, son." Charles's voice came from behind them. "Sounds like you're ready for breakfast."

"Hungry, Daddy." Raif giggled.

Lil stopped when she reached the landing. She turned to smile at Charles and greeted him, "Morning, Dad. I didn't know you guys were back."

"Good morning, baby girl," he replied. "We got in late last night."

She kissed his cheek before they continued down the wide steps together.

Lil tickled Raif as they walked down the hall toward the kitchen and said, "Why are you calling me Lil?"

"HT calls you Lil." He giggled.

"You haven't even met HT yet. Sounds like you're being a little repeat again."

"I'm repeat, huh, Daddy?" Raif giggled, his deep-blue eyes twinkling as he tried to stop her hands.

"Nah, not you!" Charles teased.

Lil strapped Raif into his booster seat and scooted him up to the table in the kitchen, since only holidays and special-occasion meals were eaten in the formal dining room. She brushed his black, wavy hair back from his forehead as she bent and kissed the top of his head. Charles went to the fridge to get eggs and cheese as she went to the toaster. They had it down to a science, since Raif ate the same thing every morning. Once Lil popped bread into the toaster, she went to the sink to clean and cut the strawberries. Raif loved strawberries; they were his favorite.

"Cheese, Daddy!"

"Yes, son," he responded. "I have it right here." He lifted the cheese up so that Raif could see it.

"Like cheese, huh, Lil?"

"Yep, you like cheese and love strawberries." She sat the strawberries in front of him. "I like you calling me Lil," she said, smiling fondly at him. He giggled as she kissed the top of his head again and went back to spreading homemade jam on the toast, strawberry of course. Placing the toast in front of him, she turned to get his milk.

"Kiss!" he mumbled and bit into his toast.

"Sorry." Lil chuckled, as she turned around and kissed his head once again.

"Go for a walk. Huh, Lil?"

"For sure, now that Dad and Papa are finally home."

He looked at Lil and asked, "HT walk and lunch, huh, Daddy?"

Lil got a sneaking suspicion that Charles was up to something. She glanced at him as he put Raif's eggs on a plate. She walked to the counter as she replied, "I'll ask HT if he would like to join us." Her mind was spinning as she poured Raif's milk. "Huh" was his way of asking questions, and the name he said was whom he was asking. He should have said, "Huh, Lil?" since he was asking her. If it wasn't the name of the person he was asking the question, then the name that followed the question was usually whom he was repeating, which was most likely in this case. She was sure Dad put him up to asking her if HT could come. She'd know in a few minutes; Raif would start babbling if she was right. She walked back to Raif, giving him a quick kiss and sat down the cup.

In between bites he said in a rush, "HT's cute, huh, Daddy? Wears do-rag. Huh, Daddy? Lil likes HT and do-rag, huh, Daddy? HT walk, huh, Lil? Lunch, huh, Lil?" He didn't really care if he got answers. He just rattled on between bites.

*Aha!* she thought with a triumphant voice in her head. *I knew it!* Dad had definitely put him up to asking. The way he was babbling and mixing up saying "Daddy" and "Lil" meant he was being a little repeat. He should've been saying, "Huh, Lil?" He had heard her talking to Mum and was repeating her, all but the walking and lunch. He definitely got that from Dad. She examined Charles's face, trying to make eye contact as he turned from the stove.

Charles couldn't hide his grin as he deliberately averted his eyes and walked to Raif with his eggs.

Lil knew he had planned the whole morning from the start, and Raif was getting two conversations mixed up, the one she had with Mum and the one she was sure Dad had worked on with him earlier. This meant that Grammy had better pack enough lunch for seven, but she probably already knew that. HT was about to get ambushed.

Lil had known this meeting was going to happen since she and HT had gotten so close and was spending so much time together. Although, it was a lot quicker than she had expected, seeing as they had just gotten home. *Poor HT. He didn't have a clue what was coming his way. However, if he planned to stay around this family, he would have to get used to them.* She bent down to get a kiss from Raif. He grabbed her hugging her tightly and then gave her a kiss, smearing strawberry jam and juice all over the front of her T-shirt and cheek.

"Love you," she said, hugging him tightly and kissed his cheek, not caring in the least that he had gotten her shirt dirty.

"Love you most, Lil." He giggled, emphasizing Lil. Just before he had turned two, he had begun adding *most* on his own and had them all saying it now.

"You're going to love HT," she said, ruffling his hair. "You two are just alike—love food and always hungry!"

He nodded and beamed with pleasure as he continued eating with gusto.

She watched Charles while he was putting the eggs and cheese away. He closed the refrigerator door and looked at her like a guilty child. She rolled her eyes. "You're slipping, Dad."

Managing to keep a reasonably straight face, his eyes widened. "Whatever do you mean?" he asked, doing his best to sound innocent.

"Raif should have said, 'Huh, Lil?' since he heard that from me, all but the walking and lunch, of course. We both know who he heard that from. How long did you work on him this morning?"

"Apparently, not long enough!" was his reply as he chuckled.

"So I take it I'll be seeing *all* of you guys later?"

He shook his head, "Not all. Jayden and Ed won't be joining us, something's come up."

"Yikes!" Lil playfully shuddered. "Aunt Abs isn't going to be too happy." She knew it was more complicated than that because they were gone twice as long as planned and knew there was no sense in asking any questions. She asked, "So is it safe to mention Jay yet? Or tell him about Ed?"

"You can, but are you ready to answer all the questions?"

"I take it JR has told you HT likes to ask a lot of questions?" Lil said, chuckling.

"He happened to mention it. The bet is still on, so how about you let HT and JR get to know each other before you let him in on JR being your—"

Lil interrupted him, "Companion. Don't worry. I'm going to let him figure that one out on his own. He already thinks we're a bunch of crazies with the security thing going on around here."

Charles laughed as he pulled her into a fierce hug. "I'm sorry. I know I can be a pain with all that."

"You're a major pain. Period," she teased, returning his hug. "But I wouldn't want you any other way. You're perfect and the world's greatest dad!"

"Love you, baby girl."

"Love you, Lil," Raif mumbled through a mouthful of strawberries.

"Love you guys most," she said kissing the top of Raif's head. "See you for lunch," she added over her shoulder as she hurried out the door.

Charles said under his breath, "Can't wait to finally meet him as me."

"Meet as me, huh, Daddy?" Raif asked.

Charles laughed and ruffled his hair.

HT had a smile pasted firmly on his face as he waited on Mrs. Peters. He was listening with only half an ear as she went on about Fluffy. He kept glancing over his shoulder toward the back, watching for Lil. It was two weeks since she came bursting into his life. He thought he would have gotten over his unexplainable infatuation with her by now. It seemed that every day he learned something more amazing about her. His day didn't seem to start until he saw her. "Finally," he muttered as he caught a glimpse of her, making his pulse quicken. She always seemed to have that effect on him. He told Mrs. Peters a big fat bold-faced lie of how he was glad Fluffy was all better. He grumbled under his breath while going to the back when he finished waiting on her. "Bloody fur ball, wonder how many lives it has left? Too many, as far as I'm concerned." His heart raced as soon as he saw Lil. He was constantly amazed by Clyde's quick reaction from just seeing her. Her hair was pulled back with a pink ribbon, matching the pink T-shirt with the bakery logo.

Lil looked up as he walked in.

"That woman never shuts up!" he said grinning. "I see why you said she's the queen of the gossips."

Lil laughed, trying to ignore the way her pulse leapt at seeing him.

His mouth curved into a smile at seeing jam smeared on her shirt and cheek. "Tough morning?"

"It was Raif. He caught me. He decided I was helping with his breakfast this morning." She thought he was talking about her shirt having some strawberry stains and being a little late.

"Nice," he said walking over to wet a hand towel. He walked to Lil and gently wiped the strawberries off her cheek and tucked a wayward strand of hair behind her ear.

She all but melted at the touch of his fingers. Tingling began at the tip of her ear and traveled through her body down to her toes.

Trying to ignore the discomfort Clyde was causing he chuckled and said, "I take it he likes strawberries."

"Loves them and anything else strawberry," said Lil.

"Our little munchkin loves bananas. We really *do* need to set up a play date with those two."

"Well, Raif just informed me he wants to join us for lunch." She didn't want him to see in her eyes that she wasn't telling him all of it, so she backed up and turned away grabbing her pink-and-white striped apron off the hook.

"Oh, he did, did he?"

She turned, looking down at her apron when she answered. "Yeah. So I told him he could join." She told herself she wasn't lying, just not telling him everything, keeping their rule still intact. Her stomach tightened. She had to give him a little heads-up and at least tell him Dad was coming too. She thought about how to tell him as she folded the apron in half. She fumbled with the apron and fussed. "I hate the neck thing on these things. They choke me to death."

"And here I thought you were just trying to show off your brilliant top." He chuckled watching her.

She tied the folded apron around her waist as she raised her head and rolled her eyes at him. All thoughts of telling him were gone.

"What? So that the customers can see the logo," he teased.

She cleared her throat as she said, *"Horny Harry."*

He laughed.

"I'll blame that one on Mrs. Peters, doing your head in," she grumbled. "Now back to Raif. I have to warn you, watch what you say because he's a little repeat and never forgets anything he hears!"

"Aha, so that's why you've been holding off letting me meet the little man. You're afraid he'll tell me how much you like me," he said with a chuckle as he followed her to the front.

"Man, you're in rare form this morning," she mumbled. "Good morning, Mum," she greeted Mary with a big smile and kissed her cheek.

"Morning, dear," she returned her greeting with a big smile. "I see our little one caught you this morning!"

"He did. We had a nice breakfast. He's joining HT and me for lunch."

Mary looked at HT. "Sounds like fun. You're in for a treat"

"So I hear. It's about time I meet the little man. He seems to be my main competition with all the ladies around here!" He teased, "I hope he likes me and doesn't feed me to his sidekicks for lunch, though."

"He'll love you, I'm sure," replied Mary with a grin, "but it wouldn't hurt to pack a little extra lunch for them."

They laughed.

After the cleanup Lil said on the way to the loo, "I'll just be a few minutes, HT. I need to freshen up a bit."

"Take your time," he replied hanging up the broom.

Lil washed up and changed into a clean T-shirt. Letting her hair down from a ponytail, she brushed it out deciding to wait until she went outside to pull it back again to give her head a break.

HT was leaning against the counter waiting for her, flipping through the pages of the latest rock magazine. He sucked in his breath when he looked up and saw her. It was the first time he had seen her hair down.

"Your turn." She smiled innocently.

"My turn?" he asked, his brow bunched up in confusion. "I'm not the one who was covered in strawberries!"

Lil glanced away, unwilling to meet his eyes as she walked over to the counter. "No," she said with a playfulness she didn't feel, "but you might want to take that rag off."

He screwed up his face and looked at her as if she'd gone a bit loopy. "What are you going on about?" he asked puzzled. "I'm only going to meet your brother."

She said in a rush. "Dad got back this morning and is coming too." Grabbing her camera, she turned and walked toward the door, picking up the food basket as she added, "I'll meet you outside."

His brow folded into deep creases as he whined, "Bloody hell, Lil! You could have warned me this morning!"

She turned to look at him. "Oopsy!" she said as innocently as she could. Her tone wouldn't deceive anyone. "What? I didn't mention it to Horny Harry this morning?" she added, looking horrified as her hand flew up to her slacked mouth.

His tone went up, "That's still dodgy!"

"Aww, suck it up, Horny Harry. You can handle it," she said with a laugh as she breezed out the door.

HT went into the loo and tried to make himself presentable as quickly as possible. He had been aware if he wanted to keep spending so much time with Lil, which he did, he would have to meet her dad when he got home. He was hoping his parents would be there though, like at dinner or even at one of their family barbeques she was always going on about. He was a bit nervous about meeting him one on one. He pulled off his do-rag and stuck it in his back pocket and ran a comb through his hair. He ran his fingers through it a few times making it lie naturally, as he stomped out the back door.

The door closed, none too lightly, behind him. "Let's get this over with," he muttered miserably, taking the basket from her. He was too nervous about meeting Charles to notice the weight of the basket.

"I'm sure the guys are waiting," she said as she swept past him before he could ask questions that she didn't want to answer.

He watched her hurry off and noticed she had pulled her hair back again. "Good," he muttered. "I need my wits about me to deal with her dad." Seeing she was almost to the steps, he called out, "Hey, slow down, what's the bloody hurry?"

She ran up the steps in the stone wall, not slowing down.

His mind started racing. Was he imagining it, or did she seem a little nervous and had just speeded up even more!

Once up top she turned and waited for him. He fell in beside her as they walked up the gravel path toward the iron gate.

"Hey, Snaggs!" Bill called out.

HT's pulse quickened. "Buggar!" he said under his breath for only her to hear. "Now this is just wrong, Lil. Now I see why you were in such a hurry to get up here," he grumbled. "You knew if I'd had time to think about it I would've realized I was going to get the double whammy!"

"Hush," she whispered back as she nudged his side with her elbow. "He'll hear you. He can hear a pin drop. I really am sorry, but I warned you about my crazy family. Now smile. A real one not one of your fake, flirty ones. He'll know the difference, and I want his first impression of you to be good."

"Fine, Ms. Bossy Pants, but you owe me for this," he whispered.

"Noted," she said and greeted Bill as they reached the gate. "Welcome back, Papa."

Bill hugged her as if they were just reunited after a long year.

"How was your trip, Papa?" she asked, as she kissed his cheek.

Shaking his head sadly he answered, "Aww, them bigwigs ain't playing with a full deck, I tell ya! They're wired for four forty and pulling about one ten. More money than brains, that's for sure!"

HT snickered.

Lil looked over at HT and smiled.

He gave her a wink.

Her insides turned to mush as she turned to Bill. "Papa, this is HT. HT, this is my papa."

HT moved forward and extended his hand. "Nice to meet you, sir. I've heard a lot about you."

Bill pumped his hand enthusiastically with a firm handshake, glad to finally meet him face to face after watching him grow up from afar. "Pleasure," he greeted with a huge smile. "No sir around here though, boy. Call me Bill. Had to come meet the chap the hens are all clucking about; seems Tessa has taken quite a liking to you!"

"I feel the same about her. She's brilliant! And *wow*, she can cook—best food ever!" said HT as he wiggled his hand behind his back trying to get feeling back.

"You haven't seen anything yet, boy. That's why we have to walk so much. She'll make a fatty out of ya!"

They laughed.

Lil linked her arm through Bill's. They walked arm in arm through the gate and up toward the house. HT closed and latched the gate and then quickly followed not wanting to miss anything Bill said. He immediately liked Bill.

Bill spoke shaking his head in disgust, making sure HT heard. He winked at Lil and continued with his cover story. "Them bigwigs were dumber than a box of rocks. If stupid could fly, them idiots would be jets!"

HT chuckled and thought, *He wasn't what he had pictured when Lil talked about him*. He was the total opposite. He was tall, at least six four, because he had to look up to meet his eyes. He was in fantastic shape and had a tough, hard look that meant trouble if you messed with him.

They walked past the glass solarium toward the steps on the back porch. HT heard the dogs barking and laughter that had to be Raif's coming from the house.

Lil hurried up the steps laughing, knowing what was coming.

"Yay, Lil's here! Lil's here! Huh, Daddy?" Raif said all excited as he came busting out the door like a shot. The dogs, wagging their tails, were right on his heels.

"I see you're all ready to go!" she said, holding out her open arms to catch him.

Raif's eyes flashed with delight as he dashed across the porch and flung himself into her arms. He hung on tightly, giggling as she squeezed him and kissed his cheek.

HT watched all smiles. He looked up hearing a man laugh. He knew it had to be Lil's dad coming out the door, because she definitely had his dark eyelashes and hair, and Raif was his mini-clone!

"HT cute, huh, Lil?" Raif said, seeing HT standing there.

"And it begins," she mumbled as she carried him down the steps. She sat him down in front of HT and ran her fingers through his dark hair as her voice rang with pride.

HT watched her face soften as she beamed at Raif.

"Raif, this is HT. HT, may I present Raif."

"Hey, little man, how's it going?" asked HT smiling. "It's nice to finally meet you."

"Nice to finally meet you," Raif repeated. He stuck out his closed fist, knuckles up.

HT chuckled as his fist hit Raif's. Once Raif opened his fingers, HT saw what he was planning and did the same. Together they pulled their hands back and made a soft "Whoosh" sound, making it an exploding fist bump.

HT glanced at Lil and winked. The look he gave her said, *"How cool is this little guy?"* He had never seen a three-year-old do *that* before.

She smiled and nodded.

The dogs were sitting like statues on each side of Raif. Sir George was looking at HT with no emotion, but he could see in Sir Tigger's eyes that he was waiting anxiously for his acknowledgment. "Hello, mates," HT said, "nice to see you again." He put out his hand and shook Sir George's paw and received and returned a head nod. HT then turned to Sir Tigger and bent over patting his head, knowing what was coming. "Hi, big fellow, where's my kiss?" He laughed, patting his head. Sir Tigger's tail was going like crazy as he whined and licked all over his face. HT raised up wiping his face and said, "Not too much there, big guy. Don't want you to get carried away with me ending up on my backside again."

The others laughed.

Raif was in awe as he watched HT. He instantly fell in love with him after he let Sir Tigger kiss him like that and wanted to impress him. His little face lit up with a huge grin as he proudly proclaimed, "Lil likes a do-rag. Huh, Lil?" He didn't have a clue what a do-rag was but knew Lil sure did love it from the way she talked to Mum about it.

"Blimey, it's going to be a long day!" Lil mumbled.

Charles came forward to introduce himself. He smiled as he extended his hand. "Hi, HT."

HT experienced a déjà vu feeling while shaking his hand. He grinned liking Charles instantly but not knowing why. "Nice to meet you, sir, I've heard so much about you, I feel like we've already met."

Charles just chuckled and teased, "All good, right?"

"Of course!" HT answered.

"Hi, JR," Raif yelled. He took off like a rocket, his little legs pumping hard as he ran. The dogs followed right behind him.

HT's eyebrows shot up at Lil, realizing he was about to meet the mysterious JR. "Another one?"

"Come on," she said as she looped her arm through his and pulled him forward. "You're going to love him, I promise."

HT just grunted.

Raif leaped in the air and landed in JR's opened arms. It was obvious from his shining eyes that Raif worshipped him. JR tossed him up high over his head as if he was light as a feather. Raif's blue eyes sparkled, and he squealed with laughter. He was breathless with excitement as he yelled, "Higher, higher!" when JR caught him. He tossed him again, making Raif laugh hysterically.

HT didn't take his eyes off JR. He thought he reminded him of someone but couldn't think who; being so nervous he couldn't get his mind around it.

JR gave Raif a quick peck on the cheek and a tight bear hug, making Raif laugh. He then put him down, affectionately tousling his hair.

Raif looked up to JR and said in an eager-to-please voice, "JR, Sir Tigger loves HT."

JR replied with genuine affection, "If Sir Tigger has given his seal of approval, he must be okay then, huh?"

"Yeah." Raif vigorously nodded. He turned to Lil all smiles. "We like him, huh, Lil?"

She looked at HT. "Yes, we do," she agreed smiling, as her stomach filled with butterflies.

HT smiled making his eyes twinkle.

Lil turned to JR and made the introductions.

JR stepped up thrusting his hand out to HT. "Hi, I'm glad to meet you," JR greeted.

"Hi, nice to meet you," HT responded as he shook his hand.

Raif puffed out his chest. "I'm little man, JR. Huh, HT?"

"Yep, little man!" said HT. "You're my new best mate, along with this sister of yours." He glanced over at Lil and winked.

"Let's go eat," Lil said quickly and leaned over to pick up the basket, diverting HT's attention from her face so that he wouldn't see her blush. "I'm sure Grammy has packed us a great lunch!"

"Hungry, huh, HT?"

"I'm starving, little man." He picked Raif up, putting him on his shoulders. "How about you lead us to a great place so that we can get started on that basket? What do you say, let's do this?"

"Let's do this!" Raif repeated excitedly, with a fist pump.

Everyone laughed.

They walked a short distance and then HT put Raif down so that he and the dogs could run to pick a spot for the picnic.

"So, Ms. Oopsy," HT teased, glancing at her. "Seems this turned into a family affair. I think we may need to discuss our very first rule!"

"What? I never lied," she replied in a honey-sweet voice, with her most wide-eyed, innocent look.

"True, but holding back can be just as bad. A real fine line if you ask me, Ms. Oopsy."

"I agree it can be just as bad," she mumbled.

"What was that?"

"I said, I agree," she replied softly.

"I heard. I just wanted to hear you say it again." He chuckled.

"Stop; don't act like I never agree with you."

He snorted, "Yeah, when it suits you."

"Of course, and adding no holding back to our rule suits me just fine!"

They laughed.

"I'm sorry I let you get ambushed, but you have to admit, there's no preparing for these blokes. It's like removing a bandage; you just have to pull it off all at once!"

"I can see that, so, you're forgiven...this time, Ms. Oopsy."

"You know," Lil said, "thinking about what we just added to our rule about holding things back...we might need to tweak that a bit."

"Already?"

She nodded.

"That was quick. What is it you need to tweak? I'm fine with it. I've already told you my life story and secrets. Well, okay. I might have a few more," he said with a wink, "but, something tells me you haven't even scratched the surface on telling me yours."

She ignored his wink and statement and said, "Now back to our rule. I want to get it right; no more being dodgy when I can't tell you things."

"See I knew you've only scratched the surface!"

"Stop. I'm trying to be serious here. Say you ask a question, and it's a family thing and you can't talk about it, so you have to hold back. That doesn't count, right?" She didn't wait for an answer and started to mumble. "If I know a secret someone has asked me not to tell, how would you know what to hold back? You can't just tell every secret, but what if it's not a secret and they want you to hold back just because. Should you? This is hard. Or maybe..."

He stopped walking. "Whoa, stop the mumbling for two seconds. You're doing my head in here."

She stopped and turned, giving him a look.

His mouth curved into a sexy grin. "Sorry, you know I like your mumbling."

"You're forgiven; now help me figure this out."

"Give me a sec to think, Ms. Bossy Pants," he replied with a chuckle. After a minute he said, "How about this? If we feel shady about holding things back, we're not being honest, and it could be considered lying. Let's say rule one, no lying, no matter what, and we let our heart decide if we are being truthful in why we're holding things back."

"So when you find out things you know I was holding bac—"

"I will know you were not being dodgy and that rule one applied," he said grinning. "So we all set?"

"Yes, all set!" she agreed with a huge smile.

"This is a *big* rule that we're making for life. We might need to share a nonfish kiss on this one! Then, you'll see just how honest I am when I say I don't kiss like a fish." He made the same fish face she had earlier.

"Tempting, but no. A handshake will do."

"Again with the bloody handshake?" He snorted, acting disgusted as he shook her hand. "But, we still need to hug on it," he added as he quickly picked her up and swung her around.

She started laughing.

He sat her down staring into her eyes. He started to lower his head to kiss her when they heard Raif.

"Let's eat here!" he said breaking their trance.

Lil quickly stepped back. Her heart did a funny little beat.

HT turned and walked toward Raif calling out, "That's what I'm talking about." His heart felt like it was going to beat out of his chest, wondering if he had read her right. *Did he really see that she had wanted him to kiss her?*

Lil took in a deep breath and slowly released it trying to calm down. She followed him mumbling, "Blimey, this is hard!"

There was a lot of talking and laughing from everyone as they ate lunch. After letting the food settle, they started on their walk. Lil followed behind the guys feeling a swell of pride at the way they were interacting with HT and their easy companionship with him. She smiled; it was as if they had known him all of his life, especially Dad and Papa. She didn't really know why, but it made her really happy. After hearing enough sounds of male bonding and banter, she wandered off and took photos. She couldn't have gotten a word in if she wanted to anyway.

When Lil saw they were heading back she joined them, walking behind Charles. Raif was fast asleep in his arms. She thought about how lucky she was, having such a great family. She let out a contented sigh.

HT lengthened his stride to walk up behind her. He had been wondering all afternoon if she wanted him to kiss her. She confused him so much that he didn't know what to think. After hearing her sigh, he decided to use it to find out.

She looked over and smiled as he walked up beside her. "I heard that sigh. It can only mean one thing. You're thinking about me," he teased, watching for the slightest reaction.

She wrinkled her nose a bit and said sarcastically, "Oh my gosh! Isn't it obvious you're all I think and dream about? You're always on my mind. Morning, noo…"

He started laughing as he got his answer—it was just wishful thinking. "I guess I deserved that one. So what's going on in that head of yours now?"

"How great my family is." She added with a chuckle, "I know they're all a really big pain sometimes and can seem loonier than a loon, but, I'm really blessed!"

"Yeah, I get that. They're amazing! Why do JR and Bill call you Snaggs?"

Lil smiled as she explained and then added after, "Looks like all of you hit it off."

"Good thing," he said grinning, "since you left me on my own."

Lil started laughing. "I got dizzy from all that male bonding and testosterone flying around. You didn't even realize I wasn't walking with you guys!"

"It's been fun," he admitted.

She pointed to his head. "I see Raif got you to put that on."

"Oh! I almost forgot. I told him he could have it after our walk." His grin widened as he teased, "Don't worry; I have plenty. Little man said you like to see me wearing one and think I'm cute."

"Oh really?" Her pulse was racing as she thought, *The little, shit!* "Hate to burst your bubble, I forgot to mention, he doesn't always get his repeating right!"

He gave her the soft sexy laugh that left her breathless before he ran to catch up with Charles.

# CHAPTER 9

T he next weeks flew by with Lil and HT pretty much keeping to their routine. Some days they were happy to do nothing, and other days their schedules were full. They began having dinner together, switching between their homes.

Lil loved his parents and Maddie. It was obvious that both HT and Maddie got their looks from Madison, because Maddie was a beautiful female version of HT. Her eyes even twinkled like his when she smiled. Raif and Maddie became instant buddies as soon as they met. For some reason Raif called her, "Miss Maddie." Nobody was sure why; he just did.

They never missed each other's texts, even when HT went to Chester for date night. HT didn't bring up them dating again, deciding to take Luke's advice and give it sometime to see where it went. He was still very much attracted to her, but then, he asked himself, *Who wouldn't be? She is amazing!*

Saturday morning Lil awakened later than usual. She felt groggy and out of sorts and more irritable than she could remember ever being. Her nerves were on edge, and her emotions were in chaos. She threw off the bed cover and dragged herself up to sit on the side of the bed. She yawned and then mumbled, "Thank God, when this horrible mood strikes after my curse, it only lasts for a couple of days." She reluctantly slipped into her pink slippers and made her way to take a shower, yawning again. It took a while for her to get started, but once she took her shower and got dressed, she felt better and made her way to the bakery, trying to forget it was HT's date night.

She heard HT up front as she entered through the back door and tied on her apron. A surge of heat rushed through her body at hearing his throaty laugh. It inflamed her. She had convinced herself that she was getting immune to the way he made her body react. Gritting her teeth in frustration, she grumbled under her breath, "What's wrong with me? When is this going to stop?" She stomped to the front, reassuring herself it was just hormones causing the reaction.

HT looked up seeing her come in and glanced at the clock, as if he didn't know exactly what time it was. He had been watching for her for the past half hour. "Running a little late I see. Must be nice," he teased with a wink. "You'll have to remake your tea; the cup I made is cold by now."

"It'll be fine," she grumbled, as she walked to it and drank it down, making HT chuckle.

A few hours later while trying to start a pot of coffee, she could barely concentrate as she listened to HT and JR talking and flirting with a couple of girls. HT's chipper voice and flirting all morning had been grating on her last nerve. She glanced over just in time to see HT wiggle his brow at JR as the girls walked away giggling. Her bad mood that had started in the morning grew steadily deeper. She bit the inside of her mouth, concentrating on stopping herself from throwing the pot at HT's head. She turned back to start the coffee maker, slamming the pot underneath to catch the coffee and turned toward the back. As she reached the doorway, she heard HT say something, but it didn't register. She turned and snarled, "What?"

"I asked, do you need any help with anything?" he repeated with a smile.

"No, I got it," she said with a disgusted huff and walked to the back.

HT's smile faded. A crease lined his forehead, since he was learning what her looks meant. The way she was staring him down meant she was annoyed with him about something. He turned to JR. "She's been like that all morning. It's like she hates me!"

"Don't be daft; she doesn't hate you," said JR with a chuckle, knowing it was her curse making her such a bitch, but he couldn't help winding him up. JR followed him to the back.

HT, not giving up, sweetly asked her, "Are you sure I can't help out?"

Her eyes snapped back to him with a chilling look. "For God's sake. Yes, I'm sure!" she replied forcefully.

He put up his hand. "Okay just asking, calm down."

His cavalier attitude irritated her even more. "Don't tell me to calm down." She grabbed a bag of icing sugar from the shelf and stomped off to the baking room.

JR grinned wickedly and said, "Whoa, maybe she does a little, mate. I'm sure the temperature in here just dropped, drastically. Telling her to calm down was a bad mistake, drives her mental."

"You think?" HT asked sarcastically.

"What did you do, bro?" asked JR egging him on.

HT threw his arms upward with a look of puzzlement. "Who bloody knows? When you find out, let me know!"

JR gave him an ironic "ha!" shaking his head. "Don't drag me into this. I'm out of here before she starts on me," he said hurrying to the back door.

HT fired off at his departing back, "Cheers!"

JR opened the door laughing, knowing what cheers meant. "Hey, I'm here for you mate."

"Yeah, I see that mate!" HT said sarcastically.

JR laughed harder as he went out the door.

"Tosser," HT grumbled as he returned to the front.

Lil shook her head in disgust at herself, fighting back a burning guilt. She knew she was being a bitch but couldn't stop herself. Taking in a few deep breaths she pushed her emotions down, getting herself back in control.

A few hours later, after eating lunch on their hill, neither of them were talking as they lay looking up at the sky. It was an overcast day with the sun not showing its face, making it slightly cool, which didn't improve Lil's mood. She didn't want to admit to herself it was driving her mental because it was date night. It frustrated her even more that she couldn't get a hold on her emotions. It had been weeks; the attraction should be long gone. She kept reminding herself she didn't care in the least whom he was seeing or what he was doing, but she knew that was total crap. It did her head in whenever he left. She still hadn't asked if he had a girlfriend. She didn't want to know and wouldn't admit to herself why.

HT looked at his phone and frowned. It was time for him to get going, and he had to admit he didn't want to go. He looked at Lil thinking maybe he would stay and finally start helping her in the darkroom. She was probably in such a bad mood all morning because she was stressed from having so much to do. He asked, "How about I stick around and help you out in the darkroom?"

She didn't hear him, wondering with irritation what it was about him that fascinated her so much. She frowned, attempting to rationalize why she was still unable to find a flaw that would turn her off. Lost in deep thought, she nearly jumped out of her skin when HT reached over and lightly tapped her on the nose with his fingertip.

"Hello!" he said with a sexy chuckle.

Her eyes jerked open as she sat up. She snapped, "What the hell, HT? You scared the crap out of me!"

The glare she gave him made him sorry he'd asked in the first place. "I asked if you wanted me to stick around and help you, but forget it. I'd rather go to Chester where they like my company." He was suddenly anxious to get going, keeping his temper under control, before she could say anything else. He stood up, shifted his weight from one foot to the other, and then stretched the muscles in his neck by rolling his shoulders, working out the stiffness. He was really taking a moment to regain his composure after putting up with her mood all morning.

Lil saw the hurt expression flash across his face and felt even worse for taking her bad mood out on him. She had been such a bitch she couldn't stand herself. She managed to get the scowl off her face and gave him a faint smile. "Sorry, I've been a bear all morning. You know I love your company."

He gave her a hand up as he assured her, "No worries. You're probably just stressed and tired. We had a lot of photo sessions this past week." In a halfhearted attempt to tease her out of her mood, he added, "If I'm totally honest, you do look a bit knackered."

"Cheers!" She chuckled as she let out a slow sigh of relief, knowing he didn't know what was really going on in her head.

"Right then," he said, glad the tension was over. "Do I chance a hug?"

She playfully rolled her eyes as she leaned in and teased, "If I must!"

They hugged, and he lightly kissed her forehead, his routine whenever he left her. Heat flooded through her body again making her quickly step back.

"I'll see you tomorrow," he said with a little sigh, dropping his shoulders. He folded his arms across his chest and stuck out his bottom lip to make a pouty face. He then turned and stomped down the hill. Turning back around when he reached the bottom, he gave her the smile that made his eyes twinkle and dimples run deep. "Did that work? Can I stay?"

She shook her head laughing. "Pouting only works for Raif."

He laughed as he turned and strolled off, automatically singing his favorite song about her being beautiful. He thought, *If I ever do get to record a song, this will be my first and my first music video, too!*

Lil watched him walk away and said with a groan, "It worked if you wanted to make me hot from head to toe. When is that smile and those twinkling eyes of yours going to quit working on me? And that bloody wink of yours is wicked! Note to self: buy that bloke a pair of bloody sunglasses!"

The next afternoon, Lil packed their lunch with all of HT's favorites, still feeling guilty for being awful to him the previous day. The sun was burning brightly in the sky as she made her way to the top of the hill. She was feeling tired from working until midnight in her darkroom and then back at it at six this morning. Spreading a quilt over the ground, she lay down, getting comfortable. The sunny day began to brighten her mood as her weariness slowly faded. She turned looking toward the sky and closed her eyes, feeling like she was floating on one of the white, fluffy clouds. Her thoughts drifted to HT as a soft, pleasant breeze brushed across her face. Maybe, it was time to show him her darkroom. She would be sharing something she had never shared with anyone, giving up her private haven, but she was ready to share it with him.

Her mind took a three sixty, going to where she didn't want it to go. What was he doing that it took him to almost midnight before he sent his text?

HT quietly approached and sat down thinking she was asleep. He was trying to decide whether or not to wake her and tell her his news or let her sleep. He went with letting her sleep, knowing she'd probably worked most of the night. He stretched out beside her, stacked his hands behind his head, and stared up at the sky thinking, *What a brilliant night!*

Lil hadn't noticed HT had joined her. She was too disgusted as she realized she was becoming one of those lame girls obsessed with him. She couldn't stop thinking about him and was unable to stop the fierce way her body reacted to him. A voice inside her head shouted, *You need to get your bum back to training with JR and get a handle on this!* She let out a disgusted groan. Whatever it took, she had to stop this insane obsession with him.

Hearing her he leaned in and whispered, "What's up?" by her ear.

She gasped and jerked up into a sitting position as she scowled. "What the hell, HT! You did it again! I swear you're going to give me a bloody heart attack!"

"Sorry." He chuckled, trying to ease the tension and get her to laugh. He winked and teased, "So should I take credit for that groan? Come on admit it." He said giving her a slow smile, "You were lying there fantasizing about me. Well, here I am in the flesh; you don't have to fantasize anymore!"

It was as if he could read her mind, upsetting her even more. Her gray eyes darkened to a charcoal color as she snarled, "Have I ever told you just how unbearable you are and how absolutely without a doubt are the most annoying person you can be, with all that flirting rubbish of yours?" She instantly regretted her words seeing the hurt expression on his face again; it dissolved all her anger.

HT tapped his chin with a forefinger; his right eyebrow arched slightly as he softly said, "Hum, maybe…let me think. Yes—I don't know—I mean. Right. I think I remember now," he replied in a normal tone. But his tone rose as he said, "I'm almost positive you never mentioned unbearable or annoying. By the way, have I ever told you just how unbearable and absolutely annoying it is when you're being such a total bitch! I was hoping you'd be in a better mood. You're worse today than yesterday!"

She smiled tiredly and teased, "You're always so nice!" hoping her humor would ease the tension.

He instantly felt bad for snapping, seeing how tired she looked with dark rings under her eyes, which meant she had worked all night. Knowing she was trying to lighten the mood and was sorry for snapping at him, he replied with a cocky expression, "Almost as nice as you!"

She playfully tossed her ponytail over one shoulder, fluttered her lashes, and teased, "I know; I'm always *so* nice!"

He laughed, shaking his head. "It's hard trying to stay mad at you."

"I'll be sure to add that to my long list of things to remember about you," she said smiling.

Pushing hair behind his ear in a quick brushing gesture, he smiled and asked, "You get all caught up?"

"Yep, and I've decided it's time to show you something."

"Hot damn! Now we're talking!" he said, waggling his eyebrows up and down. "I knew I would break you down." He leaned forward, staring straight at her chest while rubbing his hands together. "Okay," he joked, licking his lips, "let's see them beauties!"

She couldn't keep from laughing as she pushed him back. "You're such a tosser, HT, or should I say 'Horny Harry'? What on earth is up with you?"

He gave her sexy grin. "I was convinced for a second there that you were hitting on me after you finally came to your senses. It's fine with me if you want to keep deluding yourself! We'll play it your way." His eyes sparkled as he continued teasing. "Let's act like you don't think I'm hot and sexy...and a great catch, I might add. So we'll keep acting like we're not going to date and fall madly in love, get married, and have at least half a dozen kids."

She shook her head laughing. "Oh! I see we moved from dating right into marriage!"

He shrugged with a sheepish grin. "Sometimes persistence pays off!"

"But in this case, you just do my head—"

He raised his hand waving her off. "You know I'm over all that dating rubbish and just like winding you up being *Horny Harry*."

"I know, but it just hits me the wrong way sometimes."

"Noted," he said with a nod. "No more *Horny Harry*!"

"Good. So...what's really going on? I'm taking it's something amazing?"

"You know me so well. Guess what happened? Come on! Guess! Guess! Guess!" He started tickling her.

"HT, stop!" she said giggling, fighting off his hands. "I'll have to go pee, and you'll have to wait to tell me."

He stuck out his chest. "Guess who's in a band?...Me! Me! Me!" he said as he pointed his thumb to himself. "Lee found the guys; they're twins and just moved here from London. Cody plays drums and Jody plays lead guitar! We met last night and ended up jammin' all night. I just got home!"

"Yay!" Lil squealed in delight as she threw her arms around his neck and squeezed. "That's brilliant! No wonder you're so hyper!"

He hugged her tightly and for a lot longer than usual. She playfully moaned. "You're squeezing the stuffing out of me."

They laughed as he let her go.

He opened the basket and peered in. "What's to eat? I'm starving."

She took out a plate of meat pasties wrapped in plastic. "Your favorite," she replied, smiling as she handed it to him.

"That's my girl." He chuckled, taking the plate and unwrapping it. "I was going to call you last night to tell you, but I wanted to tell you in person," he said between bites. "See what you miss not going to date night with me? Oh yeah, sorry my text was so late. Before I knew it, it was almost midnight."

"No worries, I was still awake."

"Not still working, I hope."

"No, well, okay, I had just finished," she said as she handed him a bottle of water.

"So much for getting some sleep. What time did you start this morning?"

"Early. Enough worrying about me, and technically"—she playfully slapped his arm—"you've never asked me to go to Chester with you."

"You got me there." He grinned as he opened his water. "It's time you meet my mates though. I have to admit that I've been stalling. I wanted you to get to know the real me before you hear them bust my nads with their stories."

"So when do I get to hear...I mean, meet them?"

He playfully groaned. "That's what I'm afraid of!"

She laughed.

"Anyway," he said grinning, "after we eat lunch, I want to get the garage cleaned. We're starting practice soon. Wanna help? I still have a lot of stuff in there. Dad said I could put it in the storage shed with his stuff." He tilted his head with a concerned look. "Unless you're too tired."

"Stop! I'm fine. I want to help. Tell me about the twins. Do they look alike?" she asked handing him a brownie.

He replied between bites, "Same height and maybe same hair color. Hard to tell. Jody is a little more slender, and his blond hair is longer than mine." He pointed to just above his shoulder. "About here I'd say. He did my head in all night the way he kept putting his hand in it and flipping it from side to side over the top of his head." He illustrated the movement and flipped his.

Lil laughed as she started packing up the basket. "I can tell you're in a hurry to get started on the garage. I've never seen you eat so fast."

"I know. I feel like half of it is still stuck in my throat." He playfully groaned, helping her pack. He stood, picked up the basket, and held out his hand.

As he pulled her up, she asked, "So what does Cody look like?"

"He looks like the jock of the two. His hair is short, almost a buzz cut, not sure on the color, and he's more muscular. He wants everybody to know he works out though," he said as they walked down the hill and up the path toward the house.

"Now how do you know that?" she asked.

HT dropped the empty lunch basket on the porch. "Because the bloke wears a T-shirt that is two sizes too small to show off his chest and bulging arms." He turned and took a few steps up the walk, but Lil didn't follow.

"Let's go this way," she said.

HT turned back around with a quizzical look as he retraced his steps. "Okay, you lead the way, I guess," he said as he took her hand, wondering where they were going.

They walked to the stone wall again but instead of turning left toward their hill, she pulled him to the right, following the gravel path that ran alongside the wall leading toward his house.

HT joked when the wall turned to the right, "Are we turning or going over the top?"

"I would like to see you try to climb over." She chuckled.

"I would if I could. It's a long walk to my house down that super long bloody drive of yours."

She just rolled her eyes and pulled him to the right to continue following the path alongside the wall.

"So is this just another way down to the gate?" he asked after walking about twenty feet.

She stopped, lightly withdrawing her hand from his.

"Okay, okay," he teased. "I'll keep my mouth shut. No more questions."

"I doubt that," she teased back and pointed up to the iron railing on top of the wall.

He looked up puzzled. "What am I looking at? All I see is a high wall covered in ivy, entwined with like a gazillion little lights and cameras."

"Look at the points on the rail."

"Still looking, still not seeing, and still confused. I'm getting a crick in my neck, so you want to give me a clue here?" He looked at her, making his brow go up and down and said, "Get to the point!" He chuckled at his own joke. "Get it? The point!"

"Yeah, I got it funny guy. Really look at the one I'm pointing at."

"And?"

"For God's sake, HT, you're more observant than this!" she said, flexing her hand up and down as she pointed.

"As Bill would say, cool your jets." He chuckled. "I got it. It's just a bit taller, right?"

She nodded. "The lights on it will be brighter than the rest when it's dark outside." She put her hand through the ivy, and he heard a click. She gave a little push to the gate camouflaged with the ivy.

"What the—" he exclaimed as he went through.

She made a tsk sound as she followed him. "Looks like we forgot about me being a lady, huh?"

He quickly moved to close the gate. "Sorry, my lady," he said, giving her a little bow.

She laughed playfully giving him a dismissal wave. "You're forgiven peasant; just don't do it again," she said snobbishly.

He chuckled and turned to see it put them just behind the pool house. "Come on, Lil, you should have shown me this weeks ago!"

She made a sad face. "Sorry."

"Got it. Rule one?"

She did a quick nod and said, "Look on the bright side. All that walking did you some good. Keeps those lungs built up for your singing, and I might add"—she patted his stomach—"it helped work off all those pasties you are always wolfing down; have to keep that body in shape for all of our lady customers."

HT laughed and threw his arm around her shoulder, pulling her close and giving her an affectionate squeeze. "I don't have to worry about being a fatty in this family," he said as they walked. "You guys walk me to death!" He began tickling her with his other hand.

She laughed and gently pulled away, needing to put some space between them. Her entire body was on fire. *Bloody hormones!* she thought.

He caught her hand; their fingers automatically entwined as he started babbling on about meeting the twins and what music they were going to start with at practice.

Lil tuned him out as heat waves shot up her arm. She focused on pushing down her emotions and didn't realize she had tuned him out until he gave her hand an affectionate squeeze.

"Hey, I'm talking here. You should at least try to act like I'm not boring you to death. What are you thinking about, anyway?"

"That I could use some tea," she quickly said evading his question. She teased with a grin, "All that babbling of yours is doing my head in."

"Uh-huh, my babbling!" he teased back.

"I don't babble. I mumble!" she playfully huffed making him laugh.

They went into his house, and Lil ran to the loo as HT made tea. She quickly drank it down before they went to work on the garage. Lil was barely speaking. She didn't get much of a chance, even if she had wanted to. She would nod or smile at appropriate intervals while HT continued to ramble on about the band. She was happy to see him so excited. They moved everything to the shed and cleaned thoroughly.

HT plugged in the fridge after they cleaned it. "There," he said, "now all we need to do is stock it with drinks and some snacks, and we're good to go."

Lil snirled her nose, "That loo needs some attention, or I won't be using it."

"With all that tea you put away, there's no doubt *you'll* be using it the most, announcing to everybody you have to take a pee every five minutes. You must have gone in the house a dozen times since we've been here." He laughed and added, "Go in to get tea, go back in not twenty minutes later to let it out, and then come out with more tea to start the process all over again!"

"That's because I'm normal and not a bloody camel like you!"

He threw his head back and laughed. "I'll clean the loo later. Let's go eat dinner; I'm starving. And no back talk or rolling those eyes at me," he teased, taking her hand as they started walking. He began swinging their arms as they walked and he sang "Best Song Ever."

# CHAPTER 10

Saturday morning before dawn, Jayden and Ed had just gotten home and were heading to meet the guys for a quick meeting. They made their way through Charlie's study to the fireplace. Ed flipped the hidden switch on the side, making it move away from the wall. They went through the opening, and Jayden tapped the switch on the wall making it move back. They hurried down the secret passage and steps to the command room. Charles, Bill, JR, and Luke were waiting on them. After hugs and backslapping, coffee was passed around as they sat down to start their meeting.

Charles looked at Ed and started. "Any problems I should know about?"

Ed shook his head. "Everything went like clockwork getting in and getting them. It was getting them and us out without being seen that was the pain in the arse."

"So you know what's going on yet?" asked Jayden. "It took forever because they were definitely waiting on us to move them."

Charles stood and went to lean against a desk and then folded his arms across his chest. "Those agents you just got out were buried too deep undercover to be blown like that. I don't think it's a coincidence that Lord Cunningham had just updated their info in his report at the last meeting. Even though I don't have conclusive evidence, I'm sure someone on the council is leaking reports on E's agents, which in turn puts ours in danger. I'm trying to get my head around why it's only her agents getting killed when some of our agents are on the same op. It's like I've got all the pieces of a jigsaw puzzle spinning in my head but can't fit them together."

"Who sees the reports?" asked Jayden.

"All twelve members, well eleven not counting me, but I decided I'm putting a stop to that. I told E to inform the council members they are to pass their reports to Lord Rothford from now on. He's been her right-hand man for ages, taking over for his father. As it is now, whoever is responsible could be standing right next to me, and I wouldn't know it. There's a missing link; I'm just not seeing it yet and tying it all together."

"So what's our orders?" asked JR.

"Luke has been going over the member's personal finances with a fine-toothed comb, but nothing has raised a flag yet," Charles replied. "So we will concentrate on one member at a time, following him twenty-four-seven. I'll bring in Joe, Ben, and Jake on this one. This bloke is smart; he's very efficient and knows how to cover his tracks. We need to find out if he's just after the money, or if he's been a spy all this time, and we just didn't see it. I'm leaning toward it's the money, from the way the old man is going over his ledgers. And then again, he might not have anything to do with this one."

Jayden and Ed gave JR a weird look.

JR mouthed the word, "Dreams."

They nodded back.

Luke looked at his watch and stood up. "I need to slip back into the house before HT gets up, to go over a few things with him since me and Mags will be staying a few extra days in Chester. He told me last night he's not going, so Mags wants to head that way when Maddie gets up. She wants to be there when her sister arrives. She usually stays about three days."

"HT's not going to Chester?" Charles asked with a raised brow. "He never misses Saturday night hanging out with Lee and Sloan!"

"I know. You blokes have him all buggered about golf tomorrow. And you," he said looking at Bill, "go easy on him, old man. Be nice."

"What?" Bill asked, feigning innocence. "I'm always nice!"

"Sure you are." Luke chuckled, still looking at Bill so that Charles couldn't read his face to see he was about to talk total rubbish. "Just don't scare him to death out there. He's not played in a while, and I'm sure he's going to be nervous and intimidated knowing how well you guys play. I go easy on him when we play because we play for fun. It's not serious like when we all play! It doesn't help that I can't be there. So no turning into a nutter when you get aggravated at him. He doesn't know you're just full of hot air."

"Then let's just hope I don't get aggravated!" Bill said grinning.

They all laughed.

"I've never mentioned I play there, so try not to mention it," said Luke. "I don't need him to start asking me a million questions about why I never mentioned it."

They nodded.

"So you going to be in Chester for three days then?" Charles asked Luke.

"Yeah, I figure while Mags visits with her sister, I'll go over some old files on the council that I keep in my office in the cellar. Maybe I can find something," replied Luke.

"Sounds good. I guess we're done here then," Charles said and looked over at Jayden. "I need a quick word before you head out."

"Sure." Jayden nodded.

"I need to get going, too," said Ed. "There's a big society thing tonight, and the duke should show his face since he's not been around for a few weeks, and I need some shut eye. I got stuck flying the chopper all night."

"Hey! It was your turn," said Jayden.

"Whatever," Ed replied with a grin. He looked back to Charles. "I'll hang around those tossers from the council tonight; maybe I can hear something. You should go as Lord Stutter, man," he added with a little laugh.

"Oh damn!" teased Charles. "You know I would love to go, especially as him, but when I tucked Raif in he said something about a gettin'-loose night."

Again, they all laughed.

After good-byes, handshakes, and guy hugs were given, Luke and Ed left.

'What's up?" Jayden asked Charles.

"I'm assigning you to HT."

"For how long?"

"Permanently."

"Why?"

"Because I said so." Charles chuckled.

"Yeah, right. Since when does that work on us?" grunted JR. "Try again! What's really going on?"

"When did you boys get so smart mouthed? Like the old man here, you guys forget who's the boss."

They just grinned.

"Okay, here it is. I've been having dreams, and I think they're connected to our old men's deaths. The feelings I'm getting are more intense than I've ever had, and, well, they're starting to worry me. So I want you close," he said, with a tone they knew meant not to argue. "You guys and Lil will be together all the time around the village since she and HT are now joined at the hip."

"I thought you liked HT," said Jayden.

"He does." JR laughed. "He's just not liking that Snaggs has met her match."

Jayden's brows rose. "The hell you say?"

Charles grumbled. "She's gone and fallen in love with him. Of course she won't let herself face it. And I just want it on record that when we're all living in hell around here, because she's driving HT and herself mental, it's all on Mary with that rubbish of letting things play out. She gave me strict orders, no matter how tough this gets, and it will, knowing how stubborn Lil is, we have to stay out of it!"

"And I want it on record that I told you idiots this was going to happen when you let Mary hire him," Bill said sarcastically.

"What the bloody heck has been going on around here? She's in love with him? I don't believe it! How does HT feel about her?" asked Jayden.

"Oh, he loves her too but doesn't know it. Come on I'll walk with you to the bakery so that you can see your folks, and I'll fill you in. You're going to like HT. Hey, I just thought about something. You're just the bloke HT needs to make him realize it," JR said with a chuckle. "How about we make a bet and mess with his head at the same time? You know a little initiation into the family."

"Sounds like fun," Jayden said with a little laugh, as they went out the door.

Charles grunted as he told Bill, "One good thing: JR likes HT, so I don't have to worry about him killing him anymore."

Bill chuckled.

The sun was beginning to rise casting a beautiful orange glow as HT made his way to the bakery. He decided not to go to Chester so that he could help Lil in the darkroom, and he wasn't taking *no* for an answer. He couldn't remember the last time he had missed hanging out on Saturday night and never thought a time would come when he would rather stay here than go to Chester. Of course, that was before meeting Lil. Now it seemed right.

He opened the door and went into the bakery singing, "Kiss you…" He was feeling so elated; it was hard to imagine that his good mood could be dented. He was ready to wish everyone a good morning with a winning smile until he saw Lil. He stopped short, not expecting to see her since he was early, but there she was at the counter with a huge smile on her face with some bloke he hadn't seen before. He slowed his pace, allowing time to assess the bloke for a second before he was noticed. He was almost as tall and muscular as JR. His muscles were bulging beneath his T-shirt, which stretched across his chest and shoulders. He thought, *This bloke looks like he could bench press one of the ovens*. He had a sickening twist in his stomach, seeing the way Lil was looking at him.

Putting on a fake smile, he walked up next to her. "You're bright and early."

"I am," she stated, still looking at Jayden. "I've got a wedding session this morning at ten and need to leave here by nine, so I came in early."

Her answer was completely unexpected, and he was disappointed by her less-than-warm welcome when she didn't turn to acknowledge him. "You never said anything about a session today. You can't go without me!" he said, sounding as if he was teasing, but really wasn't. "Who's going to help you?"

"Jayden has offered," she said, finally glancing at HT. "Well, Jay as I call him. Jay, this is HT. HT, this is Jay."

"Hi, nice to meet you. I've been hearing a lot about you this morning," said Jayden smiling, as he leaned forward with his hand outstretched.

Keeping the smile plastered on his face HT greeted him. "Hi," he managed to say, sounding friendly as he extended his hand.

A small group of customers trickled in and stood in line. Jayden looked at Lil and smiled. "I'll go so that you can get some work done. I'll see you around nine."

She returned his smile, making her eyes sparkle. "Great, see you then." She smiled happily and turned to wait on the customers.

"So how long have you known him? Haven't seen him around before. Is he one of the clingy ones you dumped? He's not Spanish. Can't be the fish dude from last year."

"Not now, HT. We'll talk later," said Lil not really listening, while waiting on a customer. She didn't realize the tension she was feeling came out in her tone, making her words sharper than intended, and sounding as if she was blowing him off.

Jayden had just told her she couldn't let HT know he was family for another week because he and JR had a bet going. She was feeling guilty and disgusted with herself because she agreed to keep quiet. She was stressed, not sure what to expect and worn out with their bloody bets. She was reasonably sure whatever they were betting on wasn't going to be good for HT. She'd told Jayden firmly that she was telling HT about him and JR next Saturday night if she had to walk to Chester to do it!

They stayed busy with a steady stream of customers and didn't get a chance to talk. It was nearly nine o'clock before Lil knew it, and Jayden returned to collect her.

"Give me five minutes, Jay," she said smiling as she turned to go to the back.

"No worries," he said following her. "I'll just grab a bite. I'm sure I'll have my weight back and get these puny arms built back up in no time hanging around here!"

HT's frown deepened while listening to Jayden. He thought, *Puny! How much bigger could a bloke's muscles get without exploding?* He was waiting on Mrs. Kelly. "Six apple turnovers it is," he said practically throwing them in a bag.

Poor Mrs. Kelly was going to get home and realize her apple turnovers were now slightly squashed and oozing out cherries!

Fifteen minutes later, Lil and Jayden walked to the door.

HT looked to see that "Muscleman," as he called him, was carrying her equipment in one arm, where it took him both. He managed to grin and called after them, "Don't work too hard."

"K, see you later," she said as they left.

HT's expression tightened seeing how great her bum looked in her short, tight jean skirt, showing off her long, perfectly toned legs. *Huh, what's up with her having on a skintight top and short skirt? And, her hair is down. She never looks like that when I go with her on photo sessions!* He was jolted back at hearing Mary's voice.

"HT, HT, earth to HT," Mary said, laughing.

He jerked his head up to see the long line of customers staring at him. He was trying to refocus and realized he was digging his fingernails into his palms. "Sorry

Moms, I was miles away." He chuckled not looking her way. It was the first time he could remember having to make himself smile and flirt. He wasn't feeling it at all.

Long hours later, as the morning dragged on, he couldn't stop thinking about Lil making cow eyes at Muscleman and having a nickname for him. He glanced at the clock, annoyed that it hadn't seemed to move since the last time he had looked. It didn't help that he was counting the minutes until Mary locked the door. It was the longest bloody morning of his life, even though they had been swamped.

Mary finally went to lock the door after twelve. Half an hour later, everyone else had left after helping with the cleanup; all that was left to do was the sweeping and cleaning of the loo. It gave him more time to imagine Lil with Jayden, and it wasn't a pleasant thought. He was on edge as he swept, listening for the backdoor and wondering what was taking her so long. He looked at the clock and saw it was after two. He mumbled, "She should have had her arse back here by now."

*Maybe I should text her to ask if she's coming or if I should go ahead and eat. Yeah, right, like I'm waiting on her to eat.* He stopped. *What am I doing? This is mental.* "So she stood you up," he grumbled. It was another first, which he didn't like at all. Now he knew how the girls felt when he had stood them up. He finally gave up and relocked the front door as he went out in a rotten mood.

He walked home deeply distracted, not paying attention that the sky changed rapidly, from a sky blue to a deep gray and a light rain had started. He finally realized it when the rain began to come down harder and ran the rest of the way home. He grumbled as he went through the front door pulling off the wet do-rag and ran his fingers through his wet curls. "Well this day turned to total crap!"

He headed upstairs to get out of his wet clothes and take a hot shower. The whole time in the shower, he was still struggling with his thoughts of Lil smiling at Muscleman. He wrapped a towel around his waist, not bothering to towel off. He walked over and jumped on his bed, landing on his back. He thought he might be able to take a nap.

He hadn't slept much the night before, anxious about playing golf in the morning. He loved playing golf. It had been a hard decision not to join the circuit, but he had to choose between golf and music. He couldn't do both.

He lay there tossing and turning, not being able to sleep, as he thought about Lil. *Feeling like I'm more than just a little obsessed here. Get over it already. So she stood you up for lunch!* The thing really annoying him was that she never told him about the photo session, and she had gone with Muscleman. No, what really had him mental was wondering if she was going out with him. Actually, it was making him a little sick to his stomach. He finally gave up and got out of bed mumbling, "Okay, it seems I've developed something of a small obsession here."

He grabbed a pen and his songbook off his desk and flopped down in the armchair. His mind was whirling, trying to get his emotions under control. He stared down at the song he'd been working on and muttered, "Nobody compares." He grumbled as if talking to Lil. "Yeah, nothing compares to you tearing my heart out fawning over some big, muscled bloke! Whoa, hold up. What the bloody heck is going on? I'm really jealous. So this is how it feels!" He sighed and closed the book, tossing it onto the side table. He wasn't entirely sure how to process it. "Wait a minute here; let me think about this for a sec," he muttered. "Maybe what Dad said is right, that she's a challenge, and it just drives me mental because she only wants to be best mates."

He thought about it for a moment. All the feelings he tried to convince himself he didn't have came rushing in. It was like the floodgates to his true emotions had opened, and he was forced to admit how he felt. He chuckled. "Nope, I'm absolutely, positively crazy about her, and it's not as a bloody mate! It took seeing her with Muscleman to make me man up and face it." He couldn't move fast enough. He jumped up and pulled on his clothes talking to himself. "I'm going to Lil's and get my girl." He stopped. "Bloody hell, she's not mine!" He chuckled in confidence. "Not sure how, but one day she will be if I have anything to do with it. Well, Dad, I'm absolutely sure I'm crazy about her, so I'm taking your advice. I'm going after her with everything I have!"

He darted to the door, pulled it open, and sprinted down the hall to the back stairs taking them two at a time and flew through the kitchen and out the back door. His stomach growled, reminding him he hadn't eaten all day. He muttered as he hurried passed the pool house. "The little minx has had me so upset, I forgot to eat. Little minx! I like that!" He laughed and thought, *Another first, giving a mushy pet name to a girl or even wanting to!*

# CHAPTER 11

HT turned to go up the steps at Lil's and stopped short as he heard JR yell, "Hey, bro." HT looked over to see him walking across the lawn. HT smiled and started walking toward him.

"Wow," said JR as they met, "you gave up date night to join us for gettin'-loose night? I'm impressed."

"No, actually I came to bum dinner," said HT as they walked to the front door. "I decided not to go to Chester. You know, rest up for golf tomorrow."

"Hmm," replied JR and added just to annoy him, "I thought maybe you didn't like Snaggs going off with Jay this morning!"

"Who is that bloke, anyway?" asked HT, his voice was full of disgust. "I can't believe you let her go off with him without following and don't tell me you did. I saw you in and out of the bakery all morning!"

"What's wrong, Romeo?" asked JR, his mouth twisted into a smirk. "You finally realize how you feel? Sucks having competition, huh, bro?"

"Ah, sod it off," grumbled HT, not thinking twice about saying that to him since they had become mates over the weeks. It didn't surprise him that JR knew how he felt about Lil before he even did. He was scary as hell the way he just knew things. Still grumbling he asked, "What's gettin'-loose night, anyway?"

"Just wait. You'll see. You're in for a big treat!" He batted his eyelashes at HT and in a flirty, girly-girl voice gushed, "Oh my gosh, HT! Maybe Jay will be here!"

"Cheers! If that was supposed to be funny, it needs work," HT muttered as he opened the heavy oak door.

JR laughed as HT held open the door for him to pass through.

They entered the front foyer and continued down the wide hallway on polished floors made of oak, matching the staircase and door. The walls were filled with large oil paintings HT was sure was of their ancestors. As they moved down the hallway, he heard loud music blaring. He muttered, "Whatever is going on is obviously in full swing." He walked into the huge family room decorated in shades of blue and beige. The light-colored paneling and the two crystal chandeliers made it feel warm and inviting, along with the glass vases on the tabletops and mantel, filled with the flowers from the garden.

Raif was the first one he saw as he entered. He was dancing with Moms and wearing the do-rag he had given to him.

Raif looked up and grinned. "Hi, HT!" His big blue eyes sparkled with excitement as he proudly announced, "We're gettin' loose, huh, Mummy? Come on, HT, get loose!"

"I'll just watch for right now, little man," replied HT with a big smile. He took a quick glance around the room looking for Lil. His heart soared when he spotted her dancing with Grammy. He thought, *I'd be happy to just stand here and watch her all night!*

Her hair was still a little damp, just starting to curl up. He loved it down. He looked around the room and saw Abs and Joe dancing, and, wonder of wonders, Joe was actually laughing. He didn't think the man knew how! He didn't see Mr. C. (that's what he now called Charles) or Bill. But most important—she was alone—no Muscleman.

Lil looked up, surprised. She called out smiling as she pushed her hair back. "C'mon, HT, dance."

Heat rushed through him taking his breath away and making his heart beat overtime. He stared, knowing in his heart she was the one, his soul mate. He was in love with her. No, he was insanely, wildly, ridiculously head over heels in love with the little minx. He now knew that his going into the bakery that morning not looking for a job was fate. He'd never considered falling in love a possibility. He honestly never believed a girl would make him feel this way.

"C'mon," she said, "when Raif calls a gettin'-loose night, we all have to come and dance."

His eyes opened widely acting silly, and with a horrified look on his face, he frantically shook his head.

She laughed, making her eyes sparkle.

Charles and Bill came dashing into the room.

"Hey!" Bill complained. "No fair. You started gettin'-loose night without us."

He and Charles ran over and joined in.

Raif ran up and tugged on HT's hand. "Get loose, HT," he coaxed with a sweet grin.

"That sounds like fun, little man, but I'm not good at dancing," HT said grinning.

"Please…" he begged with a little whine, still tugging on his hand.

HT gave up with a chuckle as he let Raif pull him toward the middle of the room. "What are we doing here, little man?" he asked with a little laugh.

"Do like this," Raif said, bending his little arms at the elbows and started pumping them up and down over his moving hips.

"All right, I'll give it a try just for you," he said as he took his do-rag from his back pocket and tied it on, pushing his curls up. He mimicked Raif's movements the best he could. "I'm not real good at this, little man!"

"That's okay, HT," he giggled. "Mum says just have fun!"

"Right then, that I can do!"

The next song was a twisting song.

"Now this one I can do, little man. I've had plenty of practice. I used to twist to this with Mum and Dad."

Everyone was twisting, singing along, and acting silly when Raif screamed. HT jumped, thinking something was wrong, but then they screamed on the song, and he realized that Raif had just screamed a little early. He hadn't heard the song in a while and had forgotten about the scream.

"Again, Lil! Twist again, Lil!" Raif shouted all excited as the song ended.

Lil hit the replay button and scooped up her camera. Everyone continued on, having a good time.

Raif screamed again like before, again HT jumped. He muttered under his breath, *"The little shit is going to give me a heart attack!"*

Raif ran over and pushed the replay button again as the song ended, and every-one just kept on twisting.

HT looked over to Lil raising his eyebrows with a pained look as he mouthed, "Bloody hell!"

She laughed and twisted her way to him. "It's the last time," she said. "He loves to twist, so we have to cut him off at three."

"My legs are screaming at me!" he playfully moaned.

"Already? You're in big trouble then. He's just getting started. The cup shuffle will be next."

He leaned forward, his voice just above a whisper, "Another one of my secrets—I'm total rubbish at dancing."

"Right! Like I believe that. Oh, by the way," she teased, "we do that a few times too."

"Oh no!" He groaned as he rubbed his stomach. "All this on an empty stomach."

Raif ran up and moved in between them. His back was to Lil as he began twist-ing with HT. He sang, "Twist...aww...ooo...twist."

HT smiled as he bent down to help him sing. Raif's chest puffed out in delight as he smiled from ear to ear. HT leaned in more so that they could scream together! When the song was over, HT picked Raif up, laughing, and twirled him around.

It sent Raif into a fit of hysterical laughter.

HT sat him down.

Raif said, still chuckling, "Love that song. You love Beastles, HT?"

HT suppressed a chuckle and wasn't going to correct him that the band's name was The Beatles. "Sure do, little man. One of my favorites. Maybe we should start a band."

Raif giggled. "You're silly, HT. I'm too little," and wrapped his arms tightly around HT's legs. "I love you, HT!

HT's heart melted bringing tears to his eyes as he lovingly patted his back. He felt his throat swell with emotion as he replied, "Love you most, little man."

Lil's heart felt like it was going to swell up and burst watching him with Raif.

"Break time for me," Mary announced. "I need to get dinner in the oven. I'll be right back. Don't start the shuffle without me," she said as she hurried out.

"I'll help," HT called after her as he headed to the door. "It'll give me a chance to grab a bite. I'm starving. I got stood up for lunch! Believe it or not, I haven't eaten a bite all day!"

Lil couldn't take her eyes off HT as he hurried out. The feelings of love were so overwhelming that they took her breath away. She had never felt anything like it. Raif, pulling at her hand, snapped her out of her trance.

"C'mon, Lil," he said, "let's twist again."

"Again?" she asked with a chuckle.

He nodded vigorously.

"All right then."

Raif clapped his hands with delight.

Five minutes later as HT popped the last of a pasty in his mouth, he walked over to Lil. "That will hold me until dinner," he said patting his stomach. "Now, how does that shuffle thing go?"

Lil arched an eyebrow and looked at him with a hint of skepticism. "I just can't believe you don't dance."

"Well, you're about to believe it," he teased as the words from his dad replayed in his head: *You'll be doing things you never thought you'd do.* He added with a playful grin, "Just know I wouldn't do this for anyone but you. Well, okay, maybe little man too." He chuckled.

"I'm flattered, but let's just say I'm highly skeptical. The way you sing, I'm sure you're another Justin and just winding me up!"

He gave a small ironic laugh as he shook his head. "I wanna hear you say that in about ten minutes."

Lil thought his laugh suggested he was joking, knowing what he was pulling with the guys at golf. "Mm-hmm, I'm still not buying it, but, I'll show you the steps," she said, her tone somewhere between skepticism and curiosity.

HT laughed the whole time. He got the steps easy enough but had no rhythm to go with them.

"HT," said Lil impatiently a few minutes later, "either you're still trying to wind me up or you really are total crap at this. Loosen up some; you're way too stiff." She put her hands on his waist trying to make him move as he did the steps.

Electricity shot through him at her touch, and he quickly inhaled. He let out a low groan and covered it up with a little laugh. "I warned you. Mum made me promise that I wouldn't try to dance when I'm on stage, disgracing them all!"

"I can see why. You're total crap!"

They laughed as Lil kept trying to make him loosen up and move his body.

When Mary came back in, everyone lined up as Lil started the song.

HT and Lil laughed while they danced having the best time ever! She teased, "At least you're getting the steps right!"

"Okay, Ms. Cheeky," he replied.

Raif yelled when the song was over, "Again, let's do it again!"

"Count me out," Mary announced, heading to the door. "Dinner will be ready in about ten minutes."

HT quickly followed her and called out, "What's that, Moms? You say you need some help?" making everyone laugh.

After starting the music, Lil slipped out the door to join HT. She found him setting the table in the dining room and munching on an apple pasty.

"You're going to spoil your dinner," she teased. "What happened to date night?"

"I figured I would stay around here and rest up for golf. I need to show these blokes a thing or two. That and I really wanted to talk you into letting me help you get caught up in the darkroom. Thought it was time you let me help! I hate you being so exhausted, doing it all on your own."

"You're right. It's time I let you help."

"I'm right! Oh no!" he whined with a horrified look and long-suffering groan. "I know that tone of voice, and it always makes me nervous. You're trying to rope me into something!" He teased, "Let's have it. What mountain do I have to climb? How many miles do I have to hike? Oh no! It's not a dance contest is it?"

"Stop." She giggled. "I decided it's time I quit stalling and show you my darkroom. That's what I was going to show you last week but then we got sidetracked. So much for resting, huh? All that gettin' loose in there!"

"I don't think that's what I was doing! So back to your darkroom. When?"

"Soon. No more stalling. I promise. Now, back to your dancing. You're right! You're no Justin! But I have to say, you have him beat in the singing and looks department."

"Now, you're just scaring me here," he teased. He asked on a huge sigh, "Are you sure you're not trying to get me in some village dance contest?"

She grinned, rolling her eyes.

"Did it go all right today? Did you miss me? And what I really want to know is, how much rubbish was my replacement?"

She replied with a smile, "Wedding—was great. Miss you? Yes, I did, and Jay did fine, and he's not your replacement, silly."

He playfully winced. "She smiles as she twists in the knife. You could have said he was total crap after making me starve all day."

"Enough already," she said with a little chuckle. "I'm really sorry for making you starve and for being so short with you this morning. I didn't realize I had been until after I left; then it hit me." She started to mumble. "My head was all over the place. JR sprung the news on me first thing this morning about the shoot. One of his friend's wedding photographer bailed and needed a favor, so of course he volunteered me. Jay heard JR and said he knew the bride and was going, so he offered to help. I had to stick around with him for a while since he helped me."

HT started to laugh.

"See," she teased. "You can tell I'm sorry when I start that rubbish."

"Or when you're tired, nervous, in a hurr—"

"All right, all right." She grinned. "Anyway, I was going to call you when I saw I wasn't going to make it back, but I left my phone lying on my bed. See? I'm all flighty without you. I need you to keep me organized. Again, I'm really sorry."

"Yep, I agree; you totally need me." He lightly tapped the end of her nose with his index finger. "You're forgiven for starving me and giving me attitude this morning, and you're never flighty. But no more going off on photo sessions without me, giving my job away! And, no more standing me up when it comes to food! Next time, I might pass out from starvation!"

"Promise." She chuckled. "No more standing you up. Thanks for staying home to help me get caught up. How about we take the night off and start tomorrow after golf and lunch?"

"Sounds like a plan," he said nodding.

Dinner was the same as always; the conversation flowed very loudly. Everyone was light hearted, laughing, joking, and talking over everyone else. Of course, the guys wouldn't let HT live it down that he couldn't dance. Even stern-faced Joe was full of smiles and in on it.

After letting them wind him up for a bit, he laughed and said, "Ha-ha! Bi—" he stopped, remembering Raif was sitting there.

The guys laughed harder, knowing exactly what he was about to say. Apparently 'little repeat' knew too. He said, "Bite me! Huh, HT?"

HT muttered, "That kid is a bloody parrot."

His remark had everyone laughing.

# CHAPTER 12

It was near dark by the time the cleanup was done. It hadn't taken long since everyone chipped in. Like dinner, it was a family thing.

"Let's go for a walk to our hill, HT," Lil said as she headed to the kitchen door.

He let out a low, faint growl and muttered teasingly, "I've never seen a girl who likes to walk so much, and now, I have to add dancing to the list. You're killing me!"

She turned and grinned. "You know you don't have to do anything you don't want to."

"I can't imagine not wanting to do anything you want me to do," he replied with a wink and closed the door behind them.

It was a clear, cloudless sky with a huge full moon. There was just a hint of a breeze, making it a perfect midsummer night. All of the twinkling lights in the garden and around the walls were on. The water was softly splashing in the fountain and waterfall, making it even more romantic.

Lil could hardly contain her excitement as she placed her arm through HT's. She playfully bumped her hip against his as they walked.

He fell a little to the side as if she'd hit him hard. "Easy there, killer," he joked, enjoying the feel of her against him.

Her head was tilted toward the garden. A radiant smile spread across her face as she said with a soft, contented sigh, "Isn't it beautiful? It's so breathtaking!"

"Ummm," he replied in a raspy hushed tone looking at her. "I agree. I'm looking at the most beautiful thing I've ever laid my eyes on. It truly makes my heart race." He quickly looked out at the garden as she glanced his way.

"Mine, too," she said softly.

Just after they turned left on the path leading to the waterfall, Lil gently removed her arm and came to a halt. "Hey, speedy," she said, "this way."

HT stopped and turned to see what was wrong. He walked back a few feet softly chuckling. "Why do I feel like I'm about to discover another family secret?"

She reached into the ivy wall, just like before when she had opened the gate by his house.

He heard a familiar click, as she pushed it open, making it swing to the left and followed her through. It was just light enough to see they were standing on a cobblestone terrace. He saw a Victorian bench and an unlit lamppost that matched the ones in the garden. The bench faced outward so that you could sit and enjoy watching the stars come out. "Brilliant," he said, not really knowing what to say. It was cool she had her own hideaway spot, but he didn't know what the big deal was. He could tell she was excited while showing him though, and added, "Great spot! Can't see this when we're up on top, or when we're walking, the way that wall blocks it." He stared up at the sky, watching the stars light up as it grew darker, feeling a deep sense of peace.

"Psst! Hey, HT!" she whispered.

"Huh?" he muttered, still gazing up.

When he didn't turn around, she chuckled. "H...Teee, turn around!"

He turned to look at her, slightly dazed. It took a moment for his eyes to focus. She flipped a switch, making beams of light stream out of two big windows and a door. The lights glowed in a warm, inviting way as if they were casting a magical spell from what looked like the front of a small fairy-tale cottage sitting *inside* their hill! She flipped another switch, and the lamppost and thousands of small twinkling lights entwined in the ivy covering the front sprang to life. The door and windows were rounded, and the window boxes were filled with bright pink and white flowers, making it even more cheerful and magical.

"Bloody hell," he muttered.

Lil was facing him, not wanting to miss his reactions. She reached behind her, turned the knob, and pushed it open. "Want to go inside?"

His mouth spread into a gorgeous smile, making his eyes twinkle brighter than the lights. Connecting with her eyes, he shook his head slowly, trying to sound uninterested. "Naw, you go ahead."

"Oh! My bad," she said, trying to hide her grin. "I thought you'd like to see it."

"It's cool, I guess," he teased with a little shrug, "but, I'll just sit out here and wait on you." He let out a sigh. "I'm knackered from all that gettin'-loose rubbish!"

"Oh, poor baby. I'm so, so sorry for dragging you down here then," Lil replied. "You rest, and I'll be out in just a sec." She chuckled as she turned and walked in.

He laughed as he eagerly followed her, not knowing what to expect. He stood with a dropped jaw while scanning the enormous, rectangular-shaped room. "I have never seen anything like this in my life! Unbelievable!" he muttered.

The walls and high ceiling were covered in the same blond stone as Lil's house. He looked up and continued to mutter. "That ceiling is a tall one." He saw the floor was covered in the same black marble as the mantel on the electric fireplace standing on the right wall and the four large pillars holding up the ceiling. "How in the bloody hell did they get those tall things in here?" he said, still muttering, not expecting an answer. He noticed there was an arched doorway with a rounded door on each of the three walls. He looked over to the right just past the fireplace and saw a huge flat-screen television hanging on the wall. "Wicked telly." He chuckled. "That sucker's screen is the size of a cinema's."

"Not quite." Lil laughed.

"Quiet, woman," he teased glancing over at her with a wink. "I'm trying to take this all in!" He looked at the back wall facing them, missing the blush covering her face from his wink. The back wall was lined with bookshelves, half filled with photo albums.

He looked past the bookshelves to the second arched doorway. Seeing a single red light bulb above the door, he knew it was Lil's darkroom.

His smile grew as he glanced at her and gestured toward the door. "Let me guess. That's your darkroom back there?"

"Yep, that's it!" she said with a smile. "Let's go this way first, though." They walked toward the door beside the fireplace. As they walked beside a long snack bar, Lil pointed to the right at a small kitchen in an alcove. "It's small," she said, "but it has everything you need: refrigerator, stove—"

"Blah, blah, blah!" He chuckled.

"Why do I put up with you?" She chuckled.

"Because you love me. I'm sweet, loving, caring—"

"And totally full of crap!" she teased as they reached the door. She opened the door, and he followed her in. They were standing in an enormous bathroom. The floor, walls, double vanity with his and hers wash basins, and large walk-in shower, which could easily fit six people with room left over, were made with black marble and granite. A clear glass enclosed the front of the shower with its four gold water-spouts on each of the three black granite walls.

HT shook his head in amazement. "I've never seen anything like this before."

"It's a little overdone! Don't you think?"

"No way, it's wicked!" he said. "Even the toilet is black." He noticed it had a gold handle, matching the gold fixtures on the double vanity and shower. A large, gold-framed mirror was on the wall above the vanity. Three small black wicker baskets were spaced across the top of the vanity, one in the middle and one in each corner. The one in the middle, between the sinks, held hand soap and a stack of thick pink hand towels. The one in the right corner was full of bathing products while the one on the left was empty.

HT looked at Lil and teased, "Where's the spa tub?"

"I know. What a dive!"

They laughed.

"This place is absolutely brilliant, but...I've waited long enough. Show me your pride and joy." He smiled widely.

"Follow me," Lil said happily, as he followed her out.

As they walked HT chuckled. "This place reminds me of the Potter movies. All it needs is a few broomsticks, owl cages, and—oh—how about a few magic wands floating around?"

"I never thought about that. It does. I love those movies. Actually I love going to the cinema."

"Me too."

"Then we should go. I haven't been in a while."

"Like a date-date? Like me and you?" he teased.

"Again, making fun of me, Mr. Smarty-Pants." She grinned. "I let the first one slide, but that one is going to cost you. So yes, like best mates, date-date, like me and you. You have to pay, of course, and you're buying me dinner before the movie."

"Only if you buy the popcorn and of course ice cream after!" He grinned.

"Deal." She nodded and put her hand out.

"Again with the handshake." He grunted, making her chuckle as he shook her hand.

They reached the door to her darkroom. "Now the moment we've been waiting for—drum roll, please," said Lil with an excited smile as she turned the knob. HT hit his legs with his hands making the sound as she pushed open the door and announced, "My pride and joy—my darkroom."

"And the crowd goes crazy, as they stood up and cheered!" He said as if an echo, "Yay...ay...ay."

She just shook her head chuckling as he followed her in.

"Whoa. Look at this place. This is absolutely amazing," he said, walking further into the room. "This room is the best yet!"

Lil looked at him surprised, seeing he meant it. For some reason she hadn't expected him to show such enthusiasm about her little, private sanctuary.

"I was expecting to see a closet-sized room, but it's huge in here," he said looking around. He could smell ink and chemicals, with a touch of peppermint—coming from her, of course, as they stood. He walked slowly, looking to his left at a long workbench stretching to the back with developing equipment lying on top. He stopped walking, seeing all the shelves underneath were full, holding all her supplies and noticed clotheslines with clips on them hanging overhead.

"Do I get to wear what you do? The rubber gloves, those geeky goggle things for my eyes. And oh, one of those long white jackets," he teased, nodding his head.

"That's three, Mr. Smarty-Pants," she said shaking her head. "For that one, you now have to dress nice for our date-date. Let's say a blazer is a must, no wearing a T-shirt either, and you have to take me to a fancy restaurant."

"Aww man." He groaned with a wink. "But if I wear a blazer you have to wear a dress."

She nodded.

"Right then," he said with a grin. "Back to working in here. For real. I can't wait. We hang the wet photos on all these lines right?"

"Yep!" she said smiling.

He looked to the wall on his right and saw they were covered with the same type of lines. He looked at the back wall and saw more lines, but the top six held photos. He looked above the photos and saw a big sign that read: **Story of Our Lives**, in bold black lettering. He was drawn to it. He looked at the first two photos. They were of him from the first day at the bakery. The first one was of him as he choked on the soda, making him smile as he read what it was labeled: "Day 1, Our Beginning!" The other one was of him singing while he was sweeping. He stepped sideways as he started to study each one. They read like a storybook. They were each labeled with the number of the day it was taken. Some days had more than others, but they were all pictures of them.

Leaning forward as he stared at each one in awe, he said in a soft tone, "The quality is fantastic. Nobody sees what you see in things. You capture it on film for others to admire. You're absolutely brilliant," he praised, looking over at her.

"Thank you." She beamed, not even trying to hide her pleasure as a feeling of warmth rose inside her. She didn't know when a compliment had pleased her more.

"You're welcome." Once he worked his way back to stand beside her, neither of them spoke as they stood close together staring at the first photos. He turned to her and asked, "How many times have you made this wall?"

"This is the first time," she said softly, looking at him. "You're the *only one* I've ever let in here, too. I've never wanted to share it with anyone before you."

He looked back at the wall. He was doing all he could to keep from kissing her. His heart was beating so hard and loud that he just knew she had to hear it.

She looked back at the photos feeling a hot rush surge through her body. She sighed and, in a hushed tone, said, "I started back here first, and I'm going to work my way around to the other wall."

"We're going to fill these walls up a lot over our lifetime. I love this sign," he said looking up. He repeated the words, "'Story of our lives.' I like that. I believe I feel a song coming on."

"I'm sure it will be great. Can't wait to hear it!"

"Along with an awesome music video you can shoot," he said grinning at her.

"I'm in." She smiled. Their eyes met, sharing a moment. For a brief second, she had a feeling he was thinking about kissing her and realized how much she wanted him to.

He was exercising as much self-control as he could, wanting to pull her close and kiss her breathless. He looked away, trying to snap out of it. He took a small step backward toward the door. "We still have one more room," he said as he turned and rushed out, eager to make his escape and breathe in air that wasn't filled with her scent. He took in a few deep breaths trying to clear his head. *I almost blew the whole we're-best-mates thing right there!* He shook his head in disgust knowing if she realized that he had fallen in love with her, she would cast him aside like poor old Fish Face. He had to take it slow and hope she returned his feelings one day and would give them a chance.

She let out a huge sigh as he ran out. She went out closing the door behind her, pushing back the thought of wanting to kiss him, along with all the other feelings she didn't want to face. She walked to the last door and found him standing there checking it out. The door was different from the other two. It was rounded like the others but made out of old wooden planks. It was held together with black iron rivets, bars, and hinges, with a large black iron ring for a handle in the middle of the door.

"I love this door! It looks like it came off an old pirate ship. It really matches this place," said HT as she pushed it open and walked in.

The room was massive, with the same colored stone and black marble floor.

HT's mouth dropped as he stared at the wall facing them. It was covered in glass. He slowly walked toward it. "That's the backside of the bloody waterfall," he said softly in awe.

"So you like?" Lil asked with a raised brow. She didn't turn on any lights. The lights coming from the waterfall, along with the fireplace on the left wall with its artificial flames, was enough.

"Like isn't the word I would use. Actually I can't think of words to describe it. I know I keep saying this, but I have never seen anything like it! How is this possible?" He stood in front of the glass and said more to himself than her, "When I looked through it from the outside all I saw was blue tile."

"The reason you couldn't see through from the outside, it's a double waterfall," said Lil.

He looked up studying the waterfall. "What makes the water keep flowing?"

She pointed down. "The water from both waterfalls goes there, and a pump takes it back up top."

"Really?" he said, looking where she pointed and then at her.

She shrugged with a cute grin. "I don't have a clue!"

He chuckled and shrugged. "You had me believing it." He found himself wanting to kiss her again, so he quickly turned and said, "I have to check this place out again!" He looked to his right as he walked across the room noticing the fireplace and the large piles of Lil's photo albums stacked on the floor neatly beside it, reaching to the corner. He stopped, wondering why they weren't on the empty shelves. His mind started racing. The shelves above the desk sitting by the entryway were half empty, and the basket on top of the vanity in the loo was empty. He turned to look at her. "For me?"

She nodded as her lips curved into a smile.

"Brilliant, I'll bring some stuff over after golf."

"That works for me," she said as they walked to the entrance door.

"Who did all this?"

"I'm not sure who originally put it in here, but Dad and the guys did all the remodeling so that I would have my very own hideaway. Papa and Uncle Carl—"

"The bloke who lived in my house, Bill's friend?"

She nodded. "You really do listen!"

"Even when you mumble," he teased.

She playfully rolled her eyes. "Anyway...Papa and Uncle Carl kept knocking heads on how to make it special. Dad got tired of all the bickering and told them to pick a room, and he would take care of what was left. Uncle Carl did the one with the waterfall and Papa the loo. So Papa bet Uncle Carl his room would be the best. Nobody won because, well, I didn't have one. They're both brilliant!"

"I'll say." HT nodded.

HT opened the door and held it for her. She flipped the switch turning off the inside lights, leaving the ones around the patio on. He followed her out, closing the door behind them. Night had fallen, and the moon had risen high. The sky was now alive with thousands of stars as they walked through the gate. Their fingers automatically entwined.

HT said, as they strolled toward the house, "Seeing as the only furniture there is a small pedestal table and couple of armchairs sitting by the fireplace, we should try to find a sofa and a few more tables somewhere."

"No problem there," Lil responded. "That big barn with the thatched roof is packed full of furniture from when we redid the house in London and anything else we need. Mum said I could have whatever I wanted. I just never got around to it."

"See, you were just waiting on me to help," he said. "Want to go on a treasure hunt after golf? And lunch of course! Oh wait," he added quickly, "we're going to work in your awesome darkroom. I can't wait to get started in there."

"Don't be silly; we can work in there anytime. Let's find some treasures to spruce the place up a bit, make it have a lived-in look. I'll have lunch waiting up on top, and you can give me all the details of the game." Laughing, she teased, "But if you don't get some sleep and rest those legs, they might not be good ones!"

"Let's hope they're good ones." He groaned. "I'll never live it down if they're not! I just hope they don't turn the dogs on me after what I'm about to do. You know how serious they are about their golf!"

"You worry too much; it'll be fine. It will give you and the guys something to laugh about for years to come!"

They arrived at the porch and faced each other.

"Years! I like the sound of that." He chuckled.

"Of course years, silly. We're best mates for life!"

HT, getting lost in the moment once again, leaned in to kiss her and remembered at the last second he couldn't, and lightly touched his lips to her forehead. He lingered a little longer than usual, breathing in her scent!

A heated flash burned through Lil as she took a few steps back with her heart pounding. She wanted him to kiss her and not on the forehead. She loved his masculine scent, but it was driving her insane. She needed to get away from him before she did something crazy.

"Thanks for sharing your hideaway with me," he said. "We need to think of a name to call it."

She turned and went up the stairs as she said, "You're very welcome. I love sharing it with you." She turned as she opened the door and added, "I agree; we do need a name. I'll let you do the honors. I'll love whatever you choose; I'm sure it will be perfect! Now get going so that you can get some sleep."

He saluted her with his right hand and clicked his heels together. "Yes, ma'am, Ms. Bossy Pants." He chuckled with a wink.

She laughed, shaking her head. "Don't forget to have fun tomorrow, Mr. Smarty-Pants," she called back as she hurried inside. She stood by the door with her heart still racing, listening to him sing as he walked off. "Ugh," she mumbled, disgusted with herself as she went to the stove to make tea. "What the hell! I can't be blaming my hormones on my curse; it was over last week! I wanted to attack him twice tonight. I definitely need to get my bum back to working out with JR so that I can get my head straight; this has gone on long enough!" She let out a long sigh as she sat the teakettle on the burner and pushed back her emotions once again.

# CHAPTER 13

H T was feeling great when he woke up the next morning. He wasn't the least bit nervous. Actually, he couldn't wait to get started, especially after all of the laughter and rubs he took at dinner.

He returned Lil's morning text, smiling. She had complete confidence that he could pull it off. "Man, I love her!" he muttered. *Enough,* he told himself. *It's time to get my mind around the golf game. I have to show these blokes what I'm all about when it comes to golf.* "Nice, I like that," he said, picking up his song-book and quickly adding to the song he had started about watching Lil dance. "Show you what it's all about," he said as he wrote. He put down his book and hurried across the room carrying his duffel bag. It was jammed full of stuff to take to Lil's later. He hurried down the stairs to the front door and laid his bag beside his backpack, which held his nicely folded golf clothes, hat, a few balls, and his shoes. He had tied one of his old do-rags around four of his favorite clubs and had them leaning against the door. He grinned and said, "All set to give you tossers a run for your money. Now to grab a quick bite to hold me over."

He had just finished eating when he got a text from Lil, sending small sparks through him. He read,

"Good luck and don't forget to have fun." ☺

They didn't really text each other much, mostly because they were always together and didn't need to. Plus, he had in the back of his mind that she hated it. What did she say? *The texting, the calling, too clingy...* He heard JR's horn.

He returned her text:

"Thanks and I will, Ms. Bossy Pants. They're here to get me now!" ☺

He slipped on his backpack and scooped up his golf clubs. He stood waiting with his hand on the doorknob until he heard the horn again. Dad told him, "Bill is very impatient and hates to wait," Lil had told him, "Papa is a whole different person when he's playing. Wind him up, and you'll kill three birds with one stone, as they say. He will complain and whine so bad, he will get Dad and JR frustrated for you. Don't let him intimidate you, though. If he gets too bad, Dad will back him down." To that he'd replied, "Bloody hell, he gets that bad?" making her chuckle. He heard the horn again. This time it was more insistent. He opened the door, took a deep breath, and went out.

As soon as he stepped outside JR jumped out, dressed in the latest golf apparel, and walked to the rear of the car. He opened the boot as HT walked up.

HT nearly lost it, seeing the expression on JR's face. "Morning, bro." He smiled, as he put his clubs in the boot. "You look quite dapper this morning. I didn't know they made those things big enough to fit you. I was going to borrow some of my old man's clothes, but since it was an old-guy thing wearing that stuff, I changed my mind!"

HT had dug out an old pair of washed-out black jeans, a size too small, wanting them to be super tight. They were already cutting him in half and smashing his junk, but what was a little pain compared to the fun he knew he was going to have. *Yep!* he thought seeing the look on JR's face. *Having sore junk was going to be worth it.* He had on his favorite faded black T-shirt that Mum was always threatening to toss in the trash and his favorite pair of well-worn black boots. Of course, to finish the look, his do-rag. He had it pushed up so far that his long curls were piled sky high. So high that he resembled a rooster! Now he was glad Sloan hadn't gotten around to trimming it yet.

"What's the hold up?" Bill yelled from the car. "Get a move on. Don't stand out there jawing all morning!"

HT looked at JR with a raised brow.

"He hates waiting." JR chuckled. "Just ignore him if he gets fired up."

HT nodded as he opened the car door and slid in the back seat with Bill. He held up his backpack. "I brought snacks just in case we get hungry."

Bill stared at him with his mouth gaped open, not believing what he was seeing.

It was hard for HT to maintain a straight face. He saw that Bill and Mr. C. were dressed from head to toe in golf gear not yet released to the public. He chuckled to himself; he had the same outfits. Bruce always sent him the newest merchandise in clothes and equipment. He wished he had a pair of the short pants on now; his jewels and Clyde were killing him.

"Good morning, Mr. C. Great day for golf, huh? But, maybe I shouldn't go. I didn't realize there was a dress code."

Bill jerked his head to glare at him and said gruffly, "This is just how *real* golfers dress. I was under the impression you knew more about golf than that, boy!"

"You're dressed all right, HT," said Charles. He got the feeling that something just wasn't right. "I have to say I'm surprised Luke didn't give you something to wear, though."

HT just shrugged not wanting to lie and replied, "Mum was in a hurry to get to Chester to see my aunt," and left it at that. He quickly went to work on Bill, hoping to get him complaining and change the subject. He started to squirm and lightly bounce on the seat trying to act like Raif. It worked instantly.

Annoyance flashed across Bill's face as he growled, "Sit still over there, boy. You're as nervous as a long-tailed cat in a room full of rocking chairs!"

Luke told him not to let Charles and JR see or hear him aggravate Bill because they would catch on. So he made sure they heard him say, "Sorry Bill, I'm just excited you let me tag along. I can't wait to play. I haven't played in a while. Hope I get at least a hundred. How many holes are we playing, anyway?" he asked.

"Usually eighteen," replied JR.

HT leaned toward Bill and said in a low voice so that only he heard, "Buggar, hope I can last that long. I've never played more than nine and then we take breaks!"

Bill sucked in his breath like he had been hit in the gut and shifted in his seat uncomfortably. "Un-be-lie-va-ble," he grumbled shaking his head.

"Can I drive the cart?" HT asked.

"No carts boy, we walk," Bill stated in frustration.

HT made his brow shoot up as if shocked. He whispered with a little whine to his tone, "All eighteen holes?"

Bill jerked as if someone had stuck him with a sharp pin and shook his head again.

HT quickly looked out the window so that Bill couldn't see the smug smile on his face. He was starting to wonder where they were playing. Chester would be packed this morning and Manchester too. The only other course was...his mouth dropped open as they pulled up to the main gate at Highcliff Castle. He never dreamed in a million years that they would be playing here. "We're playing here?" he blurted out all excited, not having to put on an act. He almost started bouncing again for real.

"Yeah," Charles answered and added to avoid suspicion, "We've taken advantage of the course since we took over the security contract."

"Brilliant," HT said as the gates opened, and they drove up the long drive. He was so excited that he couldn't believe he was actually playing there. He got himself under control enough to remember he needed to work on Bill. "At least we don't have to worry about people wanting to play through if we're moving too slow. That's cool, huh, Bill?" He decided to still play Raif, continuously asking "Huh," knowing it quickly irritated him.

Bill just grunted as they got out of the car. They walked to the rear of the car, and JR opened the boot.

Charles's eyes widened with surprise and then slid into narrow slits of suspicion seeing HT's clubs tied in a do-rag.

Bill didn't care to hide his disgust at seeing them. "Bloody hell, boy! Where's your golf bag? And who plays with four clubs?"

HT ignored his question and let out a little sigh as if disgusted with himself. "Oh man, I forgot to get balls and those little pins that you set them on out of Dad's bag. I bet you have plenty I can use, huh, Bill?"

Bill replied practically spitting, "No, I don't. I don't share or lend my stuff!"

A small smile began to play across Charles's lips watching HT; things started falling into place. HT was winding them up, and Luke had put him up to it!

HT saw Charles staring at him with a knowing grin. He shot him a mischievous grin as he raised his brow up and down and winked.

Charles shook his head grinning, seeing a ten-year-old Harry looking at him with his twinkling green eyes shining and dimples running deep. "I have plenty," Charles said.

"So do I, bro," added JR, "don't worry about it."

"Great!" He nodded. He waited for Bill and then followed slightly behind. It was going to be easier having to only worry about JR hearing him. He muttered under his breath as if talking to himself, "Well, that was just rude. What's it to him if I didn't bring a bag? I hate those things. They're so heavy with all that extra rubbish you have to lug around."

He grinned hearing Bill grunt.

"You go first, HT," said JR once they reached the first hole. "Show us what you got!"

"Sure!" He grinned. "Want to make it interesting and make a wager? Dad and I always do. You know like the loser washes dishes or something."

"Yeah, good idea," Bill said smugly, certain HT was going to lose and couldn't wait to see him wash all those dishes. "Whoever loses has to wash and dry dinner dishes all by their lonesome every night for a month."

"That's too long, Dad," JR said.

"Fine," Bill grumbled and added bitterly, "we will make it a week."

HT nodded. "Sounds good."

"Are you sure, bro?" asked JR. "No offense, but mate we're good."

"It's fine, bro," HT said, sounding sincere. "I don't want Bill thinking I'm a chicken. How about we bet on the last nine? That way it gives me a little warm up time since it's been a while since I've played."

"For sure," said Charles hiding his grin.

HT glanced over at the castle and grinned, thinking about seeing that view when he was ten. He thought about the girl in the maze whom he hadn't thought about in years and got a little chill. Not a bad one; it was more like a *déjà vu* moment.

"You going to take a swing or stand there gawking all day?" asked Bill testily.

"Sorry Bill, chalk it up to nerves." HT took his first swing hitting the ground making a divot. "Oops," he said innocently, as he replaced the clump of dirt and grass. "I just hate it when people don't replace them, huh, Bill?"

Bill's voice had taken on a hard edge as he practically spit out every word. "Don't play with such bad players that do that in the first place, boy."

HT shrugged and smiled to make light of it. "First time for everything, huh, Bill?"

Bill's stare was intense.

"No worries," said Charles, deciding to help HT and, of course, Luke. "Just keep your eye on the ball on your next swing."

HT, playing his role, nodded and smiled softly. "Thanks for the help, Mr. C.," he replied politely before taking another swing. This time he let go of his club letting it sail. It went about thirty feet through the air. "Wow!" he laughed; he didn't think it would go that far. "That has to be a record," he added, as if he did it all the time. "That sucker had to go at least twenty feet, huh, Bill?" He just stood there not going after his club.

Bill pinched the bridge of his nose between his thumb and forefinger, taking a moment to compose himself. He then said with a frown and nodding toward the club, "Don't just stand there, boy! Go get your bloody club!"

"I'll just use this other one and get it when we walk that way," said HT, picking up an iron and letting out a loud grunt. The grunt was for real; his junk was killing him. "No sense walking more than I have too, huh, Bill?" he added.

"That's an iron boy. You need to use a wood to tee off," grumbled Bill. "And, quit that damn gruntin'," he added, shaking his head in disgust.

"Sorry," HT said, not moving.

"Well, go, boy! Get out there and get your bloody club; quit being so lazy," Bill grumbled, shaking his head in disgust again. "That boy is so lazy that he calls the dog in to see if it's raining!"

HT was ready with an excuse. He said with a stricken expression, "I know you don't like waiting Bill. I was trying to save time."

"That's fine, bro," said JR, feeling sorry for him and looked frustrated and almost angry at Bill.

HT went after his club with an arrogant grin. He nodded gratefully at JR when he got back. "Thanks for sticking up for me, bro. Hopefully my nerves will settle down." He decided to keep JR feeling sorry for him.

JR nodded back with an encouraging smile.

HT kept his act going as they played another four holes. He took a few more shots than they did and made another divot, let his club go again, and said "huh, Bill?" to death. He made sure to hit his ball over by Bill's when he could so that only he could hear him whine and carry on. He would sigh disgustedly and make a big deal of laying his clubs down and then let out an even heavier sigh and a loud grunt when he had to bend over to pick them up.

On the next hole, while JR went up to tee off, HT leaned over to Bill so that his voice wouldn't carry over to JR and whined, "I'm really tired. These clubs are too heavy, and my feet are killing me. I can't believe we don't even have a golf cart, huh, Bill?"

"Stop huhing me!" Bill hissed through clenched teeth. "I feel like I'm playing with Raif!"

Charles laughed, earning a dirty look from Bill.

"What are you laughing at?" Bill asked with a sneer. "Don't act like he's not gnawing on your last nerve."

"Geez," HT muttered under his breath, making it obvious he had taken offense at his statement.

"He's not doing that bad," said Charles, egging Bill on.

"Chill out, Dad," JR said, looking at Bill after he hit the ball. "You've been riding him all morning!"

"Thanks, guys," said HT sadly, as if his feelings were hurt and went to tee off with a look of triumph on his face.

Bill clenched his jaw, trying to control the anger boiling through him. "I don't believe it!" Words seemed unable to form in his throat as he shook his head. When he finally responded, his voice was filled with anguish. "You guys haven't heard him carrying on all morning. All that grunting and whining." He mimicked HT. "I'm tired, my feet hurt, these stupid clubs are heavy!"

"That's enough; he's going to hear you," Charles stated as sternly as he could under his breath, trying not to laugh. "You're going to hurt Luke's feelings when he hears how you're being so tough on him."

JR nodded, still not catching on. "Ease off, Dad; can't you see he's just nervous."

Bill grunted and said to Charles under his breath, "I bet Luke doesn't let him carry on like a big baby out on the course like this. I taught him better!"

"Like not acting like a total tosser!" Charles said with a look.

Bill grumbled, "Bite me," as he stormed off.

When HT and Bill made it to the green, HT sat down and took his boot off. He began rubbing his foot.

"Of course them feet hurt," Bill snarled. "Serves you right. Who wears boots to play golf? And them trousers you have on are so tight that if you fart you'll blow them bloody boots off!"

HT laughed and said, "You're a riot, Bill." He hurried and put his boot back on seeing JR coming and stood up. He stretched and yawned loudly, again making sure JR didn't see or hear him.

"What an idiot," Bill muttered.

JR went first and sank his put on the first try. He picked up his ball and said, "I'll meet you guys at the next hole. I need to make a call," and walked off.

HT saw a great opportunity to drive Bill even more mental. He made the ball roll as slowly as possible from one side of the green to the other, and he moved just as slow between shots thinking about the next hole. He knew there was a pond, and you had to go over it to reach the green.

Bill tapped his foot as he watched him. He'd finally had enough and snorted loudly, "Just pick the bleeding ball up, boy! We don't have all day!" He threw his hands up in disgust as he looked over at Charles. "That boy couldn't hit water if he fell out of a bloody boat!"

Charles tried to sound irritated as he said, "You're making him nervous with all that bellyaching of yours!"

Bill hesitated, as if about to speak, then picked up his ball off the green without taking his turn, and stormed off grumbling to himself.

"He's never done that before," Charles said with a little chuckle.

HT laughed and said, "Wait till you see what I have planned on the next hole. How many balls do you have?"

They laughed as they hurried to the next hole.

After JR easily hit his ball over the water, hitting the green, he headed to the little bridge that crossed over the pond.

HT had lost five balls in the water before Bill started fussing. "For Christ sake! Just give up, boy. We don't have that many balls. Just shoot from the other side!" he bellowed almost spitting; he was so upset.

HT just laughed, acting as if he assumed Bill was joking. "My ball has to go over the water just like everyone else's."

Bill let out an exasperated huff as he ran up, grabbed the ball before HT could hit it, and threw it over the pond to land on the other side. He pointed disgustedly. HT could see his hand tremble from being so mad. "There, it went over the bloody water! Now get your arse over there and put it in the hole, and

I don't care how you do it!" he sneered. Tight lipped and red faced, he stomped off again not taking his turn.

HT turned to Charles, and they laughed again.

Charles hurried and threw his ball over as if he hit it so that they could quickly follow Bill. "Start picking his game apart. He hates that." Charles chuckled.

"Okay, just don't let him wrap a nine iron around my neck," joked HT.

They laughed as they hurried to the green.

Bill missed his putt, giving HT the chance to critique his game. With a touch of mockery in his voice, he said, "Seems like you pulled that one a little, Bill."

The muscle in Bill's jaw twitched as he muttered before taking another putt. "Tell *me* how to hit the ball? Acting like he knows it all. I got news for him. He's so dumb that he wouldn't find his own arse with directions and a map!" Once Bill made the shot, he didn't stick around to watch HT and Charles.

HT and Charles skipped their turns and hurried to the next hole following after him. Bill was so upset that he never noticed.

JR, once again, was on his phone and slow getting to the next hole. Bill looked at Charles and nodded at HT. "I'm shooting first; I'm tired of waiting on him."

HT, knowing JR was out of hearing distance, said before Bill teed off, "Me? You've held us up all morning waiting on you! You've been taking a piss out of me all morning, Bill. I don't see you going off on JR because he's on his phone." He scowled and sounded braver than he felt. "And...for your information, if you'd loosen your grip some, that ball would go a lot further. Then you wouldn't have to take so many shots to hit the green!"

"What?" Bill half shouted, genuinely stunned.

Charles tried to give him a stern look. "Bill!" he said, hiding his grin. "Just shoot. We'll take a break after this hole."

"Fine," Bill grumbled.

HT said to Charles before JR walked up. "How sad! Some people just can't take criticism. All I'm saying is," he added in a condescending way, "he has apparently received some bad information on playing! His game is lame!"

Bill's spine stiffened as he stopped midswing. He stepped backward and turned, open mouthed and blinking. He was breathing heavily as he shouted, "Boy, you suck so bad that you couldn't hit the inside of a barn from the inside, with all the doors shut."

"Whoa, Dad," JR said as he hurried up. He looked at Charles. "Now what's going on?"

"Nothing," Charles said waving him off. "Leave it. Just shoot, Bill!"

"Nothing? What the hell!" Bill said disgustedly. "Why am I doing this? I shouldn't be here going through all this torture." He mumbled after he teed off, "That boy is a poster child for birth control!"

HT quickly looked away so that JR couldn't see him grinning. He would have to remember that one; he liked it. He stopped winding Bill up for the rest of the hole, knowing he had reached the limit of his patience.

After Bill finished the hole, he tossed his club into his bag. "I'm going to the clubhouse and getting myself a few stiff drinks. Get a couple of golf carts out, JR, or we will be here all day! When he said he could shoot a hundred, I didn't know that idiot meant for nine bloody holes!" He stomped off.

"Okay, but, Dad, you need to calm down a bit," JR said following him.

Bill did a disgusted shuffle making his whole body shake as he yelled, "Don't tell me to calm down! You're just as bad as him. I thought you came out here to play golf not socialize on that damn phone all morning!"

HT and Charles snickered as they headed to the clubhouse.

"Please tell me you can back up all that rubbish you just pulled!" Charles said, "You play better, right?"

"Good enough to beat your sorry arses," HT said with a crooked grin.

"Thank God." Charles sighed making them laugh again.

HT grabbed the backpack he had left earlier by the clubhouse door. "Do me a favor. Tell Bill you rounded me up some clothes."

"You got it," Charles said as they went in. "I'll tell him when I join him for a stiff drink or two."

HT laughed again as he went into the loo.

Bill and JR were on one cart, and Charles was on the other one when HT walked out dressed, head to toe, hat to shoes, in golf apparel! Bill had disapproving lines across his forehead, clearly showing his impatience having to wait on him.

"Thanks, Mr. C.," HT said and gave Bill a cocky grin. "You think these fancy duds will help my game, Bill?"

He grumbled not caring HT could hear him, "Like those clothes could help that idiot's game!"

HT laughed as he hopped in the golf cart with Charles. "Fun time is over. It's time to teach you blokes how to play golf!"

Charles just laughed as he drove off following JR and Bill.

"I'll start," said HT with a cocky laugh as he strutted up to the tenth hole. He took a ball out of his pocket, sat it on the tee, and added in a mocking tone, "Let's see if this latest, top of the line ball helps. I've been listening to your total rubbish for weeks now, bragging on how good you blokes are. Get ready to do them dishes, Bill."

JR just stared and Bill muttered, "Of all the arrogant—"

Charles laughed, cutting him off. "Just watch, old man!"

Bill scratched his chin, finally thinking something wasn't adding up.

HT snickered as he swung his club, striking the ball with exquisite form. *Whoosh!* No hitting the ground this time. The ball headed straight for the green. He turned to look at Bill, the expression on his face was comical, making him chuckle. "Must be the ball, huh, Bill?"

JR and Bill looked at each other, dumbfounded. Then they burst out laughing, realizing they'd been had.

JR shook his head still chuckling. "Bro, that was just bad! Funny as hell, but bad!"

HT chuckled.

Bill patted HT on the back, grinning his approval. "Good one, boy! You really knew the right buttons to push! I was so mad. If I was a car, I'd been overheated!"

"I know," HT said laughing. "If I didn't know that Mr. C. had my back once he realized I was winding you up, I'd been outta here."

Bill laughed, looking at Charles. "When did you figure it out?"

"When I saw his clubs wrapped in that do-rag," replied Charles with a chuckle.

Bill grinned and said with pride, "Of course you did. Was this Luke's doing?" he asked HT.

"Yeah." HT nodded. "Seems like he can't beat you guys. Let's see if I can."

They all laughed.

HT parred or birdied every hole, not missing a shot. He was near perfection, beating them by seven strokes. The guys were in awe.

HT had just passed the porch when Lil saw him. She could see the look on his face. His expression of pure joy made her laugh as she ran down the hill and up the path toward him.

He got a little catch in the back of his throat when he saw Lil. Her cheeks were rosy, and she was smiling so big that her eyes were twinkling. He gave her a victorious smile letting his duffel bag drop. The closer she got, the faster his heart raced. He opened his arms, and she flew into them and they laughed as he spun her around.

"So I take it by that reaction it went well?" said Lil excitedly, as he sat her down.

"The best I ever shot for nine holes!" His warm smile lit up his face, knowing it wasn't the golf making him so happy.

"I can't wait to hear all about it," she said excitedly. "You can give me the details over lunch. It's already up on our hill."

HT dropped his bag by the gate as they made their way to the top of their hill. They sat down to eat, and HT opened a bottle of water to wet a napkin. "Did you get a lot done in the darkroom this morning?" he asked with a grin.

"How'd you know I was working?"

"Hmm, a wild guess!" He chuckled as he reached over and gently wiped the smudges of ink from her cheek.

Her insides reacted as if an electric current coursed through her. She could feel every nerve in her body, making her light headed. "Give me details, and don't leave anything out," she said with a little laugh, trying to keep her tone normal. She turned away from him taking in a breath and pushing her emotions back.

She laughed listening to his account of the game. He gave her the play by play of what he had done and how Charles had found him out right away and helped. He had Lil laughing so hard that she had tears streaming down her face.

"Did you know they play at Highcliff Castle?" he asked and went on without waiting for an answer. "I was so excited. I've always wanted to play there. I did walk, well ran through it when I was ten. Some bloke set a pack of dogs out after me." He chuckled and added, "My first real crush almost knocked me on my arse that day in the maze."

Lil's pulse quickened. "No way," she said, getting tingles all over.

"What?" he asked, seeing the surprised look on her face.

"You're why I haven't cut my hair. Oh, you made me so mad that day, thinking I was a boy!"

"That was you?"

She nodded.

They burst out laughing.

After a few minutes of laughing and thinking about that day, HT asked, "Who was that bloke who was trying to lock us in? The one who hit the alarm sending the dogs after me?"

"Anthony, the duke's son. He was a total brat back then, but I'm the one who had Papa hit the test alarm, and I sent only two dogs, not a pack."

"You little shit!" he said grinning and started tickling her.

She laughed. "They weren't even after you. If you would have stopped screaming like a big wuss and turned around, you would have seen they were too busy running and playing and not even running your way."

He stopped tickling her. "How did you know I didn't turn around?"

"We were following you in the Jeep," she said and burst out laughing again, her eyes gleaming.

He watched her laugh with a grin on his face. He wondered if that's why another girl had never gotten to him. He had pretty much fallen in love with her when she was staring him down in the maze with those beautiful gray eyes. When she finally managed to stop laughing and wiped the tears off her cheeks he teased, "I'm glad you think it's so funny. I couldn't remember how to get out of that bloody maze. I just knew I was going to be lunch for those dogs!"

"I heard." She chuckled. "I was hiding in that dead end waiting for you to leave. There's a little escape hatch there."

"I was wondering how you got away from me so fast."

"It's still there as a matter of fact. Now you know Dad does the security, we can start going over there."

"I take it rule one came in to play once again, not telling me he does."

She nodded. "Sorry."

"No worries. I love finding out about family secrets; it's like Christmas morning. I can't wait for the next one!"

They laughed.

"So since Mr. C. handles the security, does that mean we can check out the part of the castle you can't see on the tour?"

"Of course!" She nodded. "Actually Dad manages the estate. My granddad did before him. There's not a part of that place I don't know. I'll show you around including all the secret rooms and hallways."

"Brilliant!" He paused as a young JR flashed through his mind. He muttered, "That's why Mr. C and JR seemed familiar when we met. Mr. C. let me on the course, and JR was the long-haired—"

"He-Man wannabe," Lil interrupted. "He had Grammy shave his head that night. Oh, how we teased him forever over you."

Again, they laughed.

Lil wiped the tears away again as she teased, "So I was your first crush, huh?"

"Yeah, and you're just as cheeky now as you were then," he said with a wink.

She playfully rolled her eyes as she started packing up the basket. "Yeah, I'm the cheeky one. Come on, let's get started on our treasure hunt."

"I'm ready," he said and finished the packing as she pulled her trainers on.

He stood, giving her a hand up.

They laughed and talked about that day as they walked to the barn.

The barn was full of crates, boxes, and old trunks. There was furniture stacked everywhere. Persian rugs, tapestries, silver candlestands, tea sets, chairs—it went on and on as far as the eye could see.

HT opened the door and then followed Lil in. "This place is loaded! All this stuff come from the house in London? Just how big is your place?" HT asked as he picked up a silver candlestand to check it out.

"It's a little on the large size," said Lil, chuckling. "We all have our own separate living quarters. We share the front foyer and the sun-room that runs across the back, so it's like we all lived together. I loved it!"

"Well, it has to be massive to hold all this stuff. We should split up to save time. Why don't you look for lamps and rugs, you know, stuff like that, while I'll start in the back looking for the big stuff. We should make a pile outside and then take it all over when we're done."

"Good idea." Lil nodded in agreement. "I'll start this way," she said as she went to the left.

"And I'll head to the back," said HT, already heading that way.

Lil went through some of the crates and boxes and had a small pile started outside. She returned inside after taking a couple of rugs out and went toward the back. She watched as HT put a top hat on over his do-rag. He didn't see her as he said, "I say there, ole chap! How is your day?" Her insides reacted instantly, going warm from head to toe as she stared. "Push them back," she mumbled under her breath.

HT saw claw feet sticking out from under a cover leaning against the wall. He walked over to it and looked up seeing Lil. "What do you think we have here?" He started pulling the covers off.

She hurried over and helped pull the covers off a large carved wooden headboard.

"Look at the detail of the lion head carved in the middle! It looks so real," he said in amazement.

"It's amazing!" Lil said in awe. "I've never seen this before!"

They quickly uncovered the massive four bedposts. They were shaped like big lion's paws. "This thing is wicked!" he said. "I love it! It looks like a family heirloom. Maybe it came out of Highcliff!"

They began pulling covers off everything surrounding it. They found a large, footed-chest, two nightstands, and two high-backed chairs with the same carved lion head and paws. Lil said, "Those chairs will be great by the glass door," as they pulled the last of the covers off to find a mattress.

"For sure." HT nodded. "I'll have to get JR to help me with this stuff; it's heavy. I found a sofa and a couple of tables that will work great too!"

"I saw some great candlestands and lamps that I still want to grab," said Lil. "And, I saw some tapestries, too. They'll help keep the heat in."

"Great thinking," he said.

She ran off laughing and yelling over her shoulder, "This is fun!"

"I agree," he yelled back with a chuckle.

Lil had just walked back inside after adding more things to their pile and saw HT heading her way. She saw he had now added a blue silk scarf around his neck, making her giggle. They carried out all that they could, leaving the heavy stuff for JR to help with.

"I'll go get the tractor and trailer," HT said.

Lil bent down to pick up a tapestry. "I can take this over now. I want to grab some more film."

"Of course you do," he said over his shoulder, as he walked off, chuckling.

She was back in plenty of time to see HT riding up on the tractor, still wearing the top hat and scarf. She couldn't help but laugh as her camera clicked away.

He jumped down, tipping his hat as he bowed. He straightened up, taking her hand. "Your chariot, my lady!" He gave her a little wink as he kissed the back of her hand.

"Why, thank you, my lord! I've been waiting oh, so long," she said and then fluttered her lashes playfully at him, while she made a very deep curtsy with her make-believe dress.

"The pleasure is all mine, my lady!" he said grinning. "I like being a lord."

JR walked up laughing. "I see you two are enjoying yourselves! Looks like you could use some help."

"Great timing, bro. I was just about to call you."

They loaded all the furnishings and transferred them to the hideaway in two loads. Once the Persian rugs were down, everything else fell into place. They placed the sofa in front of the telly and the coffee table in front of the sofa, with the end tables and lamps on each side. "Perfect fit!" Lil said. She placed the armchairs and small table that had already been there against the wall near the darkroom.

While the guys hung tapestries in the *Lion's Room*, which is what HT and Lil named the bedroom, Lil placed the two remaining Tiffany lamps on the nightstands on each side of the bed.

"It's a good thing the ceiling is so high," HT remarked. "The bedposts nearly touch it. I can't wait to sleep in this sucker! I'm planning on using it a lot!"

"By yourself, of course," said JR.

"Oh man, I thought you might want to join me," HT joked.

"I like you, bro, but not that much!"

They all laughed.

JR left as HT went to hook up his laptop to the telly.

Some of HT's things were piled on the sofa, and Lil quickly stuck three of his four do-rags into her pocket. She said, "I think we did a great job; it has a lived-in feel now."

"Yeah, it looks great."

What are you doing with the laptop?" she asked, as she put his CDs on the shelves.

"I'm setting it to stream in shows from the States. Then, this black box here will record them. That is, if I'm doing it right."

"I'm sure you are. It will work perfectly. Haven't seen anything you can't do. Well, if you don't count dancing."

"Hey now, be nice. The twisting wasn't so bad."

She teased with a grin, "Promise me that's the only dance you do when you're on stage."

"I don't know if I can promise that. You know, if we make the show, you have to move a little. Maybe we can do that cup shuffle." He did a few moves being silly and acting awkward.

She laughed and said, "All your things from the sofa are put away. I'm going to the house to clean up for dinner. You can clean up here if you want."

"I will; save me a trip home."

"Everything is in the loo to take a shower. You're going to love it. I use it almost as much as my darkroom. See you at dinner."

"Okay," he called out as she went out the door.

Lil was standing at the counter cutting bread and turned smiling as HT entered the kitchen. His heart raced seeing her. "I see you're working hard," he said smiling. "Need help?"

"Sure you can toss that salad if you want."

"I can do that." It was sitting right in front of him with the dressing and tongs. He added the dressing and gave it a good toss.

"So," she asked, "have you thought of any good names?"

"I was thinking 'the Hilltop.' Then when I was hooking up the laptop, I saw carved on the wall by the telly that someone had named it 'the Cove.'"

"Really! I never noticed! I do like the name Hilltop though!" She paused a second thinking and chuckled. "Hmm, Hilltop...HT...here we go, you and your abbreviations. Next thing you know we will be calling it the HT!"

"I know you're not going to believe this," he said with a raised brow and chuckle, "but I didn't realize that! I thought Hilltop because it's our favorite spot."

"I like Hilltop!" Lil nodded with a smile. "It's perfect."

"I thought so until I saw it was named the Cove. I wouldn't mind just calling it the Cove if that's all right with you. You know, like tradition. I like all that family tradition stuff. It's up to you though, my lady."

"The Cove it remains then. Now grab the salad, and let's eat."

He flashed her a teasing smile. "Maybe I should have said, Ms. Bossy Lady."

She chuckled as she picked up the sliced bread. She pushed open the door with her backside so that he could walk through.

HT walked toward the table, seeing movement by the fireplace out of the corner of his eye. He turned to get a better look and burst out laughing. Charles, Bill, JR, and, of course, little man, were standing there with their arms straight up in the air. They had do-rags on and started bowing to him, and, of course, he heard the *click-click* of Lil's camera.

They all enjoyed a good laugh and sat down to dinner with the guys still wearing their do-rags. Their hair was pushed up as far as the do-rag would allow, knowing that HT did the same.

Dinner, as always, was the highlight of the day. The dining room was filled with talk, laughter, and clatter of knives and forks.

Lil cleared her throat and looked toward the end of the table at JR. "So, He-Man wannabe. How was your day?" she asked with a huge grin.

Everyone looked at her curiously.

HT let out a little groan. His voice dropped as he whined, "You're really going to drop me in it like this?"

Not breaking eye contact with JR, she chuckled and nodded. "Sorry, but if you only knew how we have teased him over you." She grinned as she pointed her index finger, moving it up and down, over HT's head.

"Him?" JR's eyebrows raised slightly and she nodded.

"Yep!" She laughed, happy to see his expression.

"You're still a tosser!" said HT with a sheepish grin.

Everyone burst out laughing. JR laughed the hardest.

# CHAPTER 14

After dinner, HT grabbed the bedding Lil had placed by the kitchen door, and she grabbed a bottle of cold champagne from the refrigerator. The moon was high and the stars were out as they made their way to celebrate the opening of the Cove!

Once inside, HT took the bedding and dropped it onto the bed while Lil went to the kitchenette for glasses. They met at the snack bar as HT popped the cork. He filled their glasses and held one out to her with a slight grin. "Let's toast!"

They clinked their glasses together ceremoniously. "Here's to the Cove," they said in unison and drank.

"And to being best mates for life," added Lil.

They clinked again and finished their glasses. HT refilled them. "What else?" he asked.

"Always being there for each other," replied Lil. They touched glasses and drank.

HT reached over and refilled their glasses. "What else?"

"Let's see. Oh, I know." Lil hiccupped. "To rule one! No lies!"

He ignored her unladylike hiccup as they touched glasses and drank. HT refilled the glasses, emptying the bottle. "What else?"

"Your turn," she said, "I'm feeling a little tipsy here, drinking this stuff so fast. I don't know about you, but I need to sit down!"

He said, as if he was trying hard to think, "Hmm! Let's see. I want it to be a good one. What else? I just don't know."

Lil rolled her eyes and gave him a look as she hiccupped.

"I knew I was going to get the double whammy on that one." He laughed. "Okay, I'll stop messing with you. Let's add that we stay together, you know, partners, when we're following our dreams. Me in the next big boy band and you taking our photos and making the music videos!"

"For sure, without a doubt." She hiccupped as she held up her hand. "Wait, let's give it a time frame," she said, along with another hiccup.

He chuckled shaking his head. "Only you would want to do that!"

"Well, it needs one. We can say it starts the first day of your audition. Better yet, the day you win the show! That sounds even better!"

"I love the confidence you have in me, but just in case that doesn't happen, let's just toast that we plan on staying together and decide later on the rest."

"Fine," she said, slurring her words a little with a slight wobble. "But I'm telling you, you're going to make it on that show and win. You know I'm always right!"

He chuckled as they touched their glasses together.

"To our plan together," they said and emptied their glasses one last time.

She was swaying on her feet. "Now, I have to sit down before I fall down."

"You are swaying a bit there," teased HT as he watched her stagger to the sofa. He wasn't surprised that she couldn't hold her booze. He went to the sofa and sat down as he turned on the telly. "Let's just see if I hooked this thing up right. If I did, you're going to love this bloke."

"Stop, it will work. I haven't seen anything you can't do. Well okay, maybe not dance."

"Hey, enough busting my nads already. You better hope I never get a chance to dance for you on the telly. I'd make sure you know it's just for you and with millions of people watching," he said laughing.

"Oh no!" she playfully groaned. "You're going to have plenty of chances to do it!"

They laughed.

"So who are we watching?" asked Lil as she scooted and settled beside him.

He took over one of the *Late Shows* in the States. He got his big start on a late Saturday night show, the one that's live and has been running forever. I wouldn't mind having the DVDs of the years he was on it. He's the funniest, craziest bloke ever!"

He automatically stretched his arm out, placing it on the sofa behind her head. "His name is Jimmy, and he's brilliant."

The hookup was a success. Lil gave him a smug smile. "See? Works perfect. I'm just saying, always right."

HT snapped his fingers and joked, "I totally forgot that, but thanks for reminding me every other day. You know, I'm going to prove you wrong one day. You can count on that, Ms. Smarty-Pants." He lightly tapped the end of her nose as he thought, *Yeah, on that rubbish about us remaining only mates.*

She quickly turned her head, feeling her pulse quicken from his touch and teased, "Maybe, but doubtful! Now hush, I'm trying to watch your man."

He just chuckled shaking his head, never feeling more like he wanted to kiss her.

Not even ten minutes later Lil was singing Jimmy's praises. "Oh my gosh! He is hilarious! I just love him!"

"I know! Right? He is my new favorite. Usually, I find myself getting bored with entertainment shows and turn them off after they do their monologue, especially if their guests are boring. Or if I do try to watch, the hour seems to drag on forever. Not his show. He keeps you well entertained and laughing. The hour is over in no time. His announcer or cohost—not sure what they call them over there, Higgins, is great and funny too. Man, some nights when they get going back and forth, I can't breathe from laughing so hard."

She stayed awake through the show but then fell fast asleep. HT dozed off, loving that she was lying across his chest.

Lil's alarm in the darkroom sounded off. She sat up groggy and blinked, uncertain for an instant where she was. "Ah!" she moaned letting out a loud yawn, seeing HT. She mumbled in a groggy voice while gently shaking him, "Hey, sleepyhead, wake up."

"Just five more minutes, Mum," he mumbled still fast asleep.

She giggled, saying his name as she gently shook him several more times, "HT, HT, time to wakey, wakey!"

He stirred, pushing his curls off his face and yawned asking, "What time is it?"

"Just about midnight. My alarm in the darkroom just went off. I have that set so that I won't end up staying in there all night."

HT stood up yawning as he stretched. "What? You live in your darkroom? Nah, don't believe it." He grinned holding out his hand and then pulled her up.

"I need to shut it off 'cause I set it to go off every five minutes," she said grinning and walked to the darkroom.

"Please do. I don't want that thing keeping me up all night. I'll walk you up to the house and then I'm coming back here to sleep since Mum and Dad are gone. I want to try that bed out."

"You'll have to make it up first. We never got that far."

"It's your fault it didn't get made, you know." He grabbed the top hat from the desk, putting it on as he held her hand and headed out the door.

"Mine?" she asked with a teasing smile as they started to stroll up the path.

The twinkling lights made it romantic once again.

"Yep, that's the way I see it! Corrupting a gentleman like myself, making me fall under your spell, getting me all tipsy, making me drink those evil spirits, keeping me out to all hours of the night so that you could try to take advantage of my virginity! I see how you are, you little Jezebel!"

"Yeah, right! Like you're a virgin, you gigolo!" She giggled.

"I am!"

"I know. A gigolo?"

"No," he said seriously, "a virgin." He had never admitted that to anyone before, and he couldn't believe he just had to her.

She was speechless for a second as she searched his face. He didn't appear to be joking. Her eyes went wide. "You're winding me up! That's just not possible! You're really not!"

"How can you say such a thing. I'm shocked," he teased with mock outrage.

"Come on answer the question. You're really not?"

They had arrived at the porch.

He tipped his head faintly and shrugged. "Ah, then…No, I'm really not," he replied smoothly with a cheeky grin.

"Wait a minute. The way you just said that sounds like your breaking our rule."

"I did, but it doesn't count," he teased.

"Oh! And why is that?" she asked with a raised brow.

"Because, you just ordered me to say I'm really not."

She rolled her eyes. "Quit making a joke of this."

"Okay, okay don't start kicking off. My first statement stands. Yes, I am a virgin, pure as the driven snow." He grinned. "Well…mostly!"

"I can only imagine what falls under mostly, though," she teased.

"I've never been one to gossip," he replied as he raised his eyebrows up and down. He added, "Besides, a gentleman never discusses such things with a lady."

"Oh! I'm a lady again, I see."

"Always, my lady." He grinned. "By the way, I planned on taking that little secret to my grave. You're the only one who knows, so keep it to yourself."

She gave him a look. "You know—"

"Draw in those claws," he said cutting her off. "Slip of the tongue; I know you never repeat what we talk about."

"That's right," she said with a grin. "I have to say I'm having a hard time getting my head around this. Blokes don't wait and—"

He laughed cutting her off. "Boy, I really have you rattled."

"You do." She nodded.

"Well, it was Dad's doing. He caught me and a girl in the back seat of a car a few years back. Things were getting a little intense. Anyway, he had the talk with me and told me about his first time and how he regretted it. He said I would never forget my first time, so it should be special. No doing it in the back seat of a car, just because I could. It got me thinking, and I decided I wanted my first time to be with somebody I care about." He chuckled seeing the look flash across her face. "Surprised, huh?"

"Totally. With all the girls after you, giving you plenty of chances."

His smile widened, making his eyes twinkle as he admitted, "True. But then, I have to let them try; after all, I have a rep to maintain."

"And there just went our serious conversation," she said rolling her eyes.

He chuckled and said, "Yeah, good place to call it a night!"

They laughed.

He tipped his hat and bowed slightly as he kissed the hand he was holding. "It's getting late, my lady. So I will wish you a—"

She cut his words off by putting her fingertip tip on his mouth. "Save the rest for our text! I like our little tradition we have going."

"As do I, my lady," he said with a wink. "So I will wish you a *no*-hangover morning!"

She chuckled as she went up the stairs and said, "See you in the morning, my lord." She pulled the door open and gave a little curtsey.

He laughed as she went inside. He started whistling his favorite song as he headed back to the Cove.

# CHAPTER 15

Friday evening, Lil and HT were sitting on the sofa in the Cove. They had just finished watching Jimmy, with Lil at one end of the sofa and HT at the other. She was putting the last of the photos from the wedding she and Jayden had attended into the album, and HT was working on a song.

She looked over craning her neck, trying to see what he was writing.

He looked her way. "What?"

"Nothing." She chuckled and looked back down. She waited a few seconds and looked back over staring at him.

He looked up as if he'd felt her staring. She felt an intense heat rush through her when his eyes found hers and quickly looked away.

"Okay, what's going on in that head of yours?"

She looked back at him. "Just thinking that it's eight thirty on a Friday night and here you sit with me. Since you've been hanging out with me you haven't had much of a life compared to what you had."

He thought, *You are my life,* but grinned and replied, "I like my life now, thank you very much. What, you trying to get rid of me already?" he teased.

"Stop, you know better. What are you working on over there, anyway? You look a bit frustrated, and you're carrying on like you're in pain every time you scrawl something down." She chuckled. "I can't tell if it's making you happy or miserable."

He pointed to the songbook and grumbled. "Trying to get a song out of this mess. It's from gettin'-loose night." This book was his second draft, the toned-down version from his original songbook where he wrote down his true feelings. He didn't hold back when he wrote in that one. She would know for sure how he felt if she saw it. He had even drew little hearts and had written "HT loves Lil" all over it.

She scooted closer to him and started to read some and mumbled out loud, "Guys said, 'Hey, c'mon, hair wet, down.'" She read on, "Music loud, dance." She whistled lightly. "Blimey, so this is how you start. I can't wait to see how you put this together, making a song. Every time you sing it, it will remind us of how much fun we had at our first gettin'-loose night."

"I hope it does. That's the hard part, making sure that after I add words in, it will still remind us of that night."

"I have no doubt you'll make it work and that the song will be great," Lil said. "I'm sure when you're done it will remind us of the best night we've spent together so far."

"I agree that it's been our best night." He nodded with a wink. "Now leave me alone, woman so that I can work on this mess."

"How rude!" she teased.

He looked back down at his book. He thought the song would remind him of the best night of his life...when he knew he had fallen in love with her. Thinking about that day got him thinking about Muscleman. He hadn't seen him all week, which meant Lil hadn't either. They had been together, except for the few hours they slept, so he knew she never went back out with him. Maybe it wasn't a date after all. His phone rang, and he knew it was Sloan by the ringtone. He stood up, running his hand through his curls, pushing them back off his face. He asked, while walking toward the alcove, "Want a brew?"

"No, thanks. I'm good," she answered. She got an uneasy, sick feeling in her stomach thinking he wanted privacy to answer it.

"I'm shocked. After all, it's been over an hour!" He laughed as he answered his phone.

"Yeah, whatever," Lil replied. She tried to tune out his conversation as she worked on her album. She couldn't concentrate. Her leg was bouncing, making the album go up and down as she listened. She was trying to tell herself it was none of her business. She peeked up seeing him by the snack bar with the sweetest smile as he talked.

"I know, I know. Okay, I promise." He paused and then said, "Sloan, I promise. I won't stand you up tomorrow."

Lil mumbled, "Well...answers that question. Her name is Sloan." Images of what she might look like spun through her mind almost making her dizzy as she continued to listen.

"Okay, okay, I will. I promise." He laughed in a teasing way and then said, "Yeah, same place." He paused as he listened and then continued, "You too! Enough already! Bye!" He walked back to the sofa and asked Lil, "Sooo, you ready to go with me to Chester?"

She didn't realize he'd asked her a question. She was concentrating on keeping her hands steady as she continued sliding photos into the album. *I'm just upset because he hasn't mentioned Sloan*, she thought.

"Hey, you!" HT said with a chuckle as he sat down.

She looked at him, but her eyes were unfocused, so deep in thought. "Huh?" she asked quizzically.

"You look sort of spacey."

"What's up?" She slammed the album shut and rose from the sofa. She went over to the desk. "Maybe I will get something to drink," she said, dropping it onto the desktop. She needed to settle down a bit.

"I knew it was about time for more tea. I asked if you're ready to go to Chester with me?"

"Sure." She stuck out her tongue as she reentered, holding up a fizzy drink.

"It doesn't surprise me," he said shaking his head. "Now go back and make your tea, and stop being so stubborn."

"This is fine," she mumbled as she sat down beside him.

He grinned, his green eyes dancing. "Man, I've never met a person more stubborn than you. Anyway, Lee has been driving me mental wanting to meet you. So tomorrow is as good a day as any—that is, if you're ready to meet him."

"Are you sure you're ready?" she asked taking a slow drink as she thought, *Humph, what about Sloan?* It brought a pang of jealousy she hadn't expected, and she buried it refusing to examine why.

"I'm ready. Wait," he teased, "maybe I'm not with that smart mouth of yours. I don't need him to see how you're always busting my nads. You guys will tag team me."

"I like him already," she said with a grin. "Sooo, tell me, tell me. Is he cute? Is he taller than me? And most importantly, does he have a girlfriend?"

His heart jumped, not being able to read her expression. Then he saw the gleam in her eye and knew she was winding him up. "He doesn't, as a matter of fact," he said trying to sound serious. "Don't worry. I've told him how it is with us."

She slowly said, "As in?"

He shrugged as he replied, "That he won't be stepping on my toes; we're just best mates and not dating."

"Oh, that's good," she said, trying to reassure herself it was.

His eyes twinkled as he added, "Yep, I made it very clear. No strings between us, boy. No commitments, no answering to each other. It's just good old lust and hot raw sex. Best I've ever had! I even told him you were a tad bit on the noisy side when you...you know, reached your peak!"

"HT!" she said a little shocked, although the thought had her going all hot, making her blush.

He laughed.

"You're such a tosser!" she said grinning, as she slapped him on the arm.

He pinned her on the sofa, tickling her. "That's what you get. Besides my mates in Chester and I decided a long time ago we don't interfere in each other's love lives...which means no fix-ups!" Looking into her eyes and watching her laugh, drew him in, making his heart race. He was just about to lower his head to kiss her when she squealed.

"Quit! Quit! Let me up! I have to go pee!"

"Oh, that's new!" he said with a chuckle letting her up.

She said, as she ran to the loo, "I don't think I've ever laughed with anyone as much as I do with you." Before going in she added, "By the way, we didn't make it a rule about interfering, so think about that fix-up," and giggled as she closed the door behind her.

"Not even a chance!" he grumbled and then grinned, thinking it should do his head in how she always ran off announcing she had to go pee, but it didn't. It was one of the many things he loved about her. Her just being herself. Then he realized he'd almost kissed her. "Bloody hell! This is hard," he said with a little moan as he fell back against the sofa.

# CHAPTER 16

The next afternoon, after a busy morning at the bakery and having lunch with HT on their hill, Lil ran through her room. She discarded her trainers, T-shirt, and bra—in that order—before she reached the shower. She turned the nozzle and dropped her short pants and underwear as she waited for the water to warm. She quickly showered and dried her hair as she looked in her closet trying to decide what to wear. She was eager to meet Lee but also a little nervous, worrying if he would like her. Then she thought about Sloan and wondered what she would be wearing, what she looked like, and more importantly just how much HT liked her. *Quit this*, she told herself. *The way HT likes his ladies, she won't be around long anyway.* She grabbed her mint-green sundress and slipped it on over her head and then finished brushing her hair and pulled some of the sides back so that she could wear the hair clips that matched. She added a touch of lip gloss, blush, and finished off with her special spray behind her ears and the back of her knees. Checking herself out one more time in the mirror and pleased with what she saw, she headed for the door and hurried out. She quietly went down the hall and stairs so as not to wake Raif from his late nap.

Lil went out the front door to see HT leaning against the car with his arms crossed over his chest talking with JR. He laughed at something JR said, making her heart race and insides go all warm and tingly.

HT turned and watched her approach, giving her the smile she loved. The one that crinkled up the corners of his eyes making them twinkle and his dimples run deep. She smiled back as she sucked in a breath, her guard shot up automatically burying her true feelings deep down once again.

He whistled as he opened the car door for her. "You look particularly beautiful today, my lady. Just in case it's for Lee's benefit, remember, no fix-ups!" he teased.

She laughed as she climbed in. HT slid in beside her and threw his arm across the back of the seat.

JR started the engine. He could tell Lil was a little nervous at meeting HT's mates. He drove down the drive and asked HT to give Lil time to settle her nerves, "You see those new golf clubs coming out?"

It worked. Lil tuned out like always when she heard the word golf. She closed her eyes as she leaned against HT, using his chest as a pillow. He laid his hand on her shoulder as she snuggled in. She let out a little sigh and was sound asleep in less than a minute. He glanced down hearing her. He had to admit he was nervous about Lee and Sloan meeting her, hoping they would love her like he did.

Less than half an hour later, HT's laugh brought Lil out of a deep sleep. She sat up seeing they had pulled up by the old movie cinema.

JR asked, "This where you wanted out?"

"Yeah," said HT, nodding. "This is where we always meet."

HT hopped out and held the door for Lil, asking, "You have a nice nap?"

She nodded with a smile. "Yeah, all that babbling put me to sleep."

HT chuckled as he leaned down to look at JR. "Thanks, bro."

"No problem. Meet you two back here about ten then?"

"Yeah, that will work. Gotta get my beauty sleep for golf in the morning. I have the feeling you guys will be gunning for me!"

"You can count on it." JR laughed as HT shut the door.

Lee and Sloan were just finishing their lattes in the coffee shop when Sloan asked Lee, "Besides telling you he was bringing her for sure, what else did he say?"

"Just asked if you were coming," replied Lee. "He never said much about her all week when we talked. So I'm thinking his big crush is over," he added with a little chuckle. "It lasted a lot longer than any other girl. You know how he is. Once they get hooked, he's not interested anymore. I was hoping to be able to bust his nads a bit about one finally hooking him."

"I actually thought this one had a chance," said Sloan a little disgusted. "He seemed to really like her the way he's always going on about her, even though he wouldn't admit to it."

"Maybe we're wrong. It really is just mates between them, and we've been trying to read something into it. He swears she only likes him as a mate and that we'll see she's not falling at his feet like other girls."

They looked at each other with raised brows. Then burst out laughing.

Sloan stood up. "Fat chance of that. I've never seen one yet."

Lee grinned as he stood, picking up their empty cups. "Maybe this one will give him a taste of his own medicine."

"I would love to see it," said Sloan with a chuckle. "Don't get me wrong; you know I love the bloke, but in my lifetime, I would like to see one girl that could resist his charms when he sets his mind on having her."

"Good luck with that," said Lee. "Besides you, I haven't seen a girl he can only be mates with or one who can resist him."

They walked over to the trash bin.

"Well," Sloan said, "something has settled him down after moving out there. You see how he's changed, and I have to say I like it. We'll be able to tell what's going on when we see them together."

"True," said Lee as they walked over to watch out the window. "But if he likes her, he's going to try to hide it as long as he can from us."

"For sure. Which means we watch him like a hawk." She chuckled. "He's not going to make it easy after boasting how a girl would never hook him. What was it he said when you fell so hard for Crissy, and he was always winding you up about acting like an idiot, and you told him it would happen to him?"

"If I recall, his exact words were, 'When you hear the fat lady singing, you'll know one finally hooked me.' Actually, I was a bit of a tosser myself back then."

"Thank God those days are over; you blokes did my head in." She glanced out the window seeing Lil and HT get out of the car. "Oh, bloody hell! Look at her Lee. She is gorgeous!"

Lee whistled. "Blimey, she is fit! Remember, don't be sticking your nose in, if it turns out he really likes her."

"I know, I know. Like I could forget our agreement. No interfering in each other's love lives. I just hope that if he really does like her, we do too," said Sloan as she opened the door.

"With looks like that, I'm sure she's going to be a real piece of work," replied Lee as he went out.

"They always are, and this one is more gorgeous than he is." Sloan chuckled as she followed him out.

HT and Lil stood hand in hand, waiting. He looked across the street and spotted Lee. "That's Lee coming out of the coffee shop," he said as he waved with his other hand. "Sloan is supposed to be here, too." He saw her at the same time she saw him. "Oh, there she is." He looked at Lil and gave her an apologetic grin. "Let me say, before you meet her—sorry for not giving you a heads-up. Just remember what you said about the first time I met the guys. Well, she's like removing the whole box at once!" He chuckled. "Brace yourself, she's a bit high strung."

Lil smiled and admitted, "I heard you on the phone with her. I'm as ready as I'll ever be."

"Little minx," he teased. "You could have said. I've been a nervous wreck you were going to give me a good thrashing."

"Oh, you're not out of the woods by a long shot, mister."

They laughed as they looked to the other side of the street.

She watched Sloan waving energetically at them as she and Lee waited to cross the street. The street was so narrow that the cars had to move slowly as they passed each other giving Lil enough time to check her out. Her spine stiffened as she drew herself up straighter, squaring her shoulders, as though readying herself for a battle. Her eyes quickly looked her up and down as she thought, *She's at least as tall as me; her shape is to die for. Her hair is totally different than mine. Hers lies just above her shoulders. Okay, hers is in style as well as elegant and glamorous. And damn! She's a true blonde. She's every bloke's dream! She could easily be a supermodel. That bright pink sun top and bellowing flowered skirt she's wearing is stylish and tasteful. It looks amazing on her!*

When it was clear to cross, Sloan let out an unladylike, high-pitched squeal of delight as she raced toward HT, her hair flying behind her.

Lil's heart was about to pound out of her chest as she got closer at seeing how gorgeous she really was. Her skin was the color of fresh cream, and she had perfectly pink cheeks and lips just like a beautiful porcelain doll. Her eyes stood out the most; they were big and a beautiful shade of blue. They shone like polished sapphires. *Bloody hell! She's gorgeous*, she thought, feeling a pang of disappointment.

"Here we go!" HT said, squeezing Lil's hand before dropping it to catch Sloan.

"Harry!" Sloan shrieked, flinging herself into his open arms. "I've missed you. It's been two whole weeks."

"I've missed you too," HT said laughing as they hugged tightly.

Lil forced a smile and raised her chin a tad as she took a couple of steps sideways, giving them more space and to compose herself. She was feeling sick from the way HT was gushing over her. She was struck by a curious sense of possession, as she thought, *He's mine, bitch, back off!* She quickly turned her head, *Where the bloody hell did that come from?* not liking what she was thinking or how she was feeling; it wasn't like her at all. She decided to focus on Lee. He was as tall as HT; his sandy brown hair was cut short and stylishly swept back from his face, showing warm brown eyes. He smiled. She smiled back as she thought, *He's very attractive.* "Hi, Lee," she greeted. "Nice to meet you. HT has told me a lot about you. I feel like I know you already."

"Great to finally meet you," he replied as he moved forward. He gave her a quick brotherly hug and stepped back a little. "I feel like I already know you. You're all I've been hearing about since he met you!"

Lil felt a rush of excitement hearing that HT had really talked about her. "All good I hope."

He wiggled his hand. "Aww, so-so," he teased, making her chuckle. "Sloan and I were beginning to think Harry had lost it and you were a figment of his imagination. Now, I see why he's been keeping you to himself."

"Don't start that already," HT said as he stepped forward to give him the handshake and a guy hug. They laughed as they slapped each other on the back. "You all right, bro?" he asked as he stepped next to Lil.

"For sure, mate," replied Lee.

"Hi, Lil. I'm Sloan, Harry's other best mate since grade school." She stepped up, giving Lil a quick hug. "Oh wait, it's HT now."

Lil felt a jolt of pleasure hearing "best mates since grade school." She was relieved, not caring it shouldn't have mattered in the least what their relationship was. "Hi, Sloan"—she returned her hug with a smile—"nice to meet you."

Sloan said stepping back. "I like 'HT.' It suits him now. I've told him he's changed for the good since he's moved!"

"Don't even go there again," HT said with a mock frown, making her grin. "So have you heard anything yet?"

"Nada," Sloan said, shrugging her shoulders, and patted the pocket on her skirt. "Still waiting on that big phone call."

"You'll get it," Lee said confidently. "You're too good not to."

"Yeah, no doubt you're the best!" HT agreed. He looked at Lil. "She's waiting to hear today about a job at the theater here as an assistant to the wardrobe director." He looked back at Sloan and added, "Which she is going to get with no problem because she's the best makeup artist and clothes designer there is."

"I'll second that," Lee said nodding.

"I don't care if you're my best mates and have to say that I'm still going to accept the compliment," said Sloan laughing, making her eyes seem even more blue and beautiful. She slipped her arm through Lil's. "Let's walk this way toward the music shop. They always go there first; it's their favorite. We can chat while they drool over the guitars. I want to hear all the gossip on him! And, I'll fill you in on a thing or two!"

"Oh no!" HT groaned, making a face.

Lil chuckled and didn't try to pull her arm away as they strolled off down the street.

HT and Lee fell in behind them. "Just know whatever you hear is a load of rubbish," whined HT.

"Which one of us are you talking to?" asked Sloan over her shoulder.

"Both," he replied making them laugh.

While the guys were in the music shop Sloan and Lil kept up a constant flow of laughter and chatter standing outside waiting on them. It didn't take long for Sloan to win Lil over with her bubbly personality and charm.

When HT and Lee exited the store, HT couldn't hide his relief at seeing them getting along so well. "I'm glad to see that," he said looking over at Lee. He glanced over Lee's shoulder and saw Jayden about a third of the way down the block. He quickly stepped back between two buildings almost like he didn't want HT to see him. "What the hell," he muttered.

"You okay?" asked Lee, seeing the look on his face.

"Yeah, I just saw somebody I'm not real fond of," he replied still looking up the street. He then thought, *Something just isn't right about that bloke.*

Sloan looked up seeing them. "It's about time. Come on, Lil. It's our turn now. Let's hit the charity shops; they're my favorite!"

"Aww man." HT and Lee groaned in unison.

Lil chuckled.

Sloan stopped at the corner. "If we go straight, there're three shops. If we turn, there's only two, but there's a fantastic coffee shop that specializes in tea. I bet you're ready for a tea, right?"

Lil looked over her shoulder at HT. He shrugged as he gave her a little wink. She playfully rolled her eyes and then looked at Sloan. "Yes, I would love a tea."

"Right then, let's get a move on and get you tea," said Sloan as they turned and walked down the street chatting away.

Lil could tell Sloan knew her charity shops. She had her poking and digging around in bins and crates to find all kinds of hidden treasures. HT and Lee happily waited outside, talking about what songs they were going to start with the next day at band practice. They were happy Sloan had someone else to drag inside and didn't say a word when they would come out with bags for them to carry. After hitting half a dozen charity shops, HT and Lee were loaded down with bags. HT would just chuckle and wink at Lil when she handed him more bags to carry. He knew Sloan and Lee were both watching him intently, trying to see a sign of how he really felt about Lil. He knew they would find out knowing him so well, but he was trying to prolong it as best he could.

A few hours later, after a few teas and a lot of shopping, HT called out to Sloan before they reached the clock tower, "Take a left on Frodsham Street. I want Lil to check out that bloke's camera shop. He must have every camera and lens ever made in there."

Lil just chuckled to herself knowing exactly what was in there. Jacob was going to be surprised seeing her on a Saturday, though.

When they reached the shop, HT held open the door as Lee and Sloan went in. He smiled at Lil as she followed them. "You're going to love this place! I couldn't wait for you to see it."

Jacob hearing the bell, looked up and saw Lil. He was in his sixties but didn't move like it, the way he ran over to her. He gave her a big bear hug as he said, "It's about time. I was beginning to think you forgot about me!"

Lil laughed, hugging him back. "Not a chance. I've just been really busy."

"JR said you have been. He was in earlier and said you would be in. I've been waiting. I got that new camera in you wanted to look at. You're going to love it. It's the top of the line. Any professional photographer worth his grain of salt uses it."

"Great, I can't wait to see it!"

"Well, come on then. I have it behind the counter!" he said all excited as he ran back around the counter. He looked over at HT and Lee and chuckled. "You boys look loaded down. Just put all those bags on the counter there if you want."

HT sat the bags down before he walked toward Lil. He merely raised his eyebrows, giving her the look that made her insides melt as he walked toward her.

She felt her heart jump. "I never lied"—she chuckled—"I've just never rode the bus here. Besides, we didn't have our rule then."

"Uh, huh," he said, clearly amused by the way her eyes twinkled. He lightly tapped his fingertip to her nose. "Still a little dodgy I think, but I'm going to let you use that excuse this time. But no using it again."

"Fair enough." Lil replied with a little laugh as they walked over to the counter.

Sloan's and Lee's eyes darted between Lil and HT as Lil introduced HT to Jacob. Sloan looked at Lee. "What the bloody hell was that all about? They have rules?"

Lee shrugged. "Sounds like it."

"He's acting a little weird, right?" she asked.

"Oh yeah, he's being really weird!" Lee replied with a nod.

"I think he's dropping his guard," Sloan said, looking back at HT. "Every time he sees me watching them, he turns away."

"Oh, he knows we're watching," Lee said grinning. "I can't get a read on him or her."

"I know. She's one cool cucumber." Sloan nodded. "I do like her though. What about you?"

"I do," said Lee as Sloan's phone rang.

She cheerfully answered it. "Sloan here, what's up?" After a second she said calmly, "I'll see you tomorrow. Oh no, it will have to be Monday. Great, see you then!" She let out a little squeal as Lee hugged her.

HT hurried over giving her a hug, knowing she had gotten the job. "Congrats! Let's go celebrate, besides I'm ready to eat," he added with a grin.

Lee nodded picking up Sloan's bags. "Me too."

"We should head over to Gino's before it gets too busy," Sloan said.

"Hey, Lil," HT called out. "Get a move on. Sloan got the job, and we want to celebrate!"

"That's awesome!" Lil said as she ran over giving Sloan a big hug. She turned back to Jacob smiling. "Of course you know I want it!"

Jacob nodded with a chuckle. "Go with your mates and celebrate. I'll get it boxed up and give JR a call. Leave your shopping bags here, too."

"Thanks, Jacob. See you next week," Lil said as they went out the door.

They headed to HT's favorite restaurant for their weekly ritual for dinner—pizza at Gino's. A sexy, blonde, big-busted waitress approached, wearing a skintight T-shirt that clung to her curves.

"You just made her day, HT," Sloan teased. She looked over at Lil. "Karen has been after HT for the last year."

Karen smiled at HT and said in a sexy voice, "There's my favorite customer. I've been waiting; you're late."

HT basically ignored Karen and said, "We'll take our regular table in the back." He rested his hand on the small of Lil's back as he led her to the table.

Sloan and Lee exchanged stunned looks. They knew that sort of touch and never expected it out of him. It was intimate, claiming ownership, letting whoever was watching know "She's mine." They couldn't keep from staring, watching HT pull out a chair for Lil and then pull his over beside her. He draped his arm along the back of hers when he sat down. Lil didn't think anything of it because it was something he did all the time when they sat together.

Sloan caught Lee's eye before they sat down. He grinned, and she chuckled.

Karen walked up. "I see I have competition," she teased with a big smile at HT. She turned to Lil and gave her the evil eye and said sweetly, "You two look cute together. So how long have you been an item?"

"Oh, were just mates," said Lil, returning her fake, sweet smile.

Karen smiled thinly and gave her a "yeah, right" look. She quickly looked back at HT with a flirty smile. "Same as always?"

HT never looked her way. "Give us a sec," he said not taking his eyes off Lil's. "Pizza okay or you want to see a menu?"

"Pizza sounds brilliant."

He nodded with a grin. "Red wine or tea?"

"Wine sounds great."

"Bring us the usual," he said to Karen, still not looking her way and focusing all of his attention on Lil.

Karen sneered as she turned and stomped off.

Sloane cast Lee a quick glance to see if he was seeing what she was. She could tell he was and leaned over and whispered, "He never gave Karen a second thought. He always flirts with her, and when has he ever asked a girl what she wants to eat or drink?"

"He starts feeding her, I'm outta here," Lee whispered back with a little chuckle.

Sloan laughed and said under her breath, "Well, there's the answer we've been looking for all day; everything makes sense now. That's why he seems so different, more mature, and happier than we've ever seen him. He's in love with her!"

"I don't know if he's in love, but he has definitely been hooked!" replied Lee.

They stared at one another in disbelief and then snickered, giving each other high fives.

HT glanced over seeing them and their goofy grins. "What?"

"Oh, nothing," Sloan said smiling.

"We just heard the fat lady singing," said Lee.

"Huh?" said HT, giving them a weird look. "I'm not getting it," he added frowning and turned back to Lil.

Lil wasn't paying them any attention. She was listening to Karen whispering so that only she could hear, as she sat a wine glass down in front of her. "Ooh, you're a clever one playing hard to get. A little warning, bitch, he's mine." Karen straightened up, putting on her biggest fake smile. "Be right back with the wine."

When Karen brought the wine, HT filled his glass, passed it to Lil, and then took hers to fill it for himself. Karen quickly grabbed it and said, "Oh dear, that one is cracked let me get you another one."

Lil thought, *Cracked? Right! Stupid cow. Hard telling what you did to it.*

When dinner was over Lil went to the loo, finally giving Sloan and Lee a chance to say something.

"Well, well, I guess the mighty *really* have fallen," said Lee mockingly, as he leaned his chair back, folding his hands across his chest.

"Okay, what's the story?" asked Sloan.

He knew what she was asking, "What? We're just mates."

"Just mates!" Sloan repeated sarcastically. "Nooo"—she pointed to herself and then him and added—"we're just mates. You don't look at me like that. Try again!"

"I told you—there isn't anything going on, so drop it," he said, trying to sound convincing.

"Not a chance," she said, slowly shaking her head. "Why the *we're-just-mates* rubbish? Now get to talking before she comes back because I'm not shutting up until I hear."

"Bloody hell, you're not going to let this drop are you?" said HT grimly.

"Nope!" she said, still shaking her head and wearing one of her determined looks he knew so well.

"Fine," he said, throwing his hands up in frustration. "I'm crazy about her," he admitted reluctantly. "You happy now?" And added before they could speak. "She doesn't know, and I want to keep it that way, so this stays between us!"

"Why?" asked Sloan.

"Because if she finds out my true feelings, she'll kick my stupid arse to the curb!"

"Why are you stupid?" asked Sloan with a scrunched up face.

"She laid the ground rules from the start not to go there. She said she liked me too much, and it would turn our friendship to rubbish. She said it would end bad and blah, blah, blah and so on. She pulled the we're-better-off-just-being-mates rubbish that I usually do. I'm her best mate, nothing more! And my dumb arse has fallen head over apple cart in love with her!"

"I knew you were in love with her!" Sloan said happily, clapping her hands. "That's great. I love her! She's perfect for you!"

"Sloan, I'm being serious here. No interfering. If you do, and she kicks me to the curb, I'll never forgive you."

Lee softly whistled. "Wow, bro, you do have it bad. You're screwed!"

"Cheers!" said HT sarcastically.

"Hey, don't cheers me," Lee said with a chuckle. "I was feeling for you. I've been there. If you remember, it did my head in chasing after someone who didn't want me."

"That's because she's mental," said Sloan. "You're too good for her anyway."

Lee grinned and gave her a wink and then turned to HT. "Maybe I don't feel for you! All you did was tell me to get over it and then bust my nads about how big of a pussy I was being."

HT saw Lil coming back to the table. He lowered his voice so that she wouldn't overhear him. "You were, the way you carried on like some whipped pup! You won't be seeing me acting like that!"

"Un-huh, seems you're already doing it!" said Lee bursting out laughing.

HT stood as Lil came up. "Thanks, bro," he said cheerfully, taking Lil's hand. Lee was as tight as they came, and HT was going to hit him where it hurt. "Lee just said dinner was on him. Wasn't that nice of him? Let's go outside and get some air while he pays the check."

"Thanks for dinner, Lee," said Lil over her shoulder as HT took her hand and pulled her toward the door.

"Sure, no problem. I'll pay," Lee grumbled as he and Sloan stood. "It'll just take my whole bloody paycheck. After all it was HT who ordered an extra-large pizza just for himself!"

HT turned at the door and called out, "Don't forget the tip."

"Cheers, bro!" Lee called out disgusted. "And that comes from the bottom of my heart!"

HT laughed as they went out the door.

After the last of the hugs and exchanges of good nights were given back at the old cinema, HT said, "I'll crawl in the back; I ate too much pizza," and quickly moved forward to open the front car door for Lil. Lee and Sloan snickered. After she got in, he closed it; he then shot them a nasty look. "Oh sod it off!" he hissed as he opened the back door and hopped in. They laughed as he closed it. In the car he half stretched out on the leather seat and moaned as he unfastened his jeans.

"Too much pizza," Lil said looking at JR.

He chuckled as he drove off.

"So how was it?" JR asked Lil. "You have fun?"

"I did," Lil gushed. "Lee is great, and Sloan is amazing. I can't wait until you meet her. She's coming over tomorrow with Lee. She's funny and smart. I can't believe we have so much in common. I just know we're going to be best besties for life. And oh my God, JR, she is gorgeous!"

HT said rubbing his overfull stomach, "Oh, he saw. He couldn't take his eyes off her in the restaurant! Ain't that right, bro?" He snickered as he sat up. "I've been waiting for Lil to tell me, but since she hasn't, I'm tired of waiting, so I'll ask. Just what the bloody hell is Mr. C. into anyways that Lil has you as her bodyguard?"

"Just because I wanted pizza, I'm her bodyguard?" asked JR trying not to laugh.

"Yeah, that's why. Give me a break; everyone has one. I think it's more than just a coincidence that Joe never seems to let Moms, Grammy, and Abs out of his sight in the bakery. Not even going to talk about Jeb and Sam always out front acting like they are cleaning the windows and working on the five feet of lawn that's out there and Mack, who is in and out of the bakery all the time and stopping in for dinner and to watch the telly. He's more of a fixture at the house than I am, and that's saying something. Bill is Mr. C.'s, like he needs one. Then there's the no letting me meet little man till Mr. C. got back. And there's little man himself, who has two Cujos right on his heels all the time. And Ben, the gardener, who wouldn't know one flower from the other, not far from him when he's outside if Mr. C.'s not around, which isn't very often."

JR started laughing. "Wait till I tell Ben you called him a gardener."

"I was trying to make a point. No way anybody could think that bloke is a gardener," said HT grinning. "He has bigger muscles than all of you and meaner looking than Joe! Is Mr. C. in the mob or what? If I had to guess, I would put my money on you guys being MI6 or some kind of secret agents."

Lil and JR exchanged a surprised sideways look. Lil had to chuckle as JR quickly said, "You have a very clever imagination; I'm sure you would be great in espionage, double-oh-not-seven."

"Nice one," HT muttered, being sarcastic. He knew there was something going on besides the security company; he just hadn't figured out exactly what, yet. "Oh by the way, I saw Jayden today. Either you suck at your job and don't know he's stalking Lil or he works for you. I go with, he works for you!"

"You saw him?" asked JR surprised.

"Yeah, when I came out of the music store."

"Sweet. I just won a hundred pounds." JR chuckled.

Lil twisted in her seat to look at HT. She rolled her eyes. "Remember how I said the guys bet on everything?"

HT nodded.

"Well"—she pointed her thumb at JR—"He and Jay are the worst. They made a bet last week. Don't have a clue about what, but they dragged me into it by having me wait to tell you Jay is Aunt Abs and Uncle Joe's son. I consider him another pain-in-the-arse brother like this one!"

"But I'm her favorite." JR chuckled.

Relief flowed through HT as it registered he wasn't competition after all but hissed under his breath in frustration. "Buggar, I knew something wasn't right; I just didn't let myself see it." He glanced to the rearview mirror at JR.

JR had a smirk on his face watching him. "What's wrong, bro, all that pizza backing up?"

"You really are a total wanker, aren't you?" HT remarked dryly.

"Harsh, but true!" JR said with a shrug. "Made you come to your senses though, didn't it?"

"Yes, but you let me think that rubbish all week!"

"I know. That was a bonus!"

"Cheers!" muttered HT.

JR laughed.

"Ohh—kay," Lil said stretching out the word. "I know I'm missing something here. Care to enlighten me? What's going on?"

"Just a little pay back over the golf thing," said JR still chuckling.

Lil made a face and turned in JR's direction. "That's rubbish, but I'm probably better off not knowing. What was the bet anyways?"

"I bet Jay that HT would catch on that he was following him all week. You almost cost me some money," he said looking at HT in the mirror again. "Tonight was the deadline."

"I wish I had," muttered HT and complained. "With all the abuse you blokes put me through to be part of this family, I think you should at least let me in on what's going on with all the guards!"

"It's not really a big deal HT; it's just complicated," said Lil.

"Oh no, that's an excuse, not an answer. So tell me and let me decide."

"Fine, but you're going to think we're a bunch of loonies."

"Ah, going to?" he said with a chuckle.

"Whatever," she said with a grin and eye roll and then began to explain. "Yes, JR is my so called bodyguard."

"Duh, I know that, but why?" he muttered.

She just gave him the look and continued, "The whole bodyguard thing goes with the family business and tradition, which Dad feels he has to follow. I didn't want or need a bodyguard. It's embarrassing. So he assigned JR, making him feel he's following tradition."

"So why and when did the tradition start?" HT asked.

"It started couple of hundred years ago. Our ancestor who started the security company had a lot of influence in the government and was really wealthy." She started to mumble, "His oldest son was kidnapped when he was ten years old while he was horseback riding, right off their own property—"

"Whoa, whoa, wait a minute! Don't start that." HT interrupted her.

Lil turned around in her seat. "What," she asked innocently, knowing she must have started mumbling.

He loved the way her chin went up whenever he called her on her mumbling. Come to think of it, he loved everything about her. "I don't want to miss a thing. I've waited months to hear this. You need to breathe in and take it slow so that I can hear actual words!" He knew as soon as the words had left his mouth he'd dropped himself in the middle of it!

Her eyebrow shot up giving him a look, making her eyes sparkle.

He chuckled recognizing her expression only too well. It was the one she had when she was going to be, well, Lil.

She took an exaggerated deep breath.

"Here we go," he said under his breath.

She began talking very slowly and acted if she was using sign language. "The tradition has been passed down in our family from generation to generation."

HT burst out laughing. "Only you would come up with that! I guess I deserved that, Ms. Smarty-Pants."

She smiled and continued, talking normally, "They got him back unharmed, but it took a toll on the family. His wife lost the baby she was carrying from all the worry and stress and was really never right after that. She always thought someone was after her kids. So that's when he decided to hire each of them a bodyguard. Then went a step farther and wanted one on all his loved ones, men he could trust and were dedicated to the job. He handpicked each and every one, choosing the best, since he had realized the kid's nanny had been in on the kidnapping."

HT let out a slow whistle.

Lil smiled and added, "He built a thriving business, the country's largest security company. Word got out, and people who needed loved ones or places protected wanted to hire them. So he put together a training camp and hand-picked every man, making sure they were loyal, honest, and respectable. His only request when he turned the company over to his oldest son, the one that was kidnapped, was that the high standards he founded the company on be maintained. He also included a provision as a tradition that all close family members would be assigned a bodyguard. He never wanted another family to live in fear and go through what he had. So, as the company was handed down, his wish has been honored."

"That's brilliant! How long has your family been their bodyguards, bro?"

"From the start," said JR. "It was one of my ancestors who became the first body-guard. He was hired to protect the little guy who was taken!"

"That is really awesome," HT said as he slowly nodded his head. "That answers the bodyguard question. Now, let's talk about why your homes and mine have more security than the Queen?"

"Really! You have to ask that knowing Dad?" Lil chuckled. "You see how he is. His excuse is that he's seen a lot of bad things over the years while taking on special security jobs. It's made him a little obsessed with keeping us safe."

"You think?" said HT, making them all laugh.

Lil looked out the window and thought she wasn't lying with what she'd said. She wasn't being dodgy breaking their rule since their rule now included anything she didn't feel bad about holding back, and she had decided anything that had to do with working with the guys fell under that. That life had nothing to do with HT. She thought telling him wasn't bad at all. *I just knew he was going to think we were a bunch of...Oh, crap!* Something JR had said set off an alarm in the back of her mind. Why was Jay following HT all week? That didn't make any sense. She thought for a second. The only reasonable conclusion she could come up with clicked into place. The bet might have been if HT saw him, but Jay didn't follow him for the bet, he was working! Dad grounded Jay and assigned him to HT! (Grounded was the term the company used when they were no longer available for fieldwork.) Hoping she was just being paranoid she turned to JR and asked under her breath, "Did Dad gro—"

"Uh-huh!" JR answered cutting her off, knowing she'd finally figured it out. "It's up to you if you want to tell him."

"Bloody hell!" she said with a little groan. "You know I have to tell him. You couldn't stop him? Never mind, stupid question. How long have you known?"

"Just this week," JR said laughing.

"Time out," said HT looking confused and not liking the last of their conversation. "I suppose that made sense to you guys, but would you want to fill me in? I'm lost here, and Lil isn't even mumbling!" he said making a joke out of it, but his stomach churned and it wasn't from the pizza.

Lil ignored him; she was beyond annoyed and deep in thought. *Bloody hell, Dad! Yeah, right, if I want to tell HT. Of course I have to tell him.* She didn't realize they were home or that a light, misty rain had started to fall until she heard HT.

"Lil, I don't know if you've noticed, but I'm standing here in the rain!" He chuckled as he held the car door open, offering a hand to help her out. His mind started racing as he thought, *I let my guard down for an instant running my mouth with JR, and now she knows how I feel! That's why she's so zoned out.* He asked with a strained laugh, "What's got you so tuned out?"

She climbed out, averting her eyes and not saying a word.

There was an enormous clap of thunder as the clouds opened up and the rain came hard.

"Bloody hell! It's coming down," yelled HT laughing as he shut the door and ran to the Cove, thinking she was right behind him. Once inside, he shook off the water and grabbed the towel on the snack bar to wipe his face. "Not too bad, just a quick little shower," he said laughing, as he turned and stopped, not seeing her.

He headed for the door as she walked in drenched. "Why didn't you run, silly? You look like a drowned rat!"

Still lost in thought she walked over to the sofa with water dripping on the floor. *What the bloody hell is going on that Dad has assigned Jay to HT? How am I going to explain this one when I don't have a clue myself? Well, everyone does love him and considers him family. But...then Dad has only known him a few months. But... then he has known Luke for a while. So, okay, maybe Dad would assign him a guard. But Jay? And Rafa was considered family being so close with Jay, and he never had anyone assigned to him! This makes no bloody sense at all!*

"Hello, you're dripping everywhere, zombie lady," joked HT.

"We need to talk," she said as she sat down.

His stomach churned again as he went into the loo grabbing a towel. He took in a couple of deep breaths, trying to calm himself as he walked over to the sofa. "What's going on? Is everything all right?" he asked in a soft tone, as he sat on the edge of the sofa beside her.

She grumbled, "It was perfect up until a few minutes ago. I've got something to tell you."

"I'm listening. Nothing bad, I hope!"

"Well, it depends on how you take it. Actually, it's kind of your fault." She decided to go with the family thing.

He slightly winced as he started to wipe the rain off her. "I'm not liking the sound of that. What's my fault? What have I done now?" he asked, with a small smile. He heard his heart beat in his chest as he waited anxiously for her answer. There was a long pause, making him even more nervous, but he was ready to come clean if she had figured it out.

She raised her brow when she looked at him. "You know how everybody loves you and thinks of you as family?"

He gave her a quick nod and broke into a grin, loving the words and thought, *Okay, maybe I'm not ready*. "And?" he asked, when she paused again.

"I don't want to freak you out," she tried to smile without success. "It's sort of weird."

"I'm use to sort of weird when it comes to this family," he replied with a chuckle as his heart started beating steady again. "I guess you have to be a little weird to fit in."

"So what does that say about you?"

"I guess that I'm brilliant at being a little weird," he replied with a chuckle. "Remember? I'm a nerd; I love golf. So come on, out with it."

"Right then. I'm just going to come out with it. Jay is your bloody bodyguard!"

For a moment he blinked at her trying to take in what she said. Then it clicked. "Really?"

She nodded with a cute face. "I hope you're not mad."

"Don't be daft." He chuckled. "It's fine. You just threw me there for a sec. Is it like all the time? You know like JR is with you? But that's silly; why would I need one?"

Her chin went up a little thinking the same thing, not convinced about the whole, him-being-family, excuse. She got a little anxious knowing he was about to ask a million questions and had a way of getting things out of her, so she needed to start explaining as best she could. She started mumbling, "I'm sorry. I would have told you if I knew. I just figured it out in the car. JR said I didn't have to tell you. As if! Like I wouldn't tell you." Without pausing for breath, she went on, "Dad never said Jay was brought home to be your bodyguard, probably because he knew I would blow a gasket! Bad enough I have to have one. But then he's hung up on the whole family-honor, bodyguard-tradition rubbish, so I shouldn't be surprised. Everyone considers you family now. Yes, to answer your question, I'm afraid so. I hope you can live with him always being around."

"I'll get use—"

She couldn't be interrupted and continued mumbling on. "I went through a phase when I was thirteen complaining to Dad that I didn't want a watchdog and how I felt like JR or Jay was always up my bum! I paid for that. I never saw them unless it was at dinner or a family thing."

She paused.

He opened his mouth to speak but closed it knowing she was on a roll and just reloading air.

She never missed a beat and kept on going. "Well, of course, I hated it because I really do love them being around, but Dad being Dad had to teach me a lesson about pride and respect. He told me he was sticking to his decision, and I had to wait at least three months before they could hang out with me again." She chuckled. "I made it nine whole days."

"Nine whole days," he repeated with amusement, enjoying the different expressions crossing her face.

"It's not funny; it seemed like forever."

"Oh, you heard me that time?"

"Don't be daft. I always hear you."

"Of course you do." He chuckled as she mumbled on.

"Like I said, I knew JR and Jay had made a bet last week, but I let them know I wasn't happy about it. It's only going to get worse now that you're one of them. But then, you're just like them, the way you and JR are always winding each other up. He's just like JR; they are thick as thieves. I'm sure you're going to love Jay. You liked him when you met him, right?" She stopped and gave him an expectant look. "Right?"

He realized she had stopped and avoided the question because no, he didn't like the tosser thinking he was competition, so he joked as his eyebrows rose. "Oh! Am I supposed to reply? Are you done? Or did you just run out of things to say? If I had to guess, I would say you're just reloading air again."

She gave him one of her sarcastic looks. "You liked him when you met him, right?"

He said in a teasing tone. "I take it I can answer."

"Come on, HT. Be serious," she said with a frown.

He shrugged not wanting to lie. "I didn't get to talk to him much. I'm sure I will once—"

"Of course you will," she said cutting him off. "And another thing—" she mumbled on.

"You're fired up tonight! Glad I didn't have much to say." He chuckled. He leaned back against the sofa and stretched his legs out in front of him. He stacked his hands behind his head and let out a little moan as he faked a yawn like he was bored to death.

She stopped. "Sorry, am I boring you?"

"Who you? Naw." He grinned lazily, crossing one ankle over the other. "No place I'd rather be. You are doing my head in with all that babbling though," he teased.

"Again, I mumble, not babble."

He said under his breath, "Still does my head in."

"Heard that, Mr. Smarty-Pants. So like I was trying to explain...Jay won't interfere in whatever you're doing, which basically just means that no matter what you do or say around him, it stays between you and him—"

He interrupted her throwing his hand up. "Hold on before you launch into another round. You mean him and JR?"

She rolled her eyes playfully. "Yes, that's what I've been saying; it's a given!"

All of sudden he realized that since the three of them were so close they might discuss him with her. "They share everything with you, too?" he asked getting a little nervous.

"Don't be daft. They would never repeat anything you say or do with me or anyone else, which includes Dad and Papa. They take that honor code thing very seriously...it's like an unwritten, unspoken law. Sharing everything is just a thing between them. They've been that way since the day they could talk. Wait until you see them together. They finish each other's sentences or don't say anything at all knowing what the other one is thinking. It can drive you mental trying to have a conversation with them."

HT smiled, feeling relief.

"Like I was saying, they've never told on me and never interfered with stopping me when I was up to no good," she said with a little chuckle. "But, I won't go into that!"

"Whoa, whoa, whoa," he said. "Let's say we *do* go into that for a second. Stop you from doing what?"

"Just silly things."

"Such as?"

She made a tsk sound. "I used to sneak out."

"To be with Fish Face?"

She frowned. "Nooo. Now, where was I?"

"Oh no, you're not leaving it there, and give my ears a break. I can't handle any more of that mumbling."

She huffed and rolled her eyes.

"That's not going to work either. Come on, out with it. You know I'm not going to let it drop, so let's hear it."

"It's really nothing, and you're going to laugh at me."

"No, I won't. Tell me. Why did you sneak out?"

"You better not laugh."

"Bloody hell, Lil! Just tell me already!" He chuckled. "Blimey, you're making my head spin tonight from trying to keep up with you!"

"Fine, I snuck out to take photos."

He struggled to maintain a straight face, trying his best not to laugh. "Really? Just to take photos? Really?" he repeated, with a sound in his voice that sounded like stifled laughter.

Lil nodded. "Seriously, that's it!"

He wanted to laugh. It took a lot of restraint not to, and he managed for about ten seconds before he burst out laughing.

"Harry Thomas, it isn't funny."

"Sure, sure not funny," he said, doubling over with laughter.

She started hitting him with a pillow. "See! I knew you would laugh. It really was a big deal. Sometimes I barely made it in the house before Dad got up. He would have been furious if he found out and taken this place away from me for sure."

He held up his hands, protecting himself. "Stop, Stop," he said in surrender, struggling to regain control of his laughter. When he did, he couldn't resist teasing her. "Sometimes you're a little strange. Do you know that? Risking your neck for a great party or a bloke, I can see, but just to take photos? What a nerd!" He roared with laughter again.

Lil started hitting him again as she laughed. "You're just as big a nerd, Mr. Golf Man! And if I had gotten caught, JR and Jay would have been in more trouble than me…Proving my point—they never interfere and can be trusted!"

"Okay, okay, stop the abuse," he said laughing, holding his arms up before he grabbed the pillow from her. "I'm sorry. I really did try not to laugh."

"I know. You're forgiven," she replied with a chuckle. "Now, about Sloan," she added with a raised brow.

"Buggar," he teased. "I thought I dodged that bullet."

She playfully swatted his arm. "Why didn't you tell me about her?"

"Ouch!" he said in mock pain, rubbing his arm. "You sure are abusive tonight!"

"Quit stalling. Out with it."

"I see Ms. Bossy Pants just reported for duty."

"Do I need to grab that pillow again?" she teased, acting as if she was reaching for it.

"No, no." He chuckled, pulling her back. "I've had enough abuse tonight, thank you very much!"

"Right then." She giggled. "Let's hear it. I love her. She's amazing!"

"That's why." He grinned. "I wanted you to form your own opinion of her when you met. I was hoping you would like her. Lee and I have been lucky we've had her in our lives. She's grounded us a lot over the years."

"Aww, that's sweet. She's the lucky one, if you ask me."

All he could think of was taking her into his arms and kissing her silly. He realized he was staring and quickly looked away before she knew what he was thinking. He picked up the remote. "You won't think I'm too sweet when I don't let you snuggle while we're watching Jimmy. Your clothes are still wet." His smile was teasing as he leaned back against the sofa.

She jumped up giggling. "You know. I would really think you're sweet if I have a hot cup of tea waiting on me after I change."

He stood up grinning as he put down the remote. "What kind? My lady?"

"You pick. You always make the perfect one," she said over her shoulder going into the loo.

He called back. "I'm making it already; no need to keep blowing smoke up my arse!" He heard her laugh as he went to the stove.

She came out after changing into a pair of sweats and one of his T-shirts. "Let's watch *Gavin and Tracy* before Jimmy."

"Sure. Smithy makes me laugh," HT replied, setting her tea on the table before he sat down. "That Corden bloke is hilarious. I bet he's a riot at a party!"

"What's with you and guys named Jimmy?" she asked with a chuckle as she sat beside him. "Oh, by the way, did you know Fallon's middle name is Thomas?"

HT laughed as he picked up the remote. "No, I didn't."

"Who knows? Maybe you'll be on his show one day. Wouldn't that be funny if he started doing skits, acting like you on his show? He would be a brilliant Harry!"

HT laughed shaking his head. "Like that could ever happen."

"What? I'm being serious here." She smiled.

"I know, and I love you for it. Even if we make it on *Brit Idol* and pull off the miracle of a lifetime and win, we will be lucky to have this country know us, let alone some yank in the States who's fast becoming the best talk show host ever!"

"I don't think you give yourself enough credit."

"I think you give me too much credit."

Lil rolled her eyes and mumbled, "You just don't have a clue how talented you really are! You're going to make it big. The whole world is going to know who you are one day, and we both know I'm always right!"

HT grunted. "More like you just mumble everything to death until I give up and agree that you're right!"

"I do not," Lil protested and chuckled. "Okay, maybe I do, but it works!"

"Drink your tea." He chuckled.

# CHAPTER 17

The end of summer came too quickly for Lil's liking, but it had been the happiest one of her life. Over the summer, she and HT hung out with Lee, Sloan, and the twins as much as their free time would allow. The six of them really clicked and created a tight bond over the summer. The guys practiced at least three times a week, sometimes at Lee's, but most of the time it was at HT's so that they could swim afterward. Sundays, after practice, they all went to Lil's for the family barbecue, and it wasn't long before they joined in on Raif's gettin'-loose nights. Lil had been extra busy trying to keep up with her photo sessions. Everyone was wanting photos done, knowing she was taking a break once school started. HT, JR, and Jayden took bets on how long that would last. HT almost always helped her in the darkroom. He even began spending a lot of nights sleeping in the Cove saying he loved the bed and could write better in it. He left out the part about feeling closer to her there.

Lil was still oblivious to her true feelings for him. She had them buried deep and had herself convinced what they shared was because they had a special bond and had become the best of mates, just like she said they would.

HT, on the other hand, knew he loved her more than ever, so much that he couldn't think straight at times. He never wanted to be away from her.

It was the first Sunday of September, and the guys had entered the Battle of the Bands in Chester. The family wanted to go to cheer them on. The guys even skipped golf.

Lil and HT were in the Cove trying to pass time until it was time to head to Chester. They were doing a little cleaning to take their minds off being stressed. HT, about performing, and Lil, about meeting all the new kids in the morning when school started. She finished cleaning her darkroom and was making tea when HT came out of the Lion's Room carrying an armful of her photo albums.

"I'm going to put these back on the shelves I'm not using," he said as he walked to the bookshelves. He stacked them and decided to look through one and walked to the sofa to sit. After looking at a few pages, he glanced over at her. "Remember the day we met, when I was trying to impress you that I lived in Chester?"

"When you thought I had never ventured out of the village?" said Lil. She asked, "You want a brew?"

"Nah, I'm good. Don't want to be like you and have to pee every five minutes," he teased.

"Wow, you're a bigger tosser now than back then," she said with a chuckle, taking a mug out of the cabinet.

He just laughed knowing she would have a comeback. "Is there any part of the world you haven't traveled to?"

"I have traveled a lot, but most of those places were just quick stops when I was with Dad on business. I didn't see much while I was there, but the things I did see were amazing. I want to travel the world at my own pace while capturing it on film. No deadlines, no commitments. Some documentaries can take weeks to do."

His stomach dropped at the thought of her going off weeks at a time, without him. "Whoa, wait a minute. What about our plan together? You can't be dumping me for weeks, not even for days. We're a team, remember?"

"Don't be silly, HT. We will always be together, but we won't be joined at the hip. Our careers aren't always going to have us in the same place."

"We should make it a rule that we only take on jobs that do. I can't be doing this music thing without you! So we should say, no more than a few days apart at the most. You know, just in case our lives happen to go a little crazy."

"We can cross that bridge when we get there," she replied and thought to herself that when she started working with the guys she would be gone for more than a few days.

"I'm just saying it could cause some trouble, so we should make it a rule now. We don't want to take each other for granted and end up growing apart," he grunted.

She didn't know what to say, so she didn't say anything as she poured water into the teapot.

He pointed to a couple of pictures. "I see that it's the duke's plane you're always on because of the Highcliff Coat of Arms emblem. Just how close are Mr. C and the duke? I haven't seen him once at the castle, and we hang out there a lot." He saw a photo he didn't like and didn't wait for an answer. "Who's this bloke? You look really tight; you're all smiles and have your arms wrapped around each other. He looks really familiar." He paused, looking at the photo closer, then said looking at Lil, "I can see he's Mack's son. Looks like he spit him out!"

"Yeah, he can't deny him that's for sure." She let out a little sigh as she walked toward the sofa. She chewed on the inside of her cheek for a moment and then opened her mouth and shut it when HT burst out laughing.

"What?" she asked, pretending like she didn't know.

"Don't what me!" He chuckled. "You tell on yourself before you start that mumbling of yours. With the look on your face, I'm sure you're going to tell me something about him that you have been holding back."

She sat beside him. "Maybe I won't tell you about him now, Mr. Smarty-Pants."

"Yes, you will," he said, giving her a quick one-armed hug still chuckling.

She grinned rolling her eyes and said, "That photo is of Anthony, my partner in crime! He's the one who shut the gate that first day we met in the maze." She looked at him with a raised brow, waiting for it to register.

"Okay, by that look I know I need to connect the dots; that's all I'm getting." After a few seconds of thinking about it, his mouth dropped open. "No bloody way. You said that he was the duke's son. So knowing how this family works, that means Mack is Edward the bloody duke!" he stated shocked. "That's why the ball cap and sunglasses when he's in the bakery—in case he's recognized and why he goes by Mack."

"Really?" she teased. "Imagine that!"

"Now who's being the smarty-pants?"

She chuckled and said, "I can add more to the story of why we moved here now if you want."

"What kind of daft question is that? Of course I want!"

"You want long or short version?"

"Long. Keep my mind off the contest later. But no mumbling; I'm too nervous to follow it."

"Not making any promises; I'm nervous myself, and I still don't like talking about it. Well, the sad part anyway." She took a breath and started. "Dad and Uncle Eddie, whom you now know we call Mack in public, go way back."

HT raised his eyebrows, and Lil smiled seeing his expression. "Sorry, he's not my uncle, but I do think of him as if he were. He and Dad feel like they're brothers. Their fathers were really close, so they were practically raised together, like JR and Jay. Our families go back for generations; there's always been a strong bond that has linked my family ancestors with the duke's. It has to do with the security company. Plus, like I said before, Granddad took care of the old Duke's finances like Dad handles all of Uncle Eddie's. I'd say Dad knows more about how much Uncle Eddie's worth and what he owns than he does."

HT grunted. "I read somewhere he's like a gazillionaire."

Lil just chuckled. "To us he's just Ed, or Mack, as you know him. Anyway, their Dads were the best of mates. They both became widowers at an early age. They didn't believe in nannies, so they always had Dad and Uncle Eddie with them, and they became really close. They stayed between here and the castle." She started to mumble; her words came out fast. "Then after uni, Dad met Mum. Uncle Eddie met Aunt Victoria, Mum's lifelong best friend. She was amazing. It was like I had two Mums well, okay, three with Grammy...no make that four with Aunt Abs. Anyway..."

HT cleared his throat softly to get her attention.

"Sorry," she chuckled and continued trying not to mumble. "Anyway, Mum and Victoria who both hated all that society stuff had each other to lean on. Actually, Mum was okay with living in London longer than she and Dad had planned, because she had Victoria." She sighed. "Then one morning Victoria was hit by a car. She passed instantly."

HT whistled softly and muttered, "Bloody hell."

Lil nodded sadly. "Everyone was devastated, to say the least. Mum couldn't quit thinking of how it could easily have been Anthony and me with her. We had all crossed that street together to get to the park a thousand times. She wanted to get us away from London; plus, Dad didn't want Mum to have to deal with all the questions and fake pity from of all those society people she hated. So we all came here and never went back."

"What about Anthony? Is he still a tosser? Where's he at?"

"I never said he was a tosser," Lil said laughing. "He was just a brat for a while is all. He went to the States to visit with Victoria's family just before you moved here."

"He's the one your uncle Carl is with, then?"

Lil nodded with a smile, going all warm that he even remembered that.

"Have you been to the States?"

Lil shook her head. "Actually, I haven't. I've always wanted to go."

"Me too. We should go together."

"We will. I'm sure I'll be filming your music videos there one day!"

"There goes that imagination of yours again!" he said with a chuckle.

"You kno—"

"Yeah, yeah, yeah, you're always right," he said laughing.

"I am when it comes to that," she said grinning. "Now, back to Anthony. What I'm about to tell you stays between us."

"Really? You still have to say that?" he asked with a hurt look.

"Don't be daft, of course I don't. I just mean no one knows this but me and now you. So when Anthony finally tells Uncle Eddie, and the family blows, we play dumb."

"Gotcha." He grinned and winked.

Lil smiled; her whole body tingled, but she ignored it and went on. "He met a girl and has fallen madly in love. He told me he's staying over there, but Uncle Eddie thinks he's coming home next week"

"Whoa, she must be one hell of a girl."

"She sounds like it, the way he goes on about her. I can't wait to meet her and you him. So anyway, everyone walked on eggshells around Anthony after moving here." She started to mumble again, "We all let him get away with everything because he started playing the Mum-passed-away card. Uncle Eddie was the worst. He let him get away with murder. When he spoke, Uncle Eddie jumped."

HT pressed his fingertip lightly to her lips and cocked his head sideways giving her a look.

She playfully crossed her eyes and stuck out her tongue.

He chuckled.

She smiled and continued, "Dad knew we weren't doing him any favors, and we needed to quit feeling sorry for him, letting him be such a brat. So a family meeting was called. We were told no more; we needed to treat Anthony the same as we did before Victoria died. It worked. Then a few months before we met, Uncle Eddie moved them back to London. Anthony was not happy having to leave here and started acting up again."

"Like locking you in the maze," said HT.

Lil nodded. "He was a bigger brat than before. Dad called another meeting telling us no more. We were to quit letting him get away with it. Papa also added no more letting him eat whatever he wanted out of the bakery. He was becoming a real porker. It was no time before he turned back to the same sweet kid we all loved. We laugh now at just how big of a brat he was."

"Seems I remember you said he moved fast for a porker," said HT with a chuckle.

"I said that? I didn't say that." She chuckled.

"Yes, you did! I remember everything you said that day! Remember you're my first and only love Rosie!"

"You said I was your first crush!" She chuckled again.

"Whatever! Same thing," he said with a wink meaning it.

For the first time in a long while, she found her heart racing and felt hot from head to toe from his wink. She quickly took a drink of tea to calm down. Then she said, "Now that I think about it, he had been getting on my last nerve, and I hated him calling me Rosie. He still calls me that when he gets upset at me! Don't you start calling me that; it's rubbish."

"I'll stick to 'little minx' then."

"Yeah, I like that," she said with a grin. "Now back to Anthony; you really are going to love him. He's actually the one who got me into photography. He wanted a camera, so Dad took us to Jacob's shop. I got the camera, and he fell in love with a video camera. He's the one who talked me into taking the course with him in London last summer. He said it was time I quit developing my own film and joined the real world of digital. He assured me that I eventually would have to once I started working professionally." She rolled her eyes and chuckled. "He's always aggravating me about my darkroom. I tell him he's just jealous because it's off limits to him."

"He's never been in there?"

"No. It's always been my private space. I told you that you're the only one I've let in there."

He grinned as they looked into each other's eyes.

He got a rush thinking he knew her looks but not this one; there was something there he couldn't quite identify. His heart started beating faster; he couldn't be sure—but just maybe her feelings toward him had changed.

She almost leaned in and then JR walked in.

"Hey, you two, it's time to get going to Chester. Snaggs, you have all your camera equipment together?"

Lil jumped up; her heart was beating like crazy as she thought, *Where is this rubbish coming from, again? Bloody hell, I almost kissed him!* She quickly pushed it back and answered JR, "Yep, right there by the snack bar." She hurried to the loo to get her head together.

HT's heart raced as he stood staring at her back. He muttered under his breath, "Did I see something in those gorgeous eyes, and is it just me or were you about to kiss me?" His hope that he was right went soaring.

Two hours later at the Battle of the Bands, HT felt fine, laughing and joking around while standing backstage, waiting to go on. As they listened to the other contestants, they felt they had a great chance of winning. HT was starting to feel anxious and looked out at the packed audience, just before it was time for them to go on. He saw Raif sitting on Charles's shoulders and Maddie on Luke's, right down in front with the rest of the family. He looked out at the crowd thinking half of Holmes Cove had showed up! His heart started pumping fast from nerves. The butterflies in his stomach kicked up a gear, and he was feeling overwhelmed. A massive panic attack came crashing in. He turned white as a sheet.

Lil watched HT turn white and whispered, "You don't look so good. How do you feel?"

Swallowing deeply in between words, he mumbled, "Like I'm ready to hurl."

"You can do this," she said with encouragement.

"You think so, huh?" he said trying to grin.

"I know so." She nodded confidently. "And we both know I'm never wrong!"

That got a little chuckle out of him. "You might be wrong this time because I'm about to toss my cookies here."

"Stop! You were born to be on a stage, Harry Thomas. You're going to smash it!"

"What if I don't? What if I'm absolutely rubbish and the whole village is here to see, embarrassing the family and letting them down?"

Lil said in a soft, calming tone as she placed a reassuring hand on his arm. "Don't be daft. You could never let any of us down. Your nerves will pass the second the music starts. I'll stand just over there to the side of the stage. Look at me and imagine we're back in the garage and that it's just another practice, just you and the guys playing for fun. Once the music starts, *your zone* will kick in. It always does."

"Let's hope so," he muttered.

"Stop this right now! Now go out there like your song from our first gettin'-loose night and...show them what you're all about!"

"Okay, Ms. Bossy Pants," he said with a chuckle, drawing confidence from her. "You know I can't do this without you! You always know how to calm me."

"So that's why you keep me around, huh?" she teased.

"You learned my secret," he said chuckling, seeing that look in her eyes again as he leaned in. He lightly kissed her forehead wanting to take her in his arms and confess his love right there. It was taking all the discipline he had to keep his mouth shut but then the thought of losing her made it easy.

He heard Lee starting the intro and groaned as he gave her a quick hug. "Here goes nothing," he grumbled and quickly turned and hurried out on stage. He returned Raif's and Maddie's thumbs-up. He looked out at the crowd, took a deep breath, and turned slightly to Lil.

Their eyes locked.

She gave him the thumbs up with a confident nod and an encouraging smile.

His confidence went soaring as Lee counted them off.

Once the music started, she could tell when his zone kicked in. The twinkle was back in his eyes, and his face lit up with his thousand-watt grin. It was a confident I-got-this sort of grin. She raised her camera and started clicking, wondering how it was possible for one person to be so gorgeous.

She could see through the lens that the thrill of being on stage had taken over. Everything about him set him apart. He had that star-like quality look. He commanded your full attention as his mouth barely caressed the mic with each word. Lil watched him fold one of his arms behind his back as he sang. She knew that meant he was just as confident as he sounded. She hurried down front. She was so proud of him that she could burst with pride.

He saw she had moved down front and winked, making her heart flutter. He would walk her way as he sang and grin as she took his photo, and she knew his nerves were forgotten. It took all she had to turn the camera on the other guys before the song was over.

When they finished, the applause went on and on as HT turned to Lil. He gave her a warm, seductive smile, making his eyes glow and dimples appear. He ran his fingers through his curls pushing them back, never losing eye contact as he put his palms and open fingers together just below his waist, and gave her a slight bow, and mouthed the words "Thank you" and winked.

Her guard that had blocked out what she didn't want to know came crashing down. The feelings she had been repressing came rushing out. She finally accepted the inevitable, what she knew in her heart. She was so head-over-heels crazy in love with him it terrified her to admit it. She was unwilling to listen to her heart because of the complications and the pain he would cause her, but she couldn't deny it anymore. *Bloody hell, what have I done?* she scolded herself. She took a deep breath and tried to push her feelings to the back of her mind. She would deal with it later; it was way too much to think about at that moment.

They were the last to perform, so the other contestants were called up on stage for the results. She didn't have the slightest doubt it would be them and wanted to get the perfect shot of HT. Her camera clicked away as he looked at her when the winner was announced. Of course, they won.

He was breath taking the way he smiled at her. Her finger worked madly on the button, getting all the shots she could as the crowd applauded. He was immediately swamped by people. He graciously accepted praise, shaking hands, and returning hugs with his easy smile.

She was starting to get a little frustrated having to watch all the girls grabbing and trying to kiss him after they took his photo. She mumbled, "You can handle this. Pull yourself together and get your head back where it belongs!" Then it happened. She couldn't tear her gaze away as a girl, who looked as though she'd just stepped off the runway, walked up. She had blond hair that fell around her shoulders, and everything about her screamed sexy. Lil sucked in her breath as she watched her kiss HT right square on the mouth. She then gave him a seductive smile as she handed him a small piece of paper. He smiled and put the paper in his pocket.

Anger lashed hot inside. She had to close her eyes for a moment to fight off the jealousy that raged through her body. She took in a calming breath and opened her eyes to see the girl batting her lashes at him and fling her hair over her shoulder. Lil had never had violent notions toward anyone before, but she found herself wanting to jerk the girl bald headed. She looked away and mumbled, "Okay, maybe I can't handle this. Yes, you can!" She scolded herself again, "You've been trained for situations like this! Just concentrate, and let it go." She inhaled deeply and then slowly let the air escape from her lips, hearing JR in her head. "Block it out. Focus on your surroundings and then you deal with it when you're out of the situation." She took in a deep breath and blanked everything out of her mind but the moment. She heard Sloan screaming and turned to see her running toward her like a crazy lady, making her laugh. They hugged as they jumped up and down.

HT searched the crowd for Lil. He heard Sloan scream and looked, seeing them hug. Grinning, he quickly hurried off the stage and wove his way through the crowd toward them, thanking people as they congratulated him.

Lil saw him coming and smiled widely and waved.

His eyes twinkled as he approached, his arms spread wide. "We did it!" he yelled with excitement.

Lil quickly handed Sloan her camera and then threw herself into his open arms. They laughed as he hugged her tight and swung her around.

"You were incredible!" she said as he sat her down. "See, right again; you smashed it!"

"Hey, now, we helped," Lee said laughing as he and the twins ran up.

"Maybe just a little," Lil teased as she hugged him and then the twins.

JR and Jayden hurried up. After all the hugs, handshakes, backslapping, and congrats they made their way to Gino's to meet their families.

When Lil got home, she took a hot shower and returned HT's text, still not letting herself think. She wanted to dive under the cool bedcovers and pull them up over her head, but she picked up her tea and went to sit on the windowsill. She often sat there to think and to make decisions. She stared down at the twinkling lights in the flower garden, trying to sort out her thoughts. She was embarrassed at being such a cliché, just like all the other girls he charmed without the slightest effort. If she was honest with herself, she knew she had fallen fast and had been ignoring the truth for a long time. How did this happen? It's all his fault that I'm in this mess. Why did he have to go and spoil things, making me fall in love with him? A dreamy look came over her face, and she mumbled, "It's impossible not to be in love with him; everything about him pulled me in. He's the most amazing, gorgeous, sexiest, sweetest, and absolutely the most perfect bloke in the whole world...Stop this! Think about a way out of this and stop with that rubbish or I'll be here all night!"

She sipped her tea and thought. If he finds out I love him, it will freak him out and make him uncomfortable around me like I was with Rafa. She sighed. Mum will be happy that I learned a lesson with this mess. She heard her voice ringing in her head after one of JR's training sessions, It doesn't matter how deeply you bury your feelings, Lily Rose. You can't escape them.

She laid her head against the windowpane as she looked up at the stars. It was inevitable she'd see him date, and she couldn't continue to feel this way every time he showed interest in a girl; he would know how she felt for sure. She needed to come up with a plan. She wasn't easily dissuaded once she made up her mind. She chuckled and mumbled, "Well okay, that's just another way of saying I'm stubborn as hell!" After thinking for a bit, she let out a long, hard sigh coming up with a plan that would help get things back on track. The best thing was to back away, put some distance between them. The thought made her nauseated. She closed her eyes, thinking about what her life was going to be like without him. "Scratch that rubbish," she mumbled. She thought some more and decided. I'll keep myself busy without him and will definitely stop spending time with him in the Cove. First time we snuggle up watching the telly or he gives me one of those sexy looks and winks that has me spilling my guts, I'll be screaming how much I love him. I just need a few weeks to get my head straight and my *emotions under control so that I'll be able to handle seeing him with those cows and accept things as they are; he's my best mate.*

Liking her decision, she walked over to bed drinking down her now cold tea. She was tough, she reminded herself. She could and would get through this. It was time to get her mind back on track, anyway. She would work out more with JR and Jay. She had really slacked off over the summer, and she only had a few more months before she started working with them. She really hadn't been looking forward to school starting, but now she was glad. It was something else to help occupy her time. She laid the cup on her nightstand and climbed in thinking about HT showing interest in that cow and taking her number. She thought, *Maybe it wouldn't hurt for me to start dating.* She mumbled, hitting her pillow harder than it needed to be fluffed. "When the gang is all together, and HT has a daft cow with him, I can focus on my date." She lay down, pulling the duvet up over her head, still grumbling, "Being in love is total rubbish!"

# CHAPTER 18

The next morning, after sending HT his text and waiting for the alarm to go off, Lil was staring up at the ceiling thinking about her plan. She was having second thoughts. How could she stay a safe distance from the most important person in her life? One minute she was telling herself, *I can do this*, and the next, doubting it. She was already experiencing withdrawal symptoms, and she hadn't even started yet. *No, my plan will work*, she tried to convince herself. It wasn't going to be too difficult. She just had to keep up the pretense she wasn't madly in love with him. She got more upset as she mumbled, "No snuggle time in the Cove with him and have to keep busy without him after almost always being together since the bloody day we met! Sure no problem! So now let's just top that off with I have to act bloody cheerful all the time like it isn't killing me!" She turned off the alarm and got up. She heard HT's ringtone as she stomped off to the loo, grumbling and regretting her decision already. "Bloody hell! Somebody, just shoot me now!"

She heard the grandfather clock in the hallway chime seven thirty, when she went out of her bedroom. She mumbled in disgust, "Time to face HT and start my life of hell!" She silently rehearsed what to say when seeing him. She knew he and Mum would be in the kitchen. Mum always made cinnamon rolls for her the first day of school because they were her favorite. She paused, taking a deep breath before entering; she could smell the cinnamon in the air. She lifted her chin and squared her shoulders as she pushed open the door and called out, "Good morning," doing her best to sound cheerful. She went over and kissed Mary's cheek. "Thanks, Mum, they smell amazing. How's Raif this morning?" she asked him, seeing him in his chair munching away on strawberries.

"Want tea?" Raif asked after swallowing and before taking another bite of his strawberries.

She kissed the top of his head. "Sure do. Did you make me some?"

He swallowed and replied with a giggle, "No, HT did. Huh, HT?"

"Yep, little man!" HT said, holding up the mug. "Have it right here. Just how she likes it!"

Lil turned with a bright smile, keeping her tone light as she walked over to him. "So how many did you inhale?" she teased.

"I'll never tell." He chuckled as he handed her the mug. "I do believe it's just the right temp and kind, if I say so myself!"

As she took the cup from him, their fingers brushed lightly. It sent sparks through her body. She quickly took a sip of tea and sighed, "Aww, perfect!" then drank it down. "Thanks, I needed that!"

"Apparently!" He grinned taking her cup. "You look nice this morning, but then, you always do!"

"Thanks. I want to make a good impression. I'm meeting almost everyone for the first time!"

"They're all going to love you," he said, thinking, *Like I do!*

Lil raised her eyebrows up and down, mimicking one of his flirty moves. "I sure hope so. I'm excited and ready to have a great last year. I might even jump back into the dating game."

"Really?" He felt his shoulders slump with disappointment and quickly turned to get his head around what she'd said. He had gotten home late after a great night at Gino's and was still flying high. He knew it wasn't from winning. He was sure her feelings had changed. He just knew he had seen it in her eyes before they went to Chester, and he would have bet that she was about to kiss him before JR came in. *I'm glad I kept my bloody mouth shut before I went on stage*, he thought as he sat the cup in the sink. He gave nothing away when he turned back with a grin and teased, "Right then, let's get going so that you can get started meeting those lucky blokes."

Mary gave Lil a quick hug and said, "I packed a few breakfast rolls just in case you decide you want to eat something on the way."

"Thanks, Mum."

HT gave Mary a quick hug.

Raif was waiting with his little fist up.

HT grinned as he walked over and bumped it. They said in unison, "Whoosh!" as their hands exploded away. Raif chuckled and crammed his mouth full of strawberries as Lil kissed the top of his head.

HT picked up the bag before he opened the door.

"Don't get any ideas, mister. Those are mine," Lil joked as they went out.

After school, HT was outside, laughing and talking with Lee and the twins. He kept glancing at the door, watching for Lil to come out. He hadn't talked to her all day. They only had lunch hour scheduled together, and she never showed up. He figured she would come out with Sloan since all their classes were together. He was surprised seeing Sloan walk up by herself.

"Where's Lil?" he asked smiling.

"She's walking out with—"

Cody interrupted her. "Bloody hell! Is that Connor Lil is walking with?"

The smile drained from HT's face. A chill ran through him as he felt a dull, sinking sensation in his stomach seeing them holding hands. He sneered at Connor as he pushed his long curls from his face.

"Yeah." Sloan nodded. "He's been all over her since first hour."

"Every league in the world is after him!" said Jody in awe.

Sloan said in a low voice so that only HT heard, "Unless you're ready to come clean with how you feel, you need to quit glaring at him."

He only nodded, finding it difficult to speak.

"And smile, for God's sake," she added.

The corners of his mouth lifted into one of his flirty smiles.

"Hi, guys," Lil greeted smiling.

"Hey," they all replied.

"This is Connor," she said and pointed to the guys as she introduced them. "Connor this is Lee, Cody, Jody, HT, and, of course, Sloan, whom you've already met."

"I've known Harry or should I say HT for years," said Connor. "We just never ran in the same circles. Hey, HT?"

HT struggled not to frown as he made a polite inclination of his head. "You all right?"

"For sure," replied Connor. He looked over at Lee. "And this bloke use to be my best mate until he decided to be a rock star," he joked.

"You mean until I turned into a wanker," replied Lee.

"Well, that too, but I was being nice," Connor said with a grin. "It's been too long. We should have talked before now."

"I agree; time slipped away, I guess," said Lee as they shook hands, doing the guy hug. He asked, "So what team are you signing with? And you better say Manchester United or this little love feast is over!"

They all laughed, including HT who tried to fight it. They talked for a while, HT nodded ever so often when Sloan would nudge him in the side. *Finally*, he thought when JR and Jayden pulled up.

Lee, Sloan, and the twins walked off after saying their good-byes. Lil and Connor still had their heads together in deep conversation when HT opened the back door and slid in. He sneered as the door closed behind him. "You sure took your sweet time. Can you believe the first bloody day and she has a boyfriend? Not just any bloke, the most popular one in the whole bleeding country!"

"Well, hello to you, too." JR chuckled.

"What! You don't like him?" teased Jayden.

"Bite me," HT grumbled, making them burst out laughing.

Connor opened the door and held it for Lil to slide in. She lowered the window as he closed it. He leaned through the window looking at JR and Jayden. "Hi, I'm Connor. Lil has done nothing but brag on her big brothers all day."

"Hi, Connor, I'm Jayden." He nodded politely.

"Which makes me, JR, her favorite." JR grinned.

"She told me you would say that," Connor said with a grin. He looked at Lil and leaned in closer. "I'll see you later," he said and gave her a quick peck on her cheek.

HT turned and glared out his window as a wave of jealousy shot through him.

"For sure," she replied with a smile.

As he straightened up, Lil rolled her window up with a sigh, as if he did something for her, but it was the complete opposite.

As JR pulled off, Lil put the biggest smile on her face, hoping it looked genuine and forced enthusiasm into her voice as she gushed, "OMG! I love this school! The kids are great! And Connor is amazing! He's like the best footballer, ever! Well, soccer, as Uncle Carl calls it. You guys' favorite team, Manchester United, is even after him. You know blokes call him the next Beckham?"

HT winced and found himself gripping the edges of the seat so hard that his knuckles were white, wishing it was Connor's neck he was squeezing as he listened to her.

She looked over at HT. "Sorry, I missed lunch. I helped Sloan set up the drama room."

He told himself to smile as he looked over at her. "No worries."

"I couldn't get within ten feet of you in the halls," Lil added. "Quite popular, I see!"

"Yeah, it was a little crazy; me and the guys were mobbed all day. A lot of them saw us play yesterday. They want us to play at some of the dances."

"That's awesome!" Lil said. She tried to be carefree and happy and make light conversation the rest of the way home, hoping her voice didn't sound as phony as she felt.

HT did the same and nodded a few times as if interested.

When they arrived home, HT casually asked as they got out of the car, "We hanging out in the Cove? We'll have time to catch up on Jimmy and *Idol* before dinner."

Lil felt the familiar tug. She wanted to so bad that it hurt, but she shook her head determined to keep to her plan. "Can't. I told Connor I would go to his game. You want to tag along?"

A stab of jealousy shot through him. "Nah, I'll pass. I need to get some things that's spinning around in my head down, anyway. You know me, it'll drive me mental until I do."

Lil smiled and joked, "You getting a song about our first day of school doesn't surprise me. So I'll see you at dinner?"

"For sure," he replied with a grin, but his eyes said he wasn't the least bit happy as he turned toward the Cove. He muttered as he walked, "The song in my head has nothing to do with school. *It's about the tosser trying to steal my girl!*"

She headed to the house letting out a long sigh.

# CHAPTER 19

Saturday afternoon it was cloudy and misting as JR drove Lil to Chester. She was going to meet Connor and then the gang later at Gino's. The weather was a perfect reflection of her mood. She wasn't in the mood for laughing, talking, or pretending she was having a great time. She'd rather be in her darkroom feeling sorry for herself. Her mind drifted as she looked out the window at the passing scenery. She couldn't believe how her life had turned to total crap in less than a week. She knew it was going to be difficult, but it was a million times worse than she could ever have imagined. She hadn't expected it to be so emotionally demanding. She seemed out of sync. All week she had been asking herself how avoiding HT was helping. She didn't believe she could be any more miserable. She wanted to cave this morning and tell him how much she had missed him the past week, but she stuck to her plan. She knew she wasn't strong enough yet to keep a handle on her emotions. She had to admit that she had become quite the little actress. Every morning she wore a fake smile and acted bubbly as she went into the kitchen, knowing HT would be waiting for her with tea, talking with Dad, and playing with Raif.

She was glad that she had met Connor. He was in most of her classes and made her feel at ease from the start, making her laugh with his humor. They had lunch by themselves, because Sloan was always off visiting with someone or running around for the drama department, and HT and the guys were always mobbed with kids. She couldn't get near HT if she'd wanted to. She could see why he thought every girl was out to get him—they were! The cows were all over him; almost every female in the bloody school had the hots for him. She could tell when he was coming down the hall by his harem. That's what she and

Sloan named the mob of girls that swarmed around him all the time. If he did see her, he would smile, wave, and wink. She just shook her head a little and smiled, feeling her heart crumble inside. She covered it up well.

She hung out with Connor after school every day so that she could avoid going to the Cove with HT. She even went to most of his games, and she hated football. It was tough, but she came up with reasons not to go to the Cove with HT to watch the telly after dinner. It hurt that he didn't care. He told her no worries, he had a few things going on himself, and went home. She threw herself into working out with JR and Jay, making sure she was exhausted when she fell into bed so as not to think about how much she was missing him.

She let out a little sigh seeing Connor standing in front of the coffee shop. He reminded her of HT in many ways: down to earth, sweet, not a phony bone in his body. He was the same height, had the same built, had curly hair; his wasn't natural of course, and he was very good looking. But not gorgeous like HT. She saw Ben casually standing by Connor and Joe on the corner, making the hairs on the back of her neck go up.

"What's going on JR? Why Ben and Joe?" she asked when JR pulled into the car park.

"See how observant you are when you get back to your training workouts?"

"Cut the crap, JR. Are we on lock-down again?"

"You know if there was a lock-down, you and HT wouldn't be in Chester in the first place."

"What about HT? Is there anyone helping Jay?"

"Of course. Everything is fine. Charlie is just having his dreams and feelings that things aren't right. You know how he gets until he figures things out—extra coverage."

She huffed knowing there was no sense in asking more.

"Right then," he said grinning. "I'll walk over with you to the coffee shop. I could use a brew. What about you?"

"That's a daft question," she mumbled as they got out of the car.

HT dropped into the chair between Sloan and Lee at Gino's. The twins were sitting on the other side of Lee, and the wine was already flowing.

"Hey, bro," said Lee. "I was just saying we can head over to my place later for a real victory party. Parents are gone; told me to just make sure we clean up." He passed the bottle over to HT.

"I'm in," HT said as he poured himself a full glass of wine.

Cody, sitting on the other side of Lee asked HT, "Lil and Connor still coming?"

HT shrugged, trying to appear indifferent when it was the last thing he was feeling. "That's what she said this morning." He almost emptied his glass with a few long gulps before he asked, "You guys over your man crush with that bloke?"

"Yeah," the twins said with a laugh.

"He is a great guy, though," added Cody.

Jody nodded in agreement. "Real down to earth. Not at all as I pegged him."

"Lil sure seems to like him, so he must be all right," said Cody.

"Yeah, he is," said Lee.

HT just swirled the wine around the bottom of his glass in wide circles thinking, *The tosser sure made my life hell the past week. It's been the worst week of my life watching her with him.* He grunted. *The up side, if there is one, I wrote my first gut wrencher. Hopefully, this thing with him won't last long. I'll be crying like a baby every time I sit down to write!*

Lee pushed a wine bottle toward HT.

"Too much wine, and I'll be hungover. The guys are getting hard to beat. Hand me your flask."

"Sorry, bro, I don't have one on me. I didn't think about the party until I was here."

HT looked up to see Lil and Conner walk in, chatting away.

"Oh joy, they're here!" he said sarcastically under his breath.

Lil smiled, seeing them all sitting around their usual table and waved.

HT nodded vaguely in her direction and grabbed the bottle and uncorked it. He poured himself another glass to the top.

"What about golf?" asked Lee with a smirk.

"Cheers," HT grunted, raising his glass in the gesture of a toast, making Lee laugh.

"I'm loving this," Lee replied under his breath. "You're in love so much that it's driving you mental." He let out a loud laugh.

"Bite me!" HT grumbled and drank until it was empty. He then refilled his glass, emptying the bottle. He felt a hot surge of anger as he watched Connor put his hand in the small of Lil's back as they walked toward the table.

Sloan looked at Lee and nodded toward HT. Lee glanced over at HT and said, out of the side of his mouth, "If looks could kill, bro, Connor would be dead."

HT put on a fake grin and hissed through clenched teeth. "No such luck." He motioned to Karen by waving the empty bottle airily in one hand and holding up two fingers on the other.

"Hi, everyone," Connor greeted as they walked up.

"Hey," all but HT replied. He was downing his wine.

"What are you celebrating, HT?" asked Lil.

"Whatever you want, little lady." He grinned with a wink.

Lil's heart fluttered as she went mushy from head to toe.

He lifted his glass in salute and knocked the rest back in long, greedy gulps.

Connor pulled out the chair beside Sloan for Lil. Then pulled one over next to her and sat down as his arm went comfortingly behind her. He put his other hand on top of hers that was lying on the table.

HT's eyes turned a deep, intense green watching him. The effort of keeping himself from throwing the empty wine bottle across the table at his head was demanding all of his self-control.

Sloan caught the hurt expression in his eyes before he looked down to his empty wine glass. She knew she was witnessing the breaking of his heart. For a split second, she hated Lil, and her eyes showed it as she glared over at her.

Lil didn't see Sloan; she was too busy watching Karen walk up beside HT. Her skintight T-shirt and skirt seemed even tighter than usual. Lil expected HT to move slightly, like he always did, knowing she would try to rub her boob against him as she leaned over to set the wine down. Her insides burned with jealously at seeing him not even trying to move, as her boob rubbed his shoulder when she placed the wine in front of him and then again even longer, before standing up.

HT gave her one of his sexiest grins. "You look really nice tonight, Karen."

"You always look gorgeous," she flirted, flipping her blond ponytail over her shoulder with a giggle.

He winked, wondering what he despised more, the hair flip or the giggle. "How about you keep the bottles coming. Don't let me down now and leave me hanging without something to drink again."

"Oh, I won't," she promised with another little giggle.

HT pulled the cork from a bottle and refilled his glass. He lifted it in salute at Lee and the twins. "The nights just starting. Right, guys?"

"Yeah," they replied lifting their glasses and laughing.

Connor asked Lil, "What do you want to drink?"

"The wine is fine," she answered with a smile, wanting to jerk Karen bald headed. *What is it with him and blondes?* she thought disgustedly.

Connor looked up at Karen. "I'll take a bottle of water, please."

"For sure," she said with another flirty grin and walked off.

"Water?" said HT, his tone laced with sarcasm.

"I've got an early practice in the morning."

"That's right. The next Beckham can't be blowing off practice now," said HT not meaning it as a compliment. He raised his glass to his lips to hide his sneer.

They all laughed not having a clue HT was being sarcastic and wanted to rip Connor's head off.

Sloan's and Lee's laugh was fake because they knew. Lee raised his glass to his mouth and whispered, "Cool it, bro, you're sounding like a jealous prat."

HT gave him a little nod.

"I don't know about that," said Connor with a little chuckle, "but what I do know is the coach will have my hide if I show up hungover."

Lil looked at Conner as he poured her wine. "Thanks," she said.

"Cheers!" he replied.

She quickly looked over to HT to see if he had heard.

He chuckled with a wink.

She grinned and turned back to Connor as her heart raced.

"You still want me to swing over after practice tomorrow?" Connor asked looking into her eyes.

"For sure. We'll have a barbecue if it's nice out." She glanced over at HT and Lee. "You having band practice?"

HT didn't answer. He just bitterly stared as he thought, *That's not good. Inviting him over in less than a week, letting him meet everyone. She must really like the tosser!*

"No, I don't think we'll be up for practice," Lee answered. "We just decided before you came in we're all heading to my place later for a real victory party. We have the place to ourselves. But hell yeah on the barbeque; can't be giving up that great food!"

"I'll second that," Cody said holding up his glass of wine.

Lil laughed and thought. *Damn! For once in my life, I leave my bloody camera home. Well, I'll just have to figure something out. No way. I'm not having photos on our wall of his first victory party.*

Lee and Sloan gave each other a worried look when Karen brought the pizzas, and HT went for the bottle of wine instead.

Connor put a piece on a plate and sat it in front of Lil and then took one for himself. She nibbled on her slice ever so often and reminded herself to look interested and nod or laugh at appropriate intervals. She sipped on her wine a lot because every time she brought the glass to her lips she got to watch HT over the rim, since she was directly across from him. She didn't notice he wasn't eating because he was always talking, laughing, and drinking. He looked to be having a great time.

Lil turned back to Connor and didn't notice Karen was picking up her plate. She was about to sip her wine and then found herself taking a gulp instead when Karen all but snorted for only her to hear, "Honestly! You thought you could keep him, you stupid cow?" She then smiled and walked over to HT.

Lil watched HT give Karen a dazzling smile. There was no doubt he was making a date, the way she glanced over at Lil with a smug look. Lil just smiled as if she could care less as she brought the glass to her lips.

Karen laughed knowing different as she walked away in her high heels, swinging her hips with no difficulty.

Lil had to restrain her anger to *not* throw the glass at HT's head, seeing him grinning as he stared at her bum.

He looked back to the table and boasted with a cheeky smile and a wink, "I'm all set."

Lee and the twins laughed.

Lil wasn't sure how much longer she could keep a smile pasted on her face. She knew she needed to get her head straight, or she would never be able to keep up the appearance that she was having a great time. To keep herself from staring at HT, she turned slightly and leaned toward Connor.

HT couldn't make himself look away as he watched Connor's head bend close to the side of Lil's face, whispering something that was meant for no ears but hers. She softly chuckled. He could feel the bile rising in his throat, along with the wine, and had to swallow hard a few times to keep it down.

Lee looked over at HT who seemed relaxed, but he could see a muscle twitching in his jaw. "How you holding up, bro?" he asked under his breath.

"I'm just peachy," he cheerfully responded, but his tone indicated otherwise. He poured another glass of wine and joked under his breath, "When all else fails drink and flirt," and shifted in his chair to the table of girls sitting beside them.

Lee laughed.

"You beauties want to come to our victory party?" asked HT.

"For sure," was their reply.

The twins got up and went to their table to sit as HT continued to talk and flirt with them.

It didn't look like Lil was paying attention to their conversation as she ran her fingers lightly up and down the stem of her glass. When Karen told the two girls who were flirting with HT to back off, he was all hers tonight, Lil almost snapped the stem in two hearing HT's sexy laugh. Despite the relaxing benefit of the wine, she knew she had about all she could handle, wanting to break the fingers of the girl who was playing with HT's curls. Her voice remained light and calm, and she gave no sign of anger as she stood up. "I'll be right back," she said and hurried off.

"I guess when you gotta go, you gotta go!" Connor chuckled.

Sloan smiled; she couldn't help but like Connor. "That's our Lil," she said. "You'll get use to her announcing when she has to go and running off."

"I hope she keeps me around so that I can," he replied with a big smile.

HT, after hearing him, turned away from the girls. His insides were burning again as he was trying to decide which to do first—break Connor's nose or blacken his eyes. He was going with both and muttered under his breath, "See how much Lil would like to stare at him then."

Lee looked over at HT and saw the dark look in his eyes and knew he was about to pounce. "Let's get out of here," he said as he waved to Karen for the check.

"I was going to bail on the party, but I think I'll blow off practice instead," Connor said as he stood taking out his wallet. "Being with Lil is worth putting up with the coach tearing me a new one."

HT lost his self-control. His lips tightened into a hard line as he sneered, "We don't—"

Lee quickly jumped up redirecting the attention to him. He finished what seemed to be the rest of HT's sentence, "—want you paying on your first time joining us, bro. It's our treat this time."

Connor smiled as Lil walked up. "Great! We'll catch you outside, then."

Lee turned to HT after Connor and Lil walked off. "What the hell, bro. I know that look. You were ready—"

HT cut him off, "To smash his face in. Yeah, I was. Still might before the night is over." He stood up staggering a little. "Get the check; I'm going to the loo."

"No way! I'm not getting stuck with this one!" Lee snarled. "It would cost my checks for a whole month the way you've been putting that wine away!"

"Well, smart guy, you should have let Connor pay," snarled HT right back.

"I had to get him out of here because your sorry arse was about to pounce. You've been a complete tosser all week! But tonight it's been doing my head in worrying about you diving across the table at him. On top of that, you've been acting like a bloody dog in heat! You've made me want to hurl!"

"Whoa, bro, that's a bit harsh!" HT replied swaying a bit.

"Stop it, you two," hissed Sloan as she stood. "The whole bloody restaurant is going to hear you and then you won't have to worry about Lil finding out! Now kiss and make up, and I'll meet you idiots outside." She turned and stomped off.

They looked at each other and laughed while they did a quick guy hug telling each other they were sorry.

"I don't know about you," Lee said, "but I'm ready to do some serious drinking. I've had enough of that rubbish."

"Sounds like a plan to me. I've decided I'm staying at your house and bailing on golf, but first I need to hit the loo," said HT as he walked off.

"Don't forget the check," Lee called out at his back laughing. "I'll meet you outside."

HT laughed and threw up his hand.

After HT felt like he had peed for an hour, he washed his hands and splashed cold water on his face while taking a few gulps out of his hand. He knew he would have to drink a few gallons to help ward off the raging headache he was in for. The cold water seemed to clear his head a little. It had been a long time since he had been so buzzed. He paid the check and went outside to join the others. He looked over and saw JR and Jayden. He thought it was funny how natural it felt to look for them. Lil was right; they were great at their job. The gang still didn't have a clue they were always around. He was wondering where she was as he turned to look down the side street beside the restaurant. He saw her and Connor sitting on a bench.

Lil thought, as Connor leaned in to kiss her, *Oh no! I hope it's half decent, and he doesn't end up with all that wine I drank all over him.*

"WTF," HT growled. His eyes were blazing with fury as pain like he'd never felt before ripped through him at watching them kiss.

Lil gave it all she had, trying her best to enjoy it. She put her hand on the back of his head touching his curls. They were coarse, not soft and silky like HT's. Of course, the only time she got to freely run her hand through HT's was when she helped Sloan trim it. She found herself analyzing his kiss. He didn't try to swallow her face, which was a plus. His lips were soft, and his tongue wasn't slimy; that was also a plus. It was a nice kiss. Not the best she'd ever had but not the worst. It just wasn't doing anything for her. Actually she found herself getting bored and started to wonder how HT's kisses would be. Just his little pecks on her forehead made her whole body tingle, while Connor's was doing nothing. After what seemed like an eternity, she opened her eyes to see Connor was staring at her just as bored; they had zero chemistry.

She burst out laughing, not realizing the gang was whistling and cheering.

Connor teased, "If this is how you're going to react, no more kissing you."

"I really did try," she said, still chuckling.

"Me too," he confessed. "I really like you, and we've hit it off so well, I was hoping—" he stopped, giving her a little shrug.

"Who are you in love with?" Lil smiled.

"How can you tell?" Connor asked with a chuckle.

"Takes one to know one, I guess," said Lil.

"My sister's best friend. And you?"

They heard Karen yell, "Hey, gorgeous, wait for me. I'll only be two more minutes."

Lil sighed and replied with a chuckle, "Unfortunately gorgeous, like every other girl."

Connor laughed and said, "I should have known from the way you kept staring at him all night and digging your nails in my leg at the way he was carrying on."

"I did not," she said laughing.

"Uh-huh, I can still feel the blood running down my leg. Wanna see?" He jumped up in front of her acting like he was undoing his trousers.

"Stop! Stop!" Lil yelled, laughing and grabbing his hand. "I believe you!"

HT heard Lil yell and started toward them, but Lee grabbed him by the arm, holding him back. "She's fine, bro, she's laughing. Snap out of it."

HT forced himself to turn away hearing another round of catcalls and whistles.

"Hey, you two, it's getting a little X-rated over there!" shouted Cody, making Jody and the girls laugh. "Come on, let's go!"

Lil was still chuckling as she stood.

"Let's give HT a little show," Connor said as he gallantly leaned over and lightly kissed Lil's lips. He then turned to the gang and gave a little bow, making them laugh. He threw his arm over her shoulder as they started walking toward them.

HT saw Karen running toward him. He laughed loudly and opened his arms.

Karen jumped into them and wrapped her legs around his waist.

Lil watched HT's opened mouth kiss her hard. She turned to Connor. "Excuse me while I vomit."

He chuckled as they slowed their pace. "Just breathe, smile, and keep looking at me. I have been told I'm not bad to look at," he teased.

Lil laughed.

HT heard her laugh and kissed Karen harder. When he stopped, she yelled, "Bloody hell! That was amazing!"

Connor teased as they stopped walking. "That's not the reaction I got."

Lil laughed as she hugged him.

HT's eyes returned to Lil, hearing her laugh. He forced what he hoped was a laugh as he looked back at Karen. He removed her from him and said, "I'll have to keep working at it. Girls usually yell they're absolutely brilliant."

"Bro, that was total crap!" Lee said laughing.

The guys laughed as they all started up the street.

"You didn't really know, did you?" Lil asked Connor as they started walking.

"No, not at all. You hide it very well."

"Good. I would die if he or the gang knew. As far as HT knows, I love him as he loves me, best mates only, and I want to keep it that way."

"Right then. So how we going to do this? How can I help?"

"How about we keep hanging out and you step in when I need help just like you did."

"I can do that. But how about we take it a step further and continue on, like we're dating?" He added with a shrug, "That way girls will leave me alone and blokes you. Plus, we'll always have a date with no strings, just mates."

"Oh no," Lil laughed and added, "and avoid entanglements. I told HT all that when we met. Look where it got me!"

"Buggar!" Connor teased. "You're not going to fall madly in love with me are you?"

They laughed.

"So we going to this party or what?" asked Connor.

"For sure! But I didn't bring my camera. I didn't want to seem like a nerd, bringing it on our first official date."

"I was surprised not to see it around your neck the way you had it in my face all week!"

Lil playfully rolled her eyes. "Whatever. I called Jacob, my friend who owns the camera shop, and he's going to lend me one. He was just finishing up dinner and said he'd meet me"—she looked at her phone to check out the time—"in about another twenty minutes."

"Wow, talk about customer service." Connor chuckled. "Since we have time, how about we grab you a tea?"

Lil nodded. "See how well this is going to work?"

They laughed as they hurried to the coffee shop.

An hour later, HT was feeling no pain and getting more upset by the minute from not seeing Lil.

Lee walked up. "What's with the look, bro?"

"You seen Lil?"

"No, not yet. She'll be here. She probably just went for tea." Lee chuckled.

"Or she bailed on me to be with him," snarled HT.

Lee tried to assure him otherwise. "She'll be here, bro. This is Lil you're talking about. Call her."

"Not a chance," said HT. Changing the subject, not wanting to talk about it anymore, he asked, "What were those things we were drinking? Never drank anything on fire like that before."

"Jellybeans. Dad use to drink them back in his uni days. You have to like black licorice, that's for sure."

"I love it, so let's go have a few more." HT chuckled, heading over to the bar swaying as he went.

Lee laughed as he followed him. "Just remember to blow them out before you try to drink them this time!"

Lil and Connor walked in about an hour later. The house was packed with kids. She looked around and saw HT by the bar with the guys drinking something they were lighting on fire and shook her head watching them all swaying. She saw Sloan waving. They went over to join her.

Sloan laughed as Lil held the camera up. "Last time I ever leave the house without one of these," said Lil smiling.

"What took you so long?" Sloan asked and then threw up her hand and chuckled. "Silly question." She looked at Connor. "She and Jacob can go on forever!"

"I saw." Connor grinned, throwing his arm around Lil's shoulder.

"I see the guys are having a great time," said Lil as she lifted the camera, hitting the button a few times.

Sloan shook her head in disgust. "The idiots have been downing those drinks one after another. They're all going to be sick; better them than us, I guess."

"I agree." Lil chuckled, hitting the button a few more times.

Hours later Jayden had HT slung over his shoulder, as he went into the Cove and dropped him onto the sofa.

"No golf," slurred HT.

"Sorry, bro. That's why I had to haul your drunk arse home. See you in a few hours," he said over his shoulder heading to the door.

HT was already in the loo.

Jayden could hear his retching as he went out.

Jayden was true to his word. He went into the Cove finding HT sleeping on the floor in the loo, with one arm draped on the toilet. He laughed and yelled, "Rise and shine!"

HT whispered, his voice filled with anguish, "Go away." He could feel the throbbing behind his temples before he even tried to open his eyes. He felt cold stone under his face and realized he was on the floor in the loo. His brain was like sludge. "How did I get here?" he asked in a hoarse whisper.

Jayden barely heard him. "As on the floor? That was all you. As here in the Cove? I carried you in. Now move it."

"I'm not going," he whined.

"Oh yes you are. You'll be there if I have to haul you there and drop you on the first hole like I did on that sofa."

HT mumbled, skipping words. It hurt to talk. "You guys been in shape. They won't care. Dad playing. Have four."

Jayden laughed and said, "Now you sound like Snaggs, and they will care. They're the ones who told me I better have you ready to go. If it makes you feel better, they never let me and JR get away with it either. We were told a real man takes what's coming to him, which basically means, you knew you had golf this morning, but you kept drinking. So suck it up and deal with it."

"Tossers! The whole lot of ya," he said with a moan.

Jayden grinned and replied, "We love you, too. I'll make you some coffee and gut-rot."

"Sounds appetizing," HT said through gritted teeth as he struggled to sit up. He leaned against the toilet once he made it up to a sitting position but still not opening his eyes. The small movement exacerbated the pounding in his head. It took a few minutes to find the strength to open his eyes. The roaring in his ears was deafening—he tried to keep his eyes open, but the room was spinning around him causing bile to rush to his throat. He quickly closed them again. A cold sweat broke out on his brow.

"Buggar! How much did I drink?" he muttered. Then he remembered why he drank so much in the first place. Lil and Connor going at it on the bench came front and center along with her blowing him off missing the victory party to be with the wanker. His stomach began to knot up again remembering doing lots and lots of shots. He groaned as he licked his chapped lips. "Bloody hell, they were lit!" He tried to think, which was hard, and it made his head hurt even more. All he could remember was some sad schmuck jumping up and down on the sofa screaming love sucks at the top of his lungs playing an air guitar. The idiot thought he could fly when he tried to jump over to the love seat. He missed it by a mile and landed on his arse hitting his head on the stone tile. He muttered, "I bet that bloke's head hurts worse than mine!" Pain shot across the back of his head. He reached up and felt the huge knot and groaned. "Yep, that sad schmuck would be me."

Jayden walked back in. "You look like you're making progress. Good news. Charlie is waiting on a call. You get an extra couple of hours. Here drink this," he said, handing him a glass. "It tastes like hell, but it works. It's not as bad if you can guzzle it."

HT's bloodshot eyes looked up at him. "Thanks, bro." He took the glass and gagged it down, not stopping for air till it was gone. "Buggar! That stuff is total crap!"

"We don't call it gut-rot for nothing. Here chase it with this black coffee. It's cold so that you can get it down quicker. It makes that other work faster. Try to keep it down. It will try to back up."

HT took the cup and gagged the coffee down. "How long does it take to work? And will it help my head? It's killing me."

"About a half hour," he replied. "It won't help your head, but it will let you keep down the pills that will. I'll give them to you if you can keep that other down for at least an hour. You're lucky you landed on your arse first; otherwise, that hard head of yours would have cracked open like a coconut."

"You saw that, huh? But, how did you?"

"The way you were screaming, I thought someone was killing you. Don't worry, no one saw me. I was looking in the window. By the way, I got the whole thing on my phone if you want to watch it."

"No thanks, I'm feeling it."

Jayden chuckled and said, "If you want that stuff to work faster take a hot shower. The hotter the better. I'll set it at the temp I use when I'm in your shape."

"Thanks, bro."

Jayden turned the shower on and walked to the door. "Now quit being a little bitch and get that arse up off the floor. You're made of stronger stuff."

HT actually smiled as he stood. He swayed a little, waited a second and then made it to the shower and closed his eyes to keep his head from spinning. He steadied himself, holding onto the door handle. He felt clammy and almost hurled. He kept swallowing hard. No way he was letting it come up and have to drink it again. He took another couple of seconds and then opened the door and stepped in, clothes and all. He groaned as the hot water hit his pounding head and body. For once he hated the shower with all its powerful shower heads. He slowly removed his clothes keeping his head as even as possible. The slightest movement caused him pain. As the hot, steaming water hit his aching body he started feeling better. He stood there as long as he could. He turned it off and stepped out, wrapping a towel around his waist as he went to the sofa.

He was sweating profusely by the time he made it. He fought back his nausea as he sat not moving an inch for a few minutes.

Jayden walked up behind him and said, "Lean your head back. This will help that knot."

He laid his head against the back of the sofa and felt the ice bag. "Thanks, b—" He fell fast asleep.

Jayden went back inside the Cove an hour later to find HT in the same position, fast asleep, snoring with his mouth hanging open. He poured a hot cup of coffee and walked over to him. He lightly nudged HT's leg with his foot. "Hey, bro."

HT opened his eyes. His mouth tasted horrible but was surprised his stomach felt better. He slowly raised his head, not wanting to trigger any pain.

Jayden handed him the hot coffee and two small white pills. "This will get you up and moving and help that head."

HT swallowed the pills with a drink of coffee. "What is all this? Some kind of secret spy crap?"

"Something like that," Jayden said with a grin. "You're going to get thirsty as hell. But don't drink anything, not even water. You'll feel worse than before you started. You have about an hour or so."

"Okay, thanks again, bro," said HT as he stood up. Pain exploded across his eyes. "Never again!" he muttered.

Jayden laughed as he headed to the door. "Same last words we all say. That head will let up some in a few."

Lil woke still sleepy and wanted to stay snuggled in bed. She thought about HT and wondered how he was making out on the lesson he was learning about now. He was learning just how tough it was being part of the family. Last she saw, he wasn't in very good shape as Jay carried him to the Cove. She was exhausted, not getting in bed until after three, and then she lay there forever rethinking her plan. She didn't like to admit she was wrong, but she was so wrong thinking she was strong enough to stay away from HT. She realized one thing after watching him in action all night though, she was strong enough to handle it. Plus, she had Connor now to help her out. So her new plan was just to stick to—no snuggle time. That would be the worst, trying to keep her emotions in check. She would just have to be doing something as they watched the telly like working on an album or doing homework. She looked over seeing the time. She shot off a text to HT and headed to the loo. She was on her way downstairs when HT's text came. She said with a chuckle, "Well at least he's alive." She went to the kitchen, smelling cinnamon rolls. She saw a bag sitting on the counter by the door. "Wow! Don't I feel special. Thanks, Mum," she said cheerfully, as she scooped it up and headed out the door.

Lil sat the bag on the snack bar and went to make her tea. She then started to the darkroom and saw HT sitting on the sofa in his golf clothes with his head back on an ice pack. Her heart missed a beat, like always, at seeing him. She wanted to hit him upside the head with the bag and scream at him for carrying on the way he had all night; but mostly she wanted to scream how much she loved him. "I didn't see you over here. I thought you'd already left," she said sitting down beside him.

He jerked his head up suddenly and felt a sharp stab of pain, sending lights flashing across his eyes, and quickly laid it back down. His nose wrinkled in disgust at smelling the cinnamon and stopped himself from groaning as his stomach flipped. "Mr. C. is running late," he told her and added sarcastically, "but then, you already know that."

"No, if I did I wouldn't have thought you were gone already." She reached for the bag to get out a roll.

"Can you stop making so much noise and be still. I know that you know I'm hungover. I'm sure I was the talk over breakfast, and get that rubbish out from under my nose. We both know you already ate!"

"Nobody has said anything. Actually, I haven't—"

He cut her off. He didn't move his head when he said, "Which means nothing with this family. You guys all have that telepathy thing going on along with the little gestures and all the little innuendoes. Nobody has a chance to get away with anything in this family."

"Hey, watch it. You're one of us now, remember? And for your information, Mr. Grouch Puss, I was about to say I haven't seen a soul this morning or eaten one bite."

He was trying to shove the image of her and Connor going at it on the bench from his mind, but it only grew stronger the more she talked.

She could see the sheen of sweat across his forehead. "Do you want me to get you some aspirin or make you a cup of coffee?" she asked.

It took a great deal of effort, but he blocked out the image and turned to look at her. His beautiful, green eyes, always so bright and twinkling, were bloodshot and boring into her. He shook his head and immediately regretted it as pain exploded behind his ears. He turned his head away making him groan. "No, I don't want anything. I'm fine."

"You don't look fine!" she said a bit loudly being so concerned. "HT, you look ghastly!"

"Can you just go to your darkroom to eat that rubbish and leave me alone?" he grumbled.

"Are you sure you're okay? How's your head?"

"Shhh!" he hissed as he scowled at the ceiling and pressed his temples with his forefingers in an attempt to stop the pounding inside his head.

"Don't shush me," she said, getting annoyed. "I understand you're not feeling well but don't take it out on me." A short moment of silence passed. She made a tsk sound as she got up and went to the kitchen. "I don't know what you expected. I've never seen you drink so much," she added when she came back to stand behind the sofa.

"Don't start. I'm not in the mood to hear your condescending tone," he grumbled. Heat rushed through him, and his head felt better almost immediately.

"And I'm not in the mood to put up with you sitting there growling at me," she said with a little huff. "Lift your head. Here's a new ice bag. Has that knot gone down any?"

He whipped around to scowl at her. He let out a sigh of relief when the movement didn't unleash the hammers in his head. "I take it you talked to Jayden?"

She stared into his bloodshot eyes and thought even hung over he was still as gorgeous as ever. "No, I told you I haven't talked to anyone this morning."

"You didn't see his phone?"

"What are you going on about? You're not making any sense. Are you sure you're feeling all right? You're starting to scare me, HT. Let me see if that knot has gone down any."

He shot to his feet. "When did you see it in the first place?"

"Eh...right after you tried to fly last night. What were you screaming anyway? I hope you didn't think you were singing." She chuckled.

"You heard me?"

"Everyone within a five mile radius did the way you were carrying on."

"You were there," he muttered.

Lil stared at him blankly, trying to register what he said. Then it dawned on her, and she was stunned. "You actually thought I didn't show up at your victory party?"

Her temper started rising. "Of course, I was there! I had to meet Jacob at his shop to borrow a camera first!"

He gave her a sheepish grin. "I didn't see you come in. I guess I drank more than I thought!"

"Apparently! I was the one nagging you all night to hold the ice bag on your fat head, but I don't care how much you drank; Harry Thomas, you know better!"

JR stuck in his head. "Time to roll, bro."

"Need a second," he called out.

"Sounds like you need more than that," JR snickered as he went back out.

HT, still not taking his eyes off Lil, hurried around the sofa. "I'm sorry. You're right, I do know better. And if I hadn't been drinking so much at Gino's, I would have realized you didn't have your camera. I guess I thought you and Connor had other plans, so you blew the party off since it was a last minute thing." He added with a sly smile, "Can we chalk this up to me hitting my head?"

She had to admit she couldn't blame him for thinking that, especially with the way she had been avoiding him all week. She said, giving him a little smile, "You *did* hit that fat head of yours pretty hard. So you're forgiven this time, but, if you ever think I would put anybody before you, that knot on your head won't compare to the one I'll put there!"

HT smiled, so relieved at what she said that he felt positively energized. He chuckled and gave her a quick kiss on the forehead. "I won't, I promise. I better get going before Bill is in here dragging me out by my ear. So I'll see you after for lunch up top?"

"I'm sorry, I can't," Lil said sadly and meaning it. "Connor's coach had me take some photos of the team, and he needs them before noon. I was going to do it last night and drop them off this morning but then the party came up so I didn't get them developed. Anyway, I won't be back here in time for lunch. I'll be here for the barbecue though," she said smiling.

"I'll see you then," he said with a wink. He gave her a quick hug and another quick kiss and hurried out.

CHAPTER 20

The following Saturday night HT was sitting with the gang at their regular table at Gino's. He was joining in on the conversation and even laughed a few times, but he still kept an eye on the door for Lil. It had been another long week of hell, them being likes ships passing in the night, so the saying goes. They hadn't really talked much since the barbecue.

They were having a great time catching up and laughing about him being so hammered the night before and not being able to remember anything. It was like the tosser had never entered into their lives until Connor showed up. Lil turned her attention to Connor, and it took all he had not to break his face. JR knew he was ready to blow and told him he had a few exercises that would help. So he became obsessed with working out with JR and Jayden. Besides getting physically stronger, he felt mentally stronger. He fell asleep at night from pure exhaustion and being sore as hell!

HT tuned back in as he played with his empty wine glass. He wasn't drinking, not wanting a repeat of the week before with waking up on the loo floor. JR's mind-control exercise kicked in giving him the edge he needed, as he watched Lil and Connor strolling in, holding hands. He snorted while putting on a big smile and said under his breath to Lee, "Showtime. Have your flask ready in case I need it."

Lee chuckled with a nod.

HT looked like his normal sunny self as he acknowledged Connor with a nod and smiled at Lil. He could care less about eating but needed something to say. "Finally we can order; we thought you got lost." He looked at Karen as she walked up and gave her a wink and a big smile.

Lil quickly looked away, not wanting to watch. The image of HT kissing her the week before flashed through her mind, making her want to scratch out her eyes.

Connor felt her tense and gave her hand a little reassuring squeeze and a wink. She smiled at him. His wink did nothing for her.

"Sorry mates, practice ran over," Connor said as he pulled out a chair for Lil. "The night's all on me for running late."

"Great, you can be late all the time then," said Cody.

Lee nodded in agreement. "That's what I'm talking about. The parents are still gone, so we can head to my house again when we're done here."

As the night went on there was lots of laughing, talking, eating, and drinking. HT never drank a drop. After a while the strain was getting to him, and he felt himself losing his edge. Every time he had to smile or talk with Connor, he had to control the urge to rip off his head. He did what JR told him to do. He took himself out of the situation and sat with a table full of girls talking and, of course, flirting for the rest of the night. Before he knew it, the night was over. The guys headed to Lee's, and he went home sober thinking the night wasn't as bad as he thought it was going to be.

Lil, on the other hand, had another rough night of watching HT. She tossed and turned long after receiving his text. She couldn't turn off her mind. She tried to suppress the unpleasant memories of another long, difficult night. She couldn't believe it when Britney, the cow who had given him her number at the battle of the bands, walked in and HT ended up sitting with her and a table full of girls.

He was always smiling, happy as could be, while she had to hide how miserable she was. It hurt that he didn't seem to care they never spent any alone time together any more. She let out a little sigh and finally fell asleep.

She woke a few hours later feeling someone gently shaking her shoulder. She felt a little weird, like she was floating. She heard the grandfather clock chime 5:00 a.m. as she sat up and squinted. By the full moon, she saw her granddad, who was an older version of Dad, standing there smiling at her. She only knew him from pictures.

She exhaled and then shook her head blinking her eyes a few times to make sure she was seeing what she thought she was seeing. He nodded reassuring her she was and motioned her with his hand to follow him. It was like she was watching herself get up and slip into her housecoat and slippers. She followed him from her room and down the hall and stairs. He turned ever so often and motioned to her to keep following. He went down the hall toward Charles's study. She saw light coming out from the door, which was standing slightly ajar. He then motioned for her to go in.

Lil sat up straight in bed, her heart thumping with adrenaline. She heard the grandfather clock chime 5:00 a.m. and looked over at the moonlight streaming through her window, just like in her dream. She had to be still dreaming! She ran her hands up and down her arms pebbled with goose bumps and bit her bottom lip. "Ouch," she mumbled, "if this is a dream, it's one of the most realistic I've ever experienced." She started getting that weird feeling again, freaking her out. "Oh no! I'm getting the heck out of here before he comes back!" She jumped up, slipped on her housecoat and shoes, just like in her dream, and ran downstairs and down the hall toward Charles's study as fast as she could. Just like in her dream she saw light coming out through the ajar door. She heard the voices coming out as she went blasting in!

They all jumped up.

Lil's face was pale and her mouth was dry. Her heart was pounding as she looked at Charles. "Granddad!" was the only word she could manage. She still couldn't believe it.

Charles calmly went to her, gave her a quick hug, and then slipped an arm around her shoulders and walked her to sit by Mary, who handed her a glass of water. He tried to say something reassuring and a little humorous. "That hazy feeling will pass in a few minutes. Did your granddad send me his love?" he asked with a grin. He was all too familiar with the feelings she was experiencing.

It worked, making Lil chuckle. "I don't know about that, but I'm pretty sure he wanted me in here. Wow, it was weird." She sighed and explained briefly ending with, "I knew it wasn't just a dream when I bit my lip and it hurt. Then I started getting that weird feeling again and got the heck out of there before he came back!"

They all chuckled.

"My granddad was my first dream. He scared the bejesus out of me too," said Charles with a chuckle. "If it helps, you'll get use to Dad, and believe it or not, you'll look forward to his visits. He's always calm, and smiling, but he can do your head in, too. Unfortunately, his visits aren't always as cut and dry as the one you just had, but we'll talk later on how to read his little visits. So I guess it's time I stop acting like I don't know that you know, huh?"

Lil smiled and replied, "And I guess it's time I stop acting like I don't know you know." She nodded at Jay, JR, and Bill. "And that you haven't had these blokes training me one way or another over the years."

Charles laughed and added, "And I'll stop acting like I didn't have JR let you find all those journals at the castle to read!"

Lil's brow went up in surprise. "Now that one I didn't know," she said laughing.

"That's how I found out as a child." Charles grinned. "I found those journals. So when you started asking questions when you were ten about what we did and where we went, instead of trying to explain it to you, I wanted you to have the same experience. Now, there's a lot we need to discuss, but before I go into all of that, you need to know what you'll be giving up so that you can decide if you really want to be a part of all this. Save your questions until I'm done."

Lil nodded.

"I know you don't plan on being in a relationship any time soon, but if that changes, there are rules that you have to abide by no matter what. You can't be seen together in public. That sounds easy, but you also have to keep what you do a secret from the person you're in the relationship with. This is safety for you, from being found out—and it keeps the person you're involved with safe in case your cover is ever blown." He held up his hand, seeing she was about to say something. "I'm not saying you can never tell them, but, you do have to ask for permission from top command if you ever want to share with somebody what it is you do. I'm sure you know top command is me and why I'm telling you this."

She nodded as she replied, "I can't tell HT. I know that you know how I feel about him, but Dad he's loyal and honest and would never say a word. He's one of us now. Knowing him, he would want to join us!"

"Yes, I agree. He would be a brilliant agent with some training, and if it were up to me, I'd say you could tell him. But there's another reason why you can't tell him. Again, baby girl, this has to stay in this room."

She nodded again.

"You've heard stories about Ed and me as kids and that we had another mate that lived in HT's house and we were all really close."

"The one that passed away."

Charles chuckled and said, "We never said that. We just let people think it. He's very much alive, and like Ed, he's one of my top agents. Actually, I put the two of them as an equal to me. Anyway, he's always been the one running things behind the ops and is the best at what he does. Besides our inner circle and a few of my top agents, no one knows he's an agent."

Lil said softly, "I can't tell HT because it's Luke!"

He nodded. "Yes, it's Luke."

She looked at JR and Jayden. "You knew?" She shook her head and looked back at Charles. "Of course they know; that was daft."

Charles chuckled and said, "Luke is on his way here now from Chester, so I'll give you the quick version. He has always been our rolling stone. We never dreamed he would want to settle down and have a family. Then he met Madison and that changed. He fell quick and hard. We have never seen him so happy.

"They were together for a while when Victoria died, and he got it in his head that it wasn't an accident. And well, to put it lightly, he freaked. All of a sudden he thought he would be putting Madison and HT in danger, putting their lives at risk. He felt so guilty he quit seeing Madison. He was miserable without her and went off the rails for a while." He paused, knowing he was delivering more bad news. "After we all moved here and had proof Victoria's death was an accident, I finally talked him into giving it another chance with Madison and promised he could have both lives. He said he wouldn't make Madison and HT move here to keep them safe, especially with being HT's stepfather. That has to do with his mum. She never wanted to marry Luke's father, and she hated having to live here in the village. When we were young, she found out Luke's father was in the service and used that to blackmail him for a quiet divorce, leaving a big hole inside of Luke. Anyway, I gave him my promise, working for the service would never interfere in his life with Madison and HT. They would always be safe, and he could choose where to live, and they would never know he was an agent unless he told them. I hoped he would want to move back here one day and share his life with us, so I came up with a cover that wouldn't be questioned, just in case he ever did.

"I'm not saying he'll never come clean with Madison and HT; he's coming around. Actually, he wanted to move back when Madison got pregnant with Maddie. Plus, HT was being a bit of a tosser. Let's just say HT wasn't happy about leaving his mates, so Luke told him if he straightened up, they wouldn't move until he was done with school. Luke's cover took him away from home more than he wanted, so he decided to make the move a year earlier. He was sure HT would go along with it. The rest you know. Now, do you need time to think over what I just told you or should I start the meeting?"

Lil replied, "I've already decided if I couldn't tell him about working with you guys, it would fall under our rule. I won't feel bad about holding things back, so start the bloody meeting. I've waited a long time for this!" she teased.

They all laughed.

Charles sat behind his desk and caught Lil up on the ongoing investigation that had started months before on the security council. Once he caught her up, he said, "The council meeting is set for tomorrow at Keaton Hall for members to hand in their quarterly reports, with their updated agent's locations and new call in codes." He sighed. "The irony is, a few months ago I made sure they go only to Lord Rothford, and now it looks like he's the one leaking the reports because two more agents were killed last week. I can't find a clear motive as to why, and there's no money trail to his personal or business accounts. Luke has even traced every member of his family's accounts, all the way down to a third cousin. Nothing has raised any flags. We can't find any links connecting him to the dead agents. So either somebody is setting him up to take the fall, or I've misjudged one of the most admired, influential lords in England all these years."

"So we should ask, why would anyone frame him?" said Bill. "Ex-wife, someone he's crossed, or a business deal gone sour."

"I thought of that, too," replied Charles. "He's a widower, essentially a good guy, and respected in his business dealings."

Bill rubbed the stubble on his chin as he said, "Then he has another agenda."

Charles made a little steeple with his fingers as he said, "My gut is telling me, no. I'm still not buying that it's him. I'm missing a few pieces of the puzzle, but I'm getting there. So, before I go accusing someone and tarnishing a reputation, we need to be absolutely sure of our facts. We can't ignore any possibilities that we will regret later. We need more proof. So we're going to change those reports and set him up. The reports he gets will have fake locations, leading them to our agents, and we'll be waiting on them. Now, back to the problem at hand." He massaged his temples as if tending to a migraine. "E says he doesn't walk out of that room with the real reports or we have to take him down. She doesn't want to take any chances of him getting out that information before we can switch the reports."

"Fine," said Bill. "The old bat will have to switch them herself then. She knows nobody goes in or out of that room once the meeting starts. That's why you redid that room to have special meetings in there. What? Does she think we can become invisible now? We're good, but we ain't that bloody good! How are we going to switch the dang things before he gets out of there?"

"Hush, old man, if you can't say something we don't already know," said Charles. "If we have to show our hand before he leaves that room, E is going to serve my arse on a platter, blowing months of surveillance work, and we'll never find out who killed those agents and why."

"Right then," said Jayden. "We need to have a reason for all the council members to leave the meeting room, since you guys have to store your brief cases in the closet that you turned into a vault."

"Even if we come up with an excuse for leaving the meeting room, it better be a good one, or he'll know he's being set up," said Bill as he rubbed his jaw, thinking it over. "Besides, no one touches the door to that vault for an hour after it's closed. If they do, alarms go off. I had it set that way. Even *I* can't open it."

"Wait a minute! You had that closet made into a vault when I was staying over there a lot to use the courts," said Jayden. "Remember JR? We stayed up all night watching them. I remember because I lost in the first round the next day at Wimbledon from not getting any sleep."

"Or because you played like rubbish!" teased JR.

They all laughed.

"Yeah, well, that too." Jayden grinned. "But my point is they didn't do the ceiling; it doesn't have steel. We go through the floor on the upper level and drop down."

Charles grumbled and said, "I had the ceiling layered once I realized they didn't do it. The whole thing is layered with six-inch steel now."

Lil got excited, knowing how she could get in. "Well, I know why Granddad wanted me in here. I can switch them," she said smiling. "I know the layout of that place better than anyone. There's not an inch I don't know by heart. I can move around using all those secret passageways and doors if you don't want me seen."

"So you've been a little snoop. How does that get you into the vault?" asked Charles.

"The walls, floor, and ceiling are covered with steel," said Lil. "But, the vent down by the flo—"

Charles cut her off, "I didn't take out until a few years later."

"Yep!" Lil replied with a huge smile. "The vent in the library is on the backside of that one. I used to play hide-'n'-seek with JR and Jay using them." She looked over at Bill. "Remember, Papa? That's how I came up with the idea to put that secret hatch in the maze."

"Wait until you blokes hear this," Bill said chuckling.

"Hear what?" asked Charles.

"I used the vents to get from one room to the other." She went on telling them the rest of how she did it.

They all started laughing.

"Anyway," said Lil. "There is just a piece of paneling matching the rest of the wall that covers where the vent was. No steel was put in. I was over there when Ben was working on it. I was disgusted that he was blocking off one of my hiding places. Cut that back out, and I'm sure I can still fit through. There's plenty enough room in there for me to stand. I can hand out his case, and you guys can switch the papers and hand the case back to me."

"I'm the one who lines their cases up in the vault. I'll be sure to put his in first, that way you'll know which one is his," said Bill.

Charles nodded with a big grin and said, "It will work. Now we need a reason to get them out of there after they give their reports to Lord Rothford."

"No problem, if E can make it to the meeting," said Mary. "She can do one of her surprise visits. For security purposes the members don't know she's coming until they're already in the meeting room. And there's always a special luncheon afterward in the ballroom for her and the members, so you can switch them then."

"You're brilliant! They know they have to put their brief case in the vault until after the luncheon," said Charles as he leaned back in his chair, with approval gleaming in his eyes. "It's been a while since she's stopped in, so it won't set off any alarms. I'll give her a call in about an hour to let her know the plan. I'm sure she'll go along with it."

He looked at Lil. "Now that I know how you've been such a snoop over there, have you ever seen any members of the council?"

"I did see, ah-ah-ah, the stuttering ah-ah Lord Standish at one of those special lunches Mum and Grammy do I was hiding in the kitchen when you came in to talk to Mum."

They all laughed.

Lil's brow shot up. "OMG! I just realized! You're the stuttering bloke HT tells stories about! He said he used to get away from you as fast as he could when he was younger because you drove him mental. But once he started sticking around, he realized he liked you, and he loved hearing your stories. No wonder you took to him so quick. You've been around him most of his life!"

"Guilty as charged," said Charles grinning.

"And how about you?" she asked looking at Bill. "You took to HT way too quick!"

"I've helped keep an eye on him growing up," said Bill with a chuckle.

JR looked at Charles and said with a raised brow, "You tossers knew who he was when you let him on the golf course that day."

"Of course," Charles replied.

They all laughed again.

Mary stood and said, "I'll get breakfast going."

"I'll only be a few more minutes here," said Charles. "I'll go up and get Raif and be in to help; that way we can head over after we eat."

Mary gave him a quick kiss. "I'll get started on the pancakes. That's been his new thing the last few days to go with his strawberries."

Charles chuckled as he looked at JR and Jayden. "You guys round up what we need to fix the wall; that way we can head straight over after we eat. We also need a couple of dry runs once it's done."

"Who's telling HT that golf is off?" asked Bill.

"Luke can tell him once I fill him in with what's going on," Charles replied. He then asked, "You heard from Ed?"

"He landed in the States a few minutes ago," Bill replied with a nod. "He said he would let us know what was going on as soon as he talked to Anthony. I told him not to be firing Anthony's guards for not telling him."

Charles chuckled and said, "Ed knows the code. If it isn't life threatening they keep what they know to themselves." He nodded at Jayden and JR and joked, "Just like I would fire these two if they told on Lil and HT. I still might if they don't quit being so nosey and get out of here and do what they were told to do."

JR and Jayden just laughed as they went out.

"I'll give'em a hand," Bill said with a chuckle as he followed them.

Charles, taking a folder out of his desk, asked Lil, "You want to save me some time and fill me in with what's going on with Anthony?"

Lil shook her head as she took the file he handed her.

"I didn't think so," he said with a grin. "Now, let's get to what's in that file. Bill has your cover all set as a freelance photographer."

She glanced at the papers inside. "He did this like six months ago."

"Well, you know him. From now on, that's your professional profile, when working with the upper class, as they say."

"As Mum would say snobs."

"Correct." Charles grinned. "E's autumn ball is in two weeks, and you're now her up-and-coming photographer. The people there will be high society and connected. They will expect you to be connected too, since you're E's photographer. Your connection will be through Ed and Anthony. You're the granddaughter of Ed's second cousin, the Duke of Saxfolk. Of course, you don't mention you're related to a duke or that your grandfather is an earl. People as highly connected as you will find out and won't expect you to discuss things like that. E likes a formal photo of all her guests before they go up the staircase to the ballroom. After everyone arrives, it's expected for you to go into the ballroom and take photos. Concentrate on Lord Rothford without drawing suspicion, of course. I want to know about anyone he talks to. If he talks more than a few minutes to someone, I also want whom they talk to and so on. You won't approach guests; only speak to them when they speak first. You're there on E's time. They won't think twice about you not talking about your business or personal life. Doesn't mean they won't ask. Believe me, they'll know before the night's over; every mum with a single son will know everything about you, well, the one in that file. Anyway, they will be wanting to set you up with their son, I'm sure."

"Oh joy!" Lil muttered.

Charles chuckled and continued, "You'll use Mary's mum's, your grandmother's, maiden name and the house in London. I redid Bill's apartments so that they look like that's where you live in case someone shows up knocking on your door when you're there. That will be your home base, as we say, to get ready for an op. I've had our agent who is a personal shopper get any clothes you'll need to start with. You'll need to shop for the rest. Not when you're with Sloan or HT, of course, because you'll never wear them around them; they're for ops only. I had Bill's quarters redone because it connects to ours without going through the front foyer. That way you'll be able to move easily from his place to ours."

"Great idea. I can use my room and sleep in my own bed if I have to stay over," said Lil.

"Exactly," Charles said with a nod. "Anthony, as you know, moved into their old quarters on the other side of Bill's. No one will think twice about you two living under the same roof, because the house is huge and sectioned into so many separate living quarters. People you will be socializing will know Anthony is wanting to go into the film industry, so your cover fits right in. You're twenty-one and have graduated from Kings College with a bachelor of fine arts degree."

"Great," she teased, "Uni is all done. Boy, it was tough!"

"Not a chance. Don't start that rubbish again. You'll put your time in at Oxford, just like the rest of us had to." He chuckled. "Now to the business end. You're all set with your business cards, stationery, an answering service to take your calls, bank accounts, and everything else you might need. You need to pack a couple of sets of small bags with things you might need, like extra clothes, footwear, extra equipment, film, cameras, whatever. We will put a set in each of the choppers for emergencies. Remember when you pack, you're expected to be in the latest, top designer clothes at all times when on an op."

"I take the photos; I'm not in the bloody things," she grumbled.

He chuckled again and said, "You're the one who wants this, so you have to play the part. You'll learn what to wear to fit in with your surroundings."

"Dad, I was wondering," she said looking at the business cards. "Can I really get started? It will help with my cover, taking on real photo sessions."

"Your mum said you would ask that," he replied smiling. "Yes, we both agreed that will be fine. We'll let you take on a few sessions as long as it doesn't get in the way of your education. I'm sure you'll have plenty of clients to choose from. The phone will be ringing off the hook after the ball and people see your work."

She just smiled.

"I'll keep up with the business end. It won't be like the locals, where you do it for free. It all has to be on the up and up. There will be contracts and deadlines and everything else that goes with a business. Now, go get dressed so that we can have some breakfast before we all head to Keaton Hall. We can talk more over there as we work."

Lil felt completely elated about something for the first time since the Battle of the Bands. She jumped up and said as she ran out, "Be back down in ten."

Charles chuckled never seeing her move so fast.

# CHAPTER 21

Saturday, two weeks later at about the time Lil usually met the gang, she was in London on her way to E's autumn ball. She could barely contain her excitement knowing she was going inside the palace. This time she had plenty to be nervous about. This was where her ops and career started as far as she was concerned. She now had to play her part in front of a couple of hundred high-society people. She'd either sink or swim as Papa would say. She hadn't been able to eat anything all day, afraid it would come right back up.

She decided to wear a black dress that went to her knee, instead of a long one, so that she would be able to move more quickly. It was elegant but not too sexy. She put her hair up, except for a few curls around her face to soften the style. She wanted her makeup to be just right, only applying a little eye shadow and lip gloss.

She was in the back seat with JR, staring out the window and thinking about the last few weeks. She had stayed busy, the days flew by swiftly, but her nights were rough. It took hours before she could sleep, missing HT like crazy. They never got to spend any alone time together, which might be a good thing. She was finding it harder to smile and act cheerful around him.

She was grateful Connor was being there for her. They had bonded over their broken hearts. She liked being around someone she didn't have to act happy and bubbly with all the time. He was always trying to make her laugh and had become her partner in crime, as he called it. She had asked him if could help with her cover Saturday night because she was taking on her first professional photo session. Her excuse for not wanting HT to know was that he always helped with her sessions, and she wasn't ready to spend that much alone time with him in London. He told her no problem. He could spend the weekend in

London and go to a football game on Sunday. He needed to meet the coach and players anyway since the team's owner wanted to sign him. When he told the guys he was going, they busted his nads all week that he better not sign, because he was playing for Manchester! Her plan was to wait till the last minute to text HT that she decided to go to London to hang out with Connor and go to the game. She actually was going but wasn't looking forward to it, hating football. She attributed some of her sick stomach to having a guilty conscience at waiting to text him until after she was supposed to be at the bakery that morning. She felt it wasn't like he really cared anyways, always so busy himself.

"We're here," said JR as they pulled through the palace gates.

HT was sitting with Lee and the twins at Gino's. He was staring at his glass of wine thinking it had been two more, hellish weeks, but he had survived. He emptied his glass and poured another. He wasn't drinking much more; he had golf in the morning. He just wanted enough to help block out that Lil was in London with the tosser and hadn't cared to tell him she was going until after she had left. But then, it wasn't like they talked much anymore.

Ever since Connor came into Lil's life, Sloan and Lee had been treating him like a bomb that might go off at any moment, and they were right. Despite his best efforts, he found himself lashing out at them. He needed to get his head around the fact that Lil really liked the tosser, and he was most likely going to be around for a while.

Sloan came in and sat beside him. "You order? I'm starving!"

"Yeah." Cody nodded and asked, "Where's Lil? I thought you were going to start rounding up costumes today for the Halloween thing."

"I thought so, too. I called her earlier. She's in London with Connor and he answered her phone, said she was in the loo. She decided she wanted to go to the game with him tomorrow after all and would be getting you blokes plenty of pics of the team."

"Brilliant!" said Jody. "He say what they were up to?"

"They were grabbing a bite to eat before going to the cinema."

HT jerked up his head. "You mean the theater?" he said as the churning in his stomach cranked up a notch, not believing what he was hearing.

"No, he said cinema. He said he got tickets for...I forget which movie. I would have been more interested if it was the theater."

The guys laughed as HT emptied his glass in a few gulps. He knew it was daft, but he was crushed, feeling betrayed as he thought, *That's our special thing, only going when we really want to see the movie to keep it special. It's our like a date-date, you-and-me night.*

"We heading to my place after?" asked Lee. "Parents are still gone for another week."

"Party time," Cody said taking out his phone. "I'll call a few people and tell them to spread the word."

It took HT a couple of seconds to regroup. "I'm in," he said as he pushed his empty glass away. "I don't want any more of that. Lee, I hope you have your flask this time."

"I do." He chuckled and handed it to him.

HT took long gulps until he couldn't anymore and welcomed the burn down his throat.

Lil was in the helicopter after the ball on her way home with Charles, Bill, and JR. She and JR had met them at the airfield after they went back to the house to change. She changed her mind about staying over. She wanted to get home to develop the massive amount of film she'd shot of Lord Rothford, hoping she caught something that would help. She closed her eyes, already looking forward to the next op.

It had been a long, fulfilling night. She could never have imagined it would be so thrilling and exciting. She tried to concentrate on how brilliant it was, finally doing what she dreamed of and trained so hard for. Her mind, however, returned to HT, and she felt an intense feeling of loss. All she could think of was how miserable she felt from missing him and wishing he had been with her to meet the queen and see the palace. She was overwhelmed at first at the extravagance. They'd entered a brightly lit entrance hall, with its domed ceiling, huge stained-glass window, and glittering crystal chandelier. A wide marble hallway lined with tall vases of white roses and silver candelabras led to a grand staircase with its red velvet runner and continued on to another entrance hall. They'd walked through the tall gold-gilded doors. There were huge silver urns holding sprays of white orchids and roses in the mirror-lined ballroom that blazed with magnificent crystal chandeliers. Long tables lined the walls with champagne fountains, hors d'oeuvres and more silver candelabras. It was the most lavish thing she had ever seen. She decided the best place to take the photos was as everyone went up the grand staircase. Precisely at six, elegantly dressed men in perfectly fitted tailcoats and ladies in glittering jewels and gowns flowed in.

Her phone buzzed in her pocket, distracting her. She read:

Doognihtg, Lil ☺.

She said under her breath. "Somebody has had way too much to drink again." She couldn't help but smile as she texted back and thought of how much she loved him and was more certain than ever it was the worst thing she could possibly do.

It was just before midnight when she entered her darkroom. Time slid past as it always did when she was in there. Her fingers began to ache and a cramp dug into her back as she placed the photos in large envelopes. She checked out the time. It was just before three. She went out seeing the night light in the loo was the only light on. She figured JR had come in and switched the one off overhead. She decided to make a quick stop in the loo before she went to the house and laid the envelopes on the snack bar. She came back out thinking she needed to remember to call Connor in the morning, letting him know she came home.

She looked over at the sofa and jumped slightly as she sucked in her breath. HT scared her. He was in a sitting position with his head hung forward, snoring away. He didn't look at all comfortable. She rolled her eyes and went over to have him lie down; his neck was going to kill him. She nudged his shoulder and softly said, "Lie down, HT." He did. She lifted his legs to straighten them out and sat on the edge, by his waist, to slip a pillow under his head. She leaned down to raise his head when she saw he was staring at her. She felt his hand on the back of her neck. She didn't pull away. He slowly pulled her toward him. She couldn't think of a single reason why she shouldn't let him kiss her, erasing the last traces of her reserve. She closed her eyes as he angled her head just right to receive his kiss. She was more than ready as his mouth covered hers. She didn't expect such tenderness or wasn't prepared for the heat that jolted through her. His tongue slid lightly along her mouth, urging her to open. His tongue swept in when she did, and he growled when her tongue touched his. She kissed him back, with all of her pent-up passion, tasting him, feeling his soft lips against hers. His kiss was unlike any she could have imagined. It made her weak and delirious. She felt like she was floating as his tongue worked hers perfectly. Passion didn't describe what she felt. She let the hot sensations sweep over her as he deepened the kiss, making love to her with his mouth. He was tender, then hard, then tender, and then so heated that she thought her lips would combust. She knew he would be an amazing kisser, but she'd never imagined it would feel like this. Her heart was beating triple time, her head was spinning, and her insides felt like they were melting. He pulled her more firmly against him until her breasts were pressed against his chest and slowly moved her until she was lying beside him. She had never felt such desire, feeling his heavy arousal when he cupped her bum and drew her harder against him. His hand found her breast and began to caress, sending a jolt of heat down deep. She was burning inside and losing all control. She slipped her hand behind his neck and kissed him harder, his tongue meeting hers in a passionate duel. Her whole body was a raging inferno. The more she kissed him back, the more she wanted. The alarm she had set for three in the darkroom went off helping her to regain her senses. It took all she had to gently pull her lips away. Her breath caught in her throat as shivers raced down her spine when he nuzzled the side of her neck lightly sucking it between little kisses. She slightly moved giving him complete access loving it. Her head was spinning; she couldn't think straight. She finally had the strength to ease off the sofa onto her knees. Her heart was racing, and she could hear the warning bells loud and clear in the back of her mind. She knew she had to get out of there before they kissed again; if they did she knew she wouldn't stop.

He let out a loud groan as she pulled away and quickly got to her feet. She ran to the darkroom and turned off the alarm knowing it would go off again. She ran back out not looking HT's way hearing him slurring his words, "Hey, where did you go?"

She went for the door scooping up the envelopes off the snack bar on her way out. She cursed herself for not thinking that one through, regretting her impulsiveness as she quietly closed the door behind her.

"What's the matter with me?" she grumbled in a huff as she went through the gate. "It's pure lust; that's all there is to it. Well, I'm never doing that again," she reassured herself as her mind raced trying to think a way out of the mess she had just gotten herself into. "Maybe he won't remember," she mumbled. "Or if he does, maybe he won't realize it was me. He's clearly drunk those lighted things again. The guys said they taste like black licorice, and he definitely tasted like it, and his text said it all," she reassured herself. "That's it!" she said. "I'll just go back to London. He'll never know I was here, just like he didn't realize I was at the party!"

JR groaned behind her, making her jump. "Snaggs, I'm beat."

"Bloody hell! JR, you almost made me wet myself! Can we go after you sleep for a bit? As you heard I got myself in a little mess."

"I heard." He chuckled. "We can just go now. I'll have Ben take us so that I can sleep. Just tell me it was worth all this trouble you're causing," he teased.

"OMG! JR, he's amazing! I finally got to taste those gorgeous lips, and blimey he can kiss. I've never felt—"

He cut her off. "Too much info, too much info." He chuckled covering his ears.

They laughed.

"Give me those envelopes. I'll take them to Charlie's study while I call Ben to tell him to get the chopper ready. You need to run up to your room and put something on that neck."

"Huh?"

"Just go; you'll see," he said with a little chuckle.

HT found himself in the same circumstances as a fortnight before. He woke up on the loo floor not remembering how he got there. He barely remembered going to Lee's. He laid there waiting for Jayden to come in and work his magic. Whatever that stuff was worked fantastic. He tried to remember why he drank so much this time. He snarled as he remembered. Lil went to the cinema with the tosser. He dragged himself up to lean against the toilet. An image flashed through his mind of him kissing someone on the sofa. He grumbled wondering if that really happened, and if it did, what else he had no memory of. He muttered, "Bloody hell, that's it. No more drinking those things; I can't remember shit!"

# CHAPTER 22

When Lil got back from London that afternoon, she was still annoyed with herself at being so weak with HT. She decided if he remembered anything she would just act dumb, laugh it off, and convince him it wasn't her. After all she was in London! She hated to admit it, but she was ready to break their rule and lie if she had to. If he knew it was her, nothing would be right between them again, which made her stomach swirl with nausea.

The gang was already enjoying the barbeque when she got home. She pulled her high-collar shirt up to help cover the love bites HT had left. When she looked at him, memories swept through her, and she felt her insides instantly go hot. She cheerfully greeted everyone and poured herself some tea and sat beside Sloan. After listening to them tease HT mercilessly, it only took her a few minutes to realize he had drunk even more than he did the night he hit his head. She was relieved, but just to make sure she teasingly said, "Darn. You really don't recall any of it? I was wanting all the details I missed."

He replied smugly. "My memories are sketchy, but I remember a little…" he turned and raised a questioning brow at Lee. "Hey, bro! Did I pass out on your sofa for a while?"

"No," Lee replied shaking his head, grinning. "Maybe you did outside on the ground after you tossed your cookies. Why?"

HT shrugged with a cheeky grin. "Just thought I had a few flashbacks this morning of a little action I got. It's been doing my head in."

Lee laughed and replied, "You didn't get any action on my sofa. Where did you go after you left the house?"

Uneasiness crawled through Lil as she inwardly groaned and thought, *Buggar, that relief didn't last long.* She forced a smile and trying to get them off that conversation said, "Must have been one boozy night! It couldn't have topped the last one though. You didn't try to fly again, did you?"

HT laughed at her joke, but there was something about the way he looked at her that made her feel defensive when he stated, "I don't have a knot on the back of my head."

Lil got a chill down her spine and quickly turned away as they all laughed.

"So how was the game?" asked Jody.

Lil pasted a smile on her face as she tried to sound excited. "Great! I took some amazing photos of the players off and on the field for you." She leaned forward and sat her glass on the table giving HT a look at her neck.

"Nice!" replied Jody.

*Who cares?* HT thought seeing her neck. It made his stomach flip as jealousy ripped through him. *What I want to know is what you were doing when you got those bloody things? I would never put one of those things on a girl. They're disgusting!*

As the afternoon wore on, the mood was cheerful and fun, as always when they were all together. Lil continued to keep her eyes on anyone other than HT. It was much easier to concentrate that way. Her heart would race when she glanced at HT and found him staring at her with a look she'd never seen. It was if he knew and wasn't liking it at all!

Sunday morning after two more of the worst weeks of Lil's life, her thoughts were in a whirl as she lay in bed staring up at the ceiling. The days had dragged on as she watched HT with his harem and the girls at the bakery. On top of that, she felt paranoid at times, afraid he remembered and just wasn't bringing it up. She worried because he wasn't acting like his usual self. His behavior toward her was different. They talked and joked around, but she couldn't help but think he was a little distant. It wasn't his words; it was the look on his face, and something in his eyes, like at the barbeque. But it was so brief that she wasn't sure it wasn't just her imagination working overtime.

She couldn't stop thinking about kissing him. She touched her lips. His tongue was silky smooth, and those lips—she knew they would be soft but firm at the same time. She never knew her body could react the way it had. She was ready to do it right there on the sofa. Actually, she wanted to jump his bones every time she looked at him. Her hormones were a mess! She was sleeping less and less because when she fell asleep her dreams were filled with fantasies of them making love. She moaned thinking how she would love to feel his hands and mouth on her from head to toe for real, not just in her dreams. She tried to push her feelings back and get her guard up, but it wasn't working anymore. She dragged herself out of bed to take another cold shower. That's all she seemed to do anymore. She had to make it a quick one because she needed to get to the Cove to finish Sloan's birthday cake. There was no school the next day, and the weather was still warmer than usual, so she and the guys decided earlier in the week to turn band practice into a birthday pool party at HT's house for Sloan. They were trying to make it a surprise, but Sloan found out, and now it sounded like half of the school was coming from the way she was inviting everyone.

She hurried down to the Cove after a quick breakfast. She decided to get a batch of photos done and hanging to dry while she finished Sloan's cake. She quickly put the pink buttercream frosting on Sloan's cake and finished it off with lilac frosting roses. She then hurried back to the darkroom peeling off the plastic gloves. She hated wearing them but didn't want the ink on her fingers to get on the cake. A few hours later, her alarm went off, and she quickly cleaned her hands, looking up at one of the photos hanging on the line. Her gaze fell on HT's beautiful eyes and was getting chills. There it was, that look!

She decided she was going to come right out and ask him what was going on. She had to ease her mind of whether he knew or not. She didn't want to face it, but he had changed, and she was tired of worrying that he remembered. A faint two knocks sounded at the door shaking her from her thoughts. She immediately felt a rush of heat from head to toe knowing it was HT. It was the signal they had come up with after he scared her a couple of times when she was exiting the darkroom not knowing he was there.

"I'll be out in just a sec! And don't touch that cake!" she called out, laughing. She took a deep breath, as she dried her hands and then brushed the small curls back from around her face, which instantly fell back again as she went out.

HT put a finger full of pink frosting in his mouth as she walked out. "Oops!" he teased, his eyes twinkling. "You caught me!" His heart skipped as always seeing her.

"You're messing up my hard work," Lil said breathlessly. That warm feeling she always got when seeing him had burst into flames.

His eyebrows rose as if surprised, "Really! You made this yourself?" he asked with a hint of humor in his voice.

"Yep, I did. Made it right here. I even made those cute flowers," she boasted.

He smiled and his eyes glinted devilishly. "Ah, that explains it. Now it makes sense."

"Huh? What makes sense. Oh no!" Lil groaned, looking horrified and starting to mumble, leaving out words, "Is it bad? I had gloves on, ink on my fingers, not in the icing. Buggar! Should have licked the spoon. But I've made it like a thousand times!"

HT laughed and got another finger of frosting and held it to her lips.

She playfully rolled her eyes at him and licked a little at first, tasting it.

An intense feeling vibrated through every nerve of his body. She didn't look up to see the little beads of sweat that formed on his forehead or see the desire in his eyes.

Her brow lifted as if she was puzzled and mumbled again, "It doesn't seem too bad." She put her mouth over his finger, letting it linger, getting the rest of the frosting, trying to figure out why he thought it was bad. "It's not Grammy's, but it isn't *that* bad."

He took in a deep breath trying to get his body and Clyde back under control. He teased once he was able to talk. "I'm bad! I made you think it was bad?"

She looked up seeing his eyes twinkling. "You're such a tosser! You had me worried it was really rubbish!"

"Sorry, I couldn't help myself. It tastes brilliant, like always."

"Good," she said looking for some sign, some small indicator letting her know what was going on inside his head. She didn't see anything, but she knew him and could tell something was going on. She was ready to broach the dreaded subject and took in a deep breath. "I need to ask you something."

He shrugged. "Sure, what's up?"

She said with a slightly forced smile, "That's what I was going to ask you."

"Okay, need more than that." He chuckled.

"Since I went to London you don't seem yourself. You smile and joke around, but the few times we try to have a conversation you never seem to say whatever it is that you are really thinking." She hesitated not sure how to go about asking if he remembered.

His eyes darkened. He was still hurt, but he tried to make the effort to appear otherwise as he said, "By the way, you never said what you did that night!"

Her heart raced at seeing the look come across his face again. A look of what she could only call hurt. No, she told herself he wouldn't be hurt. He's just wondering why I bloody kissed him. She thought hard; nervous feelings kicked in as she tried to think of excuses she could use as to why. She gave up and decided to try to make a joke of it and teased, "Like minute by minute?"

A muscle tightened in his cheek. He couldn't hide the bitterness when he snarled, "No just the ones when you went to the cinema with Connor." He searched her face for a sign that she had been caught out, but there was nothing. Instead she stared at him with what looked like anger and hurt.

"Don't be an arse!"

A trace of sarcasm was still evident in his voice, as he replied, "Oh, I'm an arse because I'm upset? Or that I found out?"

She huffed with an exaggerated roll of her expressive gray eyes. "You know, Harry Thomas, for you being one of the smartest people I know, you can be incredibly thick!"

Meeting her angry eyes, he sneered, "So now I'm thick, too?"

"Yeah...well...no!" she threw up her hands in frustration. "You know what I mean." Her gray eyes held his green blazing ones.

He shook his head as his emotions erupted. "No, I used to. Well, maybe sometimes I thought I did, but now I don't have a bloody clue what's going on in that head of yours!"

"You're right. You don't have a bloody clue if you think I went to the cinema with him or anyone else for that matter!"

His mind raced as he thought, *Bloody Hell I got it wrong again!* He playfully blew air out of his cheeks knowing it made her laugh and said with a meek smile, "I'm sorry!"

It didn't work.

"You're sorry all right!" she hissed in disgust.

He held his hands up as if in surrender. "Okay, okay." He laughed, generally relieved he was wrong again. "It won't happen again! No more jumping to conclusions."

His laugh raised her temper up a notch, and it showed in the way she looked at him. "What is wrong with you lately, Harry Thomas? First you think I wouldn't be at your victory party and now this!"

"Well...would it help if I said to try to look on the bright side?"

Lil raised a skeptical eyebrow, "Oh! There's a bright side?"

His eyes twinkled the way that turned her insides to hot mush as he made an exaggerated cross over his chest. "I swear I learned my lesson and no more accusations."

She just huffed!

"Come on now," he teased, "you've said that is all it takes with Moms when you've screwed up. Lesson learned, right?" He wiggled his brow up and down.

She let out a long sigh as her body turned to mush as always. "I'll forgive you— but don't push your luck again, mister. And for the record, he got those tickets without asking me." She then added with another little huff, "Why didn't you just ask me? But then it shouldn't surprise me since I never see you anymore. You always seem too busy to make time for me."

"What?" He stared at her, open mouthed. He let loose emotion that had been building since Connor came into their lives. "I can't believe that came out of your mouth! You're the one who's always too busy for me! So busy you forgot to tell me you were running off to London and had to tell me in a bloody text after you already left!"

They stared at each other for a long, tense moment.

Lil finally broke the silence; guilt dug at her heart knowing she was to blame. "Okay, I admit that was bad. But to my defense you've been busy too, so I'm only taking half of the blame," she said with a guilty smile.

He shook his head. "I would say it's more like seventy-thirty."

"True." She nodded and added with a cute little smile, "I'm the thirty of course."

He couldn't help grinning. "Of course you are."

The tension between them was gone.

"You know," Lil said, "I think we came close to breaking our rule."

"How's that?" he asked.

"The holding back. We should have told each other that we weren't happy about not spending time together."

He nodded. "I agree. So no more holding back when we're not happy about something."

"Right, we talk about it," Lil said and then added, "which can still be a bloody problem if we're never together to talk. That's it! We're making rule two right now. No going days without seeing each other! And we make sure we take some alone time together to talk!"

He chuckled and said, "Now, there's my bossy girl and her rules. I wondered when she'd resurface." His brow shot up. "Wait a minute. Seems I wanted to make a rule like that before the Battle of the Bands so that we wouldn't have this problem."

"Here we go with the 'I told you sos,'" she teased.

"Who me?" He snorted. "What do I know, since I'm never right!"

"Stop! Now you're just gloating because you're right." She chuckled.

"I don't gloat. Well, okay, maybe I am this time, since I wasn't just right; I was *so* right," he said with a chuckle.

She playfully rolled her eyes. "Whatever. Well, at least it's a rule now, and all we have to do is agree on the time frame we can stay apart."

"We can talk about that tonight," he said with a wink. "I say we come back here after the party and talk about it."

"It's a date," she said smiling.

"See, patience does pay off," he teased. "I believe you just said we have a date! So, we finally get to snog and cuddle, right?"

Her heart leaped wishing he wasn't teasing, wanting to do that and a whole lot more. She playfully rolled her eyes again. "I have to admit I've missed all your rubbish."

They laughed together for what felt like the first time in weeks and were surprised at how good it felt.

"What time are the guys coming?" she asked looking at the cake as if to fix the frosting. She couldn't take staring into his seductive green eyes another second.

"They're on the way. You need me to carry anything over?"

"This cake, if you can stay out of it, and that bag of disposable cameras lying there. I'm not taking my camera. I'm going to put those on the tables so that everybody can help with the photos so that I can enjoy myself!"

"Uh-huh! I'll have to see it to believe it," he replied, grabbing the bag of cameras before picking up the cake. "Catch the door, and I'll be on my way. What time you coming over?"

"After I get cleaned up. I'll walk with you up to the house," she replied as she hurried and opened the door. "JR went after Sloan a while ago. They should be getting back here!"

"Is it just me, or is something brewing between those two?" asked HT as they headed up the walk.

"I know! They can't keep their eyes off each other."

They looked at each other laughing and in unison said, "Poor JR!"

They reached the porch.

"We're doing our music the first set," HT said as she ran up the steps. "And, only doing two sets so that we can enjoy the party."

"Smart thinking. See you in a bit and be careful with that cake," she teased as she hurried into the house. She felt like she was flying as she ran to her room already feeling things getting back to normal between them and loving it.

HT headed toward his house and thought she sent him soaring way up past what she called his HT zone. He chuckled; he was in Lil Zone. Nothing could touch him or drag him down. He muttered, "I'm thinking there is a song in that! Maybe I can write a happy one for a change, not another gut-wrenching one. That's all I've been able to write since the tosser came into our lives." He started singing the first song he wrote about her, his favorite. It had been a while since he'd felt like singing it.

Twenty minutes later, after taking a quick shower, Lil walked out of the loo to find Sloan waiting on her. "I was beginning to think you forgot about me!" teased Lil as she went to sit at her vanity. "I didn't wash it. Wasn't sure if I should or not since HT's is always dry."

"No worries. Doesn't matter," replied Sloan not commenting on why she was late.

"I'm ready. Let's do this!" said Lil.

"Are you sure?" asked Sloan.

"I'm sure. Give it a whack!" Lil groaned as she turned away from the mirror.

"Right then. Here we go," Sloan said with a little, nervous chuckle. She scooped up Lil's hair, twisted it a few times, and then cut just under the twists. Lil's dark hair fell to her shoulders. It tumbled in waves and curls.

"How's it look?" asked Lil.

"Let me fix it before you look; I want the wow factor," Sloan said as she started cutting and shaping it so that it lay just right, giving it a little more wave and bounce. When she was done, it looked as if she had spent hours fixing it that way, instead of it just lying naturally. She sighed and said, "All done. Hope you like it."

Lil looked in the mirror. "I love it!" she squealed. She turned her head back and forth, making it swing. She jumped up and hugged her. "It's perfect! I really do love it!"

"I left it long enough so that you have no problem if you want to put it up. Now, let's get you dressed!" In true Sloan style, her words were more like an order when she handed Lil a pair of cut-off jeans. "How about you wear these? I trimmed them a bit while you were in the shower!"

"Sloan," Lil said with a little groan as she put them on. "You cut them way too short. I have to wear a bathing suit bottom underneath them now."

"Don't be daft. They look sexy as hell. And here, wear this swimming top in case you decide to go in the pool. Now put this tank top over it."

"Wow, this sucker is tight." Lil said once she had it on.

"Just sexy tight. Here, wear these peep-toes. Show off your painted toenails."

Lil mumbled, "I'm afraid to ask, why heels?"

"Heels make your boobs and bum look better."

"All this just because you cut my hair?"

"Of course. You have to showcase my work!"

Lil rolled her eyes. "You know you're mental, right?"

They laughed as they went out the door.

JR drove Lil and Sloan over to HT's in a golf cart. He pulled up the same time as Connor's dad was dropping him off. Lil thought again how much he reminded her of HT when he got out of the car. That's probably what drew her to him in the first place. He smiled. That's where it ended; his smile was not HT's. She hopped off the cart as she said, "You're early."

"I thought you might need some reinforcements," he whispered as they hugged. He whistled as he stood back to look at her. "You look amazing!"

"Thanks," she said with a big smile.

"Hi, Connor," Sloan said as they hugged.

"Hi," Connor replied, handing her a small wrapped package tied with a purple bow. "Happy Birthday and fantastic job on Lil's hair."

"Thanks and thanks for my present. How did you know my favorite color is purple?"

"Hey, I pay attention to my other favorite girl."

Sloan just laughed as she looked around for JR. "Oh, looks like Moms could use some help over there getting the food out. I'll go see if I can help." She hurried off.

Lil and Connor looked to see why she ran off so fast. They looked at each other and laughed seeing JR was with Mary.

"Let's go say hi to HT. Plus, I want to get the disposable cameras he brought over for me and get them out on the tables before the guys get started. I want to be front and center when they do."

"Of course you do. You not having your camera around your neck is shocking to say the least." He gave her a big smile.

"Well," she replied with a little chuckle as they walked toward HT, "I couldn't leave it behind, so I gave it to JR to bring, just in case."

He chuckled as he took her hand. "Heads up on my help with HT today. I'm going to take off about four."

"No worries," Lil said with a smile.

HT's stomach turned over watching them approach.

"Hi, bro, you about set up? Need any help?" Connor asked.

HT thought, *I'm not your bro!* Finding it difficult to maintain a civil politeness, he glared at him and answered with an icy smile and strained tone. "No, we're good."

Connor saw the flicker of anger flash across HT's face and picked up on his tone. He thought, *Whoa, what's his problem? He looks as if he could rip my head off!* Connor stared at him trying to figure out what had him so mad. Then he saw it when HT looked at Lil. His eyes were shining with love as he smiled at Lil. His look held such tenderness, it made Connor's mouth almost drop open. He couldn't believe he hadn't seen it before. HT was crazy about Lil! And it wasn't as a mate!

"I love your hair," HT said with a wink to Lil, not taking his eyes off hers.

"Thanks. It feels great," replied Lil trying to calm her racing heart.

"The bag of cameras is over there on the table."

"Great. I'll hurry and get them out and then see if Mum needs help," she said. "I want to be front and center when you get started. I'm so excited to finally hear your new songs."

He tilted his head the sexy way he did and teased, "You shouldn't have missed so many of our practices."

"I know." She nodded with a sigh. "I won't be missing anymore," she said grinning.

"I'm going to hold you to that," he said, his eyes twinkling when he returned her grin.

Lil was a hair from screaming she loved him, so she quickly turned to Connor and said, "You want to help me?"

"Of course." Connor nodded and then looked at HT. "Unless you're sure you don't need help, bro." He couldn't help winding him up. "I'll be happy to help," he said with a smirk knowing now he was the last person HT would want to help.

"I'm fine," HT said, trying not to sneer at him.

"Right then." Connor smiled. He pulled on Lil's hand. "Come on, light of my life, let's get those cameras out. Best idea ever! Gives us more alone time."

Lil chuckled as they walked off and said under her breath, "Laying it on a little thick, aren't you?"

Connor just laughed.

HT muttered as they walked off, "When I'm in need of a total wanker, I'll let you know." He knew he should turn his head away and not watch, but he looked on as they started to place cameras on the tables. He couldn't take his eyes off her. When Lil bent over to place a camera on a table it gave him a perfect view of her bum. "What the bloody hell is she wearing?" he muttered.

Clyde was up and ready for duty. "Buggar! She doesn't have anything on under those things!"

"What's that, bro? You need something?" Lee asked as he looked up from the cord he was untangling.

"Nothing. I'm good," HT said, not realizing he had walked up behind him. He pulled his eyes away and back to the cord he was untangling. He said under his breath, as he pulled on the cord, "I wish I was wrapping this thing around that tosser's neck!"

"Here," Lee said, handing him his flask. "You don't sound good. Take the edge off."

HT grunted before taking a few long swallows.

When the kids started to arrive, Lil, Connor, and Sloan went to welcome them. The guys stood behind the makeshift stage talking and passing Lee's flask, trying to settle their nerves.

"It's almost time," said Lee.

HT waved at Lil when he saw her looking his way.

"They're going to start," Lil said as she hurried off.

"It took you long enough to get back here," HT said, smiling when she ran up.

"We were greeting your public," she replied returning his smile.

"That's for sure," Sloan said coming up behind her. "There is at least seventy kids here. Biggest party I've ever had. I feel loved."

"Like you don't know that," Lee said with a nervous chuckle.

"Yeah, right, like they're here for me." Sloan laughed.

"Well, I hope we don't run them off once we get started," said Cody.

They all laughed.

"Well, mates, the sooner we get this over with the sooner we can join the party," said Lee going around the speakers to their stage.

HT and the twins followed him, and Lil hurried over to where JR put her camera. She scooped it up and made her way to stand right in the front.

HT saw she had her camera and laughed shaking his head. "I knew it!"

She smiled with a little shrug.

"Silly question," said Connor standing beside her. "Do you think...that maybe...well...Lil, I think he feels the same way as you!"

"Don't be thick," Lil said with a snort over that farfetched possibility.

"I'm not joking. I see how he acts and looks at you."

Lil laughed and said, "Me and every other girl. He's good at giving the false impression that he loves you and you're his one and only; it has nothing to do with his true feelings. For God's sake, Connor. I know that bloke like the back of my hand. You forget I've watched him in action for months."

Connor just rolled his eyes knowing there wasn't any sense pushing the issue.

"Thanks for coming everybody," Lee yelled out. "We're going to start this off with something you can dance to. So let us know what you think, by dancing." He did the intro to the set asking, "Have you ever met that one person who gives you an intense rush just by their touch, and all you want to do is kiss them? Better yet, want them to *Kiss you*?"

That was the guys' cue. They started to play.

Lil had to force herself to listen and push the button; she was lost in HT's eyes through the lens! Then she smiled realizing what they were singing. That was one of her favorites. HT always acted silly, like he was now, when he and the guys practiced it, puckering his lips up and blowing her kisses, making her laugh. She clicked away on the button as he sung to her.

She turned around and snapped off a couple of rounds of the kids dancing and turned back to give HT the thumbs-up. He smiled back with that special smile she loved and the wink that always made her melt.

She really loved the second song about their first gettin'-loose night. It was her favorite. It's the night when she had fallen madly in love with him even though she wouldn't let herself see it at the time. She sang, "C'mon, C'mon," as she hit the button.

The third song was kind of new, but she had heard him hum and sing parts of it around the Cove, something about "*I would.*" She heard him sing how it was in his head about being a boyfriend and how he would say that he loved her. She saw his sly, sexy grin radiate through the camera when he sang about the bloke having twenty-seven tattoos. She lowered her camera and playfully shook her head no and made the same disgusted face she had that day, when he said he was getting twenty-seven tattoos!

He laughed and shook his head at her silliness.

Lee gave him a look as if he had completely lost his wits for messing up the lyrics with laughing. When he turned away, HT raised his brow at Lil and pointed while he mouthed, "Your fault!"

She laughed.

"I've never seen you so happy; I like it," Connor said smiling.

"He makes me happy just watching him. He's beaming up there," Lil said as she finally tore her gaze away and smiled at Connor. "He loves it; look at the way his eyes twinkle when he sings. Gives me goose bumps just watching him."

HT turned away, not wanting to watch her with Connor; he was on too much of a high.

"Let's go dance and you can get some shots out there. I know you'll wish you had," said Connor.

Lil nodded. "So true. Lead the way."

Connor added under his breath as they walked off, "How daft can you be? He's beaming, and his eyes are twinkling because of you!"

HT turned back to Lil. His expression darkened as he thought with disgust, *Of course the tosser had to be a great dancer. He's the most annoying bloke I've ever met!* He felt a tightening in the pit of his stomach, so he turned his head away and saw a blonde staring at him. She was cute and had huge boobs, way bigger than he liked. She gave him the creeps a little, staring at him like she wanted to devour him. He smiled and quickly turned his head. His eyes went straight back to Lil. His gaze darted back and forth between her and Connor looking at each other and laughing. Not thinking, he jerked his head right back to the scary girl. He saw she was still staring. She took the tip of her tongue and outlined her lips and shook her big boobs at him. He couldn't help but laugh.

Lil was watching. Her great mood vanished as she quickly turned away reminding herself it's his business and decided not to look in his direction again.

HT turned to Lee to see if he had seen the girl.

Lee had and was grinning at him. He mimicked the girl. He shook his chest at HT and nodded toward the girl and raised his eyebrows up and down as if to say, *Go for it!*

HT blew air out of his cheeks and quickly shook his head no, making Lee laugh.

When the second set was over, the guys were drenched with sweat. They looked at each other and started laughing, getting the same idea and stripped off their shirts. Off came the trainers as they raced toward the pool. Each one did a cannonball, trying to outdo the last. They were the only ones in the pool until the girls spotted them. Within minutes, a dozen girls had joined them.

Lil stood with Connor and tried not to look over at the pool but couldn't help it. Her jealousy raged at watching HT enjoying himself, laughing and splashing around.

Jody yelled, "Let's play chicken."

Nine of the twelve girls pushed each other out of the way trying to get to HT as they yelled, "I want Harry; I get Harry!" (He was still known as Harry outside of his inner circle).

HT flashed a roguish grin. "Don't fight; plenty of me to go around," he teased as a cute redhead with a perfect shape fought her way to him first.

Lil said with a grimace, wanting to slap his too-gorgeous face, "Doesn't he ever take a break from all that rubbish he spits out? How can someone be so bloody full of himself?" She couldn't stop watching as he sank down in the water and wrapped his arms around the redhead's skinny waist and lifted her up on his shoulders. She giggled as he stood. Lil sucked in her breath as the girl ran her fingers through his wet hair, getting it out of his eyes.

HT laughed and yelled, "Let's do this!"

Lil turned away from the pool as she a took a deep breath. Tears burned behind her eyes as bile rose up her throat. She was ready to scream in frustration. She was too mad and jealous to give herself the pep talk again—his love life wasn't her business. *Screw that! She wanted to rip his beautiful curls out of his head!* Her voice quivered with anger and jealousy as she turned to Connor. "His hands and, well, whatever other body parts are all over that cow, and her hands are all over him!"

"I saw that. Come on," Connor said grinning as he snaked his arm around her waist. "Let's go sit by the fire before you have a hissy fit!"

Her brow shot up. "Excuse me! Hissy fit?"

He replied with a little chuckle, "Well, whatever you call it when you start that mumbling, threatening to jerk some girl bald headed when you watch him flirt."

"You're right," she agreed with a grunt. "I do get wound up at times."

"What was that? I'm rig—"

She playfully hit his arm cutting him off. "Don't you start; I get enough of that rubbish from HT."

HT's jaw was clenched so tightly that it hurt at watching Connor and Lil laugh as they walked by the pool.

Lil didn't look his way to see it but Connor did. He shot HT back a smug expression that seemed to say, "Yeah, I know you want this!" He put his thumb through Lil's belt hoop so that HT could see his hand bounce off her bum.

HT growled as he dropped the red head off his shoulders and hopped out of the pool glaring at Connor's hand as they continued walking.

Connor looked back at HT and his mouth curved knowingly. He had his proof staring at him. If looks could kill, he was in trouble.

HT exhaled trying to keep his cool and channel JR's mind-control training so that he didn't go after Connor and break his face. His jaw and fists were clenched as his eyes bored through him, not turning away.

Connor turned back and threw his head back and laughed and thought, *How can two people be so daft? I guess I should help them out a bit. I need a plan to make the idiots realize how the other one feels.*

HT spotted Lee waving at him and stomped over by the pool house. He hissed as he glared back at Connor, "Did you see that?"

"See what?" Lee asked as he looked over to where he was glaring to find nothing that would cause the now flashing hot green in his eyes.

HT turned to Lee. "He put his hand on her arse and gave me the look."

"The look?"

"Yeah, the bloody look! The one I give blokes when I know."

"What are you going on about," Lee said with a chuckle.

"It's not funny. I'm telling you he knows that I'm jealous as hell, and I want to break his bloody neck!"

"Don't jump to conclus—"

"Oh, I saw it," HT cut in sharply as he threw himself down on the pool lounger. "He's rubbing it in my face that she's his."

"Don't get all bent out of shape over something you thought you saw," said Lee, making an effort to keep the peace between him and Connor.

HT snorted as he settled deeper into the lounge chair. "I know what I know. That wanker gave me the bloody look!"

"You're starting to get a little intense again, bro. I thought you had that rubbish under control when seeing them together."

"Yeah, I do," HT grumbled. "I'm just having a moment."

Lee laughed and said, "It happens. Here drink this; it will help," he passed a silver flask to him.

"I would rather break his face." HT chuckled darkly, taking the flask. He tipped the flask and took a long drink and then another.

"Watch it." Lee laughed. "That's my special brew."

HT grunted. "I can tell. It burned all the way down to my bloody toes."

Lee chuckled.

They sat silently, watching the blue-green ripples in the pool as they passed the flask back and forth a couple more times.

Lee's voice shook HT from his thoughts as he stood. "Come on, let's go join the others by the fire. Did you drink enough to give Big Boobs a go?" he joked.

"Not enough booze in the world," muttered HT as he got up.

Lee laughed as they walked over to the fire.

The smell of burning wood filled the air as HT dropped down on a lounger, legs placed on each side. He squinted a little trying to peer through the flames to bring Lil into focus; she was sitting across the fire from him.

"Thanks, Connor, I know I don't say it enough. I don't know how I would have handled the last few months without you," said Lil and sighed.

Connor draped his arm over her shoulders. "That's what mates are for."

"Well, you're a fantastic one," she mumbled, leaning her head over on him.

HT was watching and turned away in case they started snogging. He saw the scary chick sitting on the ground just beside his chair. Needing something to take his mind off Lil, he flashed her his flirty smile.

She giggled and ran her bare foot up his leg.

Connor felt Lil's back go straight as a poker as she watched HT. He teased, trying to get her to laugh. "Is that smoke coming from the fire or out of your ears?"

A frustrated sigh hissed out between her lips to keep from screaming. "Who is that big-boobed hussy?"

"Whoa! Hussy?" said Connor laughing. "That comment has to be one of Bill's!"

"Actually, I hear it from Grammy," Lil said. "But I will say Papa is why she calls a certain female customer that every time she comes in."

They laughed as Connor's phone buzzed. He read the text. "That's Dad; he'll be here in about five minutes."

HT turned away from the girl at hearing Lil laugh. She caught him off guard and leapt on top of him in a flash, knocking him back on the lounger with her on top. He laughed and the girl's mouth came down hard on his.

Lil heard him laugh and made the mistake of taking a glance back across the fire. "Well, I'm ready to call it a day too; I've had all I can stomach," she grumbled as she turned away.

Connor stood up holding his hand down for her. "She sure wants him."

Lil's eyes were as cool as gray storm clouds as he pulled her up. "Don't they all?" she said stomping off.

Connor looked over seeing HT trying to push the girl off him and chuckled as he hurried to catch up with Lil.

"Whoa," HT said as he pushed on her trying to get up.

It gave her enough time to ram her tongue down his throat.

He almost gagged. Her tongue reminded him of a lizard. It was cold, long, and slimy. It was shooting fast all over in his mouth and down his throat. He was sure he felt it hit his tonsils. He tried to turn his head away, but she had him pinned down against the chair. He put his hands on her shoulders pushing her back, and she sucked his bottom lip and bit it, not letting loose! He pushed again while he bolted upright on the lounge sitting them up.

She finally let loose. In a low, sexy tone, she whispered, "You like that, baby?"

He looked at her halfway in shock and thought, *No I didn't like it, you bloody vampire lizard!* She came at him again before he could stand up, this time aiming for his ear.

She bit it.

He yelled, "Bloody hell!" and jumped to his feet as he pushed her off. He saw Jayden and JR laughing as he hurried away from her. "Real funny! I'll be lucky if I have a lobe left!" he snarled standing beside them looking over to make sure she wasn't following him.

Jayden and JR laughed harder.

"Cheers!" he said with disgust.

"What, you're not saying bite me?" asked JR between fits of laughter.

Jayden chimed in, laughing. "Looks like she did that, along with some sucking!"

HT touched his lip and grumbled, "I'm glad you guys found it amusing. That bloody vampire took a chunk out of my ear!" He raised his finger to his ear and held it up. "Look, she drew blood! Some bloody bodyguards you are! You both are total rubbish at your job!"

They howled with laughter!

He stormed off.

JR's phone buzzed. Still chuckling he read the coded text. "It's Charlie. He says he needs us both in Edinburgh and to bring Snaggs. He said Joe can tail HT if he leaves the grounds. I'll get her, and we'll meet you at the chopper."

"You got it," said Jayden over his shoulder already on the move.

Lil was waving at Connor as his dad drove down the driveway. She looked to see JR running up. She began to feel a surge of excitement, knowing she was about to go on another op. She slipped her shoes off so that she could run to the secret gate.

Less than two hours later, they landed at the airfield in Edinburgh and were in the car heading to the castle. All they knew was that Charles was going to be there as Lord Standish attending the banquet honoring the Queen's Armed Forces. Lil looked out the window as Jayden drove up Princess Street. She saw the castle come into view. It was situated on rock that was formed after a volcano erupted a million years ago and was all lit up, looking like a beacon in the gray sky. She had seen the same view many times over the years, but now it seemed mysterious and dangerous.

JR's phone buzzed, and it made Lil remember she was supposed to meet HT at the Cove. She hurried to get her phone from her emergency bag. She wished she had packed something warmer. She knew by experience Edinburgh was chilly at night and sometimes downright cold this time of year. She rolled her eyes as she looked down at the short stylish sundress she had on and the thin matching jacket. It was more for fashion than warmth. When she packed, the only thing she thought about was to maintain her image—young, sophisticated, and chic. She let out a disgusted sigh as she looked at the flat, thin satin shoes she was wearing. It was either them or the silly heels Sloan had her wear to the party. She made a mental note to pack a pair of trainers. Thinking about HT teasing her it was a date, she grinned as she texted that she was sorry, that something came up, and she would have to reschedule their date-date. She had never imagined she would fall in love so soon in her life and especially not with a bloke she could never have. Every time she thought of how hopeless it was, she got disgusted with herself all over again for falling in love with him. She ignored the tearing pain in her heart and turned her phone off, not waiting on his reply and dropped it back into her bag. As they drove up to the castle, she cleared her mind. No more thoughts of him until the op was over.

"Park right by the entrance," JR told Jayden as he drove the car park to the front of the castle. "We still have about an hour. It will take at least that long to shuttle the ladies up to the great hall. Those things they call shuttles aren't much bigger than a golf cart."

"I'd say it's going to take longer than that. Most of the men will be riding too. There's going to be a lot of old farts, and they can't tackle that steep walk either." Jayden chuckled. "It's a ceremony for fifty years of service."

"True." JR grinned as he turned to look at Lil. "Charlie wants photos of everyone that is here. Then, like the ball, concentrate on Lord Rothford. Oh yeah, make sure you get photos of the old farts when they go up for their plaques and when they shoot the cannon off so that you look legit. When you're asked, and I'm sure you will be, you were booked for this at the same time as the ball; and by the way, you're also booked for E's Christmas ball. She loved your work!"

"Really?" asked Lil as they got out of the car.

"Yeah," replied JR with a grin. "Charlie said that would make you happy. He said to tell you in case someone brought it up."

A light mist started rolling in as they got Lil's bag of equipment out of the boot. As soon as they started over the old drawbridge covered in cobblestones and wood, the wind kicked up. Lil grumbled as she slipped on the damp stones. "I bet I pack a pair of wellies too!"

JR nodded. "Won't take long before you're an expert at what to pack."

"That's what Dad said. Doesn't help me now though," she mumbled making him laugh.

They started up the steep, cobblestoned incline to get to the castle. The castle was built for military defense because whoever held the castle ruled over the city, so the monarchs living quarters and main buildings were located on top. As they walked up, the air got much colder.

Lil saw the old guard quarters ahead on the right. It had been turned into a coffee shop. She could use a hot cup right about now.

They turned left up another steep incline, after passing what was now the war museum. The wind whipped around them even more once they reached the top. They continued walking across the open courtyard to reach the main entrance to the castle. JR opened the heavy wooden door. They stepped into the Great Hall where the banquet was being held.

The inside of the castle looked exactly like the outside with its dark stone walls. Lil was surprised when she scanned the huge room. "Wow," she said looking over at JR. "Whoever decorated did a fantastic job. It's not fancy, but it's beautiful and has a military look."

"And more important," JR said with a grin, "it's warm!"

Lil shook her head and chuckled. "No, what's more important is that I see a teapot and two cups over on that table which I'm sure is for us!"

He laughed as she hurried over to the table.

After tea she took out her camera. "This one is my newest, but it's not my favorite."

"Because it's digital. Not a dinosaur like the one always hanging around your neck!"

"Okay, Anthony." She chuckled. "I miss him not being around, taking a mic out of me because I don't 'join the modern world,' as he puts it."

"Hey, that reminds me. What's the deal holding out on me about him being in love?"

"Sorry he tricked me with that stupid oath we made as kids."

"The one with you not telling me or Jay?"

"Yeah." She nodded. "To tell you the truth, I didn't think it was a big deal the beginning of the summer when he told me about her but then a few months ago he told me he was in love with her and not coming home so I knew it was serious."

"That's what has Ed so worried. Sounds like he's about to go back to the States and drag him home."

They laughed.

Lil walked around and took photos of the long wooden tables covered with white tablecloths and hurricane candle holders that sat ever so often in the middle of the tables. The royal-blue candles were lit and flickering inside the glass globes. The bottoms of the holders were circled with white carnations tipped with royal blue. Her finger clicked away getting the wooden chairs, covered in white silk. Each chair had a royal blue and gold bow on the back. She went over and took photos of the elegant buffet table full of hors d'oeuvres.

She handed JR her camera when she was done. "I have to go to the loo before this thing gets started. Any idea where it is?"

He nodded over to a door. "Through that door, take a right, and it's about half-way down the hall on the left."

"Be right back," she said already heading for the door.

JR chuckled, shaking his head.

Fifteen minutes later Lil walked back up complaining. "You have to go a mile, and there are only two lousy stalls. It's going to take forever once the ladies have a few cocktails in them. I see I won't be drinking any more tea!"

"Yeah, right!" said JR.

Lil just rolled her eyes.

Lil clicked away on her camera as the guests started arriving. She acknowledged Charles with a head nod as he entered as Lord Standish. When she changed the film in her camera, she saw Bill at the hors d'oeuvres buffet filling a plate. She chuckled. As the night went on, she couldn't help herself; she drank more tea than she cared to admit. She put it out of her mind when she had to go, not wanting to tackle the long line. She was fine until she went outside to get photos of them shooting off the cannon. The cold wind almost did her in as they crossed over the courtyard, but she told herself not to think about it. The loud blast from the cannon nearly made her wet herself. She quickly handed

JR her camera and grumbled when they made it back inside the great hall. "I have to go tackle that line. I'm about to burst. See you in about an hour," she grumbled over her shoulder as she hurried toward the door. She went out the door and headed down the hallway, seeing at least twenty ladies standing in line. She stood there for a few minutes and grumbled to an older lady in front of her. "This is absolutely rubbish."

The older lady chuckled as she turned around. "I agree," she said as she held out her hand. "I'm Lady Fairchild."

Lil shook her hand and politely introduced herself. "Nice to meet you. I'm Lil."

"I know. I hear you're the queen's favorite photographer now," Lady Fairchild said smiling. "Seems she's taken quite a liking to you. She sings your praises to anyone looking for a photographer. I'm afraid I missed the ball, but I hear you're doing her Christmas ball. I would love to have a photo of my husband in his uniform tonight, if you get a chance."

"I will be happy to take a photo of you and your husband, and I'll make sure I get you a few copies. That's if we ever get out of this line," Lil mumbled. "This is ridiculous; they need more loos."

Lady Fairchild chuckled again. "I'm on the historic society committee, and I'm always complaining we need more loos. There is another one in the old guards building, beside the coffee shop."

"I saw the shop when I came in," said Lil. "If you think it's unlocked, I would gladly tackle the weather!"

"It's unlocked. If you can tackle a few flights of stairs you won't be in the weather long."

"I can. Just point the way," said Lil smiling.

Lady Fairchild pointed with her gloved index finger. Her diamond bracelet glinted as she motioned further down the long hall. "Take a left at the end, go down the stairs, then take a first right, follow that hall, and take the stairs up. There's a door that will take you outside to the old guards building. It's just a few feet across, so you won't be in the weather long. Be careful if it's raining. Those cobblestones are like ice when wet. And there's three steps taking you down to the patio in case you don't see them, so be careful. You never know if the lights are working out there. It takes an act of God just to be able to change a light bulb around here."

Lil chuckled and replied, "Thank you, Lady Fairchild. I'll be right back," and she took off running down the long hall lined with its stained glass windows facing out to the open courtyard. Lady Fairchild's directions were dead on. Lil pulled open the door to go outside and a blast of cold wind cut through her taking her breath away. She mumbled, "Bloody hell, almost don't need the loo now." The temperature felt like it had dropped twenty degrees and the wind had picked up even more. The light posts weren't working, giving her a bad case of the creeps because it was so dark. A bit edgy with her nerves now strung tight, she hurried across the cobblestones. A flash of lightning lit up the dark sky making her jump but helped her to see. A dim light shining through the front window of the coffee shop also helped as she quickly went down the three stone steps and across the patio filled with iron tables and chairs. She was relieved to find the door to the loo was unlocked and the lights were on inside. Minutes later, feeling pounds lighter, she hurried back out the door in the wind, across the patio, up the steps and across the cobblestones. She pulled on the door handle. It wouldn't budge. "You've got to be kidding! Really? It locks itself when you go out! Thanks for not sharing that Lady Fairchild. What a stupid situation I landed myself into," she grumbled disgusted. She looked around and recognized where she was. She headed down to the incline beside the war museum as lightning lit up the sky again, followed by a roll of thunder. She wrapped her arms around her body and shivered as she hurried as quickly as she could manage on the cobblestones. She turned right at the war museum and was halfway up the steep incline when she felt her breath catch in her chest. Chills went deep inside her chest, straight to her heart. An intense feeling she'd never felt before made her skin crawl. She knew without a doubt it was a warning. Her instincts kicked in, putting her on high alert. She quickly moved over and pressed her body flat against the stone wall of the museum. The cold from the stone rushed through her. She inched her way flattened up against the wall. She made it to the top and maneuvered herself around the corner to the front of the war museum scraping her palms against the rough brick. She held herself perfectly still as she looked across the courtyard to the door leading into the Great Hall where she wanted to be and then to her right to the long hallway with light streaming out through the stained glass windows where she should be standing in line for the loo. The bad feeling that had started in her chest was growing deeper in her gut. She scanned the area in all directions to determine it was empty. Another flash of lightning lit up the sky. Just when she was about to run across the square, a chill crept through her telling her not to. A movement to her left, up on the roof of the royal apartments, caught her eye. She quickly went down into a combat crouch, not wanting to be seen when the lightning flashed again. She stayed perfectly still for several heartbeats. Her ears picked up voices coming from the rooftop. A man's voice shouted in shock, "It was you?" She couldn't make out what the other one said, the voice was too low. The voice she could hear bellowed again; it was a voice filled with rage. "I trusted you! How ironic is that? You're the leak! You're absolutely mad if you think you're going to get away with it. They will figure out it was you." The one-sided conversation made it clear he was shocked that the person had betrayed him. Lil moved forward in a wide-footed crouch, taking one tentative step after another to the cannon she had taken photos of earlier. She was hoping to hear the other person so that she could tell if it was a man or woman. She only heard the man's voice again. "You murdered all those agents just to get to one?"

It stayed deadly quiet a moment. Another crack of lightning lit up the sky. The wind was fiercely blowing and going straight up her dress. She slowly turned so that it would hit her back and arched her neck in an awkward angle around the cannon to see. She looked up to the roof of the royal apartments where the voices had come from, waiting for another crack of lightning. When it did, she saw two men appear like magic up higher on the round roof of the tower. There was a very dim light coming from an open door. The larger of the two men stood behind the smaller one. Her eyes widened at seeing the smaller one's face. It was Lord Rothford. She couldn't make out the larger man's face. He had his arm wrapped around Lord Rothford's neck, and the other hand was clamped over Lord Rothford's mouth as he struggled against him.

The darkness deepened with the passing of the lightning. Her heartbeat drummed in her ears as her heart pounded, pushing adrenaline through her body. She heard a raspy, bitter laugh echo. It sent a shiver down her spine.

She continued watching in the dark, holding perfectly still as wind whipped around her. She was colder than she had ever been in her life. She wasn't sure if it was from the cold wind or that she knew what was about to happen. Every muscle in her body screamed in protest from not moving.

Rumbles of thunder rolled in the distance as a huge bolt of lightning lit up the sky again. Every tiny movement seemed magnified while the big man raised Lord Rothford as if he was light as a feather up over his head and threw him over the four-foot wall letting out another raspy laugh. She saw the look of fear and alarm on his face as he went sailing off the roof. His high-pitched scream was cut short when he hit the hard cobblestones. It took her a few seconds to shake off the horror. She knew without a doubt he was dead. No one could survive that fall. She closed her eyes for a second—just a second, to collect herself. She inhaled, held her breath for as long as she could, and then exhaled just the way JR taught her to get her nerves under control. His first rule of training rang in her ears. Control your nerves. You will be able to clear your mind and have the insight you need to focus. She felt a calm come over her when she got her nerves under control. She instantly knew what to do. She couldn't risk being seen, and she had to get herself back to the loo and wait on JR to find her. She quickly moved backward to the wall, still in the combat crouch.

She heard JR whisper near her ear so softly that she barely heard him. "Atta girl, I knew you would figure it out. Stay down and keep moving."

She had never been so happy to hear anyone in her life. She felt his hand on her arm, giving her a reassuring, gentle squeeze. In the same low tone he said, "Focus on your balance once we get around this corner. Stay down; we're going to take this incline staying in the combat crouch. I know it will be tough on your legs, but you can do it. When we reach the bottom, don't move until after a lightning flash. Then stand, take a couple of seconds to get the blood pumping back through your legs. Then, haul arse straight for the door and don't look back. You can do it, just control your breathing. It will keep your nerves at bay."

Hearing his voice and confidence in her gave her strength. She quickly moved down the incline on the cobblestones controlling her breathing and without losing her balance. They reached the bottom and waited until after another flash of lightning. They stood in unison and waited a few seconds. Lil could feel the blood pumping through her legs as she took off running toward the door. She didn't hear JR behind her but knew he was there. Just before she made it to the door Bill seem to appear out of nowhere and pulled it open for her and disappeared just as quickly, without saying a word.

Once inside, JR asked, "Snaggs, are you all right?"

Lil nodded.

"Can you finish the night?"

Her voice shivered as she said, "Yes. I'm fine; just cold."

He looked in her eyes, carefully assessing her. Seeing she really was fine, he teased. "Well, that swan dive isn't something you see every day."

Lil blinked once in surprise. Then gave him a cute little smirk. "I give it about a five. The landing was a little rough!"

His eyes were glistening, showing how proud of her he was. "Come on tough one, tell me exactly what you saw and heard on our way back. I'm sure Charlie is having convulsions by now. Seems you made a friend, too. She'll be waiting on you."

"What about—"

He cut her off as they started running. "Jay and Ben will take care of our little problem outside. You might want to fix your hair a bit. You look like you stuck your finger in a light socket."

Lil reached up and secured the pins back into her hair, filled him in and still kept up with him as they hurried down and up the stairs. They slowed to a casual walk just before they turned the corner to the long hall; neither one was out of breath. They laughed and talked as if they didn't have a care in the world as they walked past the ladies who were standing in line for the loo.

JR was right. There was a small group of people waiting with Lady Fairchild when they reentered the great hall. Lord Witmore was one of them.

"There she is," Lady Fairchild said with a smile.

"You were right," JR said grinning. "She locked herself out."

"I'm sorry, dear," Lady Fairchild said sadly. "I forgot to tell you to push the handle down so that it wouldn't lock."

"No worries," said Lil with a smile. "I just went back to the loo to wait it out. There was no way I was going to tackle that wind to walk through the courtyard. It's wicked and it's cold," she added with a little shiver, trying not to let on just how cold she really was. She nodded at JR. "I knew he would come looking for me."

"That's why I'm your favorite assistant," said JR smiling.

"Here...ah ah. You, ah ah...could...ah ah, use this," said Charles, as Lord Standish, handing Lil a hot cup of tea with a little wink.

"Oh yes. Thank you, Lord Standish," said Lil smiling, taking it from him.

"That's what got you in trouble in the first place!" added JR with a chuckle.

Lil playfully rolled her eyes and teased, "No more out of you; now where's my camera. We have work to do."

Everyone laughed.

Nearly an hour later, when the rain let up, Lil and JR made their way down the wet cobblestones. In the distance, lightning cut jagged lines in the sky as a misty rain started to fall again. The cold wind whipped their hair and clothes. Lil's teeth were chattering by the time they made it to the car. Jayden opened the boot as they came running up. Lil quickly grabbed Connor's school jacket and her other bag out of the boot as JR placed her bag with her equipment in. She hopped in the back seat shivering violently as she put on the jacket. Lil mumbled as she shivered, "I'm happy he left this in the car."

Jayden drove down the car park and pulled out onto the street. The only sound was the rain, now coming down hard hitting the roof and the wipers. As they went down Princess Street, Lil glanced out the window as she finished pulling the dangling pins out of her hair. She saw the castle, barely visible in the skyline through the pouring rain. "Are we taking the helicopter home?" she asked as she yawned sounding like nothing was out of the normal.

"No, Ben needed it," said JR.

"Oh yeah, I imagine he would," she mumbled.

"You need to talk?" asked JR.

"No. Still not thinking about it."

"Okay, just remember when you do, because of him a lot of good agents lost their lives. Get some sleep. Charlie and the guys will want to talk when we get home."

She kicked off her soaked shoes as she reached for her phone. She turned it on as she mumbled, "You mean *yell* at me for taking off like an idiot without backup. You think I've seen my last op?" She quickly returned HT's nightly text ignoring that she had a phone message from him.

"I doubt it," said JR. "You learned from your mistake. Just remember it's command, not Dad and the guys, so keep your mouth shut when they're chewing you a new one."

The car had gotten warm as toast. Lil was having a hard time keeping her eyes open. "K, love you guys," she mumbled as she lay down falling fast asleep, not hearing them say love you most.

HT woke from his dream yelling, "Where did you go?" He sat up and looked for Lil. His dream was so real that he thought he was lying on the sofa with her in the Cove. Unlike the image that flashed through his mind over the past couple of weeks, the dream was more intense. He looked at the clock on the mantel and saw it was nearing 4:00 a.m. He sat on the side of his bed for a few seconds knowing he couldn't get back to sleep. It hadn't been a good night; he'd tossed and turned a dozen times before he finally fell asleep wondering what she was doing and why it took her until almost midnight to return his text. The fact she never returned his call didn't help. Knowing he wasn't in the mood to write, he decided to go for a run to clear his mind. He got up, pulled on his sweats and T-shirt. He slipped on his trainers, tied on a do-rag, and grabbed his phone and earbuds. He walked softly down the hall and quickly jogged down the stairs and out of the house. Only the stars shared the early morning hours with him.

An hour later when he reached the top of their hill, he was winded. After walking around, shaking his legs and arms to cool down, he sat. He pulled off his do-rag and shoved a hand through his curls. The rising sun was changing the morning sky from dusty gray to orange. He looked across the garden toward the driveway seeing JR pull up in front of the house.

Lil had slept the deep sleep of exhaustion all the way home. JR woke her up as they pulled in front of the house. She grabbed her shoes and dragged herself out of the car. Her body sagged with exhaustion as she headed to the front door, tired to the bone.

HT's eyes narrowed watching Lil climb out of the car. He knew she had been with Connor, seeing she was wearing his school jacket. Her hair was a mess, half up and sticking out everywhere. His heart constricted. It didn't take a genius to figure out she'd just tumbled out of bed. He could hardly bare to think of her with him. He was waiting for the jealous anger to fill him at seeing her, but it stirred something else besides anger inside him. He finally realized he had been naïve thinking just because he had fallen madly in love with her, that given time she would fall equally in love with him. Now he felt it was mental to think he had ever seen in her eyes that her feelings had changed. Why hadn't he faced it before? "'Cause you're a wanker," he muttered. Puffing his cheeks with air, he blew it out and said, "Well that's that. Time to face the truth, mate. If she had feelings for you, she wouldn't be knocking boots with him, as Bill would say." He hurried down the hill and up the walk feeling better than he had in a long time finally coming to terms with the mess he had himself in. He was ready to let all that love rubbish go. Seeing her had his head around the obvious...she would only love him as a mate, nothing more.

Lil sat not saying a word and took all of the screaming and lecturing Charles, Ed, Bill, and Luke gave her. She knew they were right. She had screwed up taking off like she did. She was on an op, for God's sake. JR and Jay nodded at her ever so often, letting her know she was doing good. After she had answered all of their questions and described in detail everything she could recall, she wearily climbed the stairs.

The guys looked at each other smiling when she went out. "She did us proud, boys," said Bill. "She's exhausted, and yet she sat there without complaining once, answering all of our questions."

They all nodded, still smiling with pride.

Lil quickly sent HT his morning text, as she went up the stairs. She knew it was early, but if she didn't send it now, he wouldn't get it. She was physically and emotionally spent and was practically asleep on her feet. The moment she closed her bedroom door, she began undressing, leaving a trail of clothing behind her on the way to bed. She pulled back the duvet and crawled in and fell fast asleep.

Charles sat behind his desk in deep thought when Ben walked in and handed him a piece of stationary in a clear plastic bag. "You were right, boss," he said. "There's a fake suicide note admitting that he sold information; he wanted the money for his grandchildren. Says his health is failing, didn't want to put his family through his prolonged death, and besides that he couldn't live with the guilt any more. You know all the typical rubbish. Found it lying on his desk in the study. Looks like he broke his neck when he landed. I put half a glass of his favorite port on his nightstand and put him in bed with his nightshirt on, just the way you wanted. Looks like he went peacefully in his sleep."

"Good. I don't want his reputation tarnished. As I have put the word out last night that he had slipped out to go home because he was feeling under the weather, nobody but the killer will think twice when he's found this morning. His doctor is just waiting on the call to go over to say he had a heart attack."

"How well do you know that pansy Lord Witmore?" asked JR. "He was waiting with Lady Fairchild and seemed way too worried about something when Snaggs and I came back in. You think maybe he and Lord Rothford had something going on?"

Charles almost laughed out loud as he looked at Luke. "You know him best Luke, after going over his file. What do you think? You think he and Lord Rothford had something going on?"

Luke shook his head trying not to laugh. "No, he's in a committed relationship. Has been for years."

Ed hid his grin and asked Charles, "So now what?"

"We go on what Lil heard, that whoever did this has murdered all those agents just to get to one?" replied Charles. "What better way to murder an agent so that it doesn't look suspicious?"

"You take him out on an op," replied Bill.

"And you take out a few more to throw everyone off the track," added Jayden.

Charles nodded and said, "Now, we find out which one of the dead agents they were after. I want their history from the time they took their first breath. I want to know everything about them and their parents and their parents' parents."

He looked at Luke. "Get me all the reports the guys filed when we started following Lord Rothford. Start with where he went after the meetings. We need to go over again whom he saw and talked to before he filed those reports. We're missing something."

"I'm on it," said Luke as he walked to the fireplace.

Charles looked at JR. "Let Lil sleep, but as soon as she gets up see if you can get her talk to you about what she saw. Let her know because of her an innocent man died with his reputation and honor intact. He wouldn't have wanted anything more."

"I'll head downstairs and help Luke until she gets up," replied JR as he went to the fireplace.

Ben headed to the door. "I'll go get breakfast made. Raif will be up soon."

"I'll head to the bakery and rustle us up something worth eating from the girls," mumbled Bill as he followed him.

"I'll remember that next time we're out on an op. You can make your own grub."

"Don't get your kickers in a bunch. I was just messing with ya," said Bill. "I'm just going to get Raif a few strawberry muffins is all."

"Yeah, right," said Ben with a laugh as they went out.

Charles chuckled as he looked at Jayden and asked, "How is HT? Will he be heading to Chester? Or did Lil cause him another rough night!"

"He's going; he already texted me he's going to Lee's," replied Jayden. "He said he was wanting to leave after he had breakfast with Maddie. Joe said he didn't drink much after we left yesterday. He went down to the Cove for a while after the party broke up and then went home. He had just finished a run when we pulled in." His phone rang. "There he is now," he added after he read the text. "He's ready to go."

"Okay, grab something to eat before you go," said Charles. "Come on Ed, let's head downstairs. You can fill me in on our other boy while the reports are printing."

Ed whined as they headed to the fireplace, "You and Mary are going to have to go over there and make him come home, Charlie. I can't talk any sense into that hard head of his. He and Lil are like two peas in a pod, stubborn as hell and always thinking they're right."

Jayden laughed.

Ed turned around and said with a huff. "What are you laughing at? They learned all that rubbish they put us through from you and JR!"

"Hey, we learned it from you blokes!" said Jayden laughing harder as he went out the door.

Charles and Ed chuckled as they disappeared behind the fireplace.

Saturday morning, Connor was sitting in Sloan's favorite coffee shop in Chester waiting for her. He was going to get her to admit HT was in love with Lil. He knew she and Lee had to know since they all had been mates for so long. Once he got her to admit it, he was going to rope her into helping him with a plan he was forming. He figured he would kill two birds with one stone since he was elected to *dragon lady detail*, as the guys called it. They warned him that she would turn into a total "beeouch!" when she was dragging him from store to store. Since he was officially one of them now and had gotten out of it all week because of practice, he got her all day on his own. She had them, especially Lil, worn out shopping every day after school, hitting every charity and costume shop within a twenty-mile radius. She was stressed to the hilt about the Halloween dance coming up on Friday night, and they were all paying for it.

The annual event was a major production put on by the Drama Club for the school. It was the biggest dance of the year and gave the seniors a chance to showcase their skills with a chance to earn the prestigious designing award, which would look great on a résumé. Each contestant needed twenty students assigned under them to qualify. Sloan had hers the very first day.

The rules for the contest were of the twenty students there had to be a group theme consisting of nine students. Six students, as couples, were to be dressed in a theme such as a prince and princess and then the last five students as individuals with no theme. The more unique the costumes, the better. The biggest challenge was to stump the judges on who was wearing the costume. They would be using a face mask on a stick to help disguise them, but the judges were teachers and knew the students very well.

Connor smiled and stood up seeing Sloan come in. They gave each other a quick hug as Sloan said, "You're early, and here I was sure you wouldn't show up!"

"Don't be daft. I'm happy to help. You want a coffee before we get started?"

"For sure," she said as she slid into the booth.

A few minutes later, Connor returned with their coffee. After talking for a bit, Connor casually asked, "So when did you realize HT was in love with Lil?"

Taken off guard by the shift in the conversation, she replied, "The first time I—" She stopped and gave him a disgusted look. "That was mean. You made me break our friend code. Listen you don't have to worry about him trying to come between you—"

He started laughing cutting her off. "Stop," he said holding up his hand. "It's fine. We're only mates."

Sloan gave him a confused look.

"Really," Connor assured her. "Think about it. Besides the very first time we all got together at Gino's, when have you ever seen us snog?"

Sloan thought for a few seconds. "Oh my God, never!"

"Oh, we both tried, but knew after that kiss there wasn't any chemistry. We ended up confessing we're in love with someone else and they didn't have a clue. Do I need to go on, or do you know where this is heading?"

"Oh no," she said with a raised brow. "Please don't tell me you're in love with me!"

He laughed shaking his head. "I do love you as a mate. Actually, like I told Lil if I wasn't head over heels in love with my sister's best friend, Amy, I would *so* be in love with you and her. You're both brilliant. But you know how love is, it doesn't give your heart a choice. I'm sure you didn't plan on falling in love with one of Lil's brothers."

"Whoa, back that train up. What do you mean? I'm in love with JR?"

"I never said JR," Connor said with a sheepish grin.

"Bloody hell, you're a sneaky one. Does Lil know?"

"That I'm sneaky or that you're in love with JR?" he teased.

Sloan gave him one of her many looks.

"We've never talked about it. But you don't hide it very well!"

"Whatever," she said with a grin. "It's not like JR doesn't know. Enough about my sorry love life; let's get back to you and Lil. Why did you two act...wait a minute. Who the bloody hell is Lil in love with?"

"Now you know I can't tell you. But I will say that we act as if we're a couple so nobody bugs us about dating, and I help her to hide the fact she's in love with him."

Sloan's forehead had a deep crease while she thought. After a few seconds, her eyes got huge. She shook her head in amazement and said almost in disbelief, "Oh my God! How daft can I be? It's so bloody obvious now. She's in love with HT!" She started laughing. "Oh this is brilliant. They're madly in love with each other and don't know it. What's Lil's excuse? HT's afraid she will kick him to the curb."

"Lil believes he only loves her as a mate and doesn't want him looking at her like one of his harem," said Connor.

"What a mess. When did you realize how he really feels about her? Like Lil, he hides it very well."

"He does. I didn't figure it out until last week at your party. I caught him giving me the evil eye. I could tell he was wanting to rip my head off." Connor chuckled. "That bloke does...not...like...me!"

Sloan nodded with a raised brow. "That's an understatement! He's been driving Lee mental having to keep him from ripping your face off!"

They laughed.

Sloan pushed back her guilt now that she knew Lil felt the same about HT. "He'll love you like the rest of us when he finds out you and Lil are only mates. So what are we going to do about it? I take it you have a plan and need my help?"

He nodded with a sly grin. "It needs some tweaking, and it's going to be a challenge."

Her lips curved into a wicked grin. "I love a good challenge."

"So do I," Connor replied with the same grin. "I never can back away from one. So here's what I'm thinking."

A plan was forming in Sloan's mind how to help as he told her what he had in mind.

The next week, Sloan had driven them all mental again, gathering last minute items at the charity shops. She had them revisit every one over and over to rummage through their bins. She just knew somebody would have donated just the thing to make her costumes perfect. Lil had taken roll after roll of film not wanting to miss a thing in documenting Sloan's journey to her big win.

Thursday afternoon, Lil, HT, and Lee skipped out of school after lunch with Sloan. They got stuck with dragon lady detail for the last time. Connor and the twins bailed; they said they'd had enough. Lil was loving every minute of it. It felt good to really laugh hard again, not having to pretend. It was like old times, just the four of them hanging out as Sloan dragged them into charity shops. HT and Lee kept her running to the loo all day. They got bored and started horsing around. They had put on wigs, hats, scarves, skirts, and even bras—over their clothes, of course. Sloan didn't think it was too funny. She bitched and rolled her eyes at them.

Lee let out a loud groan when Sloan pushed open the door to a charity shop. "Come on, Sloan, we were just here like an hour ago."

"Yeah, I'm starving," whined HT, "and I want to check out the new guitars that came in at the music shop before it closes."

"Ooooh, look," Sloan said happily, ignoring them as she pointed toward the back of the store. "They've gotten more stuff in."

"Ooooh fun!" mimicked Lee.

Sloan just huffed and hurried off.

HT turned to Lee, grinning impishly as he pushed his long curls behind his ears and plopped a wide-brimmed green hat on his head. "Isn't this hat just to die for?"

"It's absolutely charming!" Lee exclaimed.

Lil nodded and added, "Oh yes, it is! But...this will make it perfect. It will bring out your eyes," she said slapping a large ugly red flower on the brim.

"Ummm, I think you might be right. It's definitely me," HT said as he readjusted the brim, tilting it slightly to one side and batted his eyes.

"Oh my! That ugly arse flower did it," Lee exclaimed in a high pitch tone, slapping his hand to his jaw.

They laughed as Lil clicked away on her camera.

HT looked toward the back and then at Lee. "Dragon lady isn't looking. I'm out of here. I'm heading down to the music shop."

"Not without me, you're not," Lee said following him to the door.

Lil was still laughing as she took photos of them running out. Then she decided to slip out and go next door to the jewelry store. The clasp had broken on HT's chain, and she wanted to get him a new one and didn't want Sloan to know.

It didn't take her but a few minutes, having in mind what she wanted. She thought she had gotten away with it as she closed the jewelry store door, dropping the wrapped necklace in her shoulder bag.

"I bet that's for HT!" Sloan said looking at her.

"Aaaargh, don't start. I don't need to hear how I have him spoiled."

"You do!" she said laughing. "All I'm saying is that bloke has more clothes and trainers than I do, now."

Lil rolled her eyes and said, "Nobody on the planet has more clothes than you!"

"True," Sloan said wondering how she never saw how crazy in love she was with HT. "Let's go drag them away from those guitars and get something to eat, unless you're going to buy him one of those too!"

"Aaaargh." Lil playfully groaned again.

The next morning on the way to school, Lil had her eyes closed and her head was back against the seat, listening to HT laugh with JR and Jay. She had missed their banter and loved how things were getting back to normal. Well, as normal as it could be, being head over heels in love with a bloke who would never know. Her curse had been a real buggar. It really felt like a curse. She was still emotional and irritable as ever. She could already tell she was going to be a bear today. "Damn hormones," she mumbled under her breath. She should have just slept in, since there was only a half day of school because of the dance. She was dreading the dance, knowing HT was literally going to be there with his harem.

HT looked over at her and his heart raced. It had been hard the last few weeks getting his head around the fact that he didn't have a chance with her, but he was getting there. He was having a tough time trying to get his play back though. The little minx had him feeling guilty when he tried to hook up with a girl. He felt like he was cheating on her. She had thrown him off his game since the day they met. Well, he was over all that love rubbish. It was time to bring *Horny Harry* back front and center and rejoin the living. He looked out the window seeing they were pulling up in front of the school. He saw his harem, as Lil and Sloan called them. He leaned forward in the seat and laughed. "Well, boys, looks like my harem is lined up and waiting."

JR and Jayden laughed.

Lil acted as if she was still sleeping and was having to bite the inside of her cheek to keep from calling him an arse, as he hopped out. She was not in the mood for his rubbish. She slid across the seat. "What a tosser!" she said in irritation as she climbed out, making JR and Jayden laugh again.

Twelve hours later Sloan and HT were in the drama room. She had told him about her fake crisis and was tapping her foot softly against the tiled floor, waiting on his answer.

"Sloan," said HT disgusted. "You know how much I hate that bloke, and now you want me to wear his costume?"

"Please be my Zorro," she whined.

"Fine. You can stop with the eyes," he grumbled.

"You're a lifesaver," she said as she hugged him and then handed him the costume.

He smirked. "My harem isn't going to be happy!"

Sloan groaned and said, "Whatever! Tonight, Zorro has to wear a hat, so you can tuck those curls of yours up under it, or the judges will know it's you for sure." She handed him what looked to be a top hat.

"Wait a minute..." he muttered skeptically, having a feeling something wasn't right. "Sloan, we've been through this if you're trying to set me up to be with Lil? I told you I gave up on us..."

She cut him off with a sound of disgust as she turned away so that he couldn't see her face. He knew her too well. "For God's sake, HT, I have enough things to worry about. Your bloody love life isn't one of them right now. Besides, you won't be with her. I have to talk her into wearing *that* bloody thing," she pointed to the harem costume hanging over the dressing screen.

He shook his head laughing. "She's not going to like that at all!"

"I know. I'm going to have to turn on the waterworks with her." She picked up the coin belt that went with it and said, "This is my bargaining tool. She'll be the only one to have one." She shook it making the gold coins jingle.

He grinned and replied, "I'm sure she will wear the costume."

"Again, I know. She loves me," Sloan said nodding. She saw Connor slip in the back door. She gave HT a quick hug and then lightly pushed him toward the opposite door. "Go get ready. I have to figure out how to break the news to Lil."

"Good luck!" He laughed and headed to the door.

"Same to you," she said under her breath when he went out.

Connor walked up dressed as Zorro when HT had left. "I see he fell for it."

Sloan looked at him with a frown. "He'll never forgive me if this thing goes south."

Connor looked a little worried too as he said, "Same here with Lil. We just have to make sure they don't know. I popped in to give you a little heads-up. She's in one of her moods, and I made it worse by making her so late."

"Oh boy! Well, I better make sure I give her another brilliant acting job."

They laughed.

"I better get out of here and go hide," Connor said as they shared a quick hug.

"I'm more nervous about setting these guys up and worrying if we can pull it off than this bloody contest!"

"Good luck, but you're not going to need it. With the contest anyway," he said with a little chuckle as he hurried to the back door.

"Cheers!" she muttered under her breath as he went out.

Lil came bursting through the door of the drama room a few minutes later. "I'm here," she announced expecting to see a raging Sloan. "I'm so sorry I'm late. Con..." She stopped, finding her pacing and rolling her hands.

Sloan looked at Lil shaking her head and whined, "There's no way I'm going to win. I'm not going to have time to get everyone ready and out there in time."

Lil, seeing she was upset, quickly went over and gave her a hug. "Don't be silly. This is you we're talking about. Where's my costume? We know it fits; you've made me try it on enough. Who else isn't here yet?" she asked looking around for her costume.

Sloan threw up her hands. "That's the problem. Well, one of them." She made her voice tremble as she went on. "First, Connor called to say he was running late and wouldn't make the judging."

"He what?" Lil shouted and started to mumble. "He's supposed to be walking with me. Of all the nerve! He's why I'm so bloody late. He talked me into doing photos of the team for his coach. He said it would take less than an hour. It took three! Like they couldn't wait—"

"*Hello!*" Sloan said, cutting her off. "I'm the one in a middle of a crisis here!"

"Oh right, sorry." Lil chuckled. "Continue."

Sloan nodded and continued, "That isn't the problem. I talked HT into being my Zorro."

Lil grunted, rolling her eyes. "I bet that went over well, not having those half-naked girls wrapped around him but then they will be after the judging."

Sloan cleared her throat and gave Lil one of her *Really!* looks.

Lil shrugged with a sheepish grin. "Sorry. Still in a mood."

"You're forgiven. Now to *my* big problem," she said, crossing her fingers behind her back hating to downright lie. "I left HT's sheik costume and your costume at home. I pressed them wanting them to be perfect and then I went off and left them hanging in the laundry room." She started babbling really fast. "Cody and my assistant, Lisa, ran to get them, but Mum ran to the store. Anyway, Mum is bringing them back now so that Lisa can dress Cody as my sheik in the—"

"Whoa, slow down. You're going to have a heart attack," Lil said with a chuckle. "Now I see why I drive you all mental with my mumbling."

Sloan took a deep breath getting nervous that she was overplaying it a bit. She gripped her hands together for real. Her knuckles were white as she said, "I told Lisa just to put your costume on because I won't have time to get her ready. So I still have a Ms. Zorro or whatever you want to call Zorro's love interest in the movie with that Jones lady in it."

"Sloan, slow down and just spit it out," Lil said trying to keep her patience. "Just bottom line it. What are you trying to tell me, here?"

Sloan pleaded, "Please, please, please, can I put you in Lisa's harem girl costume? I swear I'll disguise you so well that no one will know it's you! You can come back here and change costumes after the judging. There's extras over there on the table."

Lil released a heavy breath followed by a flash of irritation. "I was afraid that's what you wanted. Can't you have one less harem girl?"

Her reaction was pretty much what Sloan had expected. She shook her head, giving her best sad-eyed look. "You know there has to be nine in the group category or I get disqualified. You'll have it on for about an hour at the most!"

"Fine," Lil said with a huff. "I'm not happy about it, but I'll do it."

"Thank you, thank you, thank you," said Sloan, clapping her hands and then pointed. "It's hanging over on the screen."

Lil let out an unhappy sigh as she went behind the screen. She put on the short half-top that showed just a bit of cleavage and left her stomach bare. She then donned the bikini bottom followed by sheer pants split down the sides that tied at her ankles. She chuckled and called out as she tied them, "I feel like Jeannie in that old telly series Grammy always watches."

Sloan laughed.

After Lil slipped on the soft ballet flats, she walked out from behind the screen.

"You look amazing," said Sloan.

"I hope I don't freeze to death in this thing. There's not much to it! Are you sure no one is going to know it's me?"

"Yes, but when I'm done if you're not sure, I promise I won't be upset if you change your mind," said Sloan. She put the coin belt around Lil's waist then started covering her in veils. "Now let's get that thick hair up; bend your head over for me."

Sloan scooped up her hair and twisted it into a tight bun upon her head. "Okay, you can straighten up," she muttered with pins in her mouth. Once she did, Sloan quickly secured the bun with the pins."

Lil touched it. "It's a little tight."

"I did wrap it pretty tight, but if anybody sees that hair of yours sticking out, they will know it's you!"

Lil grumbled. "Then leave it. I don't want anyone knowing."

Sloan said, as she worked, "Now I'll wrap some veils around your head and around your face, and I'll take this heavier one and attach it so that it goes just under your eyes." She stepped back to admire her work when she was done. "Wow, I'm impressed with myself," she added, nodding her head. "I wouldn't have a clue it was you if I hadn't done it myself." Highly pleased with herself, she turned Lil around to look in the full-length floor mirror.

Lil studied her reflection with a critical eye. "You're right. I don't even recognize myself," she said, her admiration showing at Sloan's talent. Lil shook her waist, making the coins on her belt jingle and her sheer pants shimmy. She giggled. "I hate to admit it, but I feel sexy and kind of sassy!"

Sloan pulled her buzzing phone from her pocket. She grinned and thought, *Right on time.* She knew it was Connor but acted as if it was Lisa, who along with Cody had been dressed and lined up waiting to go out before Lil even came in. They were so busy trying to hook up that they didn't think twice of why she'd changed her mind on what they wore. "Great," she said grinning, "I might just pull this off. Lisa and Cody are in line with the others, and she said all that is missing is a harem girl. Let's get you out there."

They hurried to where Sloan's section was. She gave them all a quick once over and fussed like a mother hen as she put them in order as the rules stated. The singles on the left, couples to their right, and the group following behind.

Sloan put Lil in the middle of the first line of the group to take Lisa's job of leading them out and keeping the group straight. A harem girl stood on each side of her. Cody was behind her with a harem girl on each side and three more in line behind them, bringing up the rear. Lil was behind HT and rolled her eyes at hearing him flirt with Lisa. He was first in the couple pairs. Lisa was on his right, and Catwoman was on his left.

"Remember, stay positioned how I have you, stay close, and walk slowly," Sloan ordered like a drill sergeant. "And keep those masks up and no talking. I get marked down if they know who you are." The bell rang. "That's it. Time to send you out," she announced.

Lil followed HT out. The lights were still up, but the fog machines were providing a light blanket of fog, just enough to make it feel mysterious. Everyone moved slowly, making sure to keep their masks up, not giving themselves away.

They walked with the other contestant groups in a big circle around the gym. There was about twenty feet between each of the groups. That way the judges sitting in the middle could see and judge them better. Lil heard HT softly laugh, making that burning sensation in her stronger than ever. She stole a quick peek at him, seeing he was leaning over to Catwoman. She had to admit, whoever it was looked great! Her outfit was so tight, outlining her every curve, that it didn't leave much to the imagination. Lil watched as Catwoman lowered her mask and raised her hand like a paw and meow as she playfully batted at HT. Lil's stomach turned, realizing it was Britney. She turned away, rolling her eyes in disgust. The hot feeling disappeared, replaced with the sick jealous feeling she hated so much.

She took in a deep breath telling herself, *Just breathe. Control your emotions. Just two more times around this bloody gym!*

After the last lap, Lil hurried to the door to change. Sloan and Connor were waiting by the door. "Here she comes," said Sloan. "Your turn. Make it sound good," she said and hurried off.

Connor stepped in front of her.

"Bloody hell, HT, you scared the total crap out of me," she said with her hand on her heart.

"Kiss me, my pretty harem girl. I love you!" he said in a low tone.

"Huh?"

Connor burst out laughing.

"Connor?"

He nodded. "In the flesh. Sorry, I couldn't help myself."

She playfully slapped his arm and said, "I was wondering how HT got over here so quickly. Why are you dressed as Zorro?"

He pulled her off to the side. "Sloan knows me too well. She gave me my costume ahead of time in case I was running late so that I could get dressed before I got here." He grinned thinking he wasn't lying; that part was true. "I guess she didn't trust I would make it and had an extra one on hand."

"Good thing she did. You almost made me late. Wait a minute. How did you know it was me?"

"Sloan. Don't get mad. She was babbling about how you and HT saved the day. She told me you had Lisa's costume on, and it was the only one with a coin belt. She said you would probably be heading to the drama room to change as soon as the judging was over."

"And she was *so* right. I'm heading to take this thing off, now."

"You know...I was standing here thinking—"

"About?" asked Lil with a scowl.

Connor said with a grin, "Before you do, why not have a little fun?"

"How so?"

"This is your chance to have your way with HT. He won't have a clue it's you."

Lil huffed. "Don't be daft. That's just ridiculous!"

"What? I'm just saying. Give it a go; you might just enjoy yourself," he said with a slow smile spreading across his face. "If I had a chance to be myself and flirt all I wanted with Amy and get a few kisses without her knowing, I would take it!"

"Uh-huh. And what is my excuse if he realizes it's me? That's if I even have a chance to get him away from his harem and that cow Britney."

"That part is all you," he replied with a little chuckle. "But your excuse can be you thought he was me."

She rolled her eyes getting a tingling sensation, remembering every detail about that night on the sofa.

"I see those wheels spinning. You know you're wanting to. Go and enjoy yourself," he encouraged, giving her a little nudge toward the dance floor. "Just take another lap or two around the gym and think about it. You just might thank me for it later!"

Her hormones overruled her common sense. She mumbled, "Fine. I'll do it, but I'm only walking around one more time to think about it. I doubt I'll have the nerve to do anything if I do see him!" She couldn't help feeling a little excited as she went to join all the other masked partygoers.

The lights had been turned down and the fog was thicker.

Sloan was standing back listening. She walked up beside Connor when Lil left. "Wow, that was brilliant. It just might work."

"I've been known to be a bit of an actor," he bragged, "but in case this thing backfires...we know nothing!"

They laughed.

Lil eased her way into the circle with everyone walking. She walked slowly, watching, listening, and nodding as she passed others thinking the fog and low lights did make it mysterious, sexy, and alluring.

HT stood by the stage looking for Lil. He couldn't help himself; he had to tease her about her costume. He instantly recognized her coming his way. He could pick her out anywhere; he didn't need the help of the coin belt she wore. As she passed, he stepped out of the shadows and strode up behind her taking her hand.

Lil felt warm shivers run up her arm. She knew it was HT by the fit of his hand. Their hands fit perfectly together. She was just about to ask how he knew it was her when he gently pulled her to the back wall behind the stage.

He leaned forward as he teased and asked in a seductive, husky whisper, "What do I have to do to get a private dance?"

Her heart ricocheted around in her rib cage. He didn't know it was her! She decided, *What the heck. What could a few kisses hurt?* He would never know it was her. She knew exactly what she was doing, and what it could lead to. Regardless of the consequences, she reached up with a fingertip, lightly tracing his cheek and the outside of his lips. In a sexy tone, that didn't sound anything like her, she cooed in a soothing whisper, "Maybe a kiss or two."

He quickly inhaled at the touch of her fingertip. His hopes soared. He couldn't believe it; she did feel the same. His heart was about to burst with joy. His voice was velvety, low and husky with passion as he pulled her close and bent down whispering against her ear, "Sounds like a deal to me."

His breath on her ear sparked an electric current under her skin. Lil's head was spinning. She unhooked the veil from behind her ear.

He told himself to stop, they needed to talk first, but his senses were already responding when he breathed in her scent, which smelled amazing as always, just more faint. He knew she passed on the perfume, not wanting to give herself away. He began planting feathery kisses on her neck.

She closed her eyes in blissful surrender as he worked his way up to her mouth. He touched the side of her mouth with his and then brushed his lips slowly across hers. "Let's see how many we can rack up," he said with a low sexy growl before he boldly claimed her lips with a hunger too long denied.

Her lips parted, his tongue swept in stroking hers. All that mattered was the sensation of his tongue crashing against hers and the desire that curled between her thighs. She pressed herself into him and his arms slid down her bare back, sending waves of shivers to her toes. She nearly collapsed from the sensation that spread through her as she returned his passion. She was unaware of anything but him. Her mind didn't want to think; she just wanted to feel.

He felt her soft lips on his, hot, sweet, and willing, firing his blood to a raging burn. He'd never expected to be able to kiss her like this. He'd imagined it and dreamed about it, of course—so many times that the sensation of her lips and tongue seemed familiar. The image of them on the sofa flashed through his mind. Then she kissed him harder; her tongue drove him out of his mind as he deepened the kiss and lost himself in sensation.

She could feel the electricity through every inch of her body. She was grateful he had her pressed against the wall, as it was helping her stand, but the cool brick didn't help cool her body while feeling him hard, up against her.

Her kisses had him weak in the knees. He never knew he could love kissing so much, and she was amazing at it. He let out a little groan as he got himself under control and pulled away. He knew they needed to talk before things went any further. He hoarsely whispered as he took her hand, "Let's go in here."

There were a thousand reasons why she shouldn't, but she couldn't resist, almost in a trance as he led her into a small room by the stage. It was completely dark except for the E on the illuminated exit sign above the door. She could make out that he had removed his cape and laid it on the floor. He sat down and then took her hand. She felt her knees buckle as he gently pulled her onto his lap.

He lightly brushed his lips on her forehead as always and then gradually worked his way down her face until he reached her lips.

His deep, drugging kisses made her tremble and melted her insides. She heard herself moan softly with little murmurs of pleasure as she kissed him back. The hot, melting sensation he was causing made her lose all coherent thoughts. She couldn't get enough.

His arm gently cradled her head as he lowered her to the floor as they kissed. His hand softly caressed her bare abdomen, leaving tingling lines of pleasure across her skin, making her light headed with excitement. She reached up to his head, removing his hat, and small mask. She couldn't wait to run her fingers through those curls she loved so much. She slipped his do-rag off; somehow she knew he would have it on under that silly hat he was wearing. She slid her fingers through his curls.

His kisses were perfect, heightening her pleasure. She couldn't kiss hard enough, wanting more and more. His hand moved up under her top and covered her breast, his fingers tantalizing her. Sensations she had never felt before rushed through her whole body making her tremble and kiss even harder. Emotions were stirring deep, like lava starting to swell in a volcano. She moaned as he stopped kissing her. She didn't want him to quit. Then she felt his mouth on her breast and saw sparks behind her eyes. She had never felt anything like it. She thought her body would catch fire! She continued to run her fingers through his curls as he worked his magic. It felt amazing; he was amazing, knowing just what she wanted. It seemed like his mouth and tongue were everywhere.

HT knew they needed to stop so that they could talk. It was getting way out of control. He was never out of control. He could always stop but then he had never felt like this before. He found himself wanting to touch and kiss every inch of her body. He began to plant soft, tender kisses from her breast down to her stomach. She groaned as his tongue moved south past her belly button just above her costume. He loved the taste of her and the little sound she made in the back of her throat. She was like a drug he couldn't get enough of, totally consuming him, mind and body. He had never wanted to do the things he wanted to do with her. He was finding it increasingly hard to control himself. He slid his hand, lightly pushing her costume bottoms down. The jingling of the coins on her belt snapped him back. He got himself under control for a split second; with a loud groan, he stopped and rolled onto his back pulling her on top of him. He whispered, his voice huskier as he fought to control his emotions, "We need to slow—"

Lil found his lips. She didn't hear him; she was burning from head to toe. She was so hot that she felt like her blood was boiling in her veins. Her body had an uncontrollable urge of its own, like it was possessed, needing for that burning volcano to be released.

Her kiss was all it took for HT's passion to explode.

Both being unfamiliar with such loss of control, neither was capable of restraint.

His tongue working hers while he rolled on top of her. Their bodies fit perfectly, as though they were made for each other.

Her passionate response equaled his. She wrapped her arms around him, loving the feel of him on top of her...his chest against her, his legs against hers. She wrapped her legs around his as she pushed her hips up toward him feeling a throbbing...a pounding so wild, so intense it was almost overpowering.

He kissed her harder as he pressed his weight against her; ripples of pleasure were building.

They moved in matching rhythm, slow at first and then faster. Even fully clothed they felt completely naked from the way they moved and matched each other perfectly.

The impulse grew stronger and stronger as she arched beneath him, seeking release for the ache deep inside. The pleasure became intense, feeling like she couldn't get close enough. Every nerve came to life as her whole body shook with waves of pleasure with every shift of his hips. She had never felt anything like it and never wanted it to stop.

She wasn't the only one. HT could feel her whole body trembling, pushing him over the edge. His whole body was throbbing. The sweet release of electric waves of pleasure came from deep inside while heat surged through him like a wildfire.

He rolled onto his back with her wrapped in his arms pulling her on top of him. He gently caressed her back and exhaled a deep sigh of contentment. His pleasure was beyond anything he'd ever known.

Neither of them spoke as they floated back down to earth.

She could feel the gentle rise and fall of his chest as his hand gently caressed her back. Her skin tingled with his touch.

Blissful moments passed with her senses reeling as he panted against her ear. "Can you imagine doing that with our clothes off? Who should I collect all of those dances from, anyway?" he teased, trying to ease into the conversation they needed to have.

His comment shocked her back to her senses, bringing her back to reality. She snapped out of the daze her emotions had her in. Her face turned red thinking about what they had just done and felt she would die if he found out it was her. A wave of nausea hit her, feeling she needed to get as far away from there as possible, before he realized it was her. Her adrenaline pumping, she quickly moved off him into a sitting position, one hand landed on her mask the other straightened her costume as best as she could. She picked up her mask as she sprang to her feet and bolted to the door. She was out the door before he could react. She took a deep breath figuring out her next move as she tried to reattach her veils here and there. She decided to go to the loo to fix them better before heading to the drama room, since she had to go past the dance floor and down a lighted hall to get there. When her vision adjusted, she quickly raced to the loo.

At first HT thought something was wrong. Then he chuckled and stacked his hands behind his head and muttered, "She had to pee, the little minx; it took her long enough to come around." He was so happy he felt as if he was floating on air instead of laying on a cold floor. He jumped up too excited to just lie there. He picked up his cape and put it on. He then felt around for his hat. He found it and his mask and stepped out of the room smiling from ear to ear, fighting the urge to jump into the air doing a fist pump. He started toward the loo and stopped, deciding to wait there for her. He leaned against the wall with his arms crossed over his chest and sang along with the song that was playing through the sound system.

Lil raised her mask as she went in the loo just in case someone else was in there. She saw HT's do-rag hanging from it and felt herself go all hot again. She quickly unhooked it and tucked it in her waist band. Not seeing anyone, she went to the mirror to fix her veils. She looked at herself in the mirror, carefully looking for any evidence she'd just had the best night of her life! Her face was flushed and her lips were a little red and swollen but not too bad. Then she saw the side of her neck and leaned closer over the washbasin. She mumbled, "Bloody hell! HT you did it again! The last ones drove me mental trying to keep them covered. You sure like giving these awful things. What? You use them as your trademark or what?" They seemed to get bigger and darker by the second as she stared. She looked down just above her top seeing more and quickly pulled her top outward so that she could see better. Her eyes widened, and she gasped at the sight. She was covered! She started pulling out the pins in her hair hoping to cover the ones on her neck. She heard the door opening, so she darted into a stall and closed the door. She could hear someone go into another stall. She knew she had to move fast if she wanted to beat the lights going up in the gym. She finished pulling the pins out of her hair, shaking it free. She ran her fingers through her hair like a comb and pulled it over to the side into a ponytail, tied a veil around it, and let it drape down, covering the love bites on her neck. She tucked veils in her top to cover the top of her breasts. She mumbled, "At least I've learned a few things from Sloan. Thank God, he made most of them low enough for my top to cover!" She drew in a breath when she was done, knowing she couldn't cower in the loo all night. She opened the stall door and walked out, with her head held high.

She didn't see anyone, so she took a quick glance back into the mirror before going out, making sure all the marks were covered. She let out a small breath of relief seeing the lights were still low as she stepped out. She started walking by the dance floor when the lights came up. "Bloody hell, almost made it," she mumbled, knowing everyone had to lower their mask when the lights came up. She lowered hers and pasted a smile on her face as she walked toward the door to make her escape to the drama room.

HT wondered what was taking her so long. She was usually pretty quick when she went to the loo. He figured she ran into Sloan. He decided to walk over by the loo. The lights came up as he reached the loo. Not seeing her, he headed to the dance floor.

"Hey, Lil," Connor called out.

She groaned inwardly as she swung around smiling.

He was grinning as he walked up. "Where are you going so fast? Whoa...I see by your neck you found him."

"Blimey!" Lil grumbled moving her hair back against her neck and arranging the veils. "I thought I had them covered."

"Them! Just how many do you have?" Connor asked laughing, moving her hair.

"Stop! You're not helping." She grinned, slapping his hand away. "I need to get out of here before HT sees me and figures out it was me."

"He didn't realize it was you?"

She grinned shaking her head. "Nope! You're plan was brilliant!"

"Really!" he said with a little grunt wondering what went wrong.

Her eyes scanned the packed gym and then at the doors leading to the side parking lot. She knew that's where JR would be parked, and she had just decided she was going home. She didn't want to take the chance of HT seeing what apparently was his trademark on her neck. She spotted HT across the floor. She quickly stepped in and slipped her arms around Connor's waist pulling him up against her pressing her face against his chest. "Hurry, put your arms around me," she demanded with a chuckle.

He hesitated for a second and then he wrapped his arms around her. They stood like that for a moment before Connor asked, "Want to fill me in on why?"

"HT is standing in the middle of the dance floor, and I don't want him to come this way."

"How long are we doing this?" Connor asked laughing.

"It's not funny. Stop your laughing," she said with a chuckle.

HT spotted Lil; his grin slowly fell as he stood watching them hug. His stomach twisted. He couldn't believe it! Sloan must have given the tosser a costume knowing he was always running late. The sinking feeling in his stomach told him she thought he was Connor. He turned his head away, letting the truth sink in. *She would have known he already had his costume and knew he would be late. That's why she went with me so easily. She thought the tosser finally showed up!...I was sure she knew it was me.* He growled when Britney clamped her hands around his neck and pressed herself against his chest. He was so occupied watching Lil that he hadn't noticed she had walked up.

Lil took a quick peek. Pain shot through her, making her suck in her breath and spine stiffen, seeing Britney's arms locked around HT's neck and rubbing up against him.

Connor followed her gaze to see what she was looking at and looked back at her and said, "Look at me and breathe."

A cold knot tightened in the pit of her stomach as she turned back to Connor. She felt a lump in her throat and swallowed hard.

"Lil, take a minute to calm down," he said trying to defuse the situation. "She's always doing that to me and the guys. We've nicknamed her leech girl. She doesn't care which one of us she clings to. She clasps her hands behind our heads and hangs on for dear life! We have to peel her hands off to get away."

"Bloody hell!" HT roared disgustedly, reaching back and unlocking Britney's grip from his neck. He needed some air. He took a deep breath to keep from hurling. He figured he had about a minute. He turned and bolted for the door.

Rejection was clearly something she was used to. She trailed off after him not giving up.

Lil cast a dark look in their direction. Her body started shaking with hurt and anger while watching HT heading to the door, with Britney following. She swallowed past the lump in her throat. Tears burned behind her eyes, but she wouldn't let herself cry; she got mad instead. "Yeah, right, try again," she hissed as she stepped back looking at Connor. "It's exactly what I think. He's leaving with the bloody cow!"

Connor saw Sloan coming and quickly decided not to let her know something happened between Lil and HT. "Heads up, here comes Sloan," he said out of the side of his mouth as he slowly shook his head at Sloan when Lil looked her way.

Sloan nodded lightly, letting him know she understood; their plan didn't work. She walked up and asked, "You didn't change?"

Lil wanted to melt into the floor. Since that was impossible, she shook her head and replied, "I decided this was fine. I had to take my hair down though. It was giving me a headache."

"I'm so sorry," Sloan said believing her. "I'll run and get you some aspirin."

"Thanks. That would be brilliant," she joked with a strained smile. "And tea if you can find some!"

Sloan chuckled as she hurried off.

Just before HT went blasting out the door he heard Lee. "Hey, yo, Cat Lady, Romeo wants to dance."

HT turned to see Britney right behind him. He looked at Lee. "Thanks, bro. I'm calling it a night. I have to work in the morning" and out the door he went.

Lee shook his head. He wasn't sure what had happened but knew it had to do with Lil. She was the only one who could make him that upset and crazy!

The cool night air against HT's face didn't help. He ran straight for a tree.

JR and Jayden were standing out by the cars and saw HT tossing his cookies. "Bloody hell! Something happened," JR said.

Jayden hopped in the car while JR ran inside to find Lil.

Jayden pulled up. HT got in and threw his hat in the back seat. Jayden's heart dropped seeing he had a defeated look on his face. He knew the look; his heart was breaking once again.

Jayden drove off.

A wave of nausea hit HT again, and he lowered the window letting the cool night air hit his face.

"You okay, bro?"

HT nodded, still looking out. The cool air was whipping his curls all over.

"I'm here if you need to talk. What you say stays between us, which you know just means JR, right? We love you as our pain-in-the-arse little brother. You know that too, right?"

HT nodded again. "I know mate, and I feel the same about you blokes. I just can't talk about it right now." He wiped a tear off his cheek. He thought his heart was broken before, but now it had shattered into so many pieces, he knew it would never heal.

After Sloan ran to get Lil some aspirin, Connor didn't know what to say as he watched a tear slowly slide down Lil's cheek. He felt like a Judas, but he knew he was right. HT loved her, and he had to have known it was her. Something wasn't right, but he couldn't ask her any questions without dropping him and Sloan in the middle of it.

"I've got to get out of here before Sloan gets back," Lil finally said, getting herself under control.

"Let's get you out of here then," he said, concern thick in his voice.

Lil shook her head. "You need to stay and support Sloan when they announce who won. Tell her I said good luck and I'll talk to her tomorrow. I don't want you to lie to her, but if you could let her think I was afraid it was turning into one of my migraines I would appreciate it."

"Lil, there is no way I'm letting you walk out of here by yourself."

"Don't be silly. I'm fine, really. Just a little bruised ego," she said with a forced chuckle, looking at the door planning her escape route. She breathed a sigh of relief at seeing JR standing at the door looking her way. He was always there when she needed him. "Besides, JR is here," she added with a grin. "He's standing over at the side door."

Connor looked seeing JR and said with a chuckle, "And we both know whom he's looking for—Sloan."

"They don't hide their feelings toward each other well. Call me when you land," she said, giving him a quick hug and hurried to the door.

"I will, and I'll text before I take off. See you Tuesday afternoon," he called out.

She raised her arm waving, letting him know she heard him.

JR said, as she walked up, "Sloan gave me your clothes. I put them in the car."

"Cut the rubbish. I know why you're in here!" she said as they walked out.

"What? She did! She gave them to me just a bit ago." He grinned.

She rolled her eyes. "You know HT left with that cow, and you're wondering if I saw them and checking to see if I'm okay."

JR just grunted, still not figuring out what was going on.

By the time they reached the car, she had worked herself up again. Getting angry lessened the hurt. "I know you won't rat the tosser out, but please tell me Jay didn't let that cow get into the car with him!"

JR shook his head as they got into the car, starting to piece some of it together. "No, she's not in the car."

"Good. I'd hate to have to torch it."

JR howled with laughter.

She asked nonchalantly as if she didn't care, "Did he get in the car?"

"Nice try." JR chuckled. He said as he pulled out, "If you want to know what he's doing or where he's going, call him."

"Cheers!" she mumbled.

JR just chuckled.

HT trudged wearily up the stairs to his room. He sunk into his armchair staring at the ceiling. He was drained from the emotional highs and lows Lil had him on over the last couple of months. He never knew he could love someone so much or that love gave someone the power to break you. He was mentally exhausted. Enough was enough! He muttered, feeling defeated, "I just about had my head on straight and then I have to bloody screw it up again. If this is love, I want no part of it. This totally blows. Dad was right. The more you love someone, the less sense anything makes."

He felt like he was trapped in a nightmare. He tried to block it out, but his mind endlessly replayed the night over and over in his head, not wanting to believe she didn't know it was him. But the more he thought about it, he knew she didn't. They really never talked, just role-played, both disguising their voices. He hated to admit it...she totally thought he was Soccer Boy. The thought made him mad all over again. He knew he shouldn't be. It was his fault for letting his imagination run wild, convincing himself that she felt the same way. *Well, I am mad, thinking about what we did. It was the best night of my life, and she thought it was with that prat!*

Then he thought about how she returned his passion. Clyde let him know; he was standing at attention. He got up, stripped off the costume, and stomped off to take a cold shower talking to himself. "What is wrong with me? Wanting to wring her little neck one minute and then thinking sexy thoughts about her the next?" He turned the nozzle in the shower and hopped in letting the blast of cold water hit him full force. He shivered as he grumbled, "I'm done. This really did it. No more excuses. It's time to move on. No more thoughts of being with her in that bloody room, either. I'll be in here all night, and I'm freezing my nads off." He let the cold water pour over his face, allowing him to clear his mind and think a little more clearly. He made the water warm as he thought. How was he going to reclaim his life before her—or more to the point, without her? *I know I'm sick to death of acting and feeling like a total wanker over her.* He came to the conclusion if he was ever going to keep his sanity he was just going to have to get the hell away from her for a while, far away. He had to keep his distance mentally and physically. "I'll go with the twins to the States over school break next week. I'll stay with Lee until we leave. Yeah, I won't have to see her much, and it won't look weird if I stay with Lee before we go. I always wanted to go to LA. I'll get over my obsession with her over there with all of those fit girls. Yeah, right, like that would happen," he muttered disgusted. "Who you trying to kid mate? Like you can stay away from her and miss her birthday."

He got out of the shower still mad at her for breaking his heart and at himself for letting her. He wrapped a towel around his waist as he stomped to the bed. He knew he hadn't sent her a text and didn't care. He wasn't going to. She probably wouldn't even notice anyway. He lay down and settled himself in. He was going to sleep. He closed his eyes trying to remember one of JR's mind-control exercises. He focused hard, trying to forget the image of her wrapped in Connor's arms just minutes after what they had shared.

After lying there having no luck at falling asleep and ending up staring at the ceiling, he muttered, "Bloody hell." He sat up and grabbed his phone and sent a text, using the excuse she would know something was up if he didn't. He sent the text and lay back down, trying to figure out how he was going to handle seeing her in the morning. He guessed he would just try to act normal. He needed to figure out what he was going to say not being there for the results of the judging if she asked. He thought for a few seconds and decided he would wink and say something came up and leave it at that, not breaking their rule.

He looked at his phone muttering, "No text yet! *Huh!*" He threw off the cover and jumped out of bed frustrated and started to pace. "I'm not sending her another text if she doesn't text back. And I'm not calling her like when she stood me up after Sloan's party. Well, okay, she did text she wasn't coming, but that's beside the bloody point; she never called me back! And what was she doing that night?" he asked himself sarcastically. He then answered himself in the same disgusted tone, "The same bloody thing she's probably doing right now! That's it! I really, really mean it. I'm done! Now is as good a time as any to start backing away from her." He told himself sternly, "I can do this!"

He paced a few more minutes. "Bloody Hell! I'm such a wanker! How pathetic. How am I going to keep away from her if I don't have enough self-control not to text her?" He growled, as he sent her another text. He took his phone to bed. After twenty very long, frustrating minutes, he jumped up and paced angrily with his phone in hand. He sent another text and said, "I'm doing this all bloody night if I have to. You *will* answer me!"

His phone finally beeped. He sneered, "It's about bloody time!" Anger and frustration raged through him as he hurled his phone across the room hitting the wall. He heard it hit the floor with a dull thud and muttered as he threw himself down in the chair, "I hope I broke the bloody thing!"

Lil stomped up the stairs to her room. She started pacing between the fireplace and her bed trying to calm down. She was crushed and mad. Her anger was mostly over him being able to leave with that cow after what they had just shared. She didn't want to face the fact he had turned into a total tosser. For the first time ever, she seemed to really see him. As far as she was concerned, her opinion of him when they first met had been reinforced. She mumbled, "What was all that rubbish about having to care about the person he was with? *Horny toad! He didn't even know who he was with!*" She kept trying to tell herself she shouldn't be mad. It was her fault for going in that bloody room in the first place! Images sprang to the forefront of her mind of him leaving with Britney. She couldn't seem to keep them pushed back. She mumbled, "Wasn't I enough?" She could feel her throat thicken with tears she was trying to hold back. She said, wiping the ones that slipped out running down her cheek, "Of course, he had to leave with that cow, the only person in the world I hate. She must be his go-to piece."

She realized he hadn't text and mumbled, "He's probably too busy with that cow! Ooooo," she grumbled, stomping her feet in place. "I can't believe I let myself fall in love with that tosser!" She took a deep breath and decided what she needed was a long, hot soak in a bubble bath. She needed to calm down and remember that his sex life was none of her business. He was still her best mate.

She heard her phone with his ringtone. "Aaargh," she grumbled as she stomped off to the loo mumbling. "Yeah! A best mate who I would love to stick my foot up his...Enough!" she said, taking a deep breath.

She decided she didn't want to wait on the tub to fill and turned the shower head on. She'd practically tore the costume off ignoring all the marks HT put on her and hopped in. After a few minutes standing under the hot water, she started to calm down and relax as her mind cleared.

She got out of the shower and slipped on her robe and stuffed her feet into her fluffy slippers. She walked out of the loo and saw a steaming cup of tea sitting on her table. "Thanks, Mum. Love you," she mumbled and went over and picked it up taking a sip. She picked up her phone to see if he had texted again. Seeing that he had, she grumbled as she threw the phone back down, "Text that bloody cow!" She started pacing, drinking her tea, and continued mumbling, "I wonder if you made her chest look like a bloody checker board. Oh! I bet you made her purr like a cat peeling that costume off her!" Her phone sang again! She couldn't put off the inevitable; she had to answer him. She stomped over, put her cup down, and picked up her phone. "Tosser," she spat as she shot off his text. She dropped the phone down by his do-rag and stomped over to bed.

# CHAPTER 25

The next morning like every other morning, Lil instinctively reached up by her head for her phone when she woke up still sleepy. It seemed like she had just closed her eyes. "Buggar," she grumbled, not finding it. It only took moments to realize something was wrong...something...she sat up and looked across the room, seeing her phone on the table lying beside HT's do-rag. Boom! She winced and felt nauseated as the memories came rushing back. "Oh no!" she gasped, falling back against her pillow. "I've dropped myself right back in it," she mumbled. "No, I couldn't be happy that I got away with it the first time. I had to do it again, and he wasn't blasted out of his mind this time!"

She swung her legs off the bed and sat up, fighting the urge to crawl back in and pull the cover over her head, turning off all the memories. She knew the bakery would be swamped with everyone picking up orders and getting their last-minute cakes and cookies for Halloween parties, and knowing it was going to be a long morning wasn't helping her mood.

Lil let out a long sigh as she dragged herself over and picked up her phone, knowing she had to send HT his morning text. She saw Connor had just texted a few minutes before and returned it telling him she was fine and to have a safe flight. She sent HT his text and stuck her tongue out at the phone. She went to the loo telling herself to push all thought of the night before out of her mind. Hopefully, he wouldn't show up. Hard telling what time he dragged his horny bum home, if at all. She took off her robe to get dressed and looked down seeing the marks. "Oh no," she gasped, hurrying over to the mirror. She stared as she leaned in, having totally forgotten about them. "Buggar," she mumbled, turning red with embarrassment at remembering how brazen and out of control she was. "I'm going to need a lot of makeup on those," she mumbled, looking at the ones on her neck. She quickly dressed, brushed her teeth, and dug around in the makeup case that Sloan had left there and found the cover up she used the last time. She applied it to the purple marks that showed just above her pink bakery logo T-shirt. She pulled her hair over to the side, tying an orange-and-black ribbon on it, making it lie across the marks. "There," she said, "now it looks like I'm in the Halloween spirit!" She scooped up her phone not realizing she had also picked up HT's do-rag with it and stuck them in her back pocket.

The morning air was chilly, but she was in such an awful mood she never paid notice to the goose bumps up and down her arms. She reached the back door of the bakery and stood there. She couldn't seem to make herself go inside. She heard HT's ringtone. It was the first time it had taken so long for him to text back, making her mad all over again. "About time. Hopefully this means you're otherwise occupied and won't show up," she grumbled.

"He's already in there," JR said behind her.

"Bloody hell," she yelped, frustrated as she turned around. "Don't you ever sleep?"

He chuckled and said, "Get ready he's in top form in there."

"Great, that's all I need," she grumbled. "What time did he get here anyway? Or is that something else you won't tell me?"

He laughed and said, "He was here waiting on Joe to open the door."

"Probably just got home," she mumbled sarcastically. She turned back around and took a deep breath knowing she had delayed the inevitable for as long as possible, and pushed open the door.

Jayden walked up to JR when she closed the door. "How's she doing?"

"It won't take much; she's about to blow."

"Good. Moms and her letting-things-play-out rubbish," Jayden said. "Those two are doing my head in."

"All our heads. After she blows and faces the fact she wants him more than working with us, I can tell her about the plan," said JR as they headed up to the house for an emergency meeting Luke had called.

Once inside Lil tied her apron around her waist as she did her morning ritual and stuck her head in the back kitchen and cheerfully called out "Good morning" to Grammy, Abs, and Joe.

"Good morning," they called back, not looking her way, all as busy as bees.

HT heard her and let out a low growl. He felt disgusted that his heart raced as always from just hearing her. He took a deep breath and put his charm into overdrive, laughing loudly, sounding happy as ever.

Lil heard him. Her body reacted by going all hot inside as she was remembering his lips...his mouth...his hands...him pressing the hard length of his body against hers. She rolled her eyes disgusted that she had so little control over her body. How could she react like this knowing he was such a tosser? She mumbled, "Remember, he's a bloody tosser; he's a bloody horny toad; he's a bloody horny toad tosser!" She planted on a fake smile, doing her best to act normally, as she walked out front seeing the bakery was already busy, the line circled out the door.

HT saw the big smile on her face as he glanced over and quickly turned back to look at Vivian the girl next in line. He became Horny Harry as he gave her one of his sexiest grins. "Your turn, little lady, step right on up here. Hey, didn't we meet up last night? You were a harem girl, right?"

Lil groaned inwardly and walked to the counter to HT's left to make her tea.

"No." She giggled. "I wasn't picked to be in Sloan's group."

Lil could feel the anger building inside as she listened. Not thinking, she put coffee in a filter to make coffee.

"Hey, no tea this morning?" asked HT, looking over at her.

"I'll make it next. Looks like we need this," she replied seeing they really did. "You're early," she added looking at him smiling. "I didn't think you would show up today or thought you might be a little late since I *just* received your text!"

"I came in early and then lost track of time; we've been really busy. Blimey, you look knackered! Fun night, huh? Is that why it took me *three times* having to text last night for you to answer?" With one of his sexiest grins, he added, "I almost gave up. I was kind of in the middle of something!" He thought, *Yeah, like pacing and wondering what your arse was doing!*

She quickly turned back to the coffee machine trying to calm down as an image of him leaving with Britney flashed through her head. "Sorry, I was too," she said sweetly. She added on a sigh, "It was an amazing night! Actually, it was the best night of my life!" She pushed the button to get the coffee started. "How about you? You have fun?"

He turned back to the line as he shrugged as if it was no big deal. "Just another night of many, I guess," he said with a sexy chuckle wanting to strangle her for what she'd said and kiss her silly at the same time. He smiled and winked at Emma now standing in front of him and teased, "Hi, gorgeous. You were a harem girl last night, right?"

It took all Lil had not to throw the coffee pot, now filling up with hot coffee, at his head. She mumbled under her breath, "Tosser. He's trying to figure out who he was with!"

Emma's face was beaming as she returned his flirting and gushed, "Yes, I was. I was disappointed you weren't the sheik. You're why I wanted to be a harem girl. I'll be wearing it to Lee's party later if you want to hook up."

"I'll see if I can fit you in," he teased with a wink. He said to Lil not looking her way, "How about you jump in so that we can get this line down and out of here. Seems I have another date with a harem girl tonight."

He didn't see Lil flashing him an angry glare. *Damn his bloody conceit.* She picked up the cup of tea she had just made.

Mary quickly stepped in front of her, blocking her way. "Good morning, dear, you're in an awfully good mood this morning being out so late last night. Did you have fun?" she greeted with a wink while restraining her with a hand on her arm.

"Good morning, Mum. Oh yes! Connor is amazing," she gushed as she playfully crossed her eyes.

Mary suppressed a laugh, shaking her head a little, and replied, "That's great, dear. I'm glad you enjoyed yourself."

HT's eyes turned an emerald green at hearing she was still with Connor, which was why she didn't text him back right away. Of course he knew that; he just didn't like hearing her confirm it. He breathed in deeply as he told himself, *I just need to get through the morning.*

As the morning dragged on, every time HT looked at Lil he thought about the night before making Clyde rear up. It angered him over his loss of control. It had him flirting with every female that walked in the door trying to keep his mind off her.

Lil glanced at the clock and let out a heavy sigh seeing it was just after eleven. She was becoming more frustrated by the second. Her nerves were strung tight from listening to HT being Horny Harry all morning. She made the mistake of looking at him as she was putting cupcakes in a box. The sight of him winking at Ava, the girl he was waiting on, intensified her anger. She started to raise the cupcake in her hand.

Mary made a warning noise in her throat and whispered as she grabbed it, "Maybe you should go to the back, dear. We don't want the whole village talking." She added with a little chuckle, "I can't keep taking stuff out of your hands. That's the fourth time in less than an hour!"

Lil couldn't help but laugh. "I'll be all right. I just need to fix some tea; that should help." She turned and quickly walked to the drink counter.

She had just poured hot tea in a cup when she heard Rachel thanking Kent, the local butcher, for holding the door open for her. She worked at the coffee shop and had it bad for HT and never tried to hide it. Lil let out a little groan. "Not now," she mumbled. She liked her, but she didn't have the patience today, and her nerves were too strained to watch her fawn all over HT.

Mary took the hot cup of tea out of her hand. "Maybe you should go ahead and call it a day."

"Are you sure? There's still a lot to do, Mum."

"Yes, I'm sure, dear. It's slowing down, and Abs can come help up here. Just tell Tessa you're leaving."

"Okay, I'll go. If I have to listen to one more daft, giggly cow flirting with the tosser, I'm going to explode!" She quickly hurried to the back. "I'm calling it a day if you don't need me," she said as she walked in.

"Nah, we're good, baby girl," said Tessa looking up at her. "But can you grab me a tin of sugar before you leave?"

"For sure," she said as she hurried out and ran to the back wall. She grabbed the sugar off the shelf and ran back meeting Abs in the doorway.

Abs said with a smile, "I'll head up front now, dear, so don't worry and get some rest. You look tired."

"Thanks, Aunt Abs. Love you," Lil said kissing her cheek.

"Love you most, dear," she replied as she hurried off.

Lil looked over at Joe. "Uncle Joe, are you sure? I can stay; I know you wanted to polish the floors today."

Joe replied, while putting cookies in Halloween boxes, "Get yourself out of here. You got more black under them eyes than these witch cookies. Besides, I have blokes coming to give me a hand."

Tessa added, "He's right, baby girl. Go get some rest. We got this."

Lil kissed their cheeks. "Thanks, I think I will call it a day then. Love you guys," she said.

"Love you most," they replied as she hurried out.

She took off her apron and threw it on the counter as she ran for the back door.

HT called after her when her hand was on the handle, "Hey, you weren't planning on leaving without saying anything, were you?" he asked, pasting on his sexiest grin.

Lil mouthed, "Bloody hell." She managed to get the scowl off her face before turning around. She gave him her biggest smile and sweetly said, "You were busy entertaining; I didn't want to bother you. Joe is polishing the floors later, so make sure when you sweep you get up under the ovens and counters. And um...it wouldn't hurt to take a little more time in that loo." She wrinkled her nose and added with a faintly superior tone, "I think you've been overlooking it lately," and ended with a soft posh laugh.

He stared at her in disbelief. He couldn't believe what she had said.

Lil watched with satisfaction. Her barb had hit its target. She was glad to see the smug grin leave his face. "I'll leave you to it," she said as she opened the door and hurried out with a satisfied smile. She headed to the Cove, cursing under her breath all the way.

He stared at the door fuming. He muttered, "Did she really just talk to me like that?" He shook with anger. "Who does she think she's talking to? I've never met anyone who could make me so bloody mad!" He continued to grumble as he went to the back wall for the broom, "Just my bloody luck. If Moms hadn't sent me back here to sweep so that I could leave, I wouldn't have seen her snooty arse!"

He grabbed the broom and began sweeping, grumbling the whole time. "Overlooking the loo my arse! I clean it all the bloody time. She should clean it. She's the one who runs to it every five bloody minutes!"

Lil charged into the Cove slamming the door behind her. She went straight to the darkroom; its door also got slammed. She needed to decompress, and knew she could count on doing it in there. She took a few deep breaths to take in the scent of the ink and chemicals to calm her nerves and clear her mind. She went to work trying to focus and get HT out of her head. It didn't work. Every picture she developed contained that smile and those twinkling eyes! She moaned, "*Ugh*, what *is* it about you that could charm the panties off a bloody nun?"

She decided maybe a hot shower and a nap would help. She went out and headed straight to the loo, taking off her clothes as she walked. She turned on the faucet, making the water as hot as she could bear, and quickly stepped inside. The hot water ran over her, clearing her mind. It seemed to slowly bring her around. She stood for a few more minutes, feeling the tension slowly melt away.

She hopped out of the shower and realized she hadn't grabbed any clean clothes. She wrapped a towel around her head and another one around her body, picked up her trail of dirty clothes as she went to the Lion's Room to take a much-needed nap.

HT hadn't calmed down by the time he finished sweeping. He was still fuming as he walked to the back wall to hang up the broom. "There's no way in hell I'm touching that loo. Ms. Snooty Pants can do it. I'm out of here. I'm going to Lee's and get a head start on that party before she shows up with the tosser!"

Mary entered the room hearing him. She had told him he could call it a day once he was done sweeping since he came in so early. She was hoping he would go up to see Lil, not run off to Chester. It was time to step in and quit waiting for it to play out. She quickly thought about an excuse to get him up to the Cove. The mood Lil was in, it wouldn't take much more for her to blow. She quickly decided she would send the lunch she had put back for her and Charles. No way she was letting him run off to Chester without seeing Lil first. She put a smile on her face as she said, "HT, can you do me a favor?"

"Of course," he said as he turned with a huge smile. "Anything for you, Moms."

"Thanks, dear. I'll be right back." She hurried out front and returned with a canvas bag full of food. She handed him the bag. "Can you run this up to Lil? She said she was going to work in the darkroom."

"Sure," HT said, his smile was now strained. "I'll run it up, before I head to Chester."

"Just make sure she eats before you go and make her one of those special teas she loves. Otherwise, she'll be in that darkroom all day and not eat or drink a thing. You should eat something, too. I haven't seen you eat anything either."

"I can't promise she'll eat, but I'll try."

"I'm sure the tea will bring her out of that room," she said smiling. Her smile turned smug as she headed back up front.

HT went out closing the door none too lightly behind him and stomped up the path deep in thought. He couldn't tell Moms that he didn't want to see Lil. Now, not only did he have to *see* her, but he also had to *talk* to her. He would make some tea, put the food on a plate, and set it out for her on the snack bar. He would simply knock on the darkroom door and tell her Moms was worried about her, she sent food, and it was on the counter with tea. Then he was getting the hell out of there before she came out!

Lil was on her way to the Lion's Room when she spotted HT coming through the door. She stopped. "I can't believe this," she mumbled, trying to decide which would be quicker, running back to the loo or keep on going.

HT was still licking his wounds from the way she talked to him in the bakery. He laughed bitterly, not disguising the resentment in his voice at seeing her. "Talk about perfect timing!" His entire body reacted at seeing her. His brow shot up seeing the marks. The hot shower made them look even worse. The pain in his chest nearly suffocated him thinking Connor had put them there.

"Oh, bite me!" she snapped, seeing his smug face.

He recovered quickly. He was feeling the ache of a broken heart on the inside, but he was his normal flirty self on the outside. He raised his brow up and down as his mouth curled seductively. "Looks like you let Soccer Boy have all the fun!" He added with a chuckle, "You look like you got in a fight with a hoover and lost!"

Her anger instantly rose to the boiling point that he didn't have a clue he had made the mess. She glared at him wanting to scream, *"You made this mess! You conceited wanker!"* But she clamped her lips together and just rolled her eyes disgustingly at him before stomping off to the Lion's Room. "Tosser!" she mumbled under her breath knowing she should be relieved he didn't know he had put them there, but for some reason it made her furious.

He stomped the opposite way to the snack bar. He muttered under his breath, "Well, I can see why it took her forever to text me back. That wanker must get off putting those disgusting things on her!" He dumped the food out of the sack onto the snack bar not caring how it landed and turned to make her tea. He opened the cabinet then slammed it shut. "She can make her own bloody tea," he said, as he shook with jealousy. He stomped to the Lion's Room muttering, "I'm going to tell her Moms said to eat, and I'm out of here!"

By the time Lil threw her dirty clothes on the bed, she was seething with anger. She quickly went to the chest for clean ones. She took out a pair of sweats and T-shirt. She pulled the sweats on under her towel and then jerked the one off her head to put on a T-shirt, not bothering with underclothes. She wanted out of there as fast as possible. She unwrapped the towel from her body and threw it on the bed as she picked up her dirty jeans to get her phone. She pulled it out, along with HT's do-rag. "Bloody hell," she said, quickly stuffing it in her back pocket with her phone as she threw her jeans in the corner.

HT stood in the doorway watching her. He heard her but didn't see what she put in her pocket. He figured it was her phone. He folded his arms across his chest and leaned against the doorframe.

She looked up to see him standing there staring at her. She quickly looked away, hoping he didn't see the do-rag and realized he had a black one on at the bakery. She knew the one she had was his favorite blue one. She was doing all she could to hold her tongue, but it wasn't easy to keep quiet when she was so furious. She tried to shove her foot into her trainer.

With an arrogant lift of his eyebrows he asked sarcastically, "Don't you think it would go on easier if you untied it first?"

She rolled her eyes at him and shoved the other one on without untying it. The backs of them were now flattened.

A faint smile touched his lips as he lightly shook his head.

She picked up her brush repressing a strong urge to throw it at him. She jerked it through her hair a few times and then threw it back on the chest. "I'll brush it up at the house," she mumbled and turned to leave.

"Now I see why it took you so long to text me back. Soccer Boy was keeping you busy," he said with a forced chuckle, as anger surged through him making his insides boil.

"His name is Connor!" Her look turned even harder.

He gave her a cool stare and smiled, but the expression didn't reach his eyes. "Whatever!"

She knew the smart thing to do would be to get away from him until she could calm down and get her head straight. "I'm really not in a good place right now. We can talk later—" she tried to suggest, but he cut her off curtly.

"What is that supposed to mean?"

Her chest was rising and falling rapidly, as she was trying to do one of JR's calming exercises. It didn't work; she had never felt so angry in her life. "You're a smart bloke; you figure it out."

His voice was low, as his eyes locked with hers. "I'm sick of trying to figure out what you mean! So, no, enlighten me."

She lifted her chin to its haughtiest angle, returning his stony stare. "Fine, I tried, but you just keep pushing," she hissed as she glared at him. "It means, that I don't like you right now, Har—"

"Oh no, don't be pulling that Harry Thomas rubbish with me right now like you're the one who is upset. I'm the one who's bloody mad and hurt here," he continued, his voice rising. "Next time you try to pull that—I'm-better-than-you—expression you did at the bakery, I recommend you raise that chin like you just did then and look down your nose just the tiniest bit more!"

She gave a hollow laugh. "The one I gave you seems to have worked just fine!"

His upper lip curled into a sneer. His tone reflected a rage she'd never heard before. "Yeah, it did as a matter of fact. I didn't like it. Don't ever look or talk to me like that again!"

"Oh! Really?" she said hotly.

"Yes, really! Disrespect me like that again, and I'll never step another foot in that bakery! Or around you as a matter of fact! Got it?"

"Fine, sorry, got it!" she mumbled.

"I didn't hear you."

"I'm sorry; I get it!" she shouted. "Did you hear that?"

"Yes and so did everyone in the bloody village!"

"Good, now move! I don't want to breathe the same air as you!" she said, still shouting.

He was confused by her anger. He knew something was wrong. He just couldn't get his mind around what could have set her off since leaving the bakery. "All right, Lil. What's this all about? What the bloody hell did I do this time?" he demanded, his patience fraying fast.

"Nothing," she hissed angrily, as she marched past him. "Nothing at all. Don't you know the girls all think you're perfect, just the sweetest thing ever!" she spat sarcastically. She added with a huff, "More like the horniest bloody toad on this entire planet!"

He stared at her blankly for a moment and then screwed up his face and yelled after her as he followed, "What the bloody hell you going on about?"

She replied over her shoulder as she stomped to the door, "That you're a low-life pig!" She mumbled, "You don't care who you're with, as long as your Johnson's happy!"

"I heard that, and for your information, his name isn't Johnson; it's Clyde!"

She yelled, "Ooh, you're such a tosser!" and ran out the door.

He yelled, chasing after her. "Oh no, you don't! You don't get to run out of here after starting this rubbish! Get back here, Lily Rose!"

He caught her arm and brought her to a standstill just after she exited through the gate.

She turned toward him, fury on her face as she pulled her arm away. "Don't touch me!" she snarled and stormed up the walk.

He ran ahead of her and swung around to face her, planting himself in her path so that she would have to stop.

In a near shout she demanded, "Get out of my way!"

He made no effort to move.

She tried to walk around him and let out a loud sigh of frustration when he moved blocking her way. "I want to puke just looking at you!"

"Well, guess what, lady? You're not floating my boat right now either! Let's calm—"

"I will not calm down!" she screeched.

He had never seen her lose control like this; crazy lady came to mind. A sickening realization came over him; she knew it was him and now hated him for it. He felt a sense of panic in the pit of his stomach. He took in a deep breath. "Lil," he pleaded making his tone soft and even. "Let's go back inside and talk this out."

Lil's eyes narrowed as she hissed, "You go talk it out! I'm never going back in there with you!" she tried to get around him.

"Like it or not, you're going back inside, and we're talking." He quickly scooped her up and slung her over his shoulder, carrying her like a sack of potatoes, her head and arms dangling down his back.

She yelled and squirmed, hitting his bum. "Put me down!"

He pushed his way back through the gate; she grabbed onto the pole sticking out. Trying to stay calm he said, "Let go and stop wiggling before I drop you. You're no lightweight, you know."

"Aaaarrgh," groaned Lil. "You are such an arse!"

"So you've said like a million times."

Before he went back into the Cove he said, "Stay out of it, bro!" He hadn't seen JR but knew he was close. He stomped over to the sofa where he dropped her, none too lightly. She landed in a sitting position and started to spring right back up.

"Stay!" he ordered, breathing hard.

She quickly fired back glaring at him but not moving. "Don't you dare try to tell me what to do, you horn dog." She was so mad that she was struggling to breath.

"Now," he said, still breathing hard, "if you can quit slinging bloody insults at me for five seconds, tell JR you're fine." All the time he spoke, his eyes never left hers. He didn't have to look. He knew JR would be standing in the doorway.

Lil was furious, her chest quickly going in and out from breathing so hard as she just stared, defying him with her eyes.

"Now, Lily Rose!" he said sternly, as he sucked in a breath through his clenched teeth.

"Fine!" she hissed. "But only because I want to, not because you're telling me to!" She turned her head, smiling sweetly. "Hi, JR. I'm fine." She sprang to her feet and turned back to HT. She shouted, glaring fiercely as she jabbed her finger into his chest. "But this wanker may not be by the time I'm done with him! You might want to come back to check on *him!*"

HT grabbed her hand. They stood toe to toe. Their gazes were fixed on each other, both breathing hard as anger sizzled in the air between them, each daring the other to speak.

JR said with a chuckle, "I'll be clo—"

HT cut him off, still glaring at Lil. "Yeah, we know. You'll be close by if she needs you!"

JR burst out laughing as he turned to leave. "Actually, bro, I was talking to *you!*"

"Cheers, mate!" muttered HT.

JR laughed harder as he went out.

HT, still not taking his eyes off her, wanted to kiss her so bad that it hurt but strangle her at the same time. "Now, can you please quit acting like a raving lunatic so that we can talk?"

She jerked her hand away as she step sideways, looking over to the door.

"You aren't going anywhere until we talk, Lily Rose."

She huffed and glared at him taking another sidestep, ready to make a beeline for the door.

His brow went up as he shook his head with a cocky grin. "Don't even think about attempting it. I'm faster than you. We're talking about this, Lil!"

She took his do-rag out of her pocket and threw it at him before bolting for the door. "Oh no, I'm not, you tosser!"

He caught it as he ran cutting her off. His voice, almost too low for her to hear when he saw what it was asked, "This is what set you off. Where was it?"

"Stuck in the back pocket of the jeans I took off, with my phone. I picked it up with it this morning without realizing I even had it," she replied honestly.

"You realized the tosser only wears red ones," he said mostly to himself.

Lil just stared registering what he'd said. Then it dawned on her and immediately saw the way out of this mess. She was in the clear. He thought she had just now figured out that it was him by the do-rag. What luck! She never paid attention when Connor wore his at practice since it didn't do anything for her. He had mentioned once that he only wore red ones because it was Amy's favorite color.

Running his fingers through his hair, he released a slow breath. "I'm sorry." His expression became more serious, his green eyes searching hers. "We can get past this right?"

Lil nodded with a shrug. "I can see how you didn't know it was me. I didn't even know it was me when I saw myself." She looked at him with a mixture of sadness and guilt, letting him take the blame.

"I know I should have told you as soon as I realized you thought I was that wanker last night, but I was—"

"Whoa," she said throwing up her hand. "What are you going on about?" asked Lil confused.

"I thought you knew it was me. I misread your feelings. I'm really sorry I got it wrong."

"My feelings? Got it wrong? You're saying you knew it was me before we went in that room?" she snapped.

"Of course, I knew it was you. I was going to tease you about your costume. Then things got out of...Bloody hell, Lil. I never expected that to happen when I took your hand."

She found herself growing even angrier knowing he left with Britney even after he knew it was her.

HT continued on, "And when you took off afterward, I figured you had to go to the loo. Then when I saw you wrapped in that tosser's arms I realized I got it all wrong, that you thought I was him. I wasn't thinking straight. You're all I've wanted and thought about since the day we met. I've done everything I could to show you how I feel, and I thought your feelings changed."

She thought about him leaving with Britney and gave a soft snort. "Brilliant speech!"

"What does that mean?"

"That we both know you're full of rubbish! I saw you leave with that cow Brit—"

He cut her off midsentence, almost shouting. "Bloody hell! Do you think I could do that? I never left with her, and I had no idea she was following me out," he denied hotly as he ran his fingers forcefully through his curls. He gave a wicked laugh and sneered, "I know you have this illusion that I'm out there nailing everything that walks, but guess what, lady? Unlike you, I'm still a bloody virgin. I know I'm not a saint, but I won't stand here and be accused of things I've had no control over and am innocent of from the one person in the world who I thought knew me best! I'm so over being worried about you kicking my arse to the curb if you realized how I feel. I love you! There I said it, so now you know! I'm out of here. I have a party to get to!" He turned and stomped out slamming the door behind him.

HT met JR at the gate. "Sorry for being bit of a prat earlier," said HT with a sheepish grin.

"Don't be daft, bro. I'm the one at fault. I shouldn't have stuck my nose in. It won't happen again. You heading to Chester?"

"Yeah, in a bit," he replied as they did the handshake guy-hug thing. "Do me a favor and ask Mr. C if he'll call off Jay. I'm skipping golf in the morning. I don't want to wake up in the loo in the morning!"

JR chuckled and said, "No worries. Golf is off anyway. Something has come up."

"Brilliant," HT said over his shoulder as he started up the walk.

"Hey, bro," JR called to his retreating back.

HT turned walking backward. "What's up?"

"Keep your flying to a minimum tonight, aye!"

"Cheers," HT called back laughing as he turned back around.

JR chuckled as he went into the Cove.

Lil was still staring at the door. She knew that she had crossed the line. She had never seen him so mad. Then her heart soared. She mumbled, "He loves me." A dozen different emotions rose up. She wanted to run after him. She loved him with all her heart. The defense mechanism in her mind, honed by years of JR's training, asked, "Are you sure? More than the life of excitement and intrigue you love?" The very thought of not being part of the team terrified her, but somehow, standing there watching him leave terrified her more. "Yes, I'm sure," she mumbled.

"Snaggs," said JR looking at her. "Everything okay? You have a strange look on your face."

Lil looked at him smiling and said, "Oh yeah, everything is brilliant!"

"Good. So now we talk."

"Why do I feel a lecture coming on?" she joked as she followed him to the sofa.

"No, you'll like what I'm about to tell you if you're going to say what I think!"

"That I know the last few months has been on me," she said with a little sigh. "That I subconsciously buried how I feel knowing if he returned my feelings I would have to choose him or my life's dream of working with you guys. Silly me, I thought I had my guard up until I found myself madly in love with him at—"

He chuckled cutting in, "The Battle of the Bands."

She threw a pillow at him laughing as she sat down. "This is your fault you know? You and that bloody mind-control rubbish. If I had realized I was falling in love with him, I could have fought it."

"You don't really believe that do you?"

"Of course not. I was doomed the second I laid eyes on him," she said. "Thanks for the heads-up on how he felt though."

"Sorry, but I had to agree with Moms on this one. Things had to play out. You needed time to get a few ops under your belt so that there where no regrets when you made your decision. So have you decided?" he teased. "Him or us?"

"Real funny," she replied rolling her eyes. "Like there's a doubt. I knew I would pick him if he ever returned my feelings the second he did that little bow thing at Chester."

JR chuckled and said, "I've known since your guy's first gettin'-loose night. That's the night he realized he was in love with you by the way. You know, the same night you also realized you loved him but was just too stubborn to admit it?"

"Do you see everything? You're scary, you know that?"

"I prefer being called wise!"

She playfully rolled her eyes.

"So why are you sitting there? Go put that poor bloke out of his misery. What I have to tell you can wait!"

"I'm giving him a little time to calm down. To tell you the truth, I'm not sure how to tell him."

"Don't beat yourself up, Snaggs; you didn't know how he felt. But when you tell him hold that temper of yours if he says a few things you might not like to hear. You've had his head all over the place for months, especially watching you with Connor."

She said making a cute face, "Maybe I'll give him time to get a few of those lighted drinks down at the party before I confess how I feel. So what did you want to tell me? Sounds like it's something good, and I could use that now!"

"We've came up with a plan where you can still work with us and have HT."

She laughed and threw another pillow at him. "You could have started with that! You really are a tosser, you know that?"

"Yep!" He grinned and then added, "Orders from top command made me wait!"

"Which means, Mum," Lil said with a little chuckle.

"Exactly. I had to hear you would choose HT first."

"I take it we've means everyone?"

JR stood up and said, "Yep, family meeting as always."

"What is it?" asked Lil following him toward the door.

"It will work better if you don't know. You'll know when it happens."

HT started throwing clothes into his backpack. He was ready to admit defeat. He'd had enough and was going with the plan he came up with the night before. He would stay at Lee's, out of her way, and then go with the twins. He stopped, thinking he was missing something. After a moment he muttered, "Wait a minute. She had a bloody attitude all morning! Why did she leave early? And look how she talked and looked at me about sweeping and cleaning the loo. She's never acted like that no matter how much I drive her mental! It's obvious now she was mad about something when she came into the bakery this morning before she saw me acting like Horny Harry. The question is, what made her so mad? Think, mate. This is serious here. Maybe I'm trying to read something in to it, and she got mad like she said when she realized it was me after seeing the do-rag? No, I thought that! She never said that's what set her off. She said she didn't realize she'd picked up the do-rag with her phone and left it at that. And why would it matter if I had left with Britney last night? She sounded hurt and jealous and not as a mate!"

At that moment, he knew it wasn't just his imagination. Everything made sense now. He burst out laughing, and ran out the door, and down the back stairs still talking to himself. "The little minx was hurt and mad at me this morning because she bloody well knew that was me in that room with her and thought I left with Britney! She had to leave early because I was doing her head in being Horny Harry all morning! I was right," he yelled triumphantly as he flew out the kitchen door, "she does have bloody feelings for me!" He thought his chest might explode, as he ran toward the secret gate.

HT had that twinkle back in his eyes as he went bursting into the Cove.

"Hey, bro," said JR as he passed him on his way out.

"Hey," HT replied, his eyes locked with Lil's. "So it seems you have a little explaining to do, little minx," he said huskily, as he started toward her.

She put her hand up to stop him.

He frowned as he stopped walking and said slowly, drawing out the words, "You knew it was me last night, right?"

"Of course I knew it was you the second you took my hand!"

"So you're regretting what happened between us?"

She shook her head. "Don't be daft. It was the best night of my life! I love you!"

His heart soared hearing her say it, and he started walking toward her. "You love me, huh? Well, I love you most," he said with a huge smile making his eyes twinkle and his dimples appear. "You took your sweet time getting there. I didn't think I'd ever hear those words coming from you." He teased, "What? Us snogging made you realize you really do love me? Why didn't you tell me before I left out of here?"

She started backing up toward the sofa.

He stopped, confusion spread across his face. "Why are you backing away from me?"

She stopped. "Because when you touch me, I turn to mush, and we need to talk first."

He grinned and started walking again. "We can talk after a little repeat of last night."

She backed up again. "Let's see if you feel that way after we talk," she mumbled and turned going to sit on the sofa.

He followed her over and sat down beside her. He saw her neck and touched the marks. "I guess I put these disgusting marks on you!"

"What?" The one word popped from her mouth as she stared at him.

"I thought...well...maybe...I'm sorry; that was daft. It's just I've never gave those before. Do they hurt?" he asked with a grin, relieved he had been the one who had done it.

"No, they just look bad." She wasn't ready to confess that he had definitely given them before. She blurted out, "I knew!"

He repeated, "You knew?" He chuckled. "I need more than that!"

"I knew I loved you before last night."

"Okay," he said slowly, not liking the way she was looking at him. "When?"

"It's been a while."

His throat tightened knowing he wasn't going to like her answer. "How long, Lil?"

She let out a long sigh knowing her words would set him off. "Our first gettin' loose...that is, I didn't realize it...until you did that little bow thing at the Battle of the Bands."

"Is that right?" he grunted, clearly blindsided. His eyes got darker as his mind raced thinking back to the day before they left for Chester. He had to force his words out trying to fight back his temper. "You knew way back then? I can't believe this." His voice was soft, chilling. He jumped up and started pacing. "Bloody hell!" he said running his hand through his dark curls. He was suddenly furious with her. He laughed harshly. "I knew I saw in your eyes that your feelings had changed. I was so bloody sure that I almost confessed how I felt before going out on that stage! Then everything went to hell. I couldn't figure out what had caused the sudden change with you."

"I pushed my feelings back and wouldn't let myself realize I—"

He cut her off. "Of course you wouldn't let yourself realize it! That means you would have had to admit you were wrong!" He stopped pacing and stared at her. "You have this thing that no bloke is going to tell you what to do or stop you from doing it. You were too stubborn to hear me say I'd never interfere with your bloody independence! That's one of many things I love about you. I'm not too crazy about that bloody stubborn streak of yours though. I would never want you to change your life or plans for me. I just want to share them with you!"

She straightened her shoulders and raised her chin, not saying a word and refusing to meet his eyes.

"What? Now you have nothing to say?"

"Dad always paces like that when he's upset with me, and I don't like it." She gestured for him to sit. "So sit back down, and I'll talk."

"Bloody hell," he grumbled as he flopped down. "I'm sitting. Now talk!"

"I admit I tried to back away from you."

With a furious scowl on his face he asked sarcastically, "You think?" He jumped to his feet still too upset to sit and started pacing again. That nagging question in the back of his mind came rushing in. The one he asked himself after seeing her come in after Sloan's party. If she had feelings for him, how could she be with that tosser? He stopped pacing and glared fiercely into her eyes and sneered, "You and that bloody stubborn independent streak of yours. You even started up with that tosser to push me away. Am I right?"

His words stung because she knew they were true. She just looked at him not flinching.

He studied her face, and it was clear that what he said was the truth. "From the way you're looking at me, I'd say I'm right!" he grumbled. The longer he thought about it, the madder he became. "Well?"

Still no answer.

"Oh, bloody hell! This is ridiculous!" he said giving up, flopping back down at the other end of the sofa. He looked at the ceiling and inhaled a deep breath. "I have a feeling I better sit over here because I'm not going to like this!"

"You had me scared because I love you so much."

He grunted even though his heart soared again at hearing her say she loved him.

She rolled her eyes and continued, "I decided that night after the Battle of the Bands that it was best to put some distance between us. The thought of kicking you to the curb, as you put it, never came to mind. Then I met Connor the next day. I admit I tried to like—"

"Tried?" he repeated with a huff. "Looked like you were doing a real fine job of liking him to me. I thought you were going to need oxygen from you going at it so hard on that bench just after you met him!"

Frustration was mounting, making Lil snap back. "Like you and that cow Karen?"

He snarled back, "I only kissed her after watching you!"

She heard JR's words echoing in her head. "Hold your temper. You've had his head all over the place for months, especially watching you with Connor." She took a deep breath and continued, "It felt good to unburden myself of my secret, confess my feelings for you, and—"

Lil didn't get to finish. HT shot up again and started pacing. "I can't believe it. You told that tosser how you felt and not me?"

She continued talking, not stopping. "HT, I'm trying to tell you how I felt and why I did what I did. He helped me get my mind off you. The whole time I kissed him, I thought about—"

"*Hello*, I'm pacing here," he interrupted her. "Which means shut the hell up, and let me get my head around all this! And I bloody don't need to hear in detail how you felt when you were with that tosser!"

Lil huffed. "Well, if you keep jumping up after every little word, we're never going to get anywhere!"

HT's eyes narrowed as he stopped pacing and glared at her. "You think it's been easy watching you with him? Hell cannot begin to describe what I went through, lying awake night after night wondering what you were doing with that tosser! So how does it feel knowing you tore my heart out, huh?"

She stuck her nose up and her chin went forward in rebellion as she looked away, refusing to say anything else.

He growled. "For the love of God!" he grumbled and threw himself down again.

"I'm trying to tell you Connor and I are only mates. We knew right away there was no chemistry. So, since we didn't want to date anybody else, he tried to make sure he was around to help me hide my feelings from you."

"Quit deluding yourself. He has it bad for you."

"No, he doesn't. He's in love with his sister's best friend." She paused, and deeply exhaled. "I know I was wrong—"

He grunted and sneered, "You're not capable of knowing when you're wrong!"

His jibe hit home, but she just huffed again and went on. "I'm sorry I hurt you letting you think we're more than mates, but"—she cast an accusing glance—"I had no idea how you felt! I thought—"

"Oh no, you didn't think," he accused. "Or you would have realized there isn't anyone else I've wanted since the day we met!"

She rolled her eyes and said in disgust, "Give me a break! I didn't know how you felt until you just threw it at me before you stormed out of here! I never dreamed you had feelings for me the way you carried on all the time. Look at the way you are in the bakery and with your harem. Not to mention the way you were at Gino's and Sloan's party. I wanted to drown you in that pool! Then when that cow jumped on you I had all I could handle."

His green eyes became more intense as he sneered, "I didn't know how you felt the way you carried on with that tosser for months. You want to talk about Sloan's party? Look how you carried on with that wanker with those bloody short shorts you had on. I saw how his hand was all over your bum hanging out of those things!" He grunted. "You didn't see me jumping in the sack with any of them after the party! Unlike you, I couldn't look at anyone else since the day we've met let alone sleep with them!"

The last remark was a direct insult. She couldn't control her temper as her anger took over. Her tone began to rise as she said, "Whoa, wait one minute here. I've tried to ignore the implication of that comment earlier," she snarled. Her tone shot up three octaves as she continued, "I'll say this one more time, so get it in your thick head. We're only mates! Nothing ever happened between us but that one bloody kiss!"

HT jumped up and started pacing again. "Fine, you never slept with that tosser! So you're telling me there's somebody else then? I saw you that morning after Sloan's party. Why did you look...well like you just had a great night in the sack? So what have you got to say about that, eh?"

She refused to answer.

He let out a loud growl and flopped down. "I feel like a trained monkey," he muttered.

She opened her mouth, but no words came out; she was so mad. She closed it and swallowed.

"I'm sitting down over here. Talk...mumble...or whatever!" he said sarcastically.

"You're such an arse," she huffed, her patience was gone. She hopped up and started pacing. Her expression was intense, and her tone steadily grew louder as she said, "I'm really trying to keep my cool here, Harry Thomas, because I know I've put you through hell. But for the last bloody time." She started to mumble, "I've never ever done anything like what we did last night with anyone, and I've never wanted to. If I remember, you promised no more jumping to conclusions and making your bloody accusations. But you're right back at it!" She snarled looking at him, "Well?"

He just gave her a look and then slowly turned his head looking to the sofa then back at her.

"Oh, you're such a tosser!" she said with a humph and stomped over and sat back down.

He huffed and muttered, "I see you didn't mumble that!" He raised his brow staring her down and asked sarcastically, "So were you mumbling something about those marks on your neck when you got back from London or did I just miss it?"

She gave him a surprised look. She hadn't realized he saw them. She burst out laughing; she couldn't help it. For some reason she found it hilarious!

His brow rose while watching her, thinking she was mental. "What's so bloody funny?"

Between bouts of laughter she said, "The same jackass who put them on me last night did it!" She laughed even harder with tears streaming down her cheeks.

"What you playing at? I left those on you, right?"

"Of course you did you jackass!" She said as she wiped the tears off her cheeks.

"No bloody way," he muttered as the fog lifted. "It was real! Not a dream. How?" he muttered. A wide grin spread across his face as he said, "Of course, the chopper! You sneaky little minx, you came home and went back! That's why I couldn't get my head around that it was you and that it really happened!"

She nodded, still chuckling.

He moved over to gather her in his arms as she explained, "I hadn't planned on going back when I came home. I was in the darkroom and found you all slumped over when I came out. I lay you down, and you kissed me, so I kissed you back and—"

"We did something like this," he said bringing his mouth down on hers.

He kissed her with a hunger that sent them both whirling.

After a few more long kisses, Lil stopped him. "I have to tell you one more thing I've been holding back."

"Oh no," he said with a sexy growl. "Am I going to start pacing again?" he teased, nuzzling her neck.

"Hope not." She sighed, as she tilted her head to one side giving him access. "No more of those marks; you're killing me trying to cover them." He chuckled as she continued, "I started doing professional photo sessions. I didn't go to London to be with Connor; I went on my first session. I did meet him for lunch and went to the game, though. And he knew, helping me out."

He kissed his way up her throat to her ear and teased it with his tongue. He softly whispered, with a sexy growl low in his throat, "Just because I'm enjoying this, doesn't mean I wouldn't like to wring your pretty little neck for not sharing that with me instead of him." His tongue found her ear again.

"Sorry," she moaned softly as she pressed herself into him. "Since I was trying to keep my distance, I didn't want you going; I did, but I didn't. That's why I came home, to develop them." She skipped words. "Went back...wouldn't know me... poor JR so tired—"

He cut her off with another long kiss.

She continued as he brushed her cheek with a kiss. "Sloan's party... Edinburgh...session...wind blowing...slept way home. Why I looked—"

"Hush. Talk later." Another sexy growl rolled through his chest as his mouth came down on hers.

Later, after a more intense session than the night before, they cuddled in each other's arms, not wanting to let go. They talked, and laughed, while sharing teasing touches and kisses, apologizing and professing their love to each other over and over again.

HT propped his head up on his bent elbow, with the length of his body stretched alongside Lil's. He ran a finger lightly between her bare breasts down to her belly button then back up. "Sooo, do I need to run up to the house and get something to dress Clyde in for an occasion in the Lion's Room?"

"Clyde doesn't need a rain coat." She chuckled with a feather-light brush of her lips. "I've been on the pill for a few years."

"Hmm, sooo, are we taking this to the Lion's Room then?" he asked seductively, as he kissed her neck.

"Sounds amazing," she purred, "but—"

"Oh no." He softly groaned looking at her. "There's a but?" he gave a low, slow laugh. "Crazy lady just came to town, and you downed a bag of your favorite candy from Jones's shop yesterday, so I know that's not it."

She chuckled and said, "Yes, my curse, as Mum and I call it, is over. I began taking birth control pills for medical reasons...migraines, bad cramps. Mum said it unfortunately ran in the family. She knew the signs. Since the pill had helped her, I went on it, and it worked. Now, I just get a little emotional, and sometimes I'm a... well a bitch! That's where the candy thing comes in. It helps. Did you figure it out, or did JR give you a heads-up?"

"No, I figured it out on my own," he muttered as he kissed his way down her throat. "The first time you went off on me got me thinking. Then you followed it up by jumping down my throat the next day when I met you for lunch on our hill. I remember because it was the day after I met the twins. That night I almost pulled back a nub when I tried to get a piece of your candy. I think you even growled at me!" He softly chuckled and propped himself up again to look at her.

"I never growled at you!" she said grinning.

He nodded with a raised brow.

She chuckled. "I felt awful being such a wanker to you. I was fighting myself then about my feelings. I hated when you went to Chester for date night, and I wouldn't admit it to myself. You had me in a mood, first from flirting all morning and then being so late that night with your text. My mind was all over the place with what you were doing and with whom. That's when my curse started getting harder to deal with by the way. It's all your fault."

"Uh-huh. Why am I not surprised?" he teased, lazily kissing her nose.

She made a cute face. "All that flirting of yours started doing my head in big time after that. When I realized I loved you after your little bow thing in Chester I totally went mental when you flirted, and oh! when you winked at other girls. You had me wanting to pull your curls out of your head! That wink of yours has turned my insides to mush since the day we've met and I hate when you wink at other girls!"

He chuckled and said, "No more winking at other girls then! And like that day in Chester, I'll end every performance with that bow just for you. Like then, in my own special way, I'm saying I love you, and you are my life. Don't ever doubt that I love you, little minx."

"Same goes here; I love you most."

They shared another long, hard kiss.

"Why are we waiting?" he asked with a low groan, kissing her neck.

"Again, your fault," she replied with a little giggle.

He propped himself up again to look at her. "How so?"

"When we were discussing our, well, your love life, you said you wanted your first time to be special and actually so do I. Since my eighteenth birthday is next week—"

"Bloody hell," he cut in teasing. "Mum always said I would regret my big mouth one day. Time out here for a second; let's back up and talk about my flirting. You do know it's all part of an act, right? It's only genuine when it's *you* that I'm flirting with. I realized when I started this music thing it went hand in hand for getting attention. You know the blokes decided it was my job to be the flirt, and they expect me to play that rubbish up big time."

Her phone interrupted them with a text, both knowing that it was from Connor by the sound.

"Yeah, I know," Lil said ignoring her phone. She gave him a quick kiss and teased, "Lucky me, falling in love with the one who's going to be known as the biggest flirt and player in the world!"

"No, lucky me for having you," he said leaning down with another hard kiss, leaving her breathless.

Her phone dinged again after it had gone off two more times while they kissed.

HT grunted and muttered, "The tosser has a lot to say."

"It's probably the same message that's coming through. His phone must not work that well in the States. He said he was going to call." She reached over to pick up her phone and handed it to him. "How about you read while I fix us a plate. I'm starving."

He let her up and followed her. Leaning against the counter he said, "Not same text. Looks like the tosser wrote a book here!"

"Just read them," she said as she put the kettle on the burner and turned it on.

"Still bossy, I see." He chuckled and leaned over giving her a quick kiss. "Now let's see what this wanker says." He read out loud. "I know I said I would call, but I was worried you would hang up on me when I confessed something, LOL." He looked at Lil. "I bet this tosser is going to tell you he's in love with you."

Lil rolled her eyes. "Don't be daft. Keep reading."

HT continued to read, "First know, I love you." He then looked at Lil with a sarcastic look.

Lil chuckled and said, "Keep reading; he means as a mate."

"Sure he does," HT said with a huff and continued. "Sloan also loves you as you know, and just let me say I tricked her into admitting HT was in love with you."

HT kept on reading Connor's confession out loud of how they set them up. He looked at Lil when he was done, and they burst out laughing.

"Looks like I owe the toss...Connor one for helping us out," HT admitted.

"And Sloan." Lil nodded. "She was good! I never had a clue she was setting us up. I know we apologized a million times to each other, but I'm really sorry for making you think—"

He cut her off with a long, hard kiss.

"Humm." She giggled. "I love being shut up that way."

He chuckled and said, "No more feeling bad over the last couple of months and no more apologizing." They went to the sofa with the now hot food and tea. He added as they sat down, "Let's say all that rubbish over the last couple of months goes on a list. Things we never talk about again. Couples can have the same arguments again and again; sometimes it can break them up. So how about we always do that? When we talk about things, even fight over something and get it all worked out, we don't bring it up again. It goes on the list. When it's done, it's done."

"I like that," she said as she handed him a meat pasty.

After eating, and the most intense session yet, they fell asleep wrapped in each other's arms. The session was so intense that Lil tried to persuade HT they didn't have to wait until her birthday and should continue in the Lion's Room. He chuckled and reminded her it was her fault; she wanted to wait. And she was always right!

# CHAPTER 26

The next day, the Sunday family barbeque turned out to be a small victory party for Sloan because Lil and HT never made it to Lee's the night before. She had won the Halloween contest, of course. Sloan and the guys were shocked to see Lil and HT wrapped in each other's arms as they greeted them. They had pretty much been that way since the day before, not letting each other out of their sight. Sloan admitted that she had helped Connor out of love for them, and everyone got a laugh, with Connor on speakerphone, at how well they had pulled it off.

The next morning at school, Lil couldn't wait for HT's harem to see them together. She was all smiles as they walked to meet the gang, holding hands. She figured his harem would back off and leave HT alone. Boy, was she wrong. They looked like a pack of wild dogs about to charge at her when they saw them and still flocked around him when she was with him between classes. Sloan was the one who was upset. Lil just chuckled and said his harem didn't bother her, now that she knew he loved her. As the morning wore on some of the girls had resorted to childish things, like pulling Lil's hair, knocking books out of her hands, throwing things, and tripping her. She didn't tell anyone, figuring they would quit. At lunch, someone put a big wad of gum in her hair, and Sloan had to help get it out. Lil finally came clean with HT and the gang about being harassed. They were furious with her at first for not telling them. For the rest of the day, they made sure someone was always with her until she was safely in the car to go home. She made JR and Jayden promise not to tell Charles because she could handle them, and it would stop once they got used to seeing them together.

Little did Lil know HT's harem harassing her worked out perfect. JR saw the best opportunity to put their plan in place. He knew Lil always went to the loo about an hour after lunch during study hour. The next day while Jayden stood guard, JR dumped a bucket of ice-cold water over the stall on her.

She stormed out ready to tear someone's head off and found them laughing. "Why in the *bloody hell* did you do that?" She could hardly breathe, trembling and shaking so violently, not sure if it was from the shock of the ice water or being furious.

"Part of the plan." Jayden chuckled. "I'll run after HT; you get her to the car," he said running out.

"This is your bloody plan, making me get pneumonia?" she complained as she followed JR out. "You could have used warm water!"

"We had to make it look real. Come on, we don't have much time. Let's get to the car." They took off running. JR opened the boot and grabbed a blanket and a pair of his sweats and a T-shirt.

"I could have used this stuff up at Edinburgh," Lil grumbled between chattering teeth. "Buggar! It's cold out here. What's the plan anyway? I'm still not getting it!"

"You're going to have to stay tough for it to work. We're going to make HT feel guilty. Can you handle it?"

"I have to if I want to keep working with you guys."

"Well, just remember it's not your fault. It's Luke's that you can't come clean with him—nothing for you to feel guilty about, the way I see it."

She nodded and said, "I know in my heart I would tell him everything if I could, so I'm not breaking our rule. And he wouldn't want for me not to be able to do what I love because of him."

"I agree," said JR. "If we pull this off, Charlie is going to tell him you guys have to act as mates while in public solving command's rule never being seen with the person you're in a relationship with. Now it's show time; here he comes. Try to act upset; you're too calm."

"Oh, help me. I'm a poor defenseless female," she said.

"Smart arse. Get in the car and act cold at least."

"Now, that I can do. I'm freezing," she said and hopped in the back seat and huddled for warmth under the blanket, shivering.

HT jumped in and wrapped his arms around her and asked, "You all right?"

"I'm fine. Just cold," she said between chattering teeth.

"We need to get those wet clothes off you."

"K," she said her teeth still chattering.

He helped her get the cold wet clothes off and put the dry ones on, under the blanket.

"Let's snuggle so that you can get me warm," she said with a grin.

He wrapped his arms around her again and held her tight. "I'm sorry," he said sadly. "I never realized those bitches could be so evil. I should've known they would stoop this low. They're mental! I'm sure Mr. C is going to think it's my fault for not paying more attention."

"I'm afraid you're right there," said JR. "It wouldn't surprise me if he pulls Lil out of that school."

"So that's why we aren't telling him," Lil grumbled trying to sound believable.

"That cold water has made you loopy," said JR.

They laughed.

"Or, we can tell him after we see if the plan I just came up with works," said Jayden.

"What's your plan, bro?" asked HT after kissing Lil on top of the head.

"You need to talk to Connor. If he agrees, he'll become Lil's boyfriend again. This time, leave no doubt; make it official—hand holding, face sucking, hugging, and staring into each other's eyes. Whatever it takes to get those girls to believe that you and Lil were only acting like you were together to make Connor jealous. And that it had worked and Connor had come crawling back or whatever, as long as they think you and Lil are only good mates. Since Connor hasn't been here for the last couple of days, that makes it even better. You can laugh it off, saying you were just helping Lil and busting Connor's nads at the same time. Make those girls think it was all a joke on your part to get Connor going and that Lee and the twins were in on it!"

"Sounds like it will work," said JR. "They all know you guys are always messing with each other!"

"You guys in?" Jayden asked.

"I'm in," said Lil.

"Me too. I'll do anything to keep Lil safe," said HT as he gave her a wink.

Lil smiled and said, "I received a text from Connor earlier saying he landed. I'll call him to let him know what's going on. I'm sure he will be in."

"And I'll call Lee and have him pass it on to Sloan and the twins," said HT.

"Okay. I'll wait until tomorrow to see how it goes before I tell Charlie," said JR.

"Thanks, bro," said HT.

JR just nodded.

When Connor and the gang heard what happened, they all met at Gino's for dinner to work on a plan and come up with a believable story they would spread the next day. Before the night started Connor got HT off to the side and apologized for being such a tosser at Sloan's party, winding him up after figuring out how he felt. They had a big laugh, and HT told him to remember that paybacks are hell! When the night was over, HT decided he really did like Connor.

The next morning, Connor waited with a dozen roses and a big bunch of "I'm sorry" and "I love you" balloons.

HT and Connor laughed and did the guy handshake thing the best they could, while Connor held onto the balloons and flowers.

HT said loudly so that everyone would hear, "I'll leave you two lovebirds to it. I've been neglecting my ladies the last few days, helping Lil out."

Lil chuckled hearing him and seeing his harem smiling from ear to ear. She threw herself into Connor's arms, making him let go of all the balloons and flowers as they kissed, acting as if they were never letting go again. They put on one heck of a show, just like planned. HT's harem laughed, loving the great love scene going on, and chased after the balloons and picked up the flowers. Lil smiled and thanked them all as they put them in the car. Then, wrapped in each other's arms, Lil and Connor walked in to the school acting like the two lovebirds everyone thought they were.

During the day, the gang spread the story that Lil was furious at Connor for being late at the ball, which made her have to wear a harem costume. They got in a huge fight when he finally got there. She told him she was fed up with him always putting his football before her. Then she had HT act like they were dating to show him just how easy he was replaced with a bloke who was even more popular than him! Of course they weren't really together; it was just to make Connor jealous and it had worked. Kids said they witnessed Lil running out in a harem costume before the results of the contest, verifying it was true because she would never leave Sloan like that. They were the buzz of the school by lunch hour. HT's harem said they knew all along that HT didn't have feelings for her in that way. They were only best mates like they had always professed.

# CHAPTER 27

Thursday night after dinner, Lil, HT, JR, and Jayden did the cleanup while Mary and Tessa took Raif to the bakery. There was still a lot of work left to do for Lil's party.

JR asked, "Well, Jay, you ready to go face the music? Looks like your plan worked but I still have to come clean with Charlie about the water incident at school."

"Yeah, let's get it over with," replied Jayden. He looked over at HT. "Stick around, bro. I'm sure when he gets done chewing us a new one you're next."

"Lovely," muttered HT.

JR and Jayden laughed as they made their way to Charles's study for the second part of the plan. Charles was going to lay down the law to HT that he and Lil were to remain to be seen as mates only as long as he pursued his music.

"Poor baby, you're about to get your first talk to and stare down from Dad," Lil teased.

"Man," HT playfully whined, "I thought I was in the clear since Jayden's plan worked."

"It won't be bad," Lil said. "Besides, what's the worst that can happen?"

"Oh, I don't know…feed me to the fishes, turn the dogs on me, drop me out of one of those helicopters," joked HT.

"Well, yeah. I guess Sir Tigger could be a problem. He would lick you to death. He loves you as much as I do." She giggled. "Thinking about it, you'd better not go for a helicopter ride anytime soon."

"Real funny, and I love you most." He pulled her to him. "It's a good thing I love you so much, my lady. You come with a lot of baggage!"

They laughed then kissed.

"Okay, you two," JR said as he poked his head in. "You have to give your lips a rest for a few minutes. HT you have been summoned."

"At least I'll die well snogged," HT teased with a wink at Lil.

"I wouldn't get worried unless you hear a helicopter." Lil snickered.

"Little minx." HT grinned, giving her a quick kiss.

Lil played her part and walked with him to Charles' study for moral support. HT tapped lightly on the door.

Charles was sitting behind his desk. "Come in, HT," he called out.

HT looked at Lil and blew air out his cheeks.

She chuckled. "It won't be that bad. I'll wait out here."

He took a deep breath and opened the door. "What's up, Mr. C?" he asked. He walked in and closed the door behind him. He sat solemnly in the chair across from him.

"I hear there was a little trouble at school," Charles said. "Is this something I need to worry about? JR seems to think it's under control," his voice rose a bit, as he played his part. "What's your take on it? After all, it's your harem, as Lil calls them, which seems to be behind it."

"I agree with JR. It's all over now they think we're only mates, Mr. C. I still can't get my head around what those bitches did to her."

"Maybe something good came out of it. A wake-up call, letting us know when you become rich and famous, it will only get worse," Charles said with a chuckle.

HT said with a grin, "Now you sound like Lil."

"Well, just in case she's right, it wouldn't hurt to make sure Lil is not romantically connected to you. We don't need your crazy fans after her. So, I was thinking, keep up the pretense that you're mates only from now on when you're out in public. Especially at the bakery with all the gossips. What do you think?"

HT thought about it for a second and nodded. "I totally agree, Mr. C. Her safety should always come first. If we keep it up now it will make it easier as time goes on."

Charles nodded as he stood speaking with a stern voice. "One more thing. I don't want to see any more of that rubbish on her!"

HT blushed as he said, "I totally agree to that too. I didn't realize I—"

Charles put up his hand stopping him. "Let's just leave it at that." He chuckled.

HT laughed as he stood.

"So," Charles said as they went to the door. "Don't you think it's time to start calling me Charlie?" He opened the door.

"For sure, Charlie," HT replied with a huge smile, feeling genuinely flattered as they went out.

Lil was still standing just outside of the door. "Charlie? Wow, I see the meeting went well. No one-way helicopter ride, huh?" she teased.

HT gave her a wink and a quick kiss.

Charles joked pointing at her neck. "Well, I see any more of that rubbish on your neck, he might be getting that helicopter ride after all."

They laughed as they made their way to the bakery.

Friday afternoon, the gang cut out of school after lunch. HT, Lee, and Connor took the twins to the airport while Lil and Sloan shopped in Chester for something special to wear for her birthday party the next day.

Lil sat outside the coffee shop drinking her tea and heard the chimes from the cathedral behind her letting her know it was five. She realized she hadn't heard from HT in a while and looked for her phone to see if she'd just missed his call. She couldn't find it. She remembered she put it in her camera case. "Bloody hell," she mumbled, realizing she didn't have her case. "Man, I left it at Jacob's," she mumbled.

Lil looked through the window seeing JR and Sloan laughing and talking away while standing in line for their food. She smiled, loving that JR seemed to be letting his guard down some with her. She didn't want to intrude.

She asked two older ladies sitting beside her if they could keep an eye on her bags so that she could retrieve a bag at a nearby shop. She told them her friend was in line waiting on food.

"Of course, love, take your time," they said.

"Thanks," Lil said as she jumped up and took off running. She decided to go the backway, it being faster, and it would take her to the back of Jacob's shop. She knew the front would be locked since he closed at five, and he had mentioned he wanted to work on the small patio behind his shop. He told her his wife wasn't taking "I'll get to it" and made him start on replacing the broken stone blocks.

She ran past the cathedral, cutting through its small yard, and then down the thirty or so stone steps in the wall. It only took a few minutes to reach the back of the shop. She didn't see Jacob. She grabbed the handle on the door, but it was locked. A familiar feeling rushed through her. The same feeling she had gotten at Edinburgh but more intense. Protocol on what to do came front and center...You never go anywhere without backup. The guys had pounded that in her head after Edinburgh. She knew there was no way of telling what might be waiting on the other side of the door. She started to back up, but her pulse rate sped up rapidly, a sense of unease made the hairs rise on the back of her neck. She knew better than to ignore the sensation her body was feeling. *Don't wait!* A voice echoed in her head. She made a quick decision. She quickly lifted the flowerpot on a shelf, knowing a key was kept there, and summoned her courage. Quietly she unlocked the door letting herself in and eased the door shut. She was relieved to see the room was empty, and there was no sound or movement. Then, she heard muffled voices coming from up front. She couldn't shake off the chill that something wasn't right. As quietly as possible, she crossed to stand beside a filing cabinet in the hallway leading up front. A woman laughed, a high-pitched sound. She flattened against the wall. She stood there for a second as her instincts took over. Cautiously she inched herself up the hall without making a sound, trying to focus on what she was hearing. The woman's voice was strange, as it became louder.

"My father was so grief stricken over that bitch's death he never gave me the time of day. I hope he's burning in hell with that old man who turned my life to hell. Then after finding my mother's diaries, I learn I'm not his daughter, and he has a son!"

A man's voice whispered hoarsely.

The woman's voice shrieked, "Don't tell me to quiet down. I don't care if those idiots in the back hear me. They're probably both still unconscious, plus they're tied up and gagged."

Lil thought, *Both! Who else?* She quickly crouched down into her combat stance and moved to the other side of the hall to see if she could see the woman's face.

The woman went into a bout of hysterical laughter. "They're not saying a word or going anywhere. You should have cut their throats like I told you to do in the first place."

Lil heard what she thought was a slap, she knew the woman was deranged.

"Next time grow a pair and follow orders."

Lil froze, her blood icing over as she heard the man's raspy laugh. Her heartbeat started to pound in her ears. She would know that laugh anywhere; it was the bloke who threw Lord Rothford off the roof. She took a few deep breaths trying to calm down. HT's ringtone went off on her phone. The woman was still rattling on after it stopped.

"What the hell!" the woman's shrill voice yelled. "How many times is that HT going to call? This is the fifth time. Don't they realize she doesn't want to talk or that she doesn't have her phone? That stupid bitch was so busy running her mouth and fawning all over that camera, she never noticed I took her case. Getting her phone was a bonus. I knew if we followed them long enough today they would give us the chance we need. When she realizes she left it here, they will come back for her to get it, and you'll be ready." There was a pause before Lil heard another loud slap. She knew the bloke had to have a palm print on his face. "This is all your fault," she said cruelly. "You screwed up letting her see you throw him off the roof. Now we have to take her out, too!"

Lil realized with a shudder that they were after her.

"If I hadn't stayed to watch, I would never have seen her. What pleasure it was, though, to watch that old coot's bulging eyes when you threw him over." The satisfaction in her tone was evil as she continued, "It was a perfect plan to get information from those reports, if I say so, myself. Taking out all those agents was clever on my part, but the joke was on me. Taking them out and sleeping with that old coot was for nothing! His son wasn't even an agent and wasn't the cook's son!"

A phone rang.

After a few seconds the woman sneered, "That was the idiot watching her. He said she must be on her way. He thought she went inside, but he looked and didn't see her. He and the other three blokes are staying on him. He said you didn't need any help with her." She let out another chilling laugh. "He's right. One quick slice across that nosey bitch's throat will do it!"

Lil almost panicked. She closed her eyes and focused as hard as she could. She needed to warn JR. She would find Jacob and use his phone.

The woman hissed, "Get ready to gut him after you take care of her." She added with an evil laugh, "Leave her lying so that he can see her when he comes in. Those four blokes I hired will jump him from behind. I'll meet you at the hotel. I'll text him now from her phone saying she's at the camera shop, just in case he didn't see her leave."

Lil's phone sang again.

"Give me a break!" the woman spat and threw Lil's phone. "Screw the text. The way he tails her, I'm sure he'll be in right after her."

Lil could barely hear HT's ringtone.

The woman turned when she reached the door, giving Lil a straight view. "No screw ups this time," she ordered. "When you're done with them take care of the two in the back. I don't want anyone here left alive. Once you're done, burn this bloody place down. Gloves are off time is running out," she said coldly as she went out.

Lil eased her way from the doorway and then quietly stood up and quickly made her way back down the hall. She scanned the room looking for Jacob. She spotted him on the floor unconscious, and her mouth dropped open at also seeing Luke bound and gagged, staring at her. "Oh my God. Uncle Carl!" she said under her breath and hurried over to him, panic rising inside her. "Oh no! When did you get back? Were you in here to buy me a birthday present?" she asked as she started working on the knots.

Luke made a sound of frustration holding up his chin.

"Sorry, Uncle Carl," she said as she quickly removed the gag from his mouth. She started to mumble, "They're going to get JR. Oh my God, JR. You have your phon—"

"Hush that mumbling right now Lily Rose! You're an agent; act like one!"

Lil's mouth gaped open. "Luke?" she asked shocked. Her brain was having trouble with the idea.

"Yes." His voice was quiet and stern as he answered. "Now see if Jacob has a belt on. As soon as I move this leg, it's going to start gushing."

Lil quickly pushed all shock and questions from her mind until later. She went on autopilot, zoned in, and focused, as she removed Jacob's belt while Luke finished untying himself.

"Tell me what your heard," he said as he pulled off his belt and wrapped it on the top of his leg.

"It's a woman and a man. The woman is the one calling the shots. I met her at the ball. I took her photo a few times talking with Lord Rothford. The man is the one who threw him off the roof. They're after me; they know I saw him," said Lil helping him wrap Jacob's belt on his leg.

"What else?" he asked with a grunt, pulling the belt tighter. He checked his pocket. "They got my phone."

"That psycho bitch took my camera case and phone when I was in earlier. Sounds like they have been tailing us because she knows JR is always close behind me. They've just been waiting for the chance to take me out. He's supposed to slit my throat when I come in and then gut JR. There are four goons on him now."

"Help me up! We're going to help JR and take that bastard out. He's a big one, and he's good with that knife. He caught me off guard, and my kick wasn't high enough. I connected with his chest. It was like hitting a bloody tree. He grabbed my leg and sliced it pretty deep. Then it must have been the bitch that hit me from behind with something. I'm going to need some help. Grab that sledgehammer there by the door."

She quickly got it, and they moved up the hall, quiet as cats. Luke staggered a little but kept moving as he whispered, "You're going to have to bring that bastard down low enough where I can reach him. Use combat one. Your first kick will be the most important; throw your weight into it. The only chance we have is if you can take his kneecap out."

Lil nodded. She saw that Luke was leaving a trail of blood and limping badly but didn't say a word. She was to take orders and keep her mouth shut.

"You have to be quick," Luke continued whispering. "Take him by surprise. I'm not going to be able to move after we take him down, so once JR comes through that door, you yell 'right on three.' Then we're going to help him with the other bloke on your far right, so get him as close to me as possible."

They moved quickly. Once up front they saw the guy peering through the slits of the shade on the door.

They moved in. After Luke was in position, Lil handed him the hammer and quietly positioned herself just behind the huge tree-trunk size of a man. She was waiting for Luke to nod when he was ready.

When Luke nodded, she didn't have to think; her body just reacted; all of her hard training didn't fail her. She jumped up and with a side kick, she threw her body weight into her foot and connected with his kneecap. She heard it crunch. Once her right foot hit the ground, she quickly jumped up and swung her body around in full force with another perfectly executed kick. He thrust at her with the knife as she hit her mark. Her foot connected with his nose shoving the bone up into his skull. She not only heard the crunch but she also felt it vibrate up her leg. Lil was surprised he was handsome but saw the evil in his eyes and knew he wouldn't have had a problem slitting her throat like the psycho ordered.

As he fell forward, Luke swung the sledgehammer, connecting with his head. It splattered like a watermelon. He staggered upright again, as the guy hit the ground. It seemed it was all over within seconds. It went like a well-rehearsed play.

JR came blasting in.

"Three on your right," yelled Lil as she looked at the bloke farthest on her right. He reminded her of a rat, with a sharp nose, and forehead that sloped backward showing his tiny beaded eyes. Breathing hard with adrenaline pumping through her veins, she slowly edged toward Luke as if scared. The man made a grizzly snarling noise as he moved forward. She made sure Luke could reach him before she acted as if she was turning to run. When he got close, enough she jumped up and swung around striking him full force with a side kick connecting with his throat. He gasped. She knew she had crushed his larynx, taking him down. Luke didn't need to splatter his brains, but he did.

She looked to see if JR needed help. Two blokes were not moving on the ground, and he was just about to put the final kick on the third one when Joe walked up behind the bloke and twisted his neck in one swift move.

"That was quicker," he said, pulling the bloke the rest of the way into the shop and closed the door.

Lil saw Luke staggering, about to go down. "JR hurry, Uncle Carl."

JR quickly moved catching him in his arms. "Where's Jacob?"

"Unconscious, tied up in the back. There's a woman," said Lil. "She has blonde hair and was heading to a hotel!"

Joe without being told ran to the back.

"He's losing a lot of blood, JR. That tosser cut his leg," Lil said running, following JR down the hall.

"Lil, grab the door," ordered JR. Jacob was just coming to. "Joe get Jacob to our medical here. The cleanup crew will be here anytime."

"We're here," Ben said standing in the hall.

"There's a woman who got away," yelled JR. "Check the hotels. Look for a blonde; I saw one going around the corner at the end of the street to the right. Start on those hotels first."

"I'll get Jake's team on it. Charlie will be at Zone One by the time you get him there. I'll be right behind you as soon as I take care of things here," he called out to JR's back.

JR was already out the door with a limp Luke in his arms with Lil running right behind. "What the hell is Uncle Carl doing here anyway?" asked JR.

Lil didn't answer as she followed him to the waiting ambulance. Instead, she asked, "So Jacob is an agent?"

"Yes," replied JR as they hopped in the back. JR looked to see it was Sarge waiting on them and let out a huge sigh of relief. Ed was in charge of the medical team, and Sarge was his best man. He had been taking care of agents in the field ever since he could remember. "He's lost a lot of blood, Sarge. Should I lay him down?"

"No. Won't take us long to reach the chopper; better not to move him much. Keep holding him and keep that leg elevated." He then talked into the headphone speaker, "With all this blood it looks like the artery has been cut on his upper leg." He quickly stuck a needle that was hooked up to a bag of blood in Luke's arm. "Hold this up," he ordered Lil, handing her the bag. "I'm cutting them now," he said as he cut the leg of Luke's trousers around JR's hand. "Yeah, it's cut. His leg is a mess. I'll work on it in the chopper; he won't make it into ER if I don't. I hear you overhead now." He looked at JR as he put towels on Luke's leg. "Charlie says pilot the bird."

JR nodded.

They pulled into the field behind HT's old house. They reached the chopper as Charles landed.

Charles got in the back and opened the door.

JR, Lil, and Sarge hopped out of the ambulance and ran to the chopper. Luke was still in JR's arms with Sarge holding up his leg, carrying what looked to be a cooler and Lil was holding up the bag of blood.

Charles helped JR lay Luke onto the floor of the chopper. Charles took over, keeping pressure on his leg. JR hopped in the pilot seat while Sarge and Lil hopped in. Lil cradled Luke's head in her lap, still holding the now almost empty bag of blood.

"Where the hell is Dad, Charlie?" yelled JR.

"In the other chopper with Ed. He's not real happy with me for taking off and leaving him."

"I bet!" muttered JR.

Sarge slid the cooler near Lil. "Change the bag, Lil. Charlie keep pressure on his leg. I'll have to clamp that artery," he said as JR put the chopper in the air. "I'm going to need a smooth ride back here."

"You got it," JR called back.

"Dad." Lil winced looking down and seeing her lap full of blood. He was worse than she expected. "His head is also bleeding. He said that psycho bitch hit him with something." She quickly reached for a towel while Charles held the bag of blood. She lifted Luke's head, placing it on the towel.

"We have to keep him awake," said Sarge.

"Luke! Luke! You with us?" yelled Charles.

"What the hell! Luke?" yelled JR shocked.

Lil didn't realize she was crying.

Luke opened his eyes and managed a thin smile. "Hey bro. What are you crying about, baby girl? And boy what are you yelling about up there?" he slurred in Carl's accent. "Your old uncle Carl is okay. You should have seen our baby girl, Charlie, like a flying ninja."

"Save your strength," Charles ordered, "and stay with us!"

"Get this disguise off me, baby girl," Luke muttered. "Don't want anybody connecting me to Cam."

JR's voice cracked, "Cam! Don't you dare die you son of a bitch, because me and Jay will want the pleasure of doing it. I can't believe you never told us!"

"Love you, boy!" said Luke breathlessly.

"Love you most. But don't think you're off the hook." JR sniffed.

Luke chuckled.

Lil pulled off his fake nose, slightly gray mustache, beard, and fuzzy eyebrows. He opened his mouth so that she could pull his white crooked teeth out. "Love you, baby girl," he slurred.

"Love you most, now hush like Dad said and save your strength."

"Hey, Ms. Bossy, as HT calls you, I'm your command here."

"No, you're my uncle Carl right now so hush!" she said between tears and bent down kissing his forehead.

He chuckled as his head slumped to the side.

"Dad," she yelled. The look on Charles's face frightened her.

Charles's voice cracked as he yelled, "Wake up! Fight you son of bitch. Don't you dare die on me! How much longer, JR? This damn blood is coming out faster than it's going in."

Lil heard a definite note of panic in his voice.

"We're landing now. The team is in place. Ed and Dad are here."

"Thank God," said Charles.

Luke slowly opened his eyes as the chopper door flew open. Sarge ordered the team waiting with a gurney, "Move him out and get him to ER."

"Hi, old man, bro," Luke slurred as they helped lift him on the gurney.

"I hear you let some tosser carve you like a turkey!" Bill said with a nervous grin as a tear slipped down his cheek.

"Yeah, but I splattered his brains. Cracked that head like a melon. Right, baby girl?"

"Yeah, you got him." said Lil handing the bag of blood to Ed.

Luke groaned and passed out.

"Let's get him inside," yelled Sarge.

JR grabbed Lil's arm holding her back while the rest of them ran into the private medical center located just outside of Manchester.

"Let's give them some room," said JR. "We should wait out here. Sarge is the best. Uncle...ah, Luke is in brilliant hands. Buggar! This is hard to get my head around. I honestly didn't have a clue!"

"Me either," said Lil shaking her head. "Oh my God, JR. It just hit me!" she started to mumble. "HT! Uncle Carl is Luke, his dad. How can I not show how much I love and idolize Uncl...Luke around him? Bloody hell, this is messed up! Who's telling HT he's hurt? I can't be talking to him like this. He's called me like five times. That psycho bitch said so; she took my phone."

"Whoa, slow your row, Snaggs. I talked to him earlier. He's why I noticed you weren't sitting outside. At first I thought you were in the loo. He called me to ask why the hell you weren't answering your phone and that he thought he heard some lady talking when he called. I thought fast and told him you lost it, and it was probably the lady who found it. So he told me to tell you the twins' flight was delayed for a few hours, and they were going to stick around and hang out with them, and he loves you."

"Good. It gives me a while before I have to talk to him. So those ladies told you where I went?"

"Yeah, Sloan said to tell you she'd just take your bags home with her, that she wasn't waiting knowing you'd be with Jacob half the night."

Li nodded. "I think my phone is under the counter at Jacobs."

"It was," Ben said walking up. "I heard it blowing up with that god-awful ring of HT's. I put it in your case. You all right, baby girl?" he asked, handing the camera case to her.

"I'm good. Thanks for grabbing my case," she replied and kissed his cheek.

Ben nodded and looked at JR. "How's he doing?"

JR shrugged. "I think Sarge stopped the bleeding in time. Did you know?"

Ben just chuckled.

"Tosser. Of course you knew. I take it besides me, Snaggs, and Jay the family all know?"

"Not Anthony and Raif," Ben said with a chuckle. "Of course Sarge knows. He's patched him up a few times in his disguises."

JR laughed shaking his head. "I've idolized Uncle Carl, bollocks, Luke all my life! I'm trying to get my head around just how many disguises he's had over the years as Cam. You have to give it to him; he's brilliant!"

"That's why we call him Cam." Ben chuckled.

"JR, we taking the chopper home?" asked Lil.

"Should be. Why?"

"When I grab my bag to clean up, I'm leaving my camera case in there along with my phone. That way I'm in the clear when HT calls."

"That's dodgy." Ben chuckled.

"He'll just call me," added JR.

"I know," Lil said turning toward the chopper.

"Hold on, here comes Charlie," said JR grinning.

"He's going to be fine," Charles said walking up. He looked at Lil. "Now, young lady, I don—"

"I know, Dad," Lil interrupted him and mumbled, "I almost turned to go after JR when I knew something wasn't right before I went in, but I couldn't. I got such an intense feeling that I needed to go in."

"It's a good thing you did, baby girl; otherwise, Luke would have sat there and bled out before that tosser got the chance to finish him off," said Charles. "Sarge said those belts he wrapped around his leg is what saved him."

"Yeah, but it's still my fault. I'm the one who ended up outside at Edinburgh—"

"Stop," said Charles. "It's not your fault and don't start doubting yourself. Always trust those feelings we get, baby girl; we have them for a reason. What I was about to say before you interrupted is that I don't think I need to tell you how proud we all are of you. You saved Luke's life no matter how you look at it." He hugged her.

"Thanks, Dad. Just part of the team," she said grinning.

"That you are. Our little flying ninja, as Luke was babbling before they put him under," Bill said as he walked up giving her a hug. "You did brilliant, baby girl. Luke's head scan looks good. Sarge is finishing up on him now. We can see him shortly."

Charles's phone started ringing. He quickly answered it. "You get the bitch? What? Well get over to her place and tear it apart," he said as he put his phone back in his pocket. "She got away from them at the hotel. She ran out of the hotel not watching and ran right in front of a bloody delivery truck, killed the bitch instantly."

"Bloody hell!" growled Bill.

JR looked at Charles. "So why was Unc...Luke at Jacobs?"

Charles replied, "He found something while going back over reports on Lord Rothford's family. He noticed that the daughter's charge cards had been used on the same days and times he was visiting at her house. He always went there after the meetings. The guys figured he was just with his daughter since it was her house, but he wasn't. Luke contacted the daughter, and she admitted her father was seeing Lady Darby Rosewood, a.k.a. the psycho bitch, and she let them use her place. He told her he was embarrassed because she was so much younger than him and didn't want for them to be seen together. Anyway, I told Luke I would meet him back at the house, and we would get working on it. He then informed me he was in Chester as Carl tailing her. I was just leaving the castle when he called. I got a gut feeling he was in trouble, so I hopped in the chopper and headed to Chester. The old man was with Ed helping at the bakery. I knew not to wait for them or for another team to move in to find Luke, so I pulled the team on the blokes following you and Lil. I knew you and Joe could handle them. Joe could have handled them himself!"

"True," said JR.

Lil looked at JR and said disgustedly, "So you knew they were behind you when you came into Jacob's!"

"I did, but I didn't have a clue what was waiting for me inside. Thanks, baby girl, you did good. Like Charlie said, always trust your feelings. He has saved our hides many times because of his."

Lil nodded with a grin and asked Charles, "So is he really going to be okay, Dad?"

"Sarge says he'll be fine. So he will be."

"So what's the plan, son?" asked Bill.

"He's going to be talking out of his head for a while when he comes around," Charles replied. "So the question is, do I call Madison now or wait? He might say something blowing his cover."

"He won't like that," Bill said. "Better not call her yet. So what's the story?"

"We'll keep it simple," replied Charlie. "He fell out back running and hit his head on those jagged rocks where the wall ends. He called me. He didn't want Madison seeing all the blood. I flew him here. We're going to say he broke his leg. Sarge is putting a fake removable cast on his leg to give Luke time to figure out how to hide it from Madison. If she sees his leg is a mess later, it's on him; maybe he'll finally come clean with her."

"How's Jacob?" Bill asked Ben.

"Joe said he's come to, and he's fine," replied Ben. "Joe said Luke's cover wasn't blown with Jacob. He got knocked out before Luke came in as Carl, and he didn't see him when JR carried him out."

"Good," Charles said. "Luke will be glad to hear his cover wasn't blown. So this is the story. Luke went to Jacobs to pick up a birthday present for Lil. Not seeing Jacob, he went to the back and walked in seeing them tying up an unconscious Jacob."

"That will work," said Bill.

"Dad, when can we see Uncle Ca…Luke? Wow, this is going to be tough around HT," Lil said with a sigh.

"You'll do fine, baby girl, and it won't be long before we can go in. So get cleaned up. Give those clothes and trainers to Ben to dispose of."

Lil nodded as she turned toward the chopper. She looked down seeing all the blood. "Buggar," she mumbled, "these are my favorite trainers."

"Looks like I could use a shower and change of clothes myself," JR said and followed Lil to get his bag.

Less than an hour later, they all went in and sat with Luke. He was out, snoring away. The only evidence he had been hurt was the bandage wrapped around his head.

Lil said with a chuckle, "If I would have heard him snore, I would have known he was Uncle Carl!"

They all snickered.

"You guys were brilliant with your disguises so that you could spend time with each other's family," said Lil looking at Charles.

"Yeah, but you guys were raised with Uncle Carl," he replied. "It took HT forever to stick around and spend time with the stuttering Lord Standish!"

They all laughed as Charles' phone went off. "Excellent work, Jake. take it to the house," Charles said before putting his phone back in his pocket.

"Jake found something then at her place?" asked Bill.

"Yeah." Charles nodded. "You know Jake; he's better than a blood hound. He found a box under the floorboards. It is full of old diaries."

JR's phone went off. They knew it was Jayden.

"Bollocks, I still haven't told him," said JR as he read the text. "We need to go, Snaggs. HT is on his way home from the airport."

His phone went off again. They knew it was HT.

"Sorry." Lil chuckled as she jumped up and went over to Luke.

"I see you are." JR grinned. He read the text out loud, "Where's Lil? Still no phone?" He took a breath and said as he texted, "She's inside the bakery. I'm handling something right now. Found her phone; I'll take it to her in a bit and tell her that you're on your way." He looked at Charles and shrugged. "You needed help with Luke so you called me. He'll expect I know."

Charles nodded.

JR grunted hearing his phone again from HT. "I don't like this, Snaggs. You're putting me in the middle. You need to call him."

"I know. I'm sorry, but I need a little more time to get my head around this. He'll know something is up as soon as he hears my voice."

JR nodded and read her the text, "Thanks, bro. Tell her that I love her."

"That just made me feel like rubbish," Lil grumbled as she bent to kiss Luke on the forehead.

He opened his eyes and muttered, "Thanks, baby girl, for keeping my secret from him. I know it's hard."

"Hey you, you need to sleep," Lil said and lightly kissed his forehead again and then added, "Thank you for raising the most brilliant bloke in the world for me."

He muttered, "I'll remind you that you said that when you blame me when he drives you mental."

Lil chuckled and said, "Love you. Now go back to sleep."

"Love you mos..." he slurred, passing out.

Charles was standing behind Lil with his hands on her shoulders. He felt her tense. "He's fine, baby girl. Sarge sedated him pretty good so that he would sleep. As you can see, he's still fighting it coming in and out. Come on, I'll walk you and JR out."

Lil gave Bill, Ben, and Ed a hug and kiss before she followed JR and Charles out.

Once at the chopper, Charles said, "I'll give HT time to get to the bakery and then I'll call Madison and Jayden. JR hold off telling Jayden about Luke being Carl. We can fill him in later. We need him calm not worrying about him until we pull this thing off."

JR nodded.

"Love you, Dad," said Lil as she kissed his cheek.

He gave her a big bear hug. "Love you most. Make sure you release all this to-night. Get it all out and deal with it. Plus, I want every little detail. We'll talk when I get home."

She smiled and nodded. "I will. I won't hold anything back." She hopped into the chopper and waved as JR put them in the air.

Twenty-five minutes later Jayden had to park on the street down from the bakery because of the large white tent that had been put out front for the party. The whole village was invited. Like always, Grammy out did herself, making this one even more special since it was her eighteenth. Besides all the cupcakes, candies, and cookies, she had made a huge eight-tier cake. Usually, she just made a couple of big cakes, and people would stop in to wish Lil happy birthday and have a piece of cake. They always brought her a small gift, even though she told them not to.

Jayden and HT had just turned left walking to the back of the bakery when Lil and JR ran in the back door. Her face was flushed from running so fast from the chopper. JR placed her camera case on the table and headed to the main kitchen, while Lil quickly tied her apron on. Mary stuck a frosting bag in her hand and added a little frosting on her nose and cheek.

HT went in finding her hunched over one of the long counters. They were lined full with cupcakes. Most of them done.

"Wow," he said looking around at all the decorated cupcakes, cookies, and can-dies on the racks. "I'm getting a buzz from all the sugar."

"Hey, you," Lil said smiling as he walked over to her tying on an apron.

They kissed.

"Missed you," he said not caring who heard.

"Missed you more," she replied giving him another quick kiss, dreading the phone call he was about to receive.

His phone rang. He took it out of his pocket. "Hi, Mum, just got to the bakery." Silence. "Is he okay?" Silence. "K."

Again, like a well-rehearsed play, Jayden's phone rang. He answered it and said a few seconds later, "Going now." He put his phone in his pocket running to the door. "Going up to get your mum; be right back down for you," he said before he hurried out.

"Dad's been hurt," HT said looking at Lil.

Mary's phone rang. They looked at her knowing it was Charles as she answered it. "Hi, dear. Oh, I was wondering what was going on. I'll tell him. Love you most." She looked at HT. "Luke fell out back running. He hit his head and has some stitches, and he's broken his leg. He didn't want Madison seeing him with all that blood on him from his head, so Charles flew him to the medical center. He says to let you know he's fine."

HT looked at JR. "You knew, bro?"

JR nodded and said, "Luke swore me to secrecy when I helped Charlie get him into the chopper. I was on my way back when I got your text. Sorry, bro."

"No worries. I know how Dad is always worrying about us."

"You want me to go to the medical center with you?" asked Lil, hugging HT.

"No, doesn't sound like it's life threatening," he replied holding her.

Lil's head was lying on his chest. She rolled her eyes at JR, making him grin.

"Besides, you look knackered," HT teased as she raised her head to look at him.

"It's been a long day." She smiled. "Call me when you hear more."

"I will. Where was your phone?"

"At Jacobs."

Mary chimed in before HT could ask more questions. "HT's right, dear, you do look tired. All that is left to do is box all this up. Go on up to the house and have a hot bath. We don't want the birthday girl worn out!"

"I think I will then."

HT kissed her again after his phone went off with Jayden's ringtone. "I'll call as soon as I get there. Love you," he said over his shoulder as he ran for the door.

"Love you most," Lil called back as he ran out. She let out a long sigh. "Not life threatening at all!" she mumbled with a grunt.

CHAPTER 28

Lil took a long hot bath as she drank her tea. HT had called when she got out of the tub and said that Luke was fine. He was out from the pain meds. He chuckled when he told her that he was mumbling some off-the-wall rubbish in his sleep about a flying ninja saving his life and something about smashing watermelons! She had just laughed.

After she slipped her pajamas on, she grabbed her notepad and pen and jumped in the middle of her bed. It was time to let it all go, write it down as best she could, and deal with what happened. She laid her head back against the headboard, releasing everything in her mind, using one of JR's techniques. He had told her to write it all down but not to look at the paper, and it didn't matter if it was readable, it would help her to recall.

First, she put herself in Jacob's shop when she was looking at the new camera Jacob had gotten. She smiled thinking it didn't surprise her that Jacob was an agent; it was like she had already known.

She pictured the psycho woman. She wrote on paper, keeping her head back as she thought, *Seen her at ball. Was interested in JR; she kept staring. Not a big deal there; all women stare at him. Didn't see her at Edinburgh.*

"Now, what did I hear?" she asked herself out loud, taking herself back to when she entered the back door. She wrote as she mumbled, retracing her every move. "Once inside, I heard muffled voices. I moved up the hallway heard father grief stricken over death. Hope he's burning in hell with that old man who turned our lives to hell. I find out wasn't even my real father!"

Lil let out a big sigh as she continued, "The psycho shrieked, 'Don't tell me to quiet down because the idiots in the back will hear me. Still unconscious, tied up,

357

and gagged. You should have cut their throats.' Blah, blah, blah." Lil continued writing what she'd heard. Realizing she'd heard more than she thought.

Next thing Lil knew someone was gently shaking her shoulder. She saw herself still sitting up against the headboard. Granddad was smiling at her and went over to the bookcase. He opened the lid on a big treasure-chest-looking box she had never seen before, raised the lid, and took out her phone. He held it up and nodded.

Lil's eyes opened wide as she jumped awake. She wasn't afraid this time. She looked over to the bookshelf only seeing albums and books. She started talking to him, "What the bloody heck did that mean, Granddad? No treasure box. You were here, right?" She looked down at the floor seeing her phone lying in front of the shelf. "Oh yeah, you were definitely here! Not sure I'm going to get used to this!" She went after her phone. "So what's up with the phone, Granddad?" she asked as she looked it over. "No missed calls or messages." She stared at it for a few seconds and saw she had three recordings. "That's weird," she mumbled as she pushed the button to listen. "Oh my God! It's the psycho lady; she must have pushed the record button thinking she was disconnecting it when HT called." She ran over to her bed and grabbed the paper and pen. She listened to all three recordings and wrote as she listened: he blackmailed, sugar in helicopter tank, and getting my money!"

She ran out and headed down the hall. She wasn't surprised to hear footsteps downstairs. She flew down the stairs and through the hall and made it to Charles's study as he, Ed, JR, Bill, and Jayden went in.

"Hey, Snaggs," said JR smiling. "You just won me a hundred pounds. I told Jay you'd be waiting on us."

"Yeah, yeah, whatever," said Jayden with a chuckle.

"Let's get started," said Charles taking Lil's notes. He sat down behind his desk and laid them beside the box Jake had retrieved sitting in front of him. Once everyone sat, he continued, "Now we have to figure out why she murdered Lord Rothford—"

"I know why," said Lil jumping up.

"Let's hear it and don't start that mumbling," said Charles.

She took a deep breath and began, "The stupid psycho pushed record on my phone. From what I remembered and these recordings, it appears she didn't need him anymore." Lil started pacing. "But then she didn't need him at all, but she didn't know that. She found out the duke wasn't her father and knew he had a son and gave him up." Lil started to mumble, "He wasn't getting her money. She tracked the baby down. But wrong baby. She found out he was an agent. But wasn't an agent at all! I remember she said—"

"Lily Rose, stop that mumbling; you're not making a bit of sense, and stop that damn pacing!" Charles said sternly.

Lil stood still. "Sorry," she said. "She found out the duke wasn't her father and that he had a son. She thought he would get the money and that he was an agent. She had all those agents killed to cover up that she killed him? Wait a minute. I just thought of something." She looked at Bill. "When I was little, did I hear you talking to Dad about sugar in a tank of a helicopter crash?"

They all jumped up and yelled, "What?"

Lil jumped from being startled.

"What did you hear about that? Charles asked, trying to read her notes. "I can't read this rubbish!"

Lil walked over and pointed at the bottom of the paper. "Right here. That's what recorded on my phone: blackmailed, sugar in helicopter tank, and get money."

"What else did that bitch say?" sneered Bill.

"That was it. Why do I have a feeling this is bad?"

Charles let out a loud sigh. "Your granddad and Ed's, Luke's, and Bill's fathers were on that chopper!"

"That's why Granddad came to me again," mumbled Lil.

"What?" yelled Charles. "When?"

"Just now!"

"Why didn't you say something when we came in here?"

"Stop your yelling, son; you're going to wake the whole house," Bill said. "What did he do, Snaggs?"

"He took my phone out of a treasurechest-looking box. That's why I looked at my phone and saw the recordings."

"Snaggs, this is very important," said Bill. "When Charlie has dreams, they're not that cut and dry. Was there something else that didn't make sense?"

"Yeah, he walked to my bookshelf where the treasure box was sitting, but I don't have a box there! And my phone was on the floor in front of my shelf when I woke up."

Charles said with a grunt, "His way of showing you it wasn't just a dream. Sometimes I think he just likes messing with my head."

"Actually," Lil said pointing behind Charles, "the shelves looked like those!"

"How could I be so stupid?" Charles said as he ran over to a section of the bookshelves. "The old man wasn't pointing to my ledgers at all on this shelf; he was pointing to this box and his ledgers on his desk." He flipped a switch behind a book and a section of the bookshelf revolved showing another identical bookshelf with a big-looking treasure box sitting on the middle shelf."

"That's it!" Lil said excitedly. "What's in it?"

"Don't know. But I'm bloody well going to find out!" said Charles, taking it over to his desk. "This belonged to one of Dad's clients. He made me promise one day that if anything ever happened to him I would continue to take care of four of his closet clients. They were his mates. He had written ledgers on each client's estate and outlined in detail how they wanted it run. Same as any client really. I invested and distributed funds and made sure the estates were run properly until the legal heir was of age and could take over. This is the last one. I was not to open the chest until next week when the heir turned twenty-five. There's a letter in here laying out what needs to be done. See this slit?"

They all nodded.

"The old man told me I would get mail sent to a lockbox at the post. I was to put it in this box through the slot. The last time I received anything at the post was years ago."

"Your old man always liked intrigue and mystery. Open it up, and let's see what's in it," said Bill.

Charles pointed at the box Jake brought in marked Mum's diaries. "Ed pass those out so that you guys can get started on reading them while I check this out."

"You got it," said Ed as he took the box over to a table. JR and Jayden followed.

"Just scan the pages," said Ed. "It will take hours if we don't."

Charles took a small key from his drawer and opened the small lock. He raised the lid and took the envelope taped on top beside the slit. CHARLES was written across it. He opened it and took out the letter.

Lil and Bill dug into the box to see what else was there.

Charles read the letter out loud, "Hello, son, it's your father here. First, let me say how much I love you and how proud I am of you." Charles chuckled as he looked up with tears in his eyes. "He always starts my letters and notes that way. I started finding them before he passed. I have found hundreds of them over the years. He stuck them everywhere—books, shoes, under lamps. I never knew when I was going to find one. He looked down smiling and was just about to read out loud again when he saw "Stop if you're reading this out loud. I'm sure Bill is close, and this is something he shouldn't hear like this. If you're reading this it means I'm gone, and it's time to tell you whom this box belongs to. First, let me tell you a love story of sorts. One of my childhood mates, Marcus Carnet the Duke of Darthshire, whom you met a few times when you were young...Anyway, he was raised to do what was expected of him. So when his family wanted him to marry Lady Purcella because of her position in society he did. She was the evilest woman I've ever met. She hid it well behind her beauty. They had only been married a few years when he learned her true colors and turned to drink. Their marriage became in most part, in name only. He wanted an heir, so let's just say when he slept with her it was after a whole lot of drinking. When she became pregnant, he was happy because he didn't have to sleep with her anymore; even after she had a girl, he couldn't bring himself to. Anyway, he went through life like your typical tosser, too much money, women, and drink. Then he met the love of his life when he turned fifty-two. He turned into a totally different man. Problem was, besides him still being married, Lady Margaret was just twenty-one, and her family was very well off. The house of Carvish ring a bell?" Charles whistled and muttered, "Oh yeah, made them plenty of money over the years." He continued to read. Marcus tried to get a peaceful divorce, but Lady Purcella wasn't having it. She knew all about Lady Margaret and knew she was with child. The Carvish name meaning everything in high society, she said she would scream from the rooftops how their precious daughter was nothing but a man-stealing whore and that she was going to have his bastard! She could have easily turned the posh world against them. She had *that* much power, and you know back then your place in high society meant everything. So this is where yours truly comes in. I did a little snooping, and let's just say the prim-and-proper Lady Purcella had been having an affair with a mechanic for years, even before she married Marcus. You guessed it—his daughter wasn't his; she was the mechanic's."

Charles looked over to Bill. "Bloody hell! That psycho bitch used the surname—Rosewood; it's Carnet. That's why I couldn't get my mind around what was going on. I didn't connect her name to anything. I wrote those checks out of the estate to Lady Rosewood. That's why the old man was pointing to his ledgers on my desk trying to tell me. He pointed at the bookshelf wanting me to look in the chest. Damn! Why didn't he show me the bloody box when he pointed?"

"Maybe he did, son, and your subconscious wasn't letting you see it dredging up all that pain again, so he had to go to Snaggs. You said yourself you knew the dreams were related to their deaths but didn't know why."

"How did you get so smart, you old coot?" grumbled Charles knowing he was right.

"Love you most, son." Bill chuckled.

"Ed," Charles said looking at him, "I'm sure it was her mum who brought down that chopper. Look for a diary that talks about an affair with a mechanic."

"The sons of bitches," hissed Ed.

"Ah, I got that one right here," said Jayden as he continued reading. "Yep, you're right! Seems your old man blackmailed her over him."

Charles continued to read to himself. "So let's just say I persuaded Lady Purcell to give Marcus a quick, quiet divorce, or I was going to let it be known to the world she lived for a daughter who wasn't a lady after all but a bastard of a mechanic. I didn't tell Marcus that, of course. He got his divorce, and he and Lady Margaret were quietly married a few weeks before their beautiful son was born. No one knew of their marriage or son, of course. The story being told was after meeting at a social function and falling madly in love, they were going to have a huge wedding and then take a trip around the world for a year or so. They knew by the time they got back home with a new son, no one would give them a second look. Society would have moved on a hundred times over, tearing other people's lives to shreds.

"I've never seen such a devoted father over those few months, besides me of course." Charles chuckled and kept reading. "Well, Marcus's world came crashing down two months after Marcus Jr. was born. Two days before the wedding, which all of society was attending, Lady Margaret passed away while she slept in their bed. He was just feet away rocking and feeding the baby, looking out at the stars thinking he was the luckiest man in the world. Anyway, Marcus was devastated, to say the least. A few weeks later, he had a mild stroke in the middle of the night. I think it was from grief of losing her. He still never let the boy out of his sight; he worshipped him. He said it was a good thing the baby had slept in his room because he swore he saw Lady Purcella over the bassinet one night, trying to suffocate the baby. She denied it, of course. Said she hadn't been in the castle since their divorce. A month later he had another mild stroke. So he came to me to find his son a safe and happy home. He didn't think he could keep him safe and was afraid the next stroke would kill him.

"Abbey was pregnant with her and Joe's first. By that time Tessa, bless her heart, who I loved as a daughter and one of the kindest woman in the world, knew she would never be able to have one of her own. So I gave Marcus Jr. to them. I told Bill the child's mother was Marcus's head cook, who passed in childbirth and didn't know who the father was. Actually, she was pregnant about the same time and had a boy, but she was happily married. So I paid them off to move away to raise their son in Scotland and then me being me, laid the trail in case it ever got out that Marcus had a son, it was them that raised him.

"So by now, you've figured out the little boy you took to so fast is JR." Charles chuckled, shaking his head. "All of his legal papers and documents are in this chest and, as you know, his inheritance and birth has to be filed with the crown before he's twenty-five, which should be in a few days, or it will all go to Lady Darby Carnet.

"It's up to you, since JR's birth was never filed. Let her inherit everything, except the title of course, which only gets handed down to a male heir. Or JR legally becomes the duke of Darthshire and claims his inheritance from Marcus's and Lady Margaret's estates. I'm sure the way you have invested them, JR is a very rich man! Love you, your father."

Lil had been digging in the chest. "There's some baby things at the bottom. A blue nightie, hat, booties. I bet it was his first outfit. There's a silver rattler and a lot of pictures and lots of envelopes." A large picture of a group of men caught her attention. She stared at it for a few seconds and flipped it over and then back and mumbled as things clicked, "That's why she stared at him at the ball.

She knew she got the wrong bloke because he looks just like him. That's why time was running out, he will be..."

"What are you going on about?" asked Bill.

She looked up and said, "You never said JR is adopted!"

The guys all replied in unison, "Yeah, so?"

"Why?" asked Bill.

"Bloody hell! JR, you're biological father is—"

"No, no!" said Charles laughing. "I get the honors. This is absolutely classic." He waved his arm toward JR as he introduced him. "Everyone, let me introduce Marcus Allen Harold Byron, the third and the Duke of Darthshire and the Earl of Carvish."

"The hell you say," yelled JR. "I'm no bloody duke or a bloody earl."

"Oh, but you are. All the proof is right here in this box. All I have to do is file the paperwork!"

"Well, burn that damn box. I want no part of that rubbish."

"Now, son," Bill said, "you can't be doing that."

"No, I'm no son of a bloody duke. I'm very proud to be your son the greatest man on earth, thank you very much."

"Thank you, son, but think about your young 'uns down the road," said Bill.

"Sorry, bro; he's right," Jayden said. "You need to accept it. Just do what Ch—"

Charles loudly cleared his throat.

"What?" said Lil. "Pass one of his best mates off as the duke when you're the bloody duke! Bloody hell! Dad, you're the duke of Highcliff not Uncle Eddie!"

"How—"

Lil cut Charles off holding up the photo. "This photo is of dukes." She flipped it over on its back. "It's listed that the third bloke on the bottom left is the Duke of Highcliff—it's Granddad!" She started to mumble, "It makes sense now. Parts of the journals you let me read were missing. Our ancestor who started the security company was a bloody duke, and he started the bodyguard thing to protect his family!" She looked at Charles. "Right? The ones that had anything to do with you being the duke you took out!"

"The jigs up, boy." Bill laughed. "She found you out red handed!"

"He has more than just the duke title." JR snickered. "Snaggs, meet, Alfred Charles Raif Edmund Montgomery Montclair, the duke of Highcliff, earl of Saintsbury, the viscount—"

"Yeah, yeah, yeah! I have a few titles," grumbled Charles. "Okay, baby girl, I am the duke of Highcliff, and yes I removed the journals that linked me to being the duke. Everything you read in those journals was about our ancestors. But Ed is also a duke; he just didn't get the wealth and family estates from his ancestors. I got his funds back where they should be, and I'm working on getting back the estates."

"And when you do, just like all that bloody money, it goes to Anthony," Ed grumbled. "I don't want anything to do with all that rubbish either. Bad enough I have to play you!"

Charles chuckled and added, "Anyway, I hated all the attention when I was young, but Ed here loved it at the time and loved acting like his family owned Highcliff."

"Whatever!" Ed grumbled. "We were like fourteen, and it helped with the girls since they only had eyes for you. I still only got the ones who gave up on you! I didn't know we were going to keep it up my whole bloody life!"

"This is crazy," mumbled Lil.

"You're telling me," JR added with a raised brow.

"We should tell her the rest, Charles," Mary said as she entered. "We planned on telling her tomorrow on her birthday."

"Oh no! Why do I have the feeling this is going to be bad?" Lil said with a groan.

"Because it is as far as we're concerned," muttered JR under his breath.

"You know what I'm about to hear?" Lil asked him.

He nodded.

"Stop it, you two," said Bill with a chuckle. "I've never seen a bunch that don't want wealth and titles."

"Wealth and titles?" repeated Lil. She looked at Mary and asked, "Raif gets all that rubbish, right?"

"Yes, dear." Mary nodded. "He gets the wealth and titles from your father's side. But—"

"Oh no, there's a but!" mumbled Lil.

JR looked at Charles. Charles nodded with a grin.

"Sorry, Snaggs, this might sound better coming from me. There's lots of titles, more than Charlie's I know. And man are you loaded," said JR. "The house in London, yours. The castle you love up in Scotland, yours. Guess who's the heir Keaton Hall is being restored for? You! As a matter of fact, you own most of the bloody village! One of the private jets, yours..."

Lil whined cutting him off, "No way, Mum!"

"Sorry, dear," said Mary with a chuckle. "I'm afraid you get all that from my side. Years ago, one of our female ancestors had no choice and had to marry an evil man. Well, long story short, she gave birth to a daughter, and he beat her to death because it wasn't a boy. She was the queen's best mate. So the queen, let's just say, did away with the tosser and set the estate up that the daughters would always inherit not the sons so that they could control their own lives and never be put in that situation again. We decided when you were born that we would tell you when you turned eighteen. We wanted you to have as much of a normal life as you could, because mine...well was rubbish after my parents passed!"

"Like we have normal lives around here." Jayden chuckled.

"Hush, Jayden," said Mary and continued. "So because of my situation not being able to inherit until I was twenty-one, your father had E change the age to eighteen."

"I'm like JR. I don't want all that rubbish," grumbled Lil.

"Well, you don't have a choice on legal documents, dear. But people don't have to know," replied Mary smiling. "Now you see why I don't want it known we lived in London. Some of the gossips in the village might start connecting the dots. We've been living incognito here for years."

"Which I'm going to keep on doing," mumbled Lil.

"Me too," grumbled JR.

"Hey, Snaggs." Jayden chuckled. "HT already calls you 'my lady!'"

"Real funny," said Lil rolling her eyes at him. "No hinting about this rubbish around him either; he has enough to deal with because of us. I can hardly get my mind around all this, so I can't imagine what it would do to his! As a matter of fact, since I found this all out during a meeting, means I'm not going to feel bad holding this rubbish back from him, and I'm burying it so far back it will be years before I think about it!" She looked around the room. "I'm calling the code here; HT is not to know!"

They all laughed nodding their heads.

"If nobody is going to come in and tell me I'm loaded and that I'm a duke or earl," joked Jayden, "you might want to hear this!" He held up the diary he had been reading.

They all laughed again.

"He's right," said Charles. "Let's get back to the matter at hand. We can talk about all this later. What did you find, Jayden?"

"That psycho bitch had nothing on her mum," replied Jayden. "I just read that Lady Purcella slipped into the castle one night, right under the duke's nose, and suffocated Lady Margaret while she slept not ten feet away from him. He was rocking and feeding their son, well JR. She later bragged of how she tried to do the same to JR, but the Duke almost caught her. Sorry, bro, she murdered your mum."

"My mum is doing just fine tucked in her bed at home!" sneered JR.

"Okay," said Charles. "No more on all this for tonight. Our baby girl is going to be eighteen in about"—he looked at his watch seeing it was just after midnight—"well now. It's officially your birthday. Happy birthday, baby girl!"

They all said, "Happy birthday" and took turns giving her a hug.

"Now, I say we call it a night," said Charles. "Let's get some sleep; we all have a big day ahead of us tomorrow, which is going to start…" He asked looking at Mary.

"Tessa said she would be back at it about six."

"In less than six hours," finished Charles. "See you all down at the bakery. Not you, baby girl, you sleep in!"

## Two Ghosts

"So, my friend," Alfred, Charles's father, said to Marcus. "Looks like our work is done. My son knows that bitch of an ex-wife of yours got that mechanic to bring the chopper down, and your son knows about you. Shall we move on?"

"Nah, I'm not ready yet," said Marcus. "Sounds like my son might need me. Plus, one day when he accepts his position in life, he might need some help cleaning out those skeletons in my closet. I'll have to help him find my secret ledgers. I passed before I could write him a letter telling him where they are. He's going to need them one day. Plus, I want to make sure he finds my diary that's under the floorboards in the master suite when he's ready. I want him to know I found that bitch's diary saying she had murdered his mum. That I got justice by smothering that bitch the same way she murdered my Margaret, with her own pillow in her sleep. I just wish I could have strangled her while watching her eyes bulge seeing me do it and then yelled it from the rooftops that I did it!"

"Well, you had to make it look natural. You couldn't leave marks on her neck, causing a scandal connected to your good name."

Marcus nodded and asked, "How about you? You moving on then?"

"No, I don't think I will. I want to get to know my granddaughter. I have a feeling helping her is going to be more interesting than Charles. What a lass, huh? My little flying ninja!"

# CHAPTER 29

L il tried to sleep in, but she couldn't. She woke just after six. She sent HT a text and ran to the loo. She was going to the bakery to see what was going on and to hear how Luke was doing. Her phone was going off with HT's text as she threw her clothes on. Her phone quickly sang again with his second text. She smiled reading, "Happy Birthday, little minx! The Love of My Life! I'm at the bakery. Now go back to sleep!"

She laughed as she hurried down the stairs and out the front door. The weather was perfect, with no rain in sight. It was a little cool but was supposed to warm up. The sun was already trying to poke its head out of the clouds.

HT was taking off his apron when Lil went running in. "Hey, you," he said throwing it over on the counter. "You're supposed to be sleeping in, birthday girl."

She threw herself into his open arms. He kissed her breathless. "Happy birthday, love of my life. I love you," he said with a bear hug.

"Love you most." She sighed as he held her in his arms. Then she realized he'd taken off his apron. "You going to see Luke? How is he doing?"

HT looked over her shoulder at JR and Jayden as he hugged her. He raised his brow, letting them know he needed help.

"Happy birthday, Snaggs," they said in unison walking to her.

"Thanks, again," she said under her breath as she smiled and received their hugs and kisses.

"You about ready to go, HT?" asked Jayden, heading to the door.

"Yep, all set. Just need one more kiss from my girl." He kissed Lil breathless again and then hurried to the door.

"Give Luke my love," she yelled at his back as he went out. She looked at JR. "He was in a hurry. Luke *is* okay, right? Dad said he was—"

"Yeah, he's great! I just talked to Sarge, and he said he can't keep him in bed."

"Then why is HT in such a hurry?"

JR shrugged. "Maybe he just wants to make sure he's back in time for the party. Want a brew?" asked JR, trying to change the subject.

"For sure. When have you ever seen me turn down tea?" asked Lil, tying on her apron.

"True. Wasn't thinking." JR chuckled.

"I still need to do a few things," said Lil. "Can you take me over in about an hour or so?"

"Of course"—nodded JR—"and I'll even help!"

Jayden parked in the car park, and he and HT hurried into the shop. Jake was waiting on them.

"Hold still," said Jake ten minutes later.

"It bloody hurts!" grumbled HT.

"You had bigger nads when you were what, twelve?"

"Cheers," muttered HT. "You guys aren't ever going to let me live that one down!"

"Of course not. How's your dad?" asked Jake, winking at Jayden. "You never said how he broke his leg!"

"Out back running. He's doing great. Ouch! Don't you numb it or something?"

"When did you turn into such a wuss?" Jake laughed. "So this is a birthday present, huh?"

Jayden laughed as he sat down. "That's what he's calling it. Snaggs might not see it that way. She hates those things. She had a fit every time me or JR talked about getting one!"

"She's going to love it." HT squirmed.

"You keep telling yourself that, bro." Jayden laughed.

"She's not if you don't sit still!" said Jake. "I'm good, but you're making it hard here!" His movements were fast and precise. He didn't miss the slightest detail. It was perfect, and he had done exactly what HT asked for.

"Excellent!" said HT, looking at his left arm in the mirror. "Can you bandage it? I have to hide it until tonight."

"I can," said Jake as he applied goop on the tattoo. "That stuff will help with the pain for a while." He handed him a tube. "Apply that for the next few days; it will help with the healing and scabbing too."

"Thanks," HT said, putting the tube in his back pocket. "And thanks for meeting me so early."

"No worries," Jake replied.

"We better get a move on, bro, if we're going to make the party in time," said Jayden.

"I need to hit the loo first," HT said heading to the back.

Jayden and Jake did the guy-hug thing after HT left.

"Sarge said he'll be good as new in a few days," said Jayden. "Great work finding those diaries, by the way!"

"Ben said they helped. So the psycho bitch read the diaries and found out she wasn't a lady, that she was illegitimate. Can you believe she took out all those agents to get to one?"

"Yeah, crazy huh?" Jayden said and finished the story Charles wanted told. "The agent she was after was dating her at the time and read the diary she left out. After they broke up, he started blackmailing her. She took up with Lord Rothford to find his location and then when she didn't need Lord Rothford any-more...well you know the rest!"

"Yeah, she saw Lil and JR when that SOB threw Lord Rothford off the roof and wanted to take them out too. Just Luke's luck going to buy Lil a present and walking in at the wrong time. That poor bloke didn't have a chance, never being trained for com-bat. Hell he's never been out in the field! The worst he's ever had has been a papercut!"

They chuckled.

Jake said still grinning, "Ben said if it wasn't for Lil going back for her camera case, Luke would have been toast. HT doesn't have a clue what he has. She's a hell of a girl."

"Who is," asked HT coming back in. "Don't tell me you finally got one to go out with you!"

"No, actually I was talking about yours, thinking I might have a chance with her when she dumps your sorry arse for getting that tat!"

They laughed as Jake walked them to the door.

HT's left arm was starting to burn like crazy by the time he made it back to the bakery just before noon. He had put on a shirt with long sleeves to cover his lower arm. He entered the huge white tent and saw long tables covered with white tablecloths, lined with huge vases of lilies and roses, balloon bouquets, and three-tiered trays full of cupcakes, candies, and cookies. Lil spotted him and came running. "Buggar!" he said under his breath, trying to keep smiling. "She's going to throw herself in my arms, and, it's going to hurt!" He caught her and let out a grunt as he swung her around, kissing her. "You're looking beautiful as always, love of my life," he said as he sat her down.

"So do you. What's with the grunting?"

"Huh?" He chuckled, kissing her again and moaned with pleasure hoping to distract her. "Everything all done? Looks fantastic in here."

"Why are you trying to change the subject?" she asked looking at him.

"What?" he chuckled. "I'm just in a great mood. Dad is getting out later and going to be at Raif's gettin'-loose night."

"That's awesome," Lil said grinning. She already knew, of course, after arguing with Luke on the phone that he needed to stay in the hospital and not worry about her party.

HT was glad Connor, Lee, and Sloan came in, getting her off the subject. After they hugged and wished Lil a happy birthday, Lil and Sloan walked off. HT winced as he did the guy-hug handshake thing with Connor and Lee. He backed up letting them talk and looked down at his burning arm. The goop Jake had put on was oozing out from under the bandage and coming through his shirt. He quickly pulled the shirt away from his arm. It was throbbing and hurting like hell. "Man, what a mess," he muttered.

JR stood behind him. "Having troubles there, bro?"

HT jumped, turning around. "You scared the crap out of me. You guys sneak around like bloody cats!"

"Why so testy?" Jayden asked as he walked up. "Does that little bit of artwork hurt?"

"Sod it off," he said under his breath. "You guys need to keep it down; she's standing just over there and going to hear you!"

"Just wait until she sees it and finds out you didn't go see Luke! You better have one great. That is all I'm saying." JR chuckled. "I can't see her liking any though, the way she hates them. You just keep telling yourself how much she's going to like that one!"

"Whatever," he said making a face. "She's going to love it. I know my girl."

"You hope!" Jayden said laughing.

"Hope what?" Lil asked walking up.

"Yeah, bro, hope what?" asked JR.

"I need a drink. You idiots are doing my head in. Hey, Lee, hand me your flask."

Jayden and JR laughed as they walked off.

HT didn't have to worry about Lil causing him pain when she saw the tattoo; Jayden and JR were beating her to it all day. They waited to catch him off-guard and would slap his arm while Lil wasn't looking or pat him in a friendly way if she was, knowing he couldn't move away or show any pain. He called them wankers under his breath, making them laugh. He took it all with a smile on his face, knowing if the tables were turned he would have been doing the same to them.

Just before the party was over, Lil watched HT wince and jerk his arm away from JR again. Her mind started racing remembering how he had grunted when he swung her around. Then she watched him dodge a smack from Lee. She mumbled as she started toward HT, "He got a bloody tattoo!"

"I heard how big of a wuss you were this morning," said Lee laughing.

"What? It hurt!" whined HT. "It's burning like hell now."

"Hey, Snaggs. Great party, huh?" said JR seeing Lil walk up.

"Yeah, it's amazing," she said looking at HT. "HT, can you give me a hand in the kitchen?" She turned and walked off, not waiting on his answer.

"She knows," muttered HT.

"Yep! Good luck with that!" JR chuckled.

"It didn't take her long to dump your sorry arse," joked Lee.

"She's not going to dump me," said HT.

"I have my flask if she does," replied Lee.

"Cheers," HT grumbled.

JR and Lee burst out laughing as HT followed her.

"Do you need to tell me something?" Lil asked as soon as HT walked in the back.

"Hum, that I love you?"

She shook her head.

"Hum, that you're gorgeous?"

This time she cocked her head to the side giving him a look.

"Okay, okay, the guys said to tell you this falls under your gift clause, which I wasn't surprised you made." He chuckled and added, "You can be a little dodgy, and you don't have to answer any questions if you don't want!"

She rolled her eyes and huffed. "I should have known they had their hands in this."

He went to put his arm around her waist as she tried to lift the sleeve on his other arm.

"Let's see it!"

He laughed, pulling away. "No, you have to wait until later. It's part of your gift."

She huffed again and pointed at his arm. "Don't be blaming me for getting that thing! You know I hate those things. Does Madison know you got it?"

"Of course," he said, giving her a quick kiss.

"Whoa, wait just a minute here," she said stepping back. "You can be dodgy with the gift clause, but you can't lie! Harry Thomas, you freakin' lied to me! You never went to see Luke this morning!"

He shook his head. "No, I didn't, and I never lied saying I was, not one lie came out of my mouth!"

Lil huffed. "You let me think you were!"

He shrugged with a sheepish grin. "Dodgy!"

"Whatever." She chuckled as he pulled her back into his arms.

The party was a great success. The weather stayed perfect all day. Just about everyone in the whole village showed up throughout the day. The many tables of food were amazing and, of course, the baked goods were out of this world, as always! Everyone took boxes of goodies home, and Lil received so many photography supplies that even *she* wouldn't be able to use all them in a year!

Lil and HT had previously made plans to meet in the Cove before Raif's gettin'-loose party got started. Sloan and Lil headed to her room to change as HT went home with Jayden and JR to get Luke.

Luke, sitting in a wheelchair with his leg up, was waiting outside with Madison and Maddie, as the guys pulled up in a van. Jayden let down the back and then JR pushed Luke's chair up and sat on a seat beside him. He asked under his breath, "You okay, Un...Luke?"

"I'm fine. You forgive me yet, duke?" Luke asked under his breath, as HT helped Madison and Maddie climb in the front.

"I did until you said that!" grumbled JR.

They laughed.

Lil and Sloan hurried to her room.

"Now let's get you dressed in all of those goodies we bought yesterday," Sloan said as she handed her the black, lacy bustier.

Lil slipped it on and then sat on her vanity chair.

Sloan handed her the pair of sheer, black nylons with tiny diamonds running up the back of the legs.

Lil took her time putting them on. She carefully rolled each one up and attached it to the garter with small diamonds running down it. Then stood up when she was done.

"Raise your arms," Sloan instructed.

Lil did, and Sloan slipped the silky black dress over her head. It sparkled like small diamonds when Lil turned so that she could zip it. It was strapless, sexy, and sophisticated at the same time, clinging to her perfectly shaped body.

Lil sat back down. Sloan pinned up some of her hair with diamond clasps and added a little eye shadow.

"No lipstick," said Lil. "I know it's smudge proof, but it makes my lips feel weird! And no blush; I feel like a clown wearing that rubbish!"

Sloan chuckled and said, "Not a vain bone in your body. You don't need it anyway. Now for these amazing shoes!" Sloan stooped down to help her.

Lil slipped into her strappy heels, which perfectly matched her dress, adorned with just enough tiny diamonds to make them sparkle.

"That's it!" Sloan said as they stood up. "What does HT call you? Oh yeah, my lady is ready for Raif's big gettin'-loose night!"

Lil chuckled but then rolled her eyes as she headed to the door. She thought, *If you only knew!*

"I'll meet you downstairs. Take your time getting ready; there's plenty of time," Lil said before quickly going out the door.

Charles was waiting for her at the bottom of the stairs. He whistled and gave her a hug. "You look amazing, baby girl."

"Thanks, Dad." She kissed his cheek.

"Luke is in the family room, and Madison is in the kitchen with Mary if you want to see him real quick."

She asked over her shoulder as she hurried down the hall, "Sarge said for sure it was okay if he left?"

"He wasn't happy about it," replied Charles following her. "But he said as long as he didn't overdo it, he would be fine. If there was a problem he wouldn't have let him leave."

"You make this day perfect," she said smiling at Luke as she hurried over to him.

Luke smiled with tears in his eyes. "Happy Birthday, baby girl. You look beautiful," he said with Carl's southern voice.

"I love you, Uncle Carl," Lil said with a chuckle as she bent down giving him a quick kiss and hug. "I'm happy you made it, but I can't believe you left the hospital."

"Love you most, baby girl, and I promised I would be here. A little bump on the head and a little cut on my leg isn't going to stop me."

Lil gave Luke another quick kiss before she said, "I know you two want to talk before everyone gets in here, so I'll leave you to it. I want to go see what that knuckle-headed son of yours had put on his arm, anyway."

They laughed as Lil hurried out the door.

Lil went into the Cove hearing HT singing in the Lion's Room. She walked to the sofa, seeing her present sitting on the table with a single open rose entwined with a lily. She raised the throw-pillow on the sofa and put HT's necklace under it and saw his songbook. She picked it up to put it on the desk, thinking she had never seen this one before. It wasn't like his other ones. This one was thicker and had HT loves Lil written all over the front, with little hearts. She sat and flipped through the pages, realizing this was where he started. His true feelings and emotions were written on the pages. She flipped to the page where his pen was clipped and smiled seeing he had written, "Birthday song: *little things*, I love most." She mumbled, "I shouldn't read this" but did anyway. She read about loving her tea and how he loved her dimples, how she was perfect to him, and how he loved her most with all her silly *little things*. She continued to smile as she turned the page seeing he had another one about her turning eighteen, but it wasn't done. He also had started one about the talk he had with Dad. She read: "I want the whole world to know how much I love and adore her. She is my whole world. I hate we have to hide our love. Charlie is right though. Boy, that's weird calling him Charlie. Anyway as long as I pursue my music, Lil will be safe if *they don't know about us*." She flipped through more pages. It was easy to see where his inspiration came from. Their lives were on every page. Her heart swelled with love at the one he had written about their wall. "The story of our lives; I love this one!" she mumbled as she read it. Then her heart fell as she turned more pages and saw, "*My first gut wrencher. The love of my life broke my heart today; my world just got turned upside down.*" She read how he loved her first, way before Soccer Boy. As if in a trance she kept reading, turning the pages. She found one after another, with him being in pain and pouring his heart out about watching her with Connor. She found the one he wrote just the week before, after the Halloween dance. Her heart broke for him. She mumbled, "I thought he was with that cow, and he was writing this. I'm awful." Guilt rushed through her. Tears started as she read... he was heartbroken. She hated the part where he thought Connor held her in his arms, that he knew he could love her so much more. *Oh God, he thought I slept with him that night—and then he saw the marks he didn't know he left!*

HT saw her sitting on the sofa and went over to join her. He whistled. "You're absolutely gorgeous, birthday girl. I love the dress. The perfect little black dress for the perfect girl."

Her voice trembled. "Sounds like a song in the making to me." She sniffed as she raised her head, her eyes glistening with tears.

He saw his songbook in her lap and quickly went to sit down beside her. "Hey, none of that."

Her chin wobbled despite her attempt to hold it together. "I'm so sorry. I can't believe I was so awful, making you think I—"

"Stop," he interrupted her. His voice was soothing as he took her in his arms. "You don't have anything to be sorry about, silly goose. You didn't know you were hurting me." He looked at her and ran his thumbs gently under her eyes, wiping her tears. "All that is over, remember? Wiped away on that list." He lightly kissed her forehead before he teased, "Do we need to make no-more-feeling-bad-about-those-months a rule?"

She shook her head.

"Look at it this way." He grinned. "I've got some great material when the guys and I cut our first album. People like all of that sad, soppy stuff."

"Well"—she sniffed—"you'll not have another reason to write that sad rubbish about me ever again."

"Good!" He chuckled and kissed the tip of her nose.

"I have to confess, I read the birthday song you wrote for me. I still want to hear it, though."

"Later." He chuckled as he picked up her gift and handed it to her. "I had this made before school started. I was hoping I didn't have to say 'as mates' when I gave it to you."

"Huh?"

"You'll see," he said grinning.

She quickly opened the small box with a perfectly tied pink bow on top. Her face lit up, and she gave a little squeal of delight as she took it out of the box. She could tell he had put a lot of thought into it. It was a delicate silver chain with a pendant. The pendant was about a quarter of an inch wide and half an inch long, outlined with tiny topaz and amethyst stones, their birthstones. Three quarter-carat diamonds ran down the center. On the back was engraved a letter H; the H extended to form the letter T. A small ruby heart lay under the HT, and below the heart was a perfectly engraved lily and a rose intertwined. It read: HT loves Lily Rose.

"It's beautiful! I love it," she said, wiping the tears from her cheeks. She handed it to him and quickly turned so that he could fasten it around her neck. "I'm never taking it off!" she added as she turned back around.

He picked up the pendant and kissed it. "There're a million kisses. When you need or want one, just put it against your lips."

"Make it a couple million," she teased.

He kissed it again.

"Now, it's your turn." Lil chuckled as she took a small box from under the pillow.

"It's not my birthday," he said laughing.

"Just open it."

"I finally get my chain, huh?"

"How did you know?"

"I saw you come out of the jewelry store and mine had just broken, so, with the way you spoil me, it wasn't hard to figure it out," he said with a grin as he opened it. It was a silver chain like he expected, but it had a two-inch long thick cross on it. "I love it!" He handed it to her.

She slipped it over his head. "I'll take it to get it engraved like you have mine. I'll just switch it around, our very own engraving."

The cross lay in the middle of his chest, even with his heart. She picked up the cross and kissed it. "There's a million kisses for when you need one and think of me."

"I need and think of you *all* of the time, love of my life."

They shared a long kiss.

"We better cool it here"—he lightly groaned—"or we won't make it to Raif's party. You ready to go up?" he asked. His eyes were twinkling as he tried not to grin.

"Ha, ha, real funny. Let me see what you're hiding under that bandage."

"Oh, you mean this little thing?" He grinned pointing to it.

She playfully rolled her eyes. "Quit stalling."

He said as he removed the bandage, "The girl who owns my heart, my Lily Rose."

Lil was speechless as she stared at the open rose that covered about ten inches on his arm.

"There's eighteen petals, for your birthday. I wanted a lily entwined down the stem like your necklace, but with keeping us a secret, I had Jake entwine the lily through the petals instead. See you can just make out the lily," he said pointing it out.

"It's brilliant! I love it!" Lil gushed. "Does it hurt?"

"Nah, just burns a little," he said with a sexy grin making his dimples run deep. "When you see me pat my arm, you'll know I'm telling you that I love you and you are my life!"

Tears streamed down Lil's cheeks. "As you are mine! I love you!"

"I love you most, little minx. Happy eighteenth birthday!" he said huskily, before kissing her.

"Knock, knock, in there," yelled JR from outside a few minutes later. "You guys still have another party to get through. Get a move on!"

CHAPTER 30

Everyone had a great time at the gettin'-loose birthday party. Lil would have hated for it to end, but she was anxious to be alone with HT. While HT went with Jayden to take Luke, Madison, and Maddie home, JR was taking Lil in the Jeep to Keaton Hall, the back way.

They had gone over in the morning to get it ready. In the master bedroom on the second floor, Lil had put in an easy-listening music CD and placed candles all around the room. They were on tall stands, on the fireplace, tables, and nightstands. She'd scattered lily and rose petals around on the floor and on the bed. She'd then trailed them out the door and down the long hallway. She'd dropped them on the thick Persian runner down the staircase. She'd then lined candles along the hallway and then down each side of the stairs. She'd put large candlestands on the first land-ing of the staircase so that HT would see her when he stood in the marbled foyer just below. She'd scattered more petals on the landing down the rest of the stairs and across the foyer.

She hopped out of the Jeep as soon as JR pulled up front. "Hurry, JR," she said laughing. "There're like a million candles that need to be lit."

"You trying to burn it down or what?" he said, laughing as he ran, following her inside.

"Of course not. You know I love this place, and after thinking about it, I'm hap-py HT and I will be filling it up with kids one day."

"When you telling him you own this place?"

"Well, we decided to give our careers a good five years before getting married, so in about five years or so!"

They laughed as they quickly went to work lighting the candles.

JR's phone dinged. "That's Jay letting us know he's on his way with HT. He's bringing him on the road, so it gives us more time. You get the ones finished upstairs and get ready, and I'll do the stairs and landing before I wait on him outside."

"Okay," Lil said. "Make sure he keeps his do-rag on until he gets in the foyer. And don't you look up at the landing."

"Again, too much info." He laughed.

She hurried to the master suite and turned the CD player on low and looked around one last time after she got the candles lit. The soft music and candles made it feel romantic. It was perfect, looking like it belonged in a fairy tale. She trembled inside with excitement, as she removed her dress and put on the wrap covering her lacy bustier. She pulled the pins out of her hair and ran a quick brush through it. She added a little perfume and went to the landing to wait on HT.

HT and Jayden were in the van heading down the drive after getting Luke inside and settled.

"Here," Jayden said as he threw HT one of his do-rags. "Snaggs gave me orders that you had to put that on over your eyes."

"Okay." HT chuckled as he tied it around his head covering his eyes.

After a few minutes when HT realized they were on the road, he asked, "Where we going? What is she up to now?"

"Sorry, bro. I'm to keep my mouth shut. Just be a few more minutes."

JR opened HT's door when they pulled up. "Hey, bro," he said.

"Hey, can I take this thing off now?"

"You have to keep it on for a few more minutes. I'm going to help you out and lead you inside."

"Where are we?" asked HT. Then he chuckled. "Never mind. Defeats the purpose of all this rubbish, I guess."

They laughed as JR helped him out and walked him inside.

"Stand right here, and look up when you take that rag off," said JR. "Give me a minute to get out of here before you take it off."

"Okay. Thanks, bro. At least I hope it's thanks." HT chuckled.

JR laughed as he hurried out.

Lil was waiting. The only light was from all of the candles flickering away, which made it perfect.

"I'm taking this thing off, little minx," he said as he untied it. When his eyes focused, she was the first thing he saw.

"Welcome to Keaton Hall, love of my life."

His voice grew husky as he walked never take his eyes off hers. "Humm, so that's where we're at, you sly little minx. You've been holding out on me again, I see."

"Yes, I have, and I'm calling the gift clause. When we first met, of course, I couldn't tell you Dad ran the estate."

"Of course," he repeated with a sexy chuckle.

"Then when I realized you love it here as much as I do, I decided what a brilliant Christmas gift it'd be for you and your family to stay here, in the main part of course!"

"Of course," he said as he slowly started up the stairs. "After all I need to make sure I like it! As you know, my plan is we're going to own and live here one day," he teased.

"Oh yes we are, and you know I'm never wrong!"

He chuckled.

Lil spoke in a seductive purr as he got closer, "Question is..."

"Oh what is the question? Love of my life!"

"Well," she said seductively. "Do you want the grand tour now?"

"Or?" he asked with a sexy grin.

She took off her wrap and held it up and over to her side and dropped it as she purred, "Later?"

He let out a soft, throaty groan as he hurried up the last few stairs to the landing and scooped her up in his arms. Her arms wrapped around him. They kissed as he carried her up the remaining stairs. When they reached the top, he let out a little moan. "Please tell me no more stairs—that our room is on this floor."

She chuckled and kissed the side of his neck and then purred in his ear, "Just down the hall. Follow the candles."

They kissed again as he carried her down the hall. The room was glowing like it was magical with all the candles flickering and lily and rose petals everywhere.

"It's beautiful and perfect, just like you," he said as he carried her to the bed and gently laid her down. His mouth never left hers as he removed his clothes and lay down, gathering her in his arms. After a long, deep kiss that made them both tremble, his hands continued to caress her as he looked into her eyes. The corners of his mouth quirked into a sexy grin. "I love what you're wearing; you look absolutely brilliant, love of my life, but..."

"But?" She laughed softly, staring tenderly into his eyes.

"Question is," he whispered in a sexy growl low in his throat.

"Oh! What is the question? Love of my life," she teased repeating him from earlier.

"Well," he said mimicking her reply and then blowing air out of his cheeks. "How the bloody hell do I get you out of it?"

She giggled. "Oh! how I love you!"

"I love you most!" he replied in a breathy tone as his mouth came down on hers!

When their bodies joined, their eyes locked; they nearly cried at the intensity of it.

# COMING IN BOOK TWO

One Year from the Day They Met

Lil and HT had gone to London to order their rings just after Christmas. They felt the best day of their lives was the day they met and would always consider that their anniversary. They wanted to make it special, something they would always remember, by giving each other commitment rings. HT wanted to have them made at Harrods, the most prestigious and best-known store in London and the world. Lil chose a silver band, wanting little HTs all around it, matching the one on her necklace. She liked it because if you didn't know they were little HTs, you would think it was just a design. HT settled on a thicker, chunky silver band with raised Aztec symbols and a tiny lily and rose entwined between each symbol. The significance was again hidden in the design so that others wouldn't know the meaning. They chose to have the insides of their rings engraved: *HT* with a heart and lily entwined with a rose in hers, and HT's with the same, just reversed. Happy with their choices, HT paid to have them made and was assured he would have them back in plenty of time before April. The design was beautiful, and it assured that their relationship would be kept a secret, since the rings looked totally different.

It was just before noon when HT put the same kind of pasties and fizzy drinks, that he and Lil had eaten and drunk the year before in a bag and made his way back to the Cove.

He lightly tapped on the darkroom door. "Hurry up in there. It's almost the time we met," he called out to Lil.

"K, be out in two seconds," she called back.

He put the pasties on a plate and opened their drinks. He placed them on the table with a lit candle and their ring boxes.

Lil came out of the darkroom and ran to the loo. "I gotta pee first!"

"Of course you do." He chuckled. "Hey, I don't have to choke myself to death this time, do I?" HT called out with a small laugh.

"I think we can skip that part," she said as she came out and joined him on the sofa.

After sharing a long, hard kiss they took a few bites of a pasty and a few sips of their drinks. Lil had told him she would never want to remove her ring once he placed it on her finger, so she wanted to wear it on her second finger, leaving her third finger open for her wedding ring one day. He totally agreed, feeling the same.

HT went first. He bent down on his knee in front of Lil and picked up her hand and said, "I, Harry Thomas"—slipping the ring on the second finger of her left hand—"commit myself to you, heart, body, and soul for the rest of my life. I will always be honest, faithful, and love you for the rest of my life. I pledge and promise I will never give you a single reason to take this ring off." He kissed the ring and then her. "I love you. You are my life and my soul mate." He sat back down on the sofa, lightly kissing the tears on her cheeks.

Lil bent down in front of him, maintaining eye contact. "I, Lily Rose"—she began, putting his ring on his second finger on his left hand—"pledge all with my mind, body, and soul, and most of all, my heart, I will always be true and faithful, loving you for the rest of my life. I promise and pledge that I will never ever give you a reason to remove this ring." She kissed the ring and then him, just as he had done, kissing the tears on his cheeks. "I love you most. You are my life and my soul mate."

He pulled her up, kissing her deeply, as they both knew they meant every word.